THE ASSASSIN

a novel by

Ronald Blythe

BLACK DOG BOOKS

First published in England 2004
by Black Dog Books
104 Trinity Street, Norwich, Norfolk, NR2 2BJ.

A CIP record of this book is available from the British Library.

ISBN 0-9528839-9-6

Typeset in 11 point Palatino

Printed in Great Britain
by Biddles Ltd., *www.biddles.co.uk*.

For
Julia Blackburn

CONTENTS

In the worst inn's worst room, with mat half-hung,
The floors of plaster and the walls of dung,
On once a flock-bed, but repaired with straw,
With taped-tied curtains, never meant to draw,
The George and Garter dangling from that bed
Where tawdry yellow strove with dirty red,
Great Villiers lies.

Alexander Pope (*Moral Essays*)

'Then we set forth again, and so to Portsmouth, seeming to me very pleasant and strong place. And we lay at the Red Lion . . . Up, and Mr Creed and I to walk round the town upon the walls, then to our inn, where all the officers of the Yard to see me with great respect . . . and so down to the town again by water and then to see the room where the Duke of Buckingham was killed by Felton.'

Samuel Pepys (*Diary*, 1st May 1661)

It is an infallible rule that all natural causes are subject to mutation, and all worldly men that hunt after fortune are sure to suffer eclipse at any moment.

The Golden Epistles

1

THE OFFICER IN THE TOWER

'Here we are, Lieutenant. We are putting you in Sir John's room.'
Strange young man. He runs his eyes over its arrangement. Clean
straw from an August field in the bed space, dry sticks on the
hearth, a massive chair and table, a cloak-peg, and the shutter
laid under the window. A freshly swept floor. My eyes also run
around, travelling swiftly from object to object until, as I had
been told, they come to rest on what all new prisoners
contemplate, the view outside. A sliver of serene sky has been
squared up by bars like a drawing. The bars themselves are
corroded but the sky is kingfisher-blue. Late summer heat blazes
into the chamber without warming it, but the stone cell is cool
and heavy with the scent of unpicked London orchards, Thames
slime, prison food, the searing reek of a nearby farriery and the
presence of latrines. As for sounds, surprisingly, the place is
soundless. I had anticipated terrible sounds. A little stink which
has been dogging my heels reminds me of the muck which
collects at Traitors' Gate when the tide stagnates. It also reminds
me that I was filthy before I arrived at the shameful steps. I take
a step or two away from the gaoler out of politeness. He at once
begins to shout for a basin, a towel, a shirt! It is not a town voice.
Neither a turnkey's voice, if it comes to that.

'So,' I tell myself, 'the watching has already begun. They will not
be rough but they will be watchful. Here beside me is not my gaoler
but my watcher.'

The discovery paralyses me. My trouble has been that the
longer I live, the less I would be seen. My watcher would not go
unobserved, what with his bullock-eyes, his milky teeth, his
nimble height and other things. The basin and towel arrive. Also

a garment. He shakes this out and it becomes a voluminous affair made of thick linen and drawn-thread lace, very elaborate – the kind of first shirt which a sister would have made for a going-away brother. The watcher is proud of it:

'Sir John left it here, Lieutenant, but it has been through the wash. It will be long on you, but have it, have it.'

The thought of having to scrub my thin and dirty self in front of Bullock's-eyes unnerves me. And when he explains that, 'I am required to dress your arm', the old hysteria overcomes me.

'No, no! My arm is a nuisance, nothing more. Why I can hardly bear to look at it myself. But thank you. See where it lies, rolled under my coat here like a black cucumber!'

The gaoler or whatever he is retreats politely murmuring 'Lieutenant' and leaves. His fat key in the small lock makes it scream. I take off all my clothes for the first time since I set out from Portsmouth and pat and splash myself from head to foot. There is no razor, no comb, no oil, just tepid water from a summer butt. I pour some of it over my hair and watch it make runnels down my belly and then chase itself in dusty beads across the floor. No sooner am I in the big shirt than Bullock's-eyes appears, now with a servant. So he had watched. The Tower, I learn, is an observatory, the mightiest in the kingdom, where such as I must be forever beneath the lens.

'Your arm is bad, Lieutenant.'

'Nothing can be done. It was a battle wound and now it is simply an attachment.'

'It looks bad.'

'*I* look bad – I am not for looking at.'

He smiles. Twenty-eight or so and still with all his teeth. He hands me the comb. 'It was Sir John's but you may have it.' He pulls the table into a pool of sunshine and lays out paper, pens and ink, then leaves. I sit staring at these items until my cell breeds shadows, then do what I think is required of me.

I, John Felton, Gentleman of Ovington, did for this Realm's good, destroy His Grace at nine in the morning at the Greyhound, Portsmouth, with my knife. I, only I.

And I sign it. After which I stretch out on my last bed, feeling for

2

the dried flowers among the cornstalks and wondering 'when?'
When, not how. How was not to be contemplated. Let others
dwell on how. At dayspring my gaoler, who is also something
else, arrives like a secretary to collect signed papers, looks
eagerly at what I have written, and is indignant. Had I no notion
of confession? This was no way to confess! A couple of sentences!
It was neither adequate nor grateful. Assassins, even more than
common murderers, have a duty to supply society with a
heartfelt read. Assassins need to be more than just sorry, they
need to explain themselves. Although in his estimation few of us
can be too sorry. Two sentences and one of them only three words
long! Why, the riffraff strung up every day of the week managed
better than this, and they without so much as a normal repine to
their names. Two bare lines and one small scrap of remorse. I was
not making his new job easy. And had I considered the
hangman's feeling's? Hangmen have feelings, you know. Life
isn't easy for hangmen, what with all the cold-shouldering and
the having to receive Holy Communion wearing gloves.

'This job of your's', I ask him. 'What job?'

The lustrous eyes widen. His is a new, one might say novel,
appointment and I was to be the first to justify it. Tower
confessions were to become a model of their kind. Considering
the status of the prison, the general standard of both its voluntary
and persuaded confessions was appalling. The interrogated and
the condemned alike no longer gave a damn *how* they said it – not
even when he told them that from now on their confessions
would live in our archives for ever.

'Just imagine', I whisper to them, 'your words in History's ear!
So show a bit of style. I hoped for more from you, Lieutenant
Felton. You were to be my exemplar. Yours was to be the first
half-leather binding on the Confessions shelf.'

To soften his disappointment I forage around in my pocket
with my good hand for the copy of the statement which I had
tucked into my hat as I left St Dunstan's Church less than a
fortnight ago, although it seemed in another lifetime. The
original, discovered when they examined me at the Greyhound,
had created such an effect that I now waited with half a smile to
see what would happen now. The gaoler who is not a turnkey or
an examiner reads.

3

That man is cowardly and base and deserveth not the name of a gentleman or a soldier that is not willing to sacrifice his life for the honour of his God, his King, and his Country. Let no man commend me for doing it, but rather discommend themselves as the cause of it, for if God had not taken way our hearts for our sins he (George) would not have gone so long unpunished.

Readers will no doubt recognise the style as that of *The Golden Epistles*. I was strictly tutored in unoriginality. My deed itself followed the precedent of nobodies cutting the cackle, as it were. Be certain, the Duke would not have been *talked* out of office – out of a whole heap of offices. If it is any comfort to him in Hell he can say he died for England and virtually without pain. A single mortal blow comes more as a surprise than anything else. I watch my apologia being read very slowly and with the courtesy which one gives to a sonnet. Whilst too concise for hard covers, it surely would not disgrace the Confessions shelf? But my friend for whom I must soon find a name is now staring at me over the paper with disbelief. He looks as if he is about to take me through an act of contrition.

'You quote. What do you quote from?'

No answer. We each have our holy writ and this comes from mine, although I have doctored it a little. Anyway, it is not for distribution.

'My name is Jack Wren, since Whitsuntide Master of Confessions to his Excellency the Governor.'

But he neither offers his hand nor bows. He is offended. I realise that it is I who has to find my way into some kind of personal statement. If he or some other Tower inquisitor squeezes words from me, what use is that? I notice the actual quantity of paper which lies on the table, enough for volumes of confession. Malfeasance, treachery, guilt, roaring remorse, limp excuses, all had to run into chapters. I touch the sheets with my finger-tips and they say, 'It takes time to write a book.' Suddenly Tyburn seems as far off as all our deaths do in ordinary circumstances. I could be like that Arabian queen who spun-out tales to save her head, I suppose. Mr Wren might like this. His snowy smile was taking over. He scrunches up my apologia and flicks it to a corner. It was at this moment that Mr Golding's most

4

sensational and least praiseworthy book floats into my head, *A Brief Discourse on the Late Murther of Master George Saunders: A Worshipful Citizen of London: And the Apprehension, Arreignment and Execution of the Principall and Accessories of the Same.* Until now I had always been embarrassed that he wrote it. How a scholar who opened Ovid and John Calvin for the common reader could have descended to such Newgate stuff was a mystery. And yet, I had often reminded myself, Mr Golding was very English and the English love a scaffold – so that could be it. Certainly the confessions contained in this work were made in great style. Could it be that pretty Jack Wren, Confessions Department, hoped for a return to Elizabethan values? I turn my mind back to Mrs Saunders' guilty howls as they rang the changes on 'Let my fate be a lesson to you', and get going. Seated comfortably at the table, I have soon covered three foolscap sheets, and with some excellent flights of penmanship in the margins. If sunny Jack must have something lurid for his archive, well here was the best I could do.

> Good people I am come hither to die the death whereunto I am judged, as worthily and as deservedly as ever died any. I had a very Good Lord Duke, and might have still, had not the Divel kindled in my heart, first the hellish firebrand of a grudge, and afterwards a murderous intent towards him I held it against, and the carrying out of this intent with a Tenpenny Knife. I would, if he could hear me, lie prostrate on the ground at his Grace's feet and ask mercy of him through plentiful tears. I do ask mercy of my Saviour, and of sweetheart Charles, divine King, and of all virtuous men inhabiting the round world, whom by deed and ensample I have so wickedly offended. I especially ask mercy of that Lady his Grace's wife and of the Child within her belly, and of their Magnificences his Grace's kinsmen, and of my own disgraced Family, and all whom I have hurt by hurting my Lord Duke. I am abashed and ashamed and tears blind my face. Unworthy of pity, I beseech you for Christ's sake pity me. I thank God the Judge that the law has caught me and so has prevented me from holding the rein and bridle to sin further, to the danger of my Eternal damnation. I thank Jesu that I have been found out, brought to judgment, fatherly correction and amendment of life before I am justly carried to where I must step up on air on the Awful Day. Pray for me. *Me, me, adsum qui feei, in me convertite ferrum ...*

5

There was very much more, and all in my best hand. I could have gone on for days. And it was dreadfully old fashioned – who would have thought that we were living in the seventeenth century! I sand it and suddenly feel genuinely sad. For the truth is that my life ended with the ending of George's life. From the moment when my blade felt for his heart nothing has mattered. Nor ever can. I thought I had better translate the Latin tag in case the ignorant Tyburners take me for a Catholic. I add, 'Here am I who did the deed. Turn your sword on me.' Mr Wren returns, sees the pile of manuscript, beams, might have hugged me had I been closer, picks up the papers like a college examiner and begins to confess something himself as he skims what I have written. He is twenty-seven (good guess), and a gentleman from Dorsetshire. He has a wife and they live on Tower Green, lucky to have been allotted the end house. I must have seen it. It is the tall one. He laughs on and off with all his teeth. Something tells me that he is never to be laughed off, that he gets what he wants. He is like the teacher who reduces one to misery with his patience. His reading is now no more than a flippant glance as he shows that he can take a joke. Taking my seat at the table, he continues to tell me his life story whilst at the same time folding my Confession into paper darts and whizzing them through the window.

'What if somebody reads them?'

'They won't. The moat is full of such stuff. It sails down from the ramparts and swims out from the jakes. What a style, Lieutenant! What a plagiarist! I quite enjoyed the line from Virgil – that doesn't often get into the moat.'

He took my good arm and led me round the cell.

'You are frightened, aren't you?'

'Yes, very.'

'But not of me?'

'Of everyone now.'

'Does your book advise you what to do about fear?'

'My book ... ?'

'Your *Golden Epistles*. They found it by the town gate at Portsmouth.'

I felt tremendously relieved. 'The *Epistles* say that it is the man that is feared that hath need to fear. May I have my book?'

'Certainly. Your book, any book. We are always interested in what our prisoners read. And in what they write. You are to write what happened in Portsmouth, and why it happened. And with no remorse if you can help it as it rather ruins objectivity. Keep God out of it, too. Or rather allow us to accept that He is omnipresent. Unless, of course, He was in it – if you get my meaning.'

'But the time, sir. You are asking for a tale which cannot be told without time.'

'Forget time, never mind time. Who is mentioning time?'

He circles me. He is as excited as if it was himself who was about to write a book. I can smell him warming to its possibilities as he strolls around the room, making the floorboards squeak and kicking up the dust. He is boy-acrid still, I note. He will go home to the tall house on the Green and tell his wife, 'I've done it! I've done it! I've set Felton to his task. He knows now what he's got to do. Nothing like it will have come out of the Tower since Sir Walter's *Geography*. This is what prisons should be for – authorship!' Being such a young twenty-seven he will probably grow facetious and entertain her with references to 'author's block' and 'thereby hangs a tale'. I realise my importance to him and I breathe again. When a threat of immediate execution vanishes even a few weeks more of life offer a future as remote as old age. I tell him that I am a slow writer, which is no more than a fact.

He repeats, 'Forget time, bugger time.'

It dawns on me that I am the Tower's current prisoner number one – there has always to be the captive oriole, the golden gaolbird non-pareil who will sing the country's crimes. I am he. I pat the pen-feathers, stroke the paper, reams of it having appeared from nowhere. A matins bell clinks faraway. I see that my cell is full of unimprisoned life, a dragon-fly, bluebottles, a harvest spider, floating herb-robert seeds, a little rat with a crumb. It might have been my chamber at Ovington. I recover my aplomb. It is the moment to take charge, which is best done with a proverb. As you know, ours is the age of the concluding proverb, but all I can bring to mind is, 'I wept when I was born, and every day shows why'. Which is not strictly true.

'Oh, poor Lieutenant!' exclaims the archivist, his bullock eyes flooding with tears, 'you are our deliverer! But don't tell anyone that I told you so.' He heaves me to him, adding, 'The whole story, mind you! No cuts. Let's have it all.' He rummages around in his head for a proverb to remind me that 'everyone stretches his legs according to his coverlet' and rattles his way out. His healthy stink having gone with him, I am able to detect another essence which, though faint and delicate, masks for a second that of the scummy moat. It is the scent of an August stream where the water drowns hanging blackberry and sloe, and upholds the fat carp, the scent of the Thames as it snakes through the Bethnal meadows. If paradise is what we each most long for, then mine will be a river. No glass streets for me.

Wren gone, I stretch on the bedstraw as Sir John must have done, his hip where mine is now. I count the wall stones, not having to count the days. All prisoners count; their existence becomes a kind of abacus. There are two hundred and thirty-one stones in the window wall. Some are signed. Maybe I shall be pardoned, released, sent packing. Sir John and I will meet again and he will say, 'What did you make it? I made it two hundred and thirty not counting that cobble.' Who was it that first imprisoned another man? 'Put this fellow in prison and feed him with the bread and water of affliction', ordered King Ahab, laying down the incarceration laws for evermore. Some poor fellow like me, though not an assassin or King Ahab would not have been there to give his orders. Lieutenant John Felton, Assassin. One stroke with my good hand, and the worst character description until Kingdom come. Yet boy David did no less and look at his reputation! 'Little David! Little David!' they cried as the cart was dragged through Kingston. I think it was the first time I have ever been praised. *The Golden Epistles* say 'that all worldly men who hunt after fortune are sure to suffer eclipse at any moment.' My little shadow blotted out Buckingham's sun at its zenith. The squibbers have been quick to assess me:

> Canst thou be gone so quickly, can a knife
> Let out so many titles and a life?
> Though I did good, I did it the wrong way,
> And they fall into the worst of ills
> That act the people's wish without their wills.

My horror now is not the rope but the having to see myself, not just the assassinating me, but that me from which I have averted my interest since I was of age to take stock. Having stared into books instead of mirrors, it is dreadful to come face to face with autobiography. Wren will not be pleased with a nice selection from my reading. He wants background, motive and deed. Telling the last two will be brief enough, but telling all the rest will take space. And to tell it to myself – that will be novel. Will having to look at my life, all of it, demand the same nerve as having to look at my black arm? Innocent arm which cannot be raised, which has struck no blow, which dries and withers but cannot be shed! A limb from a vault which hides in my sleeve. I too have hidden from my own eyes. It will be interesting to see who I am when I confess myself to myself. But for convenience, and in order to give myself a little arm-room, I address myself to Wren. He will drain away the morbidity and leave me clarified. He worships me, like all the others he recognises me as the criminal liberator of the state. He trembles in my presence. He would kiss my arm better if he could. But it is just as well that, as avenging god and Tower of London librarian, we cannot expect to be mates. I doubt his claim to be a gentleman.

Morning after the first night of my captivity. I am cold. What will it be like in November? Sunbeams rain in. I leave the palliasse and crouch where they fall. Sudden heat, it is amazing. Then I dress and wait. What I dreaded hasn't occurred. I thought that, as so often they do, yesterday's decisions would have vanished with the darkness, but they haven't. Sleeping on them has proved them to be right. I am choosing a pen when my gaoler comes in with breakfast. He is all combed and talkative, and on the verge of doing a little dance-step out of some kind of inner joy, which brings to mind George on 23rd August.

'We have been shopping in East Cheap. Christ, the crowds! We did our best to take the wall but were shoved this and that way by laced mutton and shag-rags. *Foutre!* It is nicer in here. My wife bought woollens and I searched for tobacco. There was talk all over the place about the Duke's funeral, and how it should be celebrated.'

'You cannot mean "celebrated".'

'I do mean celebrated, Lieutenant. A right do for a wrong 'un,

9

is what they are saying. They are dressing the maypoles and flagging Smithfield, and talk of fireworks and Te Deums.'

When I reproach him, he reddens. He carries meat, bread and milk. And, hey presto! like a conjurer, he produces my *Golden Epistles*. I watch dumbfounded as a trickle of grit from the Portsmouth town gate, where I had left it, runs out of its pages. He waves the book above his head, like a bone for a dog. Am I supposed to leap for it? Then his antics subside and he hands it to me as reverently as I take it. To think that the last time I touched it I was Felton of Pentlow, veteran of Cadiz and the Isle de Rhé. Nothing much to be sure, but not Felton the – I cannot write it. I press the dirty binding to my lips and ask my book's forgiveness. I hear myself telling young Wren one of its lessons. 'The Romans had a law called Falcidia by which the first offense of the child was pardoned, the second punished, and for the third he was banished'.

'Sent to bed without his supper?'

'Exiled.'

'Falcidia, eh ... If only we never grew up. I loved being a child.'

'I did not.' No sooner had I confessed this to the gaoler than I regretted it. For he is instantly all attention. I can see now why he has been appointed, and what his instincts are. And where all his power lies. He is – an examiner. His ears cock up at the most innocuous things. We employed such men in the Regiment and it was incredible what they heard – as against what we heard.

'Now you must write us your "Epistle", sir. You will begin with your infancy.'

'Is that an order?'

He grins and goes away. I cannot write. The ink stiffens on the quill. I am in prison, confined, shut up, locked in. I do what all prisoners do in the first days, I fall across the bed and cry. My trial and execution are as nothing compared with my imprisonment. I would gladly fall to my death for the sake of those seconds of free tumbling through the outside air if only I could squeeze through the bars. But I am too undemonstrative to beat the walls with my fists. I weep till noon, sometimes knuckling my eyes and making them sore. Then, abruptly, it is all over and done with, and I do what I always do for release, I read. The second night I sleep hardly at all but I rest. A leisurely question seeks an answer and I take my time giving it. Regular authors will know it – should I be I or he? As a man who has spent a lifetime dodging 'I', would not 'he' be more manageable? And then what about Wren, would he accept the third person as legal tender? What I won't be able to go on with is this present tense as I am all in the past; can hope for no future. Currently I am in limbo. Painters use a maalstok to keep their eye in and their correct distance. Can a self-portrait be recognisable to the self and to the world equally? And what can be done when the image of God turns out to be image of the father? At least I won't have this to worry about. My family gave me its shield but not its face. 'Who is he like?' mother would puzzle. No answer. And now he has murdered the Duke.

2

TALES OUT OF SCHOOL

My family is seated in the Stour lands of Essex-Suffolk, where it has lived immemorially. We have undulating open country in which elm screens break up the view, and none of our towns is more than an hour's walk apart. The soil is old clay, workable clay, refusing clay, or 'loving land', as our peasants call it on account of its clinging nature. We grow good crops, and could grow anything, except that these mouse-poor days have defeated us. My family's wealth is its rank. Nothing can deprive us of this, thank God. What ever small returns that are left over after running the estate must go to my eldest brother for keeping up the rank. I, being the fifth son, have our famous name and our arms, but nothing more. In families such as ours, first-comers take all. The remainder of us have to fish around for dowries. My brother was a good catch for Parthenope my sister-in-law, who was not a gentlewoman until she wed him. I was soon packed off to bring home the spoils of war, ludicrously as it turned out, for if there are such pickings these days they are hardly likely to come to unenthusiastic soldiers like me. Also I have to admit that I obtained my commission, not to get rich, but to become changed. As it happened, soldiering changed me not at all.

Changling notions had been flying around our local fields like bees, so that not only gentlefolk but low dreamers at plough were caught up in a kind of mutability. Not one of us was content with what and who we were; all of us were at that time chasing what we might be. I have been both sea-soldier and land-soldier, yet what *am* I? What do I remain?

It was all Mr Golding's fault, if fault it be. For as long as any of us could remember he had been waving his transforming wand over our countryside. People strolling past the Great Brick House saw him as a wizard and they would wonder if they would still be the person they were when they started out. Women would glance at themselves in rain puddles, vaguely hoping that there might have been a change for the better. Boys would stretch forth their hands, dreading a paw. Lovers would not have been all that much surprised to discover themselves turned into mulberry bushes or foxes. Some would, in a discreet spot, take a quick look at what lay under their clothes, praying that all would be familiar, and not something the gods might fancy. The parson of Powles Belchamp, a Mr Nelson, would make a secret Arminian gesture, forbidden as you know, whenever he called at the Great Brick House. In church we would give covert glances to find out if anyone was not quite as he was last Lord's Day. Mr Golding sat just in front of us, worshipping but not listening, and turning his prayer-book back into Greek and Latin to pass sermon-time, his big shoulders quaking with scholarship. Now and then his wife, without looking at him, would reach across and take the book from him as though he was a fidgeting child, and he would sigh. After the blessing we would stand in respect as his squirarchal procession made its way to the west door, careful not to catch his eye. Not that he had the evil eye. On the contrary, it was a sweet eye for an old man, unfaded by reading and luminous, though lacking benevolence. One would have thought that sixty years of desk-work would have blotched it but it was as clear as a pebble in a brook. He would always pause to bow to mother – father only came on high days and holidays – and she would give her little bop, as the village women called it. And then she and his Ursula would exchange radiant smiles behind his back. Our procession followed. We were not of the parish but regular visitors, and of course our policies ran with the Golding's all across the high land, so that mother and Mrs Golding could ride side by side, each on her own property, all the way from the Great Brick House to Pentlow Hall. Should a tree come between them, they would laugh and bow, offering it to each other. Mother always came in state to Belchamp because of Mr Golding being half-brother to the Countess, and because, on her best tall mount she could take stock of the corn barns, which would rise up from the crops like black stranded behemoths. Myself looking

13

back on all this have sometimes thought that there was sufficient prosperity along those miles to have provided even a fifth son a living.

It was during such a return from Powle's Belchamp, when I was four, that the Ursulas persuaded each other that I should be tutored by Mr Golding, the man who changed one thing into another.

'Oh, could he be bothered?' asked my mother.

'Leave it to me,' said Mrs Golding.

'Will he ...?' began my mother. 'Be safe' was what she nearly asked, thinking perhaps that I might come home one evening a swan or a natterjack, or not at all myself.

'Be safe? Don't worry – look at our children.'

My mother had often done this, wondering how such dull young men could have emerged from what she thought was a very interesting union. She also knew that where offspring were concerned the Goldings were as ruthless and conventional as any parents in that they gave two of their sons a proper education for dynastic purposes and left the rest to fend for themselves as best they could. As all this family suffered from dream and inertia and was said, even in its heyday when the wool seemed to roll of its own accord from sheep to banker, not to have enough business sense to run a whelk stall, it was not long after Mr Golding's death that it slid from being our near-equals into button-making, and what kind of commerce is that? Even as early as my own childhood there was talk in the air of Goldings becoming chancers in the Americas. And then there was all the transformation notoriety. It was whispered that if a Golding could become a de Vere, what was to prevent any of us becoming nightingales? Or eldern trees, or whatever one fancied? Angels being out. This marriage which made Mr Golding, when he was little more than a boy, half-brother-in-law to the Earl, was to blight his old age, for it landed him with halls and houses and dovecotes which he had no idea how to manage, poor enchanter. So that during the time he was educating me he was forever hurrying from his study to appease lawyers and other property fiends, and losing all the way. At the same time he got quite a kick out of his many court-cases, and wiping the floor with magistrates. Except, of course, they, being what they are, would inevitably scrabble for some clause which left him in the wrong. His Ursula would wring her hands when he was in what she called 'his affidavit mood', and give thanks to Almighty God that her brothers had so entailed her houses that there was no way to her husband getting his hands on them, and that when she eventually left them for that abiding place above the firmament, they would fly back like whiplash to the Reydons. His wife's property remained a great puzzle to Mr Golding. It was not that he wanted it – he wanted very little – but that he could never work out why he could never have it. Never. He had married no ordinary woman, he decided, and the thought pleased him – and worried him. He would meet her unceremonious entry to his study with a thin smile and, as she stood talking to him, would pat her starched breast. He was very free with her in front of me.

* * *

My first day at this one-boy school started with my arriving drenched, water-logged. For not only had I run from Ovington in heavy rain, but fallen into a ditch.

'Stand by the grate and steam, boy. Remove your hat. Stand out of your shoes. Do not touch anything. When you have ceased to drip and are just damp, sit on the stool. And what ever you do, do not handle my best books.'

This was a joke. I had been building houses with his best volumes ever since I could remember, and he had stepped over me in search of a reference or his spectacles, occasionally knocking them down. It was then that I first heard his pen-scratchings and murmurs. He would say something like, 'Don't fret, poor benighted hand,' as he took up the book he was translating. 'You will soon be in decent English. Just listen to this, John' – and there would come the original paragraph and then his Englished version. He would then read the French or Latin in a comic accent and the translation with more than a touch of magnificence. 'There', he would say, 'we've done it a good turn, what!'

And so I began to open pages. Being seven, I was old for direction. About midday Mr Golding took pity on me, stopped translating and himself opened for the first and only time a book which he thought might hold a boy's attention. It was Bernhard von Breydenbach's *Peregrinations* and out of it tumbled, unfolding as it fell, a woodcut of Venice a yard long. I saw an entire city built in water, with reflecting palaces, and galleons bobbing at anchor in town squares. I was permitted to pore over this fine picture-book and a few others like it for a week or so, when they were taken away from me, like toys at bedtime. But during those few free days I was able to steep myself in decoration, in borders and head-pieces, in florid tail-ends and tortured capitals, and in the full art of illustration where gods themselves thought it an honor to present a title-page, and naked children and angels garlanded words. And then, as I have said, Mr Golding passed his hand between these delights and my gaze, tapped a chapter one and said, 'Read'. From that moment he enticed me with text and corrupted me with print. Now and then I would feel his eyes on the back of my head as I started on a particular book, looking to see what it would do to me. He allowed questions on any subject except the grammar of languages. This I was to unravel by myself, although now and then with the help of his Ursula, a highly grammatical lady. She would pounce in without knocking to 'brighten the pair of you up.' Which meant pulling a comb through my thick curls. 'What a pretty poll my blackbird has!' She would unstring Mr Golding's ruff and tie him up again in clean lace, and feel my limbs as a cook feels a chicken, pinching and assessing it, and then give me a little cake from her pocket, as if this would make me grow. Once a day, Mr Golding exercised me as he did his setter, running me through the meadows, come rain or fine. Neither of us then having a book in our hands, he had to resort to second-best – talk. Whilst never a free-thinker, he was a wildly free talker, pouring forth to the lovely golden animal and myself, and presuming on our dumbness. Quite early on I made a decision to hide from him the extent to which he was changing me, I don't know why. One day as we stood on Cavendish bridge looking at the ducks he assured me that I was certain to go to Paradise. Therefore it was commonsense not to worry over-much about what might happen to me on earth. He himself was also Elect.

I must tell you, such doctrinal barbs apart, what Mr Golding's library was like the year I matriculated. It was a long room much lived in by ourselves, by Tyto the barn owl, Rap the setter, Bufo the toad (under a damp pamment), house martins in summer, a rat in winter, a basket of cats, a lamb in springtime, a tamed badger, my own dog Tike, and thrush in a cage and, in season, quantities of butterflies and bumble-bees trying to escape through heraldic glass. Mr Golding translated by the finest of these coloured windows, looking magical in their reflections. Now and then he would shake with mirth at the nerve of some foreign author, especially if he was French. He once told me that his motive for changing so many foreign works into our tongue was not really for the convenience of those who could only read in their own language, but because he was convinced that it was a superior language. He said that his great discovery, made when he was still a Cambridge scholar, was that he himself had nothing whatever to say. So what other career was there for him than to be the man-midwife for those that had? Never, he added truthfully, had there in his case been any of that egotistical battle between the translator and his subject. Never had it crossed his mind to wish that he had been Ovid or Calvin. But he didn't say that the few times in which he had been the Author had been pitiful, such popular claptrap about murder and earthquakes as to make one embarrassed for him. Anyway, he knew his worth. He knew for instance that he was never Anon. He knew that when his name shared the page with that of a great poet or theologian it had its rightful place there. He was also the master of the puff. Who could resist buying *The excellent and pleasant Work of Julius Solinus Polyhistor. Containing the noble actions of human creatures, the secrets and providence, of nature, the description of countries, the manners of the people; with many marvellous things and strange antiquities, serving for the benefit and recreation of all sorts of persons.* Translated out of Latin into English by Arth. Golding, Gent. J. Charlewood, printer. Quarto. London, 1587.? I can feel the coins burning in my pocket as I write it. Only it was sure to have been a sell-out and long before I was born, and I doubt if one could purchase a copy now for love or money.

Sitting at Mr Golding's feet, I could smell the close feral odour of his robe, noticing at this range the extent of its embroideries. Palm-trees, water-lilies, phoenixes and some kind of text revelled along its frayed hem. The sleeves were rabbit-fur tunnels from which his hands hung uselessly whenever he wasn't writing. He was old and had finished most of his translations by the time I became his pupil, and his fame was prodigious. It was apparent when we passed people on our afternoon walks, whether gentle or simple. Since he never wore a hat, his response to their civilities was a little rattle of his fingers against his starch and a misinterpreted smile, a nodding and a noting – and, to be honest, an uncaring. He liked to think that the locals were in awe of him as a literary celebrity, whereas they viewed him uncertainly as faery.

The years travelled on, as I read Mr Golding out of house and home. There was hardly an hour when I was not devouring print and he was not turning one book into another, which is what translation means. I recall how surprised I was when I discovered that his readers actually believed that they were getting Calvin or Bucer or Aretin 'Englished', when in fact they were getting them 'Goldinged', which was quite another matter. He did to other men's works what the gods did to the Greeks. Both he and they were involved in what he once called 'the same dark philosophy of turned shapes.' 'Why,' he prophesied, 'the time would come when men could become women, had they a mind to.'

'And the reverse, sir?' I ventured.

'Oh, no. No! Never. That metamorphosis was for night-dreams, not life. In any case, what kind of woman was it who would want to be a man?'

During our walks by the Stour, which I now regard as my true education, my reading apart, Mr Golding's monologues might begin with his strict views on the religion of Our Lord Jesus Christ, continue with condemnations of the well-known heresies of the Romish Church, so dreadful that words would have failed him had he not the biggest stock of them of any scholar then alive, and then inevitably embrace what he termed his 'rescue work' of any foreign masterpiece still unEnglished. Had he been a trained historian or churchman, the reading public would have known where it stood with him. However, the truth was that he was a poet and so, of course, unsafe. If there was one thing which he taught me it was to be unsafe. The Church of England was under great obligation to him for Englishing the tracts of the Reformers as it was haphazardly intellectual itself, and relieved to have salvation in the mother tongue. Yet anxious too. Could this truly be the Protestant Word? It was not. Poetry had leaked into it. All the same, Mr Golding's translations sold like hot cakes, as unsafe things do, and were so prolific, one volume pressing on the heel of another, that, without his ever realising it, he had begun to change the English language itself. Just as a bell lets out its after-note, so in sermons and lectures from a thousand naves there was the Gospel plain and clear, plus something other, pretty enough but not quite the same sound, and this was Arthur Golding.

I was his dog, as he called me, until I was fourteen. During all that time he never once gave me set work to do or required anything in my own hand. I listened, I read, I walked. The barn owl, with eyes like suns, stared down on me knowing, as Mr Golding put it, 'more than the pair of us put together'. It was common knowledge in the village that this owl was actually Captain Manby transmogrified. The servants were decidedly respectful when they passed Tyto.

'Who was Captain Manby, sir?'

'I have no idea.'

Mrs Golding gave me the facts, such as they were, of the old disappeared seaman, adding, 'My Tyto – that rafty fly-by-night! The very idea!' To prove his glory, the barn owl spread his three-foot wings and beat the foetid air. I remember this day exactly because it was the one on which she and my mother asked audience of my famous teacher to enquire of my future. When he prevaricated they shouted at him (he was a trifle deaf).

'But where to now? He is *fourteen*.'

'Jesus College, where else?'

Knowing that my father would only send his heir to the university, Mr Golding threw this recommendation to the Ursulas like a challenge. Now they knew where they stood – as defenders of the rights of baby sons. Mother surrendered immediately. Having borne nine and reared five, and having become a Felton, she knew what to say no to.

Mr Golding was sad.

'Come in to read whenever you like, little dog'.

My boyhood, my schooling were over.

'You must have an end of terms prize,' he said. 'First in class must have a prize, what? Choose what you like within reason,' and he waved rabbity arms towards the press which held the kind of books which minor writers present to great writers. But he knew what I would choose. It lay on the table, the fat clumsy volume which had served me as the foundation of my book castles when I was a child and which, when I at last began to read it, opened my eyes more than any other work I knew. Its title was alluring – *The Golden Epistles* – its author that philosophical soldier named Sir Geoffrey Fenton. For him it was just a bad buy. But he put on a show about how sorry he was to see it go, and it would only be to someone he loved, such as myself. I wanted it so much that I could thank him profusely.

'Only to you, little dog.'

'I am all gratitude, sir.'

He did not ask me where will you go, what will you do? as he did not love me. But neither had he disliked me. My seven years nearness had not distracted him, and it was for this that he could show a parting affection. So I left.

3

GRADUATING

Memory runs our few bright days into a mighty summer. Similarly, the clarity of our winters becomes a yardstick for our bitterness. The winter I left school was bitterness itself. I walked through it clasping my school-leaving prize, freshly inscribed *Ex Libris Artur Goldiensi donari Johannes Feltonis dies natalis Christi, anno Domini 1610*. That year we kept Christmas at Pentlow, a long wade through featureless snow. Hovels, sheds, barns were no more. I remember making out the phantom church tower and plunging for it. It was mid-afternoon, lightless, yet not dark. I passed neighbours dragging faggots across the drifts. When I shouted, they shouted. I carried my book like a woman carrying a child. It was warm inside my shirt, the *Golden Epistles*, and leaped against my belly as I fell in and out of ditches. I heard my name being called, 'Mr Felton, Feltooon – Mr Felton is it?' It was as though it made a fingerpost in the desolation. Two snowmen came up and said, 'Parmenters, sir.' A pair of kestrels appeared and we all looked up. The Parmenters went ahead and I floundered in their snow-steps. They would look back to see that I had not vanished. I heard them consulting over my head – all Parmenters were tall – whether they should carry me. I was wet to the waist but fiery, not perished. I was an ivory boy, bony and enduring. When the Parmenters spoke to me the wind howled their instructions away. We had to feel our entrance to the Hall. Light spangled from every window in honour of the Christmas and there were gullies in the snow whither logs had been drawn in. Our beasts, wintering in the undercroft and shacks, bellowed mournfully. We heard music. All Pentlow, all Ovington were present inside and the mansion hummed with unseen guests. As we approached it was like putting our ears to a hive. And somewhere at the heart of these buzzing rooms would be the Ursulas in their feasting-gowns and extravagant starchings and best carcanets gliding about and giving commands. And somewhere Father would be clapping his hands and asking for silence so that he could say prayers to the Lord Jesus Christ on His birthday and wish Him and us well. Was father Elect? Did it run in families? When I asked Mrs Golding, she said, 'I hope not!' Pentlow was the seat of my uncle Sir Edmund, a widower.

* * *

I sat with them at High Table. The hearths roared and shot flames and food was carried before us for mother to poke, and then set down until not another dish could find space on the board. A carol was sung and we stood in respect. Twelve days of this! Twelve days also of my father asking where the Feltons were going? He knew all too tediously where they had come from.

'Where are you off to, little son?'

They were bringing in a pudding to flute music. I see this moment more exactly every passing year, although I now realise that father had not waited for it. His question sprang from nowhere, though having asked it so suddenly his relief was palpable. Seeing my shocked face, he hastily added, 'Not this month, eh! Not in the winter. Not until you are ready. There's no rush'.

Whilst I knew that I stood somewhere between being a child or a man, which is a disgusting state, I had no reason to believe that I had disgusted them – my parents. If I had thought of my immediate future at all it was to hide away in the warrens of our attics, or in the meadows, reading, getting through time, making myself scarce, and eventually *writing* – who knows! But 'Where are you off to, little son?' Going off somewhere to do something which might hurry me into being adult, and presentable. I admit that. Things which father had said at various moments during my childhood started to cohere, statements such as, 'I can't give you money but I have given you the Name'. And it would flourish, the Felton tree, only a little less branchy and illustrious than the Stuarts', if you would credit it.

'Your grandmother being lineally descended from the

22

Plantagenets, from King Edward Three and thus all the Saxon
kings, from Philip Three, King of France and Philip the Beautiful,
and thus from Hugh Capet himself, and so from Charlemagne –
are you following me? – she could count among her ancestors,
and thus so can you, Bigods, Mareschalls, Mowbrays, FitzAlans,
Bohuns, Tilneys, Percys, Nevilles, Staffords, Somersets, Howards
and de Veres.'

'And the Wrights', mother would wickedly include.

'Yes, yes, Wrights, Wrights'.

Her father was William Wright, once Mayor of Durham.

'Just say your name in the world and doors will fly wide.
Felton – who needs any other patrimony. And if you happen to
be in France, don't forget old Hugh Capet.'

It was during one of these recitations that mother said, 'He is
small for his name' and father said, 'There has to be the runt'.
When I told Mrs Golding this – it was too painful to be kept in –
she wept and kissed me, crying, 'No, no, you are my pretty little
blackbird. I'll give Tom Felton a piece of my mind. Why, see your
eyes, dark blue. So unusual. You will be a juicy lad yet. Put your
shoulders back. Books are bending you. *Try* growing.'

Here own sons were stout lumbering young men who, while
looking ill bred, were decidedly not, something reckoned most
distinguished in England. Suffolk and Essex were full of such
people. She petted them as she petted me, planting kisses on
their large cheeks. To her all males were trying creatures to be
hugged from going completely off their heads. She thanked God
nightly for making her female, and thus sensible. She loved
women. Her heart and arms went out to them as she gathered to
her their commonsense.

'Do you know, little jackanapes, I could *eat* a lady – I could! I could
devour your honoured mother. Do you know, I once asked Mr Golding
what kind of love this could be and he said he would look it up.'

'Our raven bird', mother was now saying as the Christmassing
got going, 'Our raven bird who must fly away.'

Christmas was when one set blood aside and condescended as
Our Lord had condescended. Father capered with the dairy girls,
slapping their arses, mother was led out by just about anyone. I
watched thinking, William had left to 'make his way', Roger too.
And now me. I was fourteen, just the age to be pushed out, just

the year for becoming a man. Would father make an announcement? Would he mount the dais with me and, holding me by my shoulders, launch me forth? It is said that English gentlefolk are more skilled in pruning family trees of younger sons and establishing them as cuttings than any other race. It was due, they said, to their stoical ability to stand the pain of it. The evergreens hung from the rafters like a gathered forest. At one in the morning our cook carried bowls of frumenty to the yard for the 'farisees', as we called the fairies. As a child I found it hard to understand why our Redeemer had so taken against the farisees, calling them every bad name which came into His head. Mr Golding explained, making an etymological note.

The company danced and drank its way to bed, holly boys and ivy girls from the village entwined by the embers, old men staggering around seeking a chance, the great people led to their chambers by trumpeters, the servants and field-folk curled under settles, myself in my room to hear the whimpering and lowing, the fluttering and honking, as Pentlow Hall itself fell into uneasy sleep. The tempest increased during the small hours, and to such an extent as to make yesterday's snowstorm seem like a spilling of cushion feathers in comparison. Whilst torpor and drink stunned our company to the sound of the northern gale, our animals quaked. This was going to be a Christmas to remember, one to measure hardship by.

It was after breakfast the next morning that my uncle Sir Edmund called the family into the painted chamber to make an announcement. This was the room in which all the Felton business was done. It reeked of codicils. At first I thought that it was to be the announcement of my leaving the nest, for both my father and he shared brotherly excitement. It was not every day that a Felton set forth. But it was to talk about a different nest altogether, the one which would contain our dust. Our vault, in other words. We all knew what for so long had been on his mind, which was that such a distinguished family should have its proper sepulchre. The Mannocks had theirs, did they not? So did the Waldegraves, the Martyns, the Edens, the Cranes ... and his tongue, even more armigerous than father's, licked its way round the county until it came to an envious halt before the sublime memorial to Speaker Cordell at Long Melford, where it became incoherent with jealousy. Feltons would never be able to afford anything on that scale. He clapped his hands for silence.

'Let me welcome Mr Underwood, Tombmaker of St Edmundsbury. Let me show you my instruction to the person to clear our way to the Lady Chapel, where we shall all lie, *Deo volente*, until Judgment Day, and from where we shall rise as a family to plead before that awful bench.'

He bowed his head and only just prevented making the sign of the Cross. Old protections die hard. So what did we think of this – a fine family tomb with alabaster displays of achievements and virtues? Would it not give the poor something to contemplate, now that the old idols had been swept from their niches leaving such blank spaces? In the highest churches in the land apostles and saints had given way to ladies and gentlemen. We were to imagine with what pride our peasantry would, half lost in prayer, catch a glimpse of our recumbency, our blazens, our mortality and its paradisal rewards. For himself he would have sleeping figures in their finery, very colourful, and seriously resting under a starry tester. Now that the Virgin, etc. had gone – their statues had filled holes in the highway – there was heaps of room. Mr Underwood, Tombmaker, would begin the matter immediately. Where death was concerned, one's arrangements could never be too soon. There were questions. Could the inscription go back to Hugh Capet? (father). What if soldiering abroad, we fell? There were rules for this emergency. A servant should boil the flesh from our heroic bones and bring them back to the Pentlow vault in a sack. Nobody of rank need be buried where they fell. The whole object of rank was to have privileges. Although one could go wrong. Our ancestor Sir Anthony had when he set up house in the holy abbey at Playford during the reforms. Our branch had taken care not to plant itself where monks throve, but continue to flourish in secularity. It knew its place. Ha-ha.

The Tombmaker wrote all this down. He also did a bit of sketching of what would lie beneath the starry tester, getting Uncle Edmund's length. It was icy in the painted chamber, with the windows curtained outside in snow. I imagined us all shut up in the vault.

* * *

I kept out of father's way after Christmas, vanishing on long winter walks. It was so cold that little could be done outside and where ever I went the land was deserted. I walked miles and always with a book. In February the river froze solid and then everybody came out to skate to Clare or downstream to Sudbury. For the old it was a curious time, the Queen having died the previous March, so that they too seemed to feel it right to pack-up, she and Mr Golding being near-contemporaries. He missed her dreadfully. And he felt rather finished, as he called it, when the Scottish king ordered a lot of bishops, most of whom had never translated a book in their lives, to make him a new version of the Bible. Worse, a terrible clergyman named Mr Wilcocks, a puritan loudmouth, had 'corrected' one of Mr Golding's most famous translations, De Mornay's *Trewenesse of the Christian Religion* and had re-published it without sending Mr Golding a penny. The world often tells the old that they are as good as dead, and this is what he was hearing.

His manner towards myself quite altered now that I was no longer his pupil. He bowed to me when I entered his study, called me Mr Felton and would ask my opinion. But he no more accompanied me on the Belchamp strolls, having another presence beside on the footpaths – Death. His steps slowed, his hand moved in flat tentative gestures over his belly, his breath rumbled and his eyes became haunted. When I once suggested that my frequent visits were becoming too much for him, he reacted quickly.

'No, no, Mr Felton. You divert me. You make me bright.'

These post-graduate months passed (it was his joke to call the Great Brick House my university) with not a word being said of my future, either there or at home. I wrote verses, hunted with father and felt strong for girls, often several times a day – but who could talk about this? The following year of Our Lord, 1606, there was trouble with our peasants when father and other gentlemen enclosed some of their commons and wastes, and for the first time in my life I experienced what it was like to be the object of spitting hatred as I crossed from Ovington to Pentlow. Fieldmen who used to wave to me and women who smiled from doorsteps ignored me. That spring Death caught up with Mr Golding. It nudged him in the lane and stood beside him at his translation desk, a cumbersome piece of furniture straight out of St Jerome's cave.

'You shall have this, Mr Felton, when I have gone to God.'

Death told him, frequently, to clear his desk but his answer was always, 'not yet' and right up until the solstice he propped himself against it, his pen working, his empty hand busy against his side, running up and down as though it might be able to make a grab at whatever it was that bolted through his guts.

'I have no pain, Mr Felton. No pain at all.'

In early May he accepted that Death would now never leave him and invited me to pray with him in Powles Belchamp church, which was just through the garden. It was raining and the leads were spouting, and the graveyard ditch running high. The slabs where we knelt also ran wet. I hoped that he would take a chair but he insisted on lowering himself like a mountain of fustian on the bricks in the north aisle, where there was nothing for him to clutch, and where he riffled through his prayer-book to find something suitable for the occasion.

'Read it, Mr Felton. And please do not touch me.'

I read, 'Extend thy accustomed goodness to this thy servant, which is grieved with sickness. Visit him, O Lord, as thou diddest visit Peter's wife's mother, and the Capitain's servant. And as thou preservedst Thobie and Sara by thy Angel from danger. So restore unto this sick person his former health, if it be thy will, or else give him grace so to take thy correction, that after this painful life be ended, he may dwell with thee in life everlasting. Amen.'

But I had barely got started when he halted me.

'Read and *pray*, Mr Felton. Don't just read.'

And I was reminded how, when we were at table and I would hold the meal up with my chatter, he would gently knuckle my head and say, 'Whistle and ride, whistle and ride'. He struggled from the floor and we returned to his study where he added to his Will in the presence of his Ursula and myself a codicil which commanded that his robe was not to be opened or removed after his disease, or that his flesh be seen by anyone, and that he should be laid in the ground coffin-less, and that before the clay thundered down on him, all should be lightly hidden with fine topsoil and daisies. His Ursula made a separate note of this as he

27

spoke, and with as little emotion as if she was telling herself to prune the fruit-trees in her kitchen-book.

All that week the house was sweetened by the smell of Death's business under Mr Golding's gown. The dogs, the tomcat, the pet hare and Tyto the owl, all drew into themselves this senescence and took to shifting uneasily, and showing signs of great sorrow, as beasts do when their friends go away. My own thoughts were selfish ones. Where would I go when he had gone? Reading them, he said, 'I won't be taking my library with me'.

His features collapsed, his size increased. So did the fatal stench. But still he stood and still he wrote. And still he ate. They say that the dying are so hungry. Every now and then I would hear Death's progress inside him, like sludge shifting in a trench. And still, miraculously, he walked, once nearly to Otten Belchamp, advertising his state, though without intention. Whilst Mr Golding had no doubt whatever that he would soon be in Heaven, those he met were quietly certain that he was on his way back to the Farisees. I begged God that I would not be present when he exploded like a puffball and his soul shot out. He died all alone in his study on May-day, his Ursula rushing out to prevent me seeing his corpse being manhandled up the stairs by the servants. He was buried two weeks later on the feast of St Euthymius the Enlightener – the thirteenth of May, who died on that day in the year of Christ 1028 by being run over in Constantinople. This saint was a great translator and had turned many Greek books into the Iberian language to help his own country. Mrs Golding, rummaging around in the library after her husband had been laid out, discovered this information and managed to live with his decay for a fortnight, quite rightly believing that he would have liked the coincidence. As mother remarked, she was full of surprises. There was a mighty concourse at the funeral, as you might expect, and a confident Luther hymn. The Earl and everybody came and black ribbons floated from Hedingham to Clare. That evening the hare and the owl left the Great Brick House and were never seen again. Mr Golding was seventy years of age when Death came. For which I thank him. He died with but one regret, which was that he had been refused permission to re-English Holy Scripture itself. He told me how, long before I was born, he had petitioned the

Queen, telling her that it would sure to be a mess if he didn't have a hand in it. But he said her answer – 'not yet' – arrived faster than horses. And then to live to see it happen without him! What a pity. And thank God he would die before its publication.

'Mr Felton, the grave is a shelter from forthcoming books.'

Mr Golding's name never hid among the small print of a title-page, but sat on it large and plain. He knew his worth, and spelt it out:

> Of truth, the skill and labour was not small
> To set each English phrase in his due place,
> And for the match the Latin therewithall,
> Of either language keeping still the grace,
> And orderly the Greek to interlace,
> And last of all to join the French thereto:
> These things (I say) required no small ado.

4

BLOIS

Not long after Mr Golding's death my parents announced my future. I had vaguely imagined that it had slipped their minds and that I would be allowed to continue pottering about the estate until I could give our name to some girl with enough money to pay for it. Whatever the dowry, we would never be more than poor relations to those who ruled the roost at Playford and Pentlow – even to my brother at tiny Ovington. But as no wife to be was in sight, I had taken to using a farm-woman for my needs. They had nothing by way of love about them, nor did I reward her with anything more than my body, not having anything other than this to give. In any case, it was a Felton principle never to pay a peasant. I was taught that the smallest token, the slightest privilege, would have him or her shooting up to the sky like a weed encouraged by a pail of water and a lump of dung. Keeping peasants low without harming them was an art in itself, as was keeping them from running off for soldiers. By him we meant a Parmenter. Any Parmenter. I do not ever remember having to learn these arts. I suppose they ran in our old blood. My hut-mistress was named Deborah and I had her discretely in my room. She was never with child.

I worked hard but haphazardly between my education and my 'future'. I took to the science of gardening. I discovered all I could about the Carolina plantations. I studied Greek. But anything I did was dubbed my 'crazes'. Father would force me to do something useful, such as taking-in land and walling it. What happened beyond our park became, in his words, 'None of our business'. Yet news leaked in. Had we heard that the new Queen was an actress? Had we heard that the Spaniards were no longer the enemy? Did we know what the French King was saying? 'There would not be a peasant so poor in all our realm who would not have a chicken in his pot every Sunday'? Did we know it was said that our Parliament was seething beneath its surface obedience? That the Queen had cut-up all Elizabeth's wardrobe for masquings and such-like? That the army was starving? That London was the poxiest town on earth – keep away, keep away!

'Father, I would see London.'

What eighteen year-old wouldn't?

'Keep away, keep away.'

The same answer to Melford fair. To anywhere.

So it was like the sudden release of the latch on the family cage when he publicly announced that I was to travel to France. We all went over to Pentlow for this stupendous event. Father straddled the time-dial in the great court, beat a drum and cried,

'You all know my son John – the scholar, shall I call him?' (Awkward assent). 'Well, he is off to Blois to manage the great horse and to talk the French language where it can be understood (pause for laughs), and to make himself a soldier'. So this was what it was all about! I was not to be put through the arcane antics of the male finishing-school in the Loire in order to rub shoulders with the young gentlemen from England who were on their way to Whitehall, or simply to a recognised culture. I was to be put through my paces and then commissioned into one of those stinking, sullenly obeying blocks of mankind called a regiment. War alone would bring my release, either via loot and fame, or via death. A second shock hit me. Had father looked at me these past months? Whilst I had put on a scrap of flesh and some inches since I left Mr Golding's reading-room, I was plainly no man-at-arms. Father continued to boost me on my heroic way, gripping my shoulder, looking down at me with pride. 'What would not I give to be his age and to sally forth!' He actually said 'sally forth', as though I was a Sir Dinas le Seneschal on the road to Tintagel. As one does at some critical moment in one's life, I found myself making a record of what was commonplace in it, in this instance my uncle's famous daisy-lawns, the whitest, they said, outside Cambridge, where in May not an inch of grass was to be seen. Those invited to view this wonderful sight had paused on the gravel walks to hear my fate. They applauded.

Mother wept. The widow Golding turned away.

There were to be subsidiary announcements. One of the Parmenter boys and an older man I had never seen before emerged from the stable arch leading three horses, including my Lento, my new servants in our livery. The unknown man looked what he was, an overdressed attendant. But Parmenter — it was Galyon — amazed me. In order to describe his transformation I must once more emphasise our necessary if sad policy of keeping the labouring kind bare-arsed-hungry, as they call it, to nip back what Mr Golding described as 'any natural supremacy'. To be fair to my family, all Parmenters were sufficiently housed, fed and clothed for decency, but of course were never allowed a stitch or crust more. This poverty didn't suit them – whom does it suit? – and yet never did it do to them what it was supposed to do, keep them down. Lean and tall, they strode around, each fresh generation of them, natural supremacy personified. All I could see of Galyon at this minute were his face and hands. The lanky rest of him was a prop for our pretentions, Capet, Plantagenet, de Vere blazing from his breast. He looked embarrassed, and hot. I could see what was in store for me. Masters who look like me, and servants who look like Galyon Parmenter have topsy-turvy times when they travel. Father said something I couldn't hear and both men came to attention. Our quarterings shimmered. Father brushed a light hand over them, getting them straight. The old servant, I could now tell that he must be forty or more, looked as if he would choke, and sweat poured into his starch. Servants and beasts then retired to more clapping and young men strode across the daisies to congratulate me with shining eyes and false envy.

I went to mother and was desperate.

'Not now, mother? Not *this morning?*'

'No, of course not, my darling. Tomorrow.'

Far off in the horseyard I could hear father shouting instructions to Parmenter and the old man. They were to keep up my state *at all times* – 'do you hear?' They were to care for me even at risk to their miserable lives – 'Do you hear me?' I was to be obeyed in *all* things – 'Are you listening? – in all things!' When I glanced imploringly at father – was I expected to make a speech? – he waved the very notion of it away as if to declare,

'Who needs gratitude?' Yelling to my new servants in our fine feathers to follow him, he vanished into uncle's armoury, where we could hear him dinning into them their responsibilities, my state, their obedience, my honour, their duty to it. A question must then have arisen because there was a long pause. Then we all heard, as distinct as a bell, 'Let me see. In sixteen-thirteen. Not a day before. Or even later if you all three go for soldiers!' But there was only his laughter.

* * *

Two days later we rode off at a showy little gallop for Gravesend. That is how it all began, the wrong-footing, the false direction, the unsuitable pace. We turned instinctively at the cross-roads to say goodbye but the ditch ashes were in full leaf early that year and Pentlow was already invisible. Father's £200 and my *Golden Epistles* topped the baggage. It was the white month when every lane in England stood proud with flowers, and may clotted the hedges, and all the mud had dried up. Father's instructions on how to get to Blois crackled uselessly in my pocket and we had hardly trotted through Chelmsford before we were enquiring the way. 'Nail-wo! – Go left!' whispered Parmenter into his horse's ear, and off we went through the marshes. Previous to this, the only journey he had made was a day's ploughing. It clearly entranced him to see field after field pass. With his straight seat and the rein hanging light between his fingers, he looked triumphant. He touched his curls to shepherds' pages, to hoers, to a parson, to vagabonds, to anyone, grinning handsomely. Not so my other servant, a Luke Allen from Lavenham, that godforsaken place. He I could tell was all of a conjecture how to rope Parmenter in, how to cope with him, how to bring him to heel. This was what was in the Lavenham man's mind as he studied the dust. Parmenter clopped on, singing.

Although it never occurred to me at the time, I suppose that this might be a good moment in which to wonder aloud about the role of Lachesis the inexorable in bringing together in the Loire valley three sets of young travellers who, when they set out from their English halls, had no knowledge of each other's existence. Unknown to us, her spindle flew. The coincidences of written romance are as nothing compared to that unsuspected drawn threadwork which pulls us into ruinous friendships. It would be of great dramatic assistance to my story if it could be stated that the modest retinues of the Villiers brothers, of John Eliot, and myself were all en-route for Blois at the very same hour, and would trot into its *place* like actors taking up their positions for what must follow. The facts are more mundane. It is simply that, there being a finite number of gentlemen such as ourselves in the world, we are bound to either know, or know of each other. Blois was where our sort had to begin to make their way. It was an antiquated riding academy, half a joke, yet still taken deadly seriously. It was a name one could drop for the rest of one's life. They say you can tell a Blois man at a glance, and that he can be found from Muscovy to Fife. Blois was the stepping-stone on to which the cadets of a great house fell when pushed from the parental nest. After Blois it was find your own feet. There must have been hundreds of youths from all over Europe, each with his small allowance and retinue of two – so that rich gentlemen should not take the advantage – in and around the city. I say this because history will insist that in 1609 Blois was Villiers, Eliot and Felton, the ruler, the conscience and the saviour of England in embryo, and that fate on the Greek scale brought us together on this spot. Unlike that of George and John, my own history would not have got much more than three mentions in the Ovington church registers had I not on the spur of the moment acted out of character, and so floated on blood into the limelight. 'Acted out of character' – how certain I have to be about this! But did I? What are we born? And I say 'on the spur of the moment', but it took five days to walk to Portsmouth with a knife, which can hardly be described as impetuous. Was I born with this knife? Was George born to be murdered? Eliot was certainly born for Parliament.

I can in retrospect see that George's role in life was to ornament it, and to receive desire. These gifts may not be on St Paul's list but they are not bad ones. Had George correctly understood them he would not now lie stinking under the Abbey floor. Just imagine, on that mid-May morning when father was pushing me off to France, George's new stepfather was doing the same for him – and his barmy brother. They showed me their joint Privy

Council pass, all of us roaring with mirth. 'We permit John and George Villiers, gentlemen, to repair unto the parts beyond the seas, to gain experience.' This was to be as funny as we first took it to be, for incredibly George was still virgin. He was backward in other things too, having no more education than what could be picked up at a Leicestershire vicarage before he was fourteen. He eyed my books nervily, as one eyes a mastiff in a gate, and would watch me read with admiration, shaking his head as the pages fled. But at the dancing-class and at the hippodrome – what a reversal of skills! His daft brother John on the other hand became vacant when he wasn't being drilled or being put through his gentlemanly paces. George showed open honour to this foolish man, as he was to do to the meanest member of his family, and so unlike myself who, apart from mother, thought little of our tribe. George demanded to know my lineage and enjoyed the notion of the FitzPagans. He himself, he told me, was descended via his mother from King Henry III.

But this is racing ahead. I am still in Essex and the Villiers still not far from Goadby. Parmenter said that he could not have imagined that there would be so much scenery. When would it stop? Was there scenery for ever? And he would twist in the saddle to take it all in. At such glad moments he would look positively seigneurial – far more so than father – and then I would think of him bent double in the February drains, his hands bleeding from the thorn-bushes which he was laying in the clay. And his shoulder-blades cutting through is shirt.

How pleased was he to be released from such labour?

'You will forgive me, sir, but I am not released.'

'I meant from the fields, Galyon.'

None of us ever found out where some of our peasants discovered their outlandish font-names.

'There is such a thing as the freedom of the fields, sir.'

'But is it not something to travel with me to France and to share the views?'

'It is something, sir.'

'You must beat him regularly to establish your mastership,' father had instructed. 'Lay about him with your crop. Sting his arse for him. Make him jump! He knows what he is and will accept your correction.'

This ludicrous advice came back to me as we swayed across the Thames on the dipping ferry. Kent bobbed before use like a foreign land. The great river was dense with ships and plangent with voices, and with the miserable dirge of marshland sheep penned on barges and on their way to the London shambles. At Rochester we stepped into the cathedral to look at the popery. Such altars! My servants were appalled. We sanctified ourselves. Parmenter fetched my prayer-book from the pannier and I read to them the proper for the Ascension, all of us kneeling. 'God is gone up with a merry noise, and the Lord with the sound of the tromp. O sing praises, sing praises unto our God, O sing praises, sing praises unto our King'.

'Do we sing?' enquired Parmenter.

'If we like.'

He sang in a light true voice a little meadow song which I no longer remember. A robed man hovered about us, fluttering anxiously. The Lavenham man beseeched God to come back to Suffolk. When we travelled on it was in self-reflective silence. You will have observed that, so far, the Lavenham man – I must call him Allen – doesn't get much of a look in, and the truth was that a kind of adult shadiness which was foreign to our youthfulness clung to him. There would be no getting to know him until he himself let out a little light. He did all and more of what was required of him. From Pentlow to Blois he protected the pair of us, fed us, kept us dainty, scolded us, led us away from a familiar to a foreign land. I thank him now for his unmemorable goodness.

It was early evening when we cantered into Dover, the very front door of England, as old Matthew Paris called it. It smelled of departure. We skinned our eyes for the famous view of France but it was curtained-off by gold mist. Though still numb-arsed from the saddle, I ran ahead in search of the double Pharos, those twinned lighthouses of the ancients whose beams were flashing even as St John was putting into words that incandescence which was Christ. And there they squatted, one on Castle Hill, the other on the western height, pink, unlit beacons which had once brought Caesars safely to our shore. After supper we walked the town again, Parmenter a step ahead wearing our livery. Women gawped at him. He looked both nervous and yet sure of himself, as the novelty of his situation began to dawn on him. The Lavenham man made us all ridiculous by pointing at me as the person who should attract attention. There were understanding grins. Ports are famous for proving that Jack looks better than his master. The late sun stared hard at the sea as if in two minds about setting. It was exciting to stroll through strange, busy streets and then to climb among the confused military outworks of centuries all fragrant with spring flowers. Just a few more weeks, and the sun would make them pestiferous. Allen gathered primroses like a child. A bugle played. We clambered over U-shaped banks and wandered from St Mary-in-Castro to the snowy drop of the cliffs to watch the tide rolling in. I remember telling myself, 'This is travel! This is what travel is!'

Except that travel knows no expurgation and doesn't give a damn what it brings into view round the corner. What we expected to see was a great harbour full of shipping, a thrilling sight for inlanders like ourselves. What we saw wiped out this happy sight, or rather be-smeared it, like a rag across a slate. Propped against the sea-wall, against moored boats, tackle, carts, sailyards, rubbish, anything which made a back-rest, were some hundred or so wounded or otherwise sick solders whose wind-burnt skin and fretful twitchings caused me at first to think that we had come upon one of those piles of old canvas which jerk with rats. As the odiousness took on human shapes, and thus growing even more horrible, I realised that we had strayed into realities too immense for any one of us at that moment to grasp. Eyes rolled in pain or desolation, or dwelt on unbelievable mutilations. We passed amputees with tarry stumps, men afloat in dysentery, thin unmarked men whitening with death, huge old carcasses crying, naked men whose wounds were healing but not closing, so that they looked as if they had been under the fletcher's knife, men whose rich young hair and beards moved with lice. No hands asked anything of us. There comes a time when begging is past. Whatever language these soldiers once spoke had coagulated into a corporate drone. I heard Parmenter asking, 'What ... what?' bending over dreadful injuries. I heard Allen imploring, 'come away, oh please come away'. I listened to a boy shrilling like a pippet. What battle?

37

'Ask a Dutchman,' replied Allen.

He then explained that what we were seeing was quite ordinary. That it was the policy of commanders to ship straight home the casualties of war. It was humane. Wars had come a long way since wounded men were left in foreign ditches. As for their destitution at this moment, did we imagine that the government would have left them in this state if it could afford to do otherwise? Governments aren't made of money. Why, he had heard it said that his Majesty wept for such as these. Imagine this too, a king in tears. It was God's truth. What I saw was the government's desire for the sea to wash all its post-battle detritus away, and I was soon to learn that Dover and all the Channel ports were in full agreement. What with being forced to billet these regiments before they set forth to lose a war, and with having to cope with them on their return, when they were in too disgusting a condition to be given house-room, it was no joke trying to uphold civilized standards on the south coast. It would be the same at Harwich. Penzance too. Each and every harbour was silted with such human refuse. There were so many of them that to just get them onto their feet would empty the poor-box. And then where to?

Parmenter walked slowly along the fallen lines, shocked, searching. Now and then his hands would go out in a small useless gesture towards someone who seemed to be calling him with his eyes. Once or twice he crouched, holding the livery skirts out of the ordure. The conduct of my other servant showed hopelessness of another sort as he stepped, not callously but very carefully between this bloody crowd towards the clean street. He was indignant for Dover, 'such a noble city, sir. What were our rulers thinking of to permit such sordid sights? Should it not be a felony for finished soldiers to exhibit themselves in such a fine place?'

'Come away.'

What now?

A Dover harbourman told us that those who could would crawl home. They'd find the road to Derby, Truro or wherever and the way back. Those who couldn't would perish and be given Christian burial. Dover did not get all the battle-wounded; each port received its share.

'Lucky for some. They'd land up on their own doorsteps.'

'Come away,' said the Lavenham man.

Just then the goodwomen arrived in their grey rank-hiding cloaks, at least a dozen of them. They set up a trestle and laid it with a mixture of food and medicines, bustling about and keeping the pity out of their faces. Goodwomen were father's nightmare. He dreaded that the Ursulas might 'go in for it'. He feared sisterhoods and had never been entirely happy with the close friendship which had sprung up between mother and Mrs Golding. Goodwomen, he said, were more out than in – it was a well known fact. They 'must' lead a life of their own, and that wasn't right. The Dover goodwomen found bits of old sailcloth to kneel on and busied themselves with the poor wrecked bodies, chatting comfortingly. One of them sent Parmenter off on an errand with a not so much as by your leave. Allen tried to indicate that I could not be ordered about like this but was ignored. The two of us were made to carry the trestle further along the quay, and to fetch water. A goodwomen asked if we could sing – had we a pipe? A drum?

'This is Mr Felton, madam, a gentleman with his servants,' said Allen.

'If you can't sing, go away.'

We returned to the inn. Allen sat me by the window and in an explosion of anger roared for this and that, throwing his weight about. Parmenter was made to stand behind my chair, where he remained still and silent. When the food came I required that they ate with me. The English Channel made prismatic reflections through the window-panes. When I crossed it to the wars, would I be shovelled back home as shit? No, only those I commanded.

* * *

In Boulogne we all three lay green and ill by the harbour wall, and holding our guts together after the ravages of *Le Mignon*, now bobbing at anchor. But the retching was over and a couple of hours collapse on a hard pavement soon steadied us. Our horses were tied up to mooring rings and were equally in need of firm ground. It did not seem inappropriate to thank God for

39

journeying mercies, after which I read aloud father's instructions. It was best that we should all three know where we were going and what we were doing. But I skipped the bits about thrashing Parmenter, and there was no mention of such correction where the Lavenham man was concerned, only a reminder to keep him in his place.

> Item 28. You are to send me report of Duke of Sully's land
> reforms and, if possible, to present yourself to that
> remarkable person ...
> Item 32. You are not to visit Paris.

The instruction sagged with do's and don'ts.

I will cut short our ride to the Loire beyond saying that M. Sully's hand was everywhere. It was Parmenter who first noticed that avenues were not restricted to country-houses but had been planted along the highways. Twinned elms ran ahead of us to infinity. Such stateliness, such divine shade! Their canopies created a dappling which played across our bodies, men and beasts, and there were alternate bursts of heat and cold as we briefly passed from the influence of one tree to the next. M. Sully's economies multiplied as we ride towards Orleans, which is the middle town of France, and a marvel to be still standing, as every invader with a military plan and a match has raged through it. Julius, Attila, the old English kings, they all came this way. But so did M. Sully to put it all back to rights. We travelled on his magnificent roads, we saw his managed woods, and the sloughs he had drained to make cornbearing acres, and his peerless meadows and his encouraged gardens. And then, winding through this earthy Duke's handiwork, we saw – the Loire! We dismounted beside it. It was as lively as cider. High above the river and extremely inconvenienced by hills, one would have thought, lived the French lords in their spiky palaces, any one of which made Hengrave look like a spice-box in comparison. These glorious seats were as fitting for eagles as for dukes and were, architecturally, quite out of control. We passed beneath them with unbelieving eyes and craned necks. Not one of them had paid heed to M. Sully's economies, needless to say, and the by-roads which approached them were full of state, with trumpets calling out and banners flying, and hound-music. We reined-in many times to let processions pass, doffing and bowing, and throwing out a right arm in what we thought was the French manner. There were no acknowledgements. We soon discovered that the French have manners but little politeness, and no consideration. These lords were people who dwelt in perpetual sunshine, inside and out, in golden rooms and golden gardens.

Parmenter was agog. As we trotted along, I told him all my father had told me about M. Sully. How he had found the most rotted-out France that ever was, and a king in a patched shirt ruling it, and how he, the Duke, had mended both single-handed, toiling night and day before Death cried, 'Come!' Which was not yet, although M. Sully was close on sixty years old.

'He loves a plough, he loves the flocks. He loves trees and good roads.'   The Lavenham man was mocking. 'So a duke loves ploughs and flocks does he?'

I quoted M. Sully. 'He called such things "France's paps".' He said, 'Suck from this green breast, not from the silver tits of Peru.'

'I wonder that my lord, your father, loves this duke, storming as he is about all the new farmsteads at home. I ask your pardon for this criticism.'

Privately, I wondered too. All my brief life our yeomanry had been in a passion of house-building. Scores of these new homesteads were visible from our parks. Down came the oaks, up went their frames, dizzy brick chimneys and all. It was the same throughout England. Where did the money come from? the gentry asked. They said that when M. Sully heard of this he felt inspired. But let him be surrounded by proud farmyards. Let him feel the independence of this go-piss-yourself breed and see how he would like it! Mercifully, father maintained, all this sticks, mud, thatch and post stuff wouldn't last. It would all tumble down in a generation or two. Unfortunately he would not live to see it.

'What my father admires in M. Sully is his aristocratic control of everything, from the court to the sty.'

This conversation took place whilst we were still in Normandy, where an enormous church all made of glass could be seen for miles. Inside, it was dark as night, a moon-drenched, starry night, that it is, all rich glimmerings and, I have to say, gorgeous dirt. We thought it badly in need of cleaning. We read its name, the Virgin of Charters.

'When your duke, sir, has finished with ploughs he could make a start on religion.'

I agreed with the Lavenham man on this point. There is nothing worse than a church in which one cannot see to read.

Since none of us is immune from the first effect of great sights, I have frequently found myself wondering how France, and the Loire in particular, first struck Villiers and Eliot. I know now that George was one of Nature's Loire-dwellers and John a cradle critic of all that this valley stood for. By the time I arrived they had already settled-in and become friends. What a lot of speculation there has been about our student years and their long shadows. What fantasies about who may have been the maker or wrecker of whom. One thing which remains uncontroversial is that we all adored the Duke of Sully. We believed that he had all the answers. He was our hero. There were not many men who could tell both king and cottager what to do for the best. As our paths crossed, the very first thing which Villiers, Eliot and myself did was to join the ranks of the Sully-men. My own conjectures on the old subject of what might have been tend to hang around the hypothesis of our meeting during a quite different studentship. Had it been Cambridge, not Blois, might not all this not have happened? I am not sure. The fact is that the three of us registered at this pompous horse academy with no previous knowledge of one another's existence.

There were a hundred or more like us, young gentlemen from all over Europe, each with his statutory pair of servants and stingy allowance, boys from Bohemia, Italy, Austria, and a number, besides ourselves, from England, all for the high horse. This was the pacing ground for second sons. Yet it does not answer the question of how it was that we three, the leading actors in a dark and future play, should find ourselves in Blois for its prologue. I suppose such coincidences must occur in the lives of those with less to do in the world. Everybody wants to know what George was like at Blois and both Eliot and myself have told them to the best of our ability, but it won't do. There is still something which has not been said, they insist. Then *you* must tell *us*, we say – over and over again. My conviction is that our fates were cast respectively in Port Eliot, Paul's Belchamp and, for George, in that Midland's parlour where his Majesty first glimpsed him, a Ganymede waiting to be uplifted to the skies. A guest who was present wrote to cousin, 'I think your Lordship has heard before this time of a youth, his name is Villiers, a Northamptonshire man (Leicestershire, of course). He begins to be in favour with this Majesty.' In favour! It was lust at first sight, then love, just as it is with all of us. George knew how to return both, something the Scotch Zeus had previously searched for in vain.

Those who feed on signs and portents have long since gobbled up the fact that soon after we three met at Blois the King of France, who was M. Sully's favourite, was assassinated. He and the Duke were at work on an amazing scheme for the federation of Europe, a scheme which would have prevented countless wars and which would have rationalised trade between the nations. Poor King Henri! He was trundling through Paris in his enormous carriage at the time, reading a letter, when a M. Ravaillac jumped on its steps and cut his throat, slicing the aorta. Sacred blood poured from the vehicle and settled the May dust in the rue de la Ferronerie. They said that the assassin had no political axes to grind, that he was mad, and that for him killing a king may have been just something to do in the afternoon. The world is apt to prefer madness to motive. I remember consulting the *Golden Epistles* when this news broke in the Horse School and read, 'God suffereth absurdities to exercise their force against such as are most strong'. Parmenter said that his grandfather, a man so strong that he could right a turned-over wagon without help, was hurried to God by falling across a cat.

'This cat, sir, lived for many years after the funeral and was known in the village as Parmenter's Dispatch.'

* * *

It was while we were on the road to Blois that I began to teach Parmenter to read. As it was among our strictest laws not to teach Parmenters anything except how to labour for us, I had to swear both him and the Lavenham man to discretion. The latter was foxed. He could read – most Lavenham folk could, having been long in the weaving line, which is a literate trade. I then saw in him more independence than my father would have liked, and that he wore servility like an apron to cover his powers. Parmenter's reading lessons took place during the afternoon, when France sleeps. One day he closed the pages of the *Golden Epistles* over my hand and said, 'Tell me a story'. As I had just read him, 'One friend ought not to say to another, I will not or I cannot, as it is the privilege of friendship to find nothing impossible', I couldn't very well refuse. We were sprawled under a hulver-tree in a warm vale full of swallows, and the Lavenham man was stewing a rabbit for dinner.

'Jonah and the Great Fish?'

Parmenter shook his head.

'The Green Boys?'

'I've heard it. Tell me one of Mr Golding's stories, and then I will tell you one.' I felt disturbed. It had always been hoped in Belchamp that the *Metamorphosis* tales were successfully restricted to us, so as not to imperil the souls of the peasants, we of course possessing the intelligence to keep them within a harmless context. So I hesitated, began to refuse, then saw something implacable in Parmenter's expression and felt a tightening of his grip on the closed book. Confused, I began to relate the first Metamorphic tale to come into my head, the one about Daedalus's other lad – not his son Icarus, whose waxed and bloody feathers fluttered on the sea – but that of his nephew, a clever youth who invented the first saw, then a compass and who, still only being twelve years of age, would certainly have gone on to invent print or whatever else was needed.

'Uncle Daedalus at once recognised his nephew's potential and the fact that here was a genius which would overtake his in life and overshadow his in history. It was what the painting masters most dread, to take on as a pupil the artist who must outshine them. To know it by the first stroke of the brush. To be known to posterity as the teacher of Signor Buonarrotti, and nothing more, might be sufficient for some men but not for others.'

I rather hoped that I had lost Parmenter with this flourish, and paused.

'Go on.'

'Well, needing like King Herod to nip trouble in the bud, Uncle Daedalus took this nephew, by name Talus, to Minerva's temple, which was the very altar of invention, and threw him from a high window. But the goddess caught Talus as he fell and changed him into a lapwing in mid-air.'

'So that he could invent plover's eggs, I suppose?' said Parmenter.

'In order that men should know that even a bird can be scared of heights. I am sorry to have to tell you that Tarus Lapwing took a cruel revenge on his Uncle Daedalus, and just as he was burying poor Icarus, who was now neither bird nor boy, just a mulch of plumage. He flapped about the grave-dirt crying Peee-wit, Peeee-wit, which in the language of that time meant something quite terrible to a parent who was laying a winged son in the tomb.'

They flock in their hundreds on the low field by Cavendish Mill, and just before snow.

Homesickness grabbed us by the throat. Our eyes were stung with tears as we watched the Suffolk lapwings. On the French roads it was the *hirondelle de cheminée* which glided past us with a tswit! And a swoop.

'The what, sir?'

'Swallows.'

'But what you first said.'

'*Le hirondelle.*'

He repeated the words in his dark new young man's voice, adding, 'I will now tell you a Mr Golding tale.' And he related 'The Transformation of Aesacus', another man-into-bird business all about a rustic prince who was caught as he slipped from a rock into the ocean and turned into a diver. Neither of us had ever seen a diver, nor knew what it was. Nor had the Lavenham man, who was listening. An anxiety then struck me, seeing their absorbed faces. What of their souls? As their master it was my duty to let nothing imperil their souls.

'Do you all know the Golding stories? All the peasantry of our country, are they familiar with them? Even the children – do they talk of apparitions and transformations? Could it be (I could hardly bring myself to say such a thing) that you all accept that you might as well turn into a bird or a tree as go to Heaven? What of our Lord Jesus Christ, who died for us?'

So I began to catechise them both, it being my duty. I prayed, 'The Lord vouchsafe to receive us into his holy household, to keep and govern us always in the same, that we may have everlasting life.'

'Amen,' they said.

We travelled to the sound of rustlings which were not made by fowls and little cries which did not come from peewits. What we heard were the Val de Loire girls who, to keep the bird metaphor, soared along with us like a pack of starlings, half running from bush to bush. To their credit, these ladies were not whores, but processions such as ours along M. Sully's highway were now so frequent that only a fool would not hope to get something from them, a coin, a husband, or just a bit of excitement. But miles before we reached the Val the Lavenham man and myself could not but notice Parmenter's brief sortees into the lane-side woodland, and hear the laughter rising to be followed by the telling silence. And then he would be seen galloping ahead in search of a spring, and when we caught up, there he would be, sluicing the love off him, my livery, like as not, tidily piled on a bank.

'He is washing the woman off him.' The Lavenham man spoke with disgust and no envy. He was never seen to wash, or at least not indecently, and carried with him a not unpleasant body stench, somewhat feral, which reminded me of Suffolk. When Parmenter shed his Felton clothes it was like a dragonfly shedding its husk. His thin nudity glittered as he splashed around and pools of pure colour shone from the hollows of his person. He danced about, waving, throwing handfuls of water into the air, yelling.

'For God's sake, sir, get him apparelled.'

The Eure fieldwomen – they followed us in groups – watched Parmenter's antics from afar, so weak with laughter that they had to cling to each for support.

'Oh for dear God's sake, sir, make him cover. Satan will be with us.'

I had them both hear Comminations – 'Turn thou, O good Lord, and so shall we be turned. Be favourable, O Lord, to the people which turn with thee.' The Lavenham man resented his

46

inclusion in such a petition. He was free-thinking and would kneel before me, but not before God. Parmenter knelt on his hunkers, mouthing the words vacantly and staring around, like a child at bedtime. During such bitter devotions I would hear in the quietness, not an inner voice, but distant cloppings and harness-jingles from sunken lanes as other Blois-venturers made their way to the Horse School.

The Duke of Buckingham was within earshot.

* * *

'Were you between Chateaudun and Vendome on Friday noon, sir?'

'Why, I suppose we must have been.' 'On that higher road?' 'Yes, again. Always ride on the higher road, if you can, Mr Felton.'

Laughter all round.

We were sitting in bedgowns waiting for clean shirts, George, his brother and myself. Our servants had rushed us to the Hotel de Saint Remi, stripped off our filthy linen, carried in food, vetted our papers, brushed our hair and patted us with rosewater. They had also forced us to wash all over in a tank by the door. They had pressed our garments and polished our swords. We sat playing cards, myself and George aged seventeen, and his older brother John. Having rode in together, we were under that curious compunction known to travellers to stay together. Who has not experienced the pain of separating from someone in who's company one has jogged along for fifty miles? Parmenter with his sixth sense smelled a rat and without a by your leave had slipped out to find other lodgings for me, but Mr John Villiers, when he realised this, and all courtesy and sentiment, spread his arms wide, shouting, 'Oh no, oh no!' We had arrived together and must therefore stay together. His voice was oddly domineering and too raised for what it had to say, the voice of a man who wasn't listened to, wasn't heard. Ever.

'Please stay with us, Mr Felton.'

These were the first words addressed to me personally by George Villiers. He might have added more but at that moment the door crashed open for another pupil's entrance, a skinny black-haired, dark-eyed creature who looked like the archetypical first-footer of a New Year's celebration. A gigantic servant, equally saturnine, proceeded him, throwing down his bag. The Villiers brothers were in a paroxism of delight.

'Then it *was* you on the lower road. Didn't I tell you, George, that rider down there, isn't that old Eliot in flight from scandal? Didn't I say it must be him? We saw you, plus that monster you call your man as we turned off at the forest. Mr Felton, Mr Eliot. Mr Felton, Mr Eliot is not respectable as he is on the run from Cornish justice, having pushed a Mr Moyle into a puddle, although do not let that stop you from shaking his hand.'

The newcomer neither offered it nor looked towards me, just nodded to the room at large. The Villiers hugged him until he gently detached himself from their warmth, but looking pleased all the same. I noted how much older he was to us and not only in year, but in every respect. He was in fact twenty and entirely grown-up. He strolled around glancing at the furniture, seeing if there was enough of it for the four of us, decided that it would do, then came to us, patting each of us in turn on the shoulder with the feathery gesture of a man who doesn't welcome too great physical nearness.

'Mr – John? – Felton.'

'I hope it will suit you, sir, for me to stay in this room.'

'Suit *me*? Will it suit you? That is what you should be asking.'

And this, I suppose, is how history comes together, casually, fatuously, with a nod and a tap and a snub, and a haven't we met before? At six the following morning we presented ourselves at the Horse School, taking care to arrive in three distinct posses, else, said George, we might look like a circus come to town. We were as clean as new pins. The drill known as *manège* is very much a public performance for no one in his right mind would be seen doing it in private. It is all about controlling a very large horse effortlessly but with panache. 'Think of Xerxes', the grooms would whisper as they heaved us up. They would have done better to tell us to manage an elephant as if it was a Spanish mare. Having sat on Suffolks since I was a child, the heighth and girth of the *manège* horses did not worry me, although I had never been instructed, as at Blois, to look down on the world as a conquered field. Crown the majesty of the horse with your princeliness, they told us. It was all in the back. From this very first day of *manège* I was laying plans to cut lessons on what I felt I already knew in order to read. I explained about the Suffolks to the Master of the Horse, but he would have none of this and ordered me to attend classes like everyone else. He took to flattering me, saying I should just see myself on Charleroi, why I was a little god! So neat. When, like the others, I had to wear the great plumed hat and carry the baton, items from the dressing-up box at the Horse School, he would bow to the floor, shaking his head and insisting that never had he seen such a future *grand maréchal!* If George happened to be watching he would applaud and agree. I must keep it up, *the manège*.

I suppose the Suffolks at plough in Pentlow had shown me that size and delicacy of movement are a common factor in both horses and riders. Dogs, too, are liberal with their nobility, lending it to their owners when an occasion warrants it. The only beasts to rival our plough-horses lived at Le Perche in the north-west fields of France. I would dearly have loved to visit them on our journey to Blois but the diversion would have been too great. Father's Suffolks were directly descended from King Arthur's battle horses. They throve on love. We blew tenderly into their silken nostrils as we thanked them for their condescension, for their coming down in the world from battlefield to cornfield, and told them that they were as good as Christians. They were sorrels with mighty heads. Their manes fell like curtains and their thoughtful eyes were full of their past. A white star shone on their brows. Their tread in the furrow was as stately as that of their ancestors in the Tintagel exercise-yards. We rode them back from their labours, our legs stretching with our years, until we were well astride. It was an honour. To be honest, the *manège* beasts were no patch on them. Groomed and practised to death, how could they be? They were equine old courtiers, affected and swanking. My heart stopped when I thought of a Suffolk ending up at Blois.

The Horse School itself was palatial. It held courses for venery as well for managing the great horse, and there were galleries where spectators could watch the making of commanders and courtiers. Its floors were paved with narrow red bricks set on edge, so that they could not crack under the hooves, and its walls were painted with the Labours of Hercules, lilies and roses, rapine, and fanciful views of the city which Alexander had built as a tribute to his beloved Bucephalus, a horse with a head like a bull. Both the Villiers boys loved chivalry, so they were entranced. Although their clothes were poverty-stricken – George's scarcely decent – I could not but notice the respect with which these French equestrians approached them. They were none of them young so perhaps it was the extreme nature of George's beauty which threw them, something which I, being his exact contemporary, found less overwhelming. George's looks were the kind which play havoc with the next generation. When he clambered onto the high horse it was King Alexander all over again. Everybody gaped and the professor-groom struck attitudes of wonder. An English god *au nez de quelqu'un!* Parmenter, attending me, stared up and past him as George was tutored in those gestures of magnificence from the saddle. In his pocket my servant carried a list of books which he was to present at the Duke of Orléan's chateau, along with a request that I might come there to read them.

* * *

On the Sunday, our first in Blois, we all four set out to pay our respects to the Duke of Orleans, a child of three, and feeling as George remarked, 'rather like the Magi'. What should we wear? A nice smile, thought George. The Duke's enormous house clung to the air above us. Its wall and towers were studded with gilded porcupines and salamanders which caught the sunbeams, and every pinnacle sported a pennant. This vision of piled and lovely rooms intoxicated George and I saw a look creep over his face which was that of someone given a ticket to Paradise. The colour scheme followed by most of the Lois chateaux was red, white and blue, a garish mixture of hues which in most instances one would avoid, but which on these rich heights became a correct declaration of good taste. The little Duke's house was red, white and blue, and all alive with leaping flags. Very pretty. We trotted through the main gate into an echoing courtyard and were received by a steward. We were just one of endless processions of *manège* students to pay this formal visit, young men on the make in France. Having been instructed what to do by the professor-groom, we spoke lavishly of the glories of baby Gaston and of how the high and mighty James adored him only a little less than the saints in heaven.

'Who shall I say called?' enquired the steward.

'You first', muttered George wickedly. He gave me a push. Well, when in Blois do as Blois does. I made a great bow and said,

'Monsieur, I am John FitzPagan Felton, Chevalier de Belchamp Walter, Belchamp Otten and Powle's Belchamp, and Cadet of the Honour of Clare.' Parmenter looked hysterical. 'Oh, I forgot', I added. 'I am Felton of Pentlow via Ovington. Yes, that's who I am.'

George said, 'I am George Villiers, late Seigneur de l'Isle Adam, of Brooksby Hall, Leicester.'

Eliot said, 'I am John Eliot of Port Eliot in the Duchy of Cornwall, and of Exeter College, Oxford.'

George's brother said, 'I am Mr Villiers.'

'No more?' asked the steward. He indicated that we should make our obeisance and we sank on the cobbles holding our hats to our hearts. 'Follow me'. We were inside. More salamanders, more porcupines, and a spring of stairs as clinging as sweetpea tendrils. We mounted. Mirrors imaged us in every direction. Monkeys, tame birds, kittens and spaniels screamed and scattered, and flutes called. We could sniff joints cooking. Halted before a closed door, we were informed of our nearness to M. le Duc, and it was true, just beyond it there was a small boy at play. More homage was required and then we were told to go. We clattered off, but I was called back and handed a card which read in English, 'Permit the bearer to read the Library. Scholar's robe. No servant'. I bowed genuinely this time. Oh, baby Gaston, how were you to know that you would continue what Mr Golding began?

Reading the Library would have taken a long lifetime. It climbed up and on like the Chateau itself with its topmost volumes crouching in the golden fenestrations of the ceiling. There were a number of other students, all male, all gowned. The Loire sun shot apologetically through the painted glass of the oriels, sorry to disturb us and throwing carmine, terre-verte, saffron and Venetian red reflections upon our absorbed heads.

Ladders ran up the laden shelves and marble philosophers with cold shoulders terminated each bay. My first action was of course to look for Mr Golding, and there he stood, all in a row, the entire Works. I ran my fingers along them. I could have done the same with my lips. I felt extraordinarily moved by his fame and so pleased for him. I imagined his translating hand under the daisies in Powle's Belchamp churchyard and, maybe, Tyto the owl seated on the leads looking down on Mr Golding's green hump. I drew out his Seneca on *The Benefitting, that is to say the doing, Receiving and Requiting of Good Turns*, and was touched to discover it to be a presentation copy carrying his signature and the legend 'Powles Belchamp Hall, 1577'. I wanted to run up and down between the students crying out, 'I knew him – he taught me!' I eased it back in silence.

I had been reading in the Duke's Library less than three months when the Lavenham man entreated me with tears to return to the Horse School and to matriculate in the sacred subjects taught there. Then to join 'my regiment'. He was so upset that I sat him down to calm himself. Out it all flooded. God had left France just as He had forsaken Suffolk. Who could abide where God was not? And must he remind me again that my body servant – he never called Parmenter by his name – was a whoremaster? And that our funds were low and, by now his eyes brooks, that he had been obliged to write to my lord your father, telling him these things?

'*What?*'

'A week ago, sir.'

He didn't blame me for my strange disobedience of a father's wishes. We were in a Godless land where the churches were stuffed with idols and the scandal of the Mass enacted daily. And where labourers were as put upon as cruelly as Jews in Egypt before God sent His plagues. I must be an English soldier. Who knows, his sacred Majesty in London would one day send in his army to cleanse this French sty and it would need gentlemen to lead it. Books came later. A man's life was action, then reading. I had got it the wrong way about.

'But our funds, Allen?'

'I eked them out and eked them out. This country is dear. There are some left. I am not a fool. But there won't be enough to cover the lessons at the Horse School if you don't start your training soon'. He quoted scripture on undefiled youth. Since we were living in the age of the epithet, and capping texts could go on indefinitely, I did not reply. What I did know was that Parmenter was costing us practically nothing, that girls fed him, if not precisely as the pelican did her brood, with practical returns for his love. It excited me to dream of him in their brown arms, tonguing their white breasts. I would be him as I fell asleep and one of his women when I woke up. It was all very confusing. But at seventeen one dreams all day of the serial joys which are waiting when the light goes out. The Lavenham man had gone back from discussing our money to the person who was also driving him crazy. He said that I was obviously too pure to know what Parmenter was up to. Momentarily forgetting himself, he went into a kind of lewd theological detail, then he drew himself back from this hell. He was severe with me – I thought he was going to shake me. I was to command him, command them both. Why did I not *command*? 'Command, sir, command!' And that Mr John Villiers – not Angel-face, his brother – surely he was mad? Oh, if only he was home in Lady Street with the flocks running through to market. Oh, if only he might get to Virginia, where the Lord had emigrated, he might be happy again. I tried to understand him, poor aged creature of forty years. I mourned for him, his day nearly over and heaven not exactly beckoning him. So I do not command, well we'll see about that. I drew myself up and pointed vaguely at the far distance.

'Return to your country and see your days out!'

'But your noble father ...'

'I will settle with him. You will have nothing to fear.'

'I will attend the Horse School, do well, and he will be pleased with me.'

'He will not believe you.'

Here he was wrong; father always believed me. Also what had begun as a bit of daring, a trying-out of authority, had suddenly coalesced into a determination to see the back of Allen. I had a vision of him in attendance for ages to come and couldn't bear it.

'Master Allen, thank you for what you have done for me. I dismiss you from my service with eight pounds and an outright gift of your horse. Let it carry you to Lavenham – or to the

Plantations if it can.'

And that would have been that, except that Parmenter then arrived in a hurry to sum-up what had just occured with his sixth or seventh sense. Allen turned on him and pounded his chest, driving his instruction home. 'Are you, thump, listening, thump? And don't you dare look at me like that!' He seized me and joined our hands together. 'Are you listening, cock-robin? You are to guard him to your last breath and to have him as your master in all things. You are to mend your ways and to fear God!' Later, we listened to him scrabbling his possessions together and harnessing Peggle. We heard him take the wrong direction. Just before this there had been a spate of farewells in emotion-thickened Suffolk. Lavenham speech was words through wool, they used to say, and you needed a local ear to unravel it. I was amazed to see Parmenter take the old man in his arms for just a moment. When we were alone he said, 'Now, little friend, what are we to do with you?'

* * *

And so our education passed. We learnt to dazzle, to catch the eye of men whom we thought could promote us, and to ape the gods. Awful, terrible, was our countenance, teenage Mars glaring from the saddle. Now and then I would catch Parmenter smothering a grin, not his fear. Both of us were leading a well-planned double life, although he knew about mine whilst I knew nothing whatever about his. He observed me work hard i.e. in the Library and play hard, i.e. in the Horse School. By making *le manège* into a silly game I found that my temper never rose when I was put through my paces. The hint of mockery with which I received the bawled orders was mistaken for a desirable arrogance in me and my frequent weariness and inattention – double lives take it out of you – were seen as officer-class languor, a sure sign of high blood. I soon began to realise that while I was nothing to look at beside George, and infinitely unimpressive beside Eliot, that in some perverse way I did look like a soldier. I resented this and would now and then turn up with wild hair and a deaf ear, galumphing about all over the place. But this behaviour too was accepted as a sign of my suitability for the officers' mess. It never occurred to me to come on with my nose in a book or to air my intellect which, if I say it myself, was – is – considerable. This would have created doubts. I began to tell myself, even at this early hour, that a lieutenancy, properly managed, would leave me adequate time for reading books, and maybe even for writing them, just as any commission allows all the time in the world for what soldiers do off the field. And my parents would love me more, and my furloughs at Ovington and Pentlow would bring out the laurels. Lieutenant Felton and, inevitably, Captain Felton. I asked Parmenter what did he think? I told him of scholar-knights, of poet-knights, of captain-visionaries with ink in their kit. I saw my tent and chapters and pages under canvas, with the blare of trumpets for bookmark. A little shed blood now and again, nothing to speak of.

Dancing classes. Eliot would have none of these. I would have had none of them either but I now saw compliancy as my best weapon, so I went. For some reason the Blois vogue was for English dances, galliards, pavanes, jigs, canaries, sarabands, Whitehall things, and all of them without women. Our instructor caned our heels as the fiddlers and drummers thumped them out. A soldier must dance. So must George Villiers, I soon realised. When George danced it was a man dancing; his masculinity was as much on display as when he fenced. His partner was a slight but robust Welshman named Lionel ap Owen, very ugly, and the pair of them stamping along in some outlandish *bourrée* which they had created was sensational. Real ladies would partner us at the Angers *bal*, and were already dreaming of partnering George. The *bal* was our passing-out parade, with not a horse present. The greatness of the Great Horse had by then to be seen in us. Although George was clearly beyond instruction where dancing was concerned, this did not prevent a little painted *Directeur* screaming such advice to him as, 'The hands, the hands! Monsieur, let fall the hands into flowers! Let them be white flowers!' And, critically, 'Has Monsieur no thin hose for his big legs?' As I may have already said, the ragamuffin outfits of the English students – there could not have been less than a hundred of us spread around Blois and Angers – enfuriated the French, who saw in them an affectation. They, although miles from Paris, would stroll down from their chateaux all got up *à la cour* to challenge what they saw as our squalor. All the same, we knew that our practise britches and slovenliness would not at all do for the *bal* and I sent Parmenter off to find feathers and plenty of ribband. I examined him too on our future, his and mine, which was another partnership.

I had it all worked out in my head. A commission in a foot regiment. A garrison of books to prevent it conquering my private life. A sensible division of the day between the field and the study, and no groaning when the King, in his fancifulness, sent us into battle. God knows there is nothing worse than the self-pity of soldiers. Mercifully, his Majesty was as poor as a church mouse and would not be able to afford the usual military larks, nor need them now that Spain was a friend.

'What do you think, Parmenter?'

I remember to this day his hesitation.

'I think you should think it over when you return home, Monsieur.'

'"Monsieur"?'

'Sir – my lord.'

'This country is pushing itself into our heads, Parmenter.'

He was on the brink of adding to this but all he replied was, 'Yes, sir, France.'

'You will be an officer's man. Turn me out well. Put a shine on me. Sleep beside me in the tent. We shall say our night prayers together and the Lord Jesus Christ will protect us and love us. What do you say?'

Parmenter's answer was a shock.

'Look at me, Mons ... Sir. Listen. You are to go home after the passing-out. You are to return to your parent's hall and tell them to make you parson at a Belchamp, or a Borley if needs be. Anywhere with an old church and a good house. *You-are-to-go-home.*' His authority was without insolence and at the same time without precedent. He added no apology for speaking to me so. 'In your bed tonight, sir, tell yourself, "It is my life, not their's." The Lord Jesus will be very glad to have you for parson, so will a Belchamp if I know anything.'

I can see him standing in front of me now, a Janus finger-post pointing to opposite directions, Pentlow-Portsmouth. I could not speak; his advice had eaten-up all my words. Looking past his earnest figure I saw my father 'Seeing me right' on the one condition that I never asked him for anything more than his gift of a good start – 'the best any young fellow from our kind of stock could have, and don't your forget it.' Were there livings within his gift? I had never enquired. Would he run to kiss me, like the ever on the look-out father in the parable, when I appeared in the drive? No. He would hurry me out of sight as he wondered what to do with me. 'He's *home* - and after all I've done for him! Dear God, what will the de Veres say!'

* * *

In my bed that night George's girl came to me. Moist from him, she put me where he had been and loved me in patios and charity, running hard little workaday hands over me, and sniffing my skin. Any attempt to describe it all at this distance will run me into writer's lust. But I can say that she smelled of mould and fruit, and I suppose George, and of mouse-nest, and that I was forced to shut here mouth with mine to mute her giggling. She was a romper. She whorled her tongue in my ear, causing a roar like seashells. This trick produced instant madness. Now she had to say shush. She was a fieldwoman but any comparison with my Pentlow hutwoman was pointless. I now understood pleasure, how to give it, how to take it. Pleasure is rare; one would not think so but it is. Rare. Why would we spend so much time seeking it if it was easy to find? George's woman – no name – was pleasure. I came with, this time, my hand over her lips in case her noises reached him. The mere sucking of my palm by this little haymaker, I can say retrospectively, carried with it more bliss than would all the arts of the stews anon. Little snoring *inconnu*, little honey-carrier, I have had to have you to have pleasure! Have you noticed how a woman will ask her pensive lover, 'What are you thinking of?' Not who, unless she feels like a row. Nobody ever, in that famous thoughtfulness which follows love said, 'A penny for her name' but even if they had I could not have given it. Not that she needed a name for my purpose. In our sleepy tangle I heard the rain, heavy summer rain drowning the thatch and hissing

57

through the cobbles, and I saw the summer lightning descending from on high like Jupitor on Aegina, all fiery spurs. It was quite a night, as they say. French thunder is so personal. I remember thinking about the crops, how they would have to be scratched to attention and made to stay upright until the scythes went in. I explored the fieldgirl softly as she slept and as the Loire shook, considered what Parmenter had said. Father's rage was much diminished in the context. A rectory, not a tent. Tithes, not laurels. The Reverend Mr Felton. Holiness was quite the fashion. It was quite in. I touched an ear with my tongue but she tore her head away and I had to comfort her back to dreams, like stroking a cat. The skies broke and the water fell in torrents. Holy Mr Felton where it never rained very much and the heavens stretched to – Heaven – where else? France was definitely less firmamental, and there were days when the clouds were spiked on weather-vanes. I used to lie in the border-Suffolk meadows thinking how suitable our skies were for the Second Coming. So much space for the Angel Host. 'I want to ask you something,' I whispered to the girl, knowing her ignorance of myself, my tongue, my new question. 'Shall I be parson – or captain?' The foreign words silently passed into her breath. No name and soon no face. But I managed to hang on to the sensation sufficiently to use it as a measure in future couplings. 'That was almost *it*!' I would tell myself, the French girl in mind. What name?

'Whore!'

Even dead asleep I found words to deny this. Scoldings beat down on us as we lay tucked into each other like conies in a burrow. So did the smell of breakfast. George was dancing round our bed, imitation white rage, a real white knife. He could scarcely speak for laughing. He called his dolt brother and the pair of them watched as the girl collected her wits and her gown, and was gone before it all started up again. She knew young men. She had thrust her way through us and made off as if we were no more than a mess of puppies.

'Oh, Monsieur de Fitzfelton!' said George. 'Parmenter!' he shouted to the attics, 'Look where you master has been loving! You must take better care of him. At this stage he can lose what else he likes but not his heart.'

For the next month or so the four of us kept common company, sharing who and what we had, but with different degrees of ease. George himself was all ease. As with sex, bodily splendours later reviewed run away with the pen. In the Blois streets, up at the Chateau, at the Horse School, or simply joining the idlers sunning themselves by the river, he destroyed ease, which I expect is why he needed to recreate it wherever he went. What was he like then? Well, think of Prince Absalom of St Stephen, or Leander 'whose presence made the rudest paisant melt'. Think of a tall lad from Leicestershire with heaps of grace and no education and a head like lovely Lucifer's. George, to do him justice, had at this time no more notion of his appearance than a hog has of its being born for roast pork. Not that I am qualified to give evidence of his beauty at this stage. Parmenter blocked my view, and was my poem in this instance. How could such flesh be so base? He was coltsfoot springing directly from clay, smooth, sky-turned, with no smear of what fed his roots, with everything denying what he was, the lowest sort.

*　*　*

Eliot was old for us. It took me many weeks to recognise that he had to be my particular friend. He hung himself up in a sleeping-net at night, like a sailor, daring us to give it a swing, which we never did. Eliot noted George as one notes phenomena, someone out of the ordinary with a future role to play. At court, naturally. Those peninsular-black eyes in the dark face would penetrate us from on high, Booby Villiers, Ganymede Villiers and the Bookworm where we radiated from the hearth. How grown-up he was, lying there. Eliot was twenty, had been to Oxford, had had a scrape with the law, and was now engaged to be married. How sappy and unlicked we three were, how just that he should soar above us! We spoke up to him. I saw at once that he possessed gravitas. Mr Golding maintained that it should not have been a woman whose name was above rubies but Gravitas. He would give it a capital. 'You have it too, dear little page-worm, but it won't begin to show until you are fifty.' So how truly distinguished to be Mr Eliot at twenty! How enviable to be a young serious man. Parmenter amazed me once by lightly grasping me by the shoulders and handling me round until I faced Eliot when he was watching the *manège*, and declaring, 'There, sir, there is our sun!' It is quite right what they say, that France breeds intimacies.

Eliot was a natural of the purified faith. His instinct was for the undiluted, undecorated teachings of Jesus. These, with no disrespect for the Saviour, he ran all the way back to the ancient philosophers, such as Plato. He hated Roman Catholics and did not really love the Church of England. What Mr Eliot loved was England itself. His country was his religion and his heretics were those who threatened its holiness.

'I suppose,' George would tease, 'that Cornwall may be called a part of England? In spite of its being no more than a rocky old foot kicking the Atlantic?' Eliot knew what was coming, or rather who, but where George was concerned his forebearance knew no bounds. Thus when George started yet again on the tale of Mr Moyle, there was no rising to his banter, albeit that Eliot's boyhood affray with this worthy had landed him with nation-wide notoriety and he had every reason to cry, 'Enough!' George would begin by being solititous. Cornwall, being no more than a ledge, was it not hard for a gentleman such as Eliot's most honourable father to find a seat?

Then it would come, along with some of that asininity forgiven in princes, 'Now, John, here is Mr Moyle taking a post-noon stroll in Port Eliot when the son of Mr Richard Eliot of that parish in the Duchy of Cornwall makes an outrageous display of his lace and is very properly rebuked. But do you, the trimmed-up pupil, learn modesty from Mr Moyle? And it is not the first lesson on public behaviour which he has given you. You do not. On the contrary, you are hot and you hit out. You, Master Eliot of Port Eliot, all of fourteen, clump Mr Moyle! And now every Englishman knows your character – a Moyle molester, and hardly fit for Exeter College where you were sent to hide until the kingdom's indignation died down. They say at Oxford that you kneel in the mud, like poor old Moyle, and cry, "Who can purge me of mine offence but only thee, O God!" What we want to know is, first, what was your sin? Scent on your black thatch? Pricked-out breeches? And, second, is it true that you shoved Moyle off a cliff? We believe that you stripped off your hose and danced on the sands with your hairy legs. Have you seen Mr Eliot's legs at

60

the swim? They are feathered like the legs of a stallion or an archangel. What a shock for Mr Moyle! You should have gone to gaol for ungodliness, not to read law at Oxford. Oh, John, to be luxurious whilst fishermen starved and festered in your coves!'

Behind this tedious mockery I could tell that George was fascinated by both Eliot and Cornwall. Mr Cade, his only schoolmaster, had read to him out of *Le Morte d'Arthur*. George, I should add, loved being read to and rarely read for himself. He could be a gannet for text if it was fed to him from someone else's mouth. His mouth would hang open for the next paragraph. 'Here,' I would say, worn-out, 'read it for yourself!' He would then hold the book like an unlettered before laying it down. The result of all this was that those who read to him became in some strange way the author of what he was hearing. Thus it was Parson Cade from Billesdon, not Sir Thomas Malory, who paraded before George that dream of knights in Cornwall. Their names, Sir Tristram, Sir Hue of the Red Castle, Sir Kay, Sir Persante of Inde, Sir Tor and all the rest of them, buzzed in his head like flies in a tinder-box. Far from being a pathetic ledge Cornwall was where he wished he came from. He was especially entranced by Sir Tristram's trial in a chapel on the rocks, as the knight, naked and accused, protested to all the other knights, 'I have fought for the truage of Cornwall!' before bursting free in a sea of blood. Mr Eliot told us about Tintagel, Dozmary Lake and Pendragon. He said he had never heard of Camelot. On a map, that is.

Eliot's fiancée was a Miss Rhadagund Gedie of Treburaye. Letters from her flew into our lodgings and were in a good hand. Eliot would rub them against his nose to smell, he said, tamarisk. Looking back, I can see that these letters were the cause of the thinnest of rifts between George Villiers and John Eliot, a division so spider-faint that only time could show it up. She made a difference. It could have been that George could not bear – endure – anything which stood in the way of full possession. Young men in barracks and classrooms possess each other in a full, legitimate comradeship. But the lady of the rocks possessed Eliot and George found his way to him barred. He may not have wanted to go that way – entirely – but it disturbed him to realise that he could not. Badly barbered, bespoke, adult Mr Eliot was out of our inexperienced reach. I see now that he was out of our hands from the start. England will always be ruled by men who have watched each other grow up. We had not watched this ruler grow up but he had us. His hammock swayed above us just as the great censer swayed above the faithful in the aisle of Norwich Cathedral, until they cut it down.

'Smell it, if you like.' Miss Rhadagund's latest letter. 'Tamarisk.'

'Bog faery,' said George. 'It smells like bog faery to me. And I should know because we have our fens.' It troubled him that a girl should have a name like the blare of trumpets. Was she conceivably descended from bog faeries? That would explain it. The fool brother went into agricultural details. George praised him with his eyes. George was such a family man, and practised in hiding the brother's deficiencies, which he did by covering them with honour, although it was obvious that he was a mite crazed. John Villiers' person was at first glance very like George's but a second look – and with such people there is always the second look – revealed the warp, the over-all misalignment which, though slight, was telling. Parmenter saw it at once; peasants are wide awake when it comes to lunacy. The brothers shared a bed and the younger would bow the elder in after prayers. We would look at our toes and shuffle our feet when George grew *exalté* about this screw-loose brother and we became even more uncomfortable when we saw that he meant it. When ever he ran into admiration, which was often, he would make one of those generous movements which one sees in paintings where the lesser figure points to the greater. At first we thought it was all a sham or all a kindness, but gradually we had to accept that George meant it. Insane or not, a brother was a brother. A Villiers. But I saw something else, or more. That whilst beseeching John to set the pace, or take the lead, George had him on a rope which he believed was invisible to us. He could be jerked to heel should he go too far. For safety's sake. John looked good as gold on the high horse and George would beam seeing him so elevated above mischief.

* * *

62

Our course passed. A future bishop drummed French into the Villiers. We all mastered equitation, court ways and the foils. Eliot, as a devout disciple of the Duke of Sully, frequently disappeared to study drainage and planting, and to pick up dangerous ideas. Our religion was a mixed business, what with the Villiers becoming giddy with papistry in the Orléans chapel and the cathedral, and Eliot feeding on the plain Word under a poplar tree, and myself holding a service for Parmenter on the river bank on warm Sundays, using the Second Prayer Book of Edward Six. Eliot would occasionally join these matins, throwing his bony length down among the water-flags, his black eyes bright with tears. It was the English language. Parmenter and I wept too for our village chancels and their ceremonies, and our own church bells. And then Mr Golding would spring into my head to do penance for 'planting in our religion uncertain stories, legends, responds, verses, commemorations and Sinodalles'. Boats passed on the violet surface, their canopies wind-filled and cracking like gunshot. They would make their way through naked children and swan-flotillas, and the white arms of women would hang from their sides, their ringed fingers feeling for marigolds or fishes. It was not easy to be stern for God.

We were to leave for Angers in August, to pass-out on the famous Parade there. It was about this period that Parmenter's behaviour grew so challenging as not to be overlooked by any of us. So far as my wants were concerned I had nothing of which to complain. Nothing. As to his friendship, for this is what I had to call it, it was faultless. My body, my horse, my commands, my state, all were properly seen to. But seen to too quickly and with that efficiency which lets you know that a servant has a life of his own. Ever since we arrived in Blois Parmenter had slipped off for an hour there, and an evening 'when I have finished' for himself. And of course there were all those free afternoons when I was reading in the Library – where was he then? He should have been kicking his heels with the other attendants, boasting about me, and not too far from my beck and call. But he wasn't. So where was he? And indeed, *what* was he? Yet all this time he remained endearingly reliable. My last sight of him each day was of him barring the shutters, smoothing my coverlet and humming his way back to the kitchens, but it was a last sight which told me pretty plainly that he was no longer doing these jobs as the servant he had been, but as somebody else. I wouldn't have minded so much, but the others were observing as well. In seagoing terms he was a craft which had cut its painter but which had not as yet left his galleon – myself – to sail on. Not to put too fine a point on it, he was independently bobbing along beside me, which was not allowed. He belonged to me. I owned him. My father had given him to me. The Villiers brothers reminded me of a further difficulty if this went on. How was I to hold my own in a decent regiment if I could not command my servant? We discussed it in the *place*. There was no real problem said John Villiers. 'Your man hasn't been broken-in – now, has he?' He thrilled with what would have to come. One good thrashing should do it. I recoiled so violently that Eliot cried, 'Whoa!' and 'Steady!' pretending to save me from falling into the town well.

5

PASSING OUT

This urban scene contains all the undimmed detail of the London day when, with the Remonstrance hammering out answers in my head, I decided to kill George. There were the August crowds hot for excitements, there were the refreshing fountains, the chattering wheels, the doves doing sentry in their *columbier*, the acrid gutters steaming with horse-piss and sending up rainbows, the pomp, the misery, the sensational public clock.

And there too at the parting of the ways were we, George and loony brother John, off to Leicestershire, Eliot off to Cornwall and his Miss Gedie and myself – if Parmenter had anything to do with it – bound for Ovington and a handy rectory. George, who always danced when he had good news, had danced to

> *Goadby, Goadby,*
> *Good old Midlands,*
> *Poor old Step-dad,*
> *Here we come!*

He was still prancing when Parmenter arrived with my marching orders from Father. I knew they would come.

St James's-tide in 1613

My ever dear Son,

Your triumphant deeds at the Great Stables have reached us. (How?) Noble lad! From now on we give you leave at all suitable times to display our Arms which, you will recall, are as following: Gule, ii Lions passant, Erm., crowned Or. To which you must

65

never forget to add a crescent to show our secondary position in the Family.

Our desire for you is: after your glorious matriculation at the Great Stables of Blois and Angers, pray proceed to a Regiment of your own choice, Parmenter to be your body servant and life man. *Do not return here.* Stand on your own two feet. Having made the severence, staunch the cut. Do not connect yourself in marriage without our permission. Remember the seat of the Pox. Remember our Lord Jesu Christ. My Lady your Mother recalls you with affection. The agent at Jewry to forward you £20 at Michaelmas in perpetuity so that you never want. You may keep the horses and the man I mentioned. O fortunate son! What prospects spread before you! It is said at Long Melford that there never has been better barley.

I am your Father, Felton of Ovington.

'So that is where you will be going when we finish?' said Eliot, touching the letter.

I nodded.

'Then we shall ride together to Boulogne – you are returning home?'

I could say yes to this; there were no English regiments abroad. But he assumed I meant Cambridge.

'*Will* you be going home?'

'I expect so.'

He gave me his worried look but said no more. The inevitable women of the Square now arrived shrilling, '*L'Anglais! L'Anglais!*' and whisking their skirts at us. George waved an imaginary apron at them, intending to be his mother in her henyard. This gesture was badly misinterpreted and there were derisive yells of '*mignon!*' Confused, George placed an arm round my shoulder in his touching way to lead us from this mob, which confirmed its abuse and it was *coquine!* until we were out of sight. John Villiers ran back after the women, chasing them, his fists up in the air like the winner of a race.

'Let us eat,' I suggested, 'then ride across the *campagne* to watch the night-harvesters.'

We spat in our hands and clapped palms in agreement. These fields were where I could just pick out Parmenter's tall form on a clear day as he farmed away or walked to the vineyards, swinging along. Free. Sliding off. No, that was not it; there was nothing furtive in him. He strode off. My father was very much against a servingman finding time for his own affairs. It was impossible, he said, for a servant to have time to himself, there being no such space in his day. The master could give him time for himself, but he could not *find* it for himself. The only way he could obtain such time was to steal it or be given it. I then thought that Parmenter's daily absences were all my fault. When had I ever told him, 'take the day – or even the hour – off?' Never. The Villiers sent their servants to the fairs and brothels, and Eliot permitted his to fish the Loire every afternoon, and thought nothing of fetching his own dinner from the buttery, or indeed mending his own shoes. I was horrified to find myself so upset by Parmenter's freedom when he was right behind me when ever I needed him, disgusted at being my father's son. He would be more comfort and my stay when I joined the regiment and do what he liked besides.

The day before the grand *bal* at Angers he made an appointment to see me. An appointment – his word! It all began easily enough. He had found feathers to stick in my hat and other tolerable finery, which he stitched together, swearing under his breath, sometimes in Suffolk, then in the Loire field language. His yellow hair hid his bent face. 'I ask your Honour for a suitable time when I may speak with you.'

I was dumbfounded.

'It would be good when you return from your reading this afternoon.' And he pushed his hair back and bowed. White and scarlet feathers swept the air. He left. I heard his light descent down the steps and a scrap of song. I felt suddenly sick, impotent. Father's incredulous features swam before me, so did an emptiness, the kind which is left by the withdrawal of caring. But Parmenter did care. If I was hollow it was because I had driven his caring from me. So it was a few hours later that I gave him, my own servant, audience, calming myself with thoughts of the condescension of our Saviour. Parmenter arrived with a woman, an old woman, at least thirty, with weathered skin and polished black hair. And grape-black eyes. She was tall like him, but plump, and he held her by the hand. He was still clinging to it when she curtsied, very low, dragging him slightly with her. But when she continued to lower her head in my presence, he tilted it back with the movement one makes when chucking a child. She smiled with dark teeth.

'Madame Oiseau – My Lord Monsieur Felton.'

The beer-coloured smile widened.

Madam's husband, Monsieur Oiseau, had died and gone to Paradise and he would marry her, prune her vines, keep her fields, give her sons. She was a papist, but who was not here? It must not be held against her. She would have a bargain in him because he was young and strong and knew how to farm. You know how to read, too, I was thinking. The childish bargain we had made out of doors soon after coming to the Loire land, that I would show him his letters if he would hide them from father, exposed itself as the treachery it surely was, my treachery to my kind. Keep them ignorant. Why give flame to an infant? Did not the Scriptures say a millstone round the neck was all too small a punishment for those who destroyed the innocence of these Little Ones? Parmenter, tall and fair, continued to hold forth on marriage and agriculture in a bi-lingual tumble so as to acquaint his women of his skills, his love and his intentions. She had obviously taken a hand with his dreadful clothes because they looked quite different with the seams tacked up and fresh strings pulling them together. In a minute he would be handing-in our livery! He opened a vellum packet and there, with its waxes dangling, were the deeds of a farm and scrap of priest's paper to say that the woman's husband had gone to God this twelve-month, *requiascat in pace*. Parmenter then undid the pouch on his belt to reveal – nothing. He shook it upside down and only seeds fell out. Laughing, and turning to her as easily as if I had not be present, he waved empty hands before her face, a take-me-as-I-am gesture which so pleased her that she very nearly did before my eyes.

'Although no Englishman is slave, sir, and I do not have to ask you to sign my freedom, it would be for me a wonderful honour to our friendship if you would write a blessing on all this.' And he waved his arm towards Madame Oiseau and some landscape which was framed in the window like a contained prospect of Eden.

'You are requiring my assent, is that it?'

'If you like, sir.'

'But you don't need it? Is that what you are saying? You would like it but you can manage without it?' I knew that I was deliberately misunderstanding him but was thrilled by his consternation and pressed on, humbling him in as many ways as I could. And especially by going on as though his partner wasn't there, which I could see made him particularly miserable. 'And,' I was about scream at him, 'What about the livery, where is it? Were you going to rob me of it? Did you think that I would forget it so that you could sell it? Or wear it when you weaned French pigs?' Abuse throws itself out like sick after the first sour mouthful. It astonishes one how much there is of it when it starts to come. Parmenter was actually holding his fingers over his face as if to protect it from this dirty jet. But then suddenly I was well again and the really rotten things weren't said, and sank back from my gullet. In the silence I began to look around for the new ink which he had just prepared me. I can't remember what I wrote. Their names, of course. What was Madame's? Thérèse. She trembled when I repeated it. My self-nausea prevented another word. I wrote what I could and pressed it into Parmenter's fist and felt his nails, broken from planting, scratch against mine as he took it. He placed it with the burial deed and the farm deed in his pouch, bowed, and the two of them left. When the Villiers returned they took my tears to be evidence of my servant's assault on his master and set-to at once to correct him. I insisted that it was unnecessary and ran after the pair. I heard John Villiers say, 'He'll warn him, he'll warn him!' and George say something like, 'Quiet! Now – quiet!' as one does to an over-excited dog, and as one has had to do many times before. There was quiet after this and not another word fled through the slats into the open air.

Parmenter and his Thérèse continued to walk when I caught up with them. He thought I had not heard all his plans for me and apologised for his casualness. The white road-dust we kicked up floated along with us. There were early-homing birds in the hedge and bees heavy with honey. He patted Madame Oiseau and said, 'A good bargain?' It was respectful fun. It was thoughtless of him not to tell me what would happen after the

Grande Equitation but of course he had it all worked out. He would not only ride with me to the port, but cross the water with me, find an attendance in Dover and set my feet on the Essex road. It was then that he entreated me not to go soldiering, stopping in his tracks and in his earnestness suddenly taking my hand and holding it to his lips. To my horror, Madame Oiseau, thinking it the done thing, seized my other hand and kissed it. Their improper warmth invaded me. In the crazy manner of such things, some advice given to me by my mother when I was twelve came back to me – 'Try not to think of what goes on in the huts.' But nothing would ever again happen in a hut where Parmenter was concerned. Barely a mile from the town he led me to a knoll and pointed to an *emplacement de ferme* which was as neatly set-out as a toy and, grinning at Thérèse said, 'Ours.' I saw his love of the land and of her for providing it. I saw too that, unlike most women, she looked younger outside a room, that her breasts had not yet fallen and, intuitively, that he had tried her. Her cows lowed in her meadow her peasants filed from her fields, dinner-smoke rose from her chimney, a husband was by her side. When he said 'Ours' she closed her eyes and said an evening prayer.

* * *

I returned and told the brothers. George cried, 'Dear God in mercy!' and 'Smart young creature to poke a fire that draws!' He was easy about it and wanted to know why I was not. Why grieve? Servants in France were four for a franc, only I must see that I treated Parmenter's successors – 'Have a couple while you are at it! – *as* servants, and not pupils. It wasn't good for them.' John said nothing. He was lolling on a bench in his awry way, the doll to George's perfectly articulated flesh, his eyes twitching and cast down. His absurd confidence sat upon him like a hen on a mistaken clutch of eggs. He was chewing at a reed as usual and, equally unthinkingly, George was covering him, the habit of his brief lifetime. I had noticed before this way which George had of diverting any studied interest which one might have taken in John towards himself, and not from vanity. For family reasons, shall we say. He was for ever, and at just the right moment,

70

jumping between his brother and the world like one of those pretty acrobats who are deployed to hide the mechanics of a scene-change. But it was not, as Mr Golding liked to announce in his mock stage-manager's voice, 'Enter Umbrarum Rex and Titan's daughter!' but Parmenter who suddenly appeared, breathless, begging our pardons, looking for – 'Yes, there it is, sir, by your foot, a paper, excuse me, I am sorry' – and kneeling to retrieve it from under the settle. All this in an instance. Just as fast and unheralded was what happened next; John Villiers's boot in Parmenter's apologising face. It shot him across the chamber in a skidding arc, all limbs and lightness and flights of blood. But the horror in George's eyes was not for the servant's injury. It was for the great injury which I could not help but have witnessed in this carefully guarded brother, his shatter-patedness. His madness. Don't let us quibble.

Lunatically convinced that the task of breaking-in my servant was his responsibility, the elder Villiers rose and took charge. By trying to stop him, George would have had to own that he was moon-crazed. It was better that his brother should be seen harsh, cruel if you must. These were sane enough things for a gentleman. So he allowed John to beat Parmenter with the small horsewhip from the gear rack, slicing the shirt from him and tripping him as in rage and pain he fled around us like a mindless colt, not knowing why or what. Eventually he collapsed and there was a last, punctuated, assault, 'It-should-have-been-done-years-ago!' and before we could prevent it, a hurling of the youth down the yard stairs. A dozen of these clung to the wall between the pavement and our door and I heard Parmenter's body flop its way from step to step until there was a sad little cry and then silence.

'It should have been done years ago,' explained John Villiers in an ordinary voice. What passed for normality in him had returned. George seized on this and added, 'These things always look worse than they are.'

'When one is just watching, you mean?'

I meant them both to know that I had missed nothing, not the madness, not the cover-up, not the hideous truth of the two of us standing there and doing nothing. I rushed down the steps. My touch revived Parmenter in an instant, in a spasm of

71

revulsion, and he was off bleeding and half-naked, weeping, shouting, stumbling. Madame Oiseau would mend him after seeing what we had done to him. George hurried to me and would have pacified me if he could. I heard him repeat something like, 'Unfortunate, so unfortunate ...' They were ringing the Angelus with its message of the day's work done. I retched over the house-ditch but no vomit came. Eve-martins joined their nests. George helped me back inside, and we all three sat manufacturing silence. When the Villiers' man arrived he was ordered to cleanse the mess but before he could begin Eliot entered and drew back from what hit him, that something terrible – not Moyle-ish – had occurred. He stared at us each in turn, not for an explanation, or for the story of what he had missed – just. We could feel him thinking 'later' when we said nothing. The man swabbed up skin and hair and put the table straight. Eliot watched for a while and then left us, striding off to where, only a week or two ago, he had separated himself from us, a gazebo high aloft. He was whistling in his lonely way.

Although there is no mention in my *Golden Epistles* of fatal returns, I recommend the subject to essayists. Having got away, for some misjudged reason you come back when you could have got clear. It is then that they get you.

6

SHOW ME YOUR FRIENDS
AND I'LL TELL YOU WHAT YOU ARE

As there appears to be a law which says that some deeds have to be the work of Malcontents, or how else could they be done, I should at this point declare the central happiness of my nature. Ask anyone. They will not immediately agree but on reflection they will answer, yes, a happy young man. Slight, cackhanded, overlooked, under-valued, but yes, a young man with enough contentment in him to make his life cheerful. They forget that we readers are in a state of intermittent uplift by what passes before our downcast eyes. I was glad and elevated enough when I rode away from Angers to the Low Countries, where James stabled his armies. Bookmen do not necessarily have to make for the study; some of them flourish in the field. Whilst recognising that reading was my vocation, I knew at once that it no longer mattered where I might do it. So off I went for a soldier, first taking leave of the Great Horse whose names were Acténn, Bayerd, Haut la Main, Créon, Tenir le fête Droite, Hérésie, Rinaldo, Jupiter, Vulcain, Charly and Trajanus, then saying farewell to the Villiers and to Eliot who looked pensive. I did not say goodbye to Parmenter and have ever regretted it. Should you read this, Galyon, know that your name has remained on my list of intercessions. God keep you, and your vines, and your damson madame, and your brood. You did well.

The Low Countries are called such because the sea is above them. They are Calvin's land and popery land, ferociously both, so that one of the first things one learns as a traveller is to steer clear of religious polarities. As nothing very definite is demanded of an Englishman, I was able to stay out of holy trouble, one way or the other. I commissioned myself to an obscure regiment commanded by a Colonel Mathers who passed me as lieutenant to a Captain Lee, a sprightly officer who could have been Irish originally but whose past lurked vaguely behind a very positive grin. Both of them went to polite lengths in affecting to know all about the Feltons, and what an honour for the regiment, etc. Where were the fighting men? Oh, the trained bands were training them. Our job was to lead them to Count Mansfeld, the great mercenary, who, suitably paid by a sacred majesty, would lead us all to victory. So, Lieutenant, take this chit to the armory, and this one to a tent-maker, and this one to a servant-hirer, purchase a wide collar and a huge hat, put up some ribband, and join us for dinner at the van der Vollenhouens, where they did you proud. All this in Arnhem. No, I would not receive payment. There was absolutely no money and how we were to restore His Majesty's son-in-law and daughter to the Palatinate was anyone's guess. God would help us when the moment came. Meanwhile it was playtime for soldiers. Had I – forgive them for enquiring – some, er, means? An officer should have means. Small ones would be something. Theirs – the Colonel bowed to the Captain – were minute. But they had them. Means.

Some time – some years – I must admit had passed then, for I could not by-road Paris for a second journey. It was easy to merge into that infestation of students which sheltered in its crannies like starlings in pediments, living on crumbs and mouthfuls of fountain water. No means arrived there, not a sou from Essex-Suffolk. Only furious letters. But one becomes practised in not being cast down by bad news in the post. I replied to it occasionally – in French, partly to show off my new learning, partly to create confusion. And, looking back, partly I now realise to affiliate myself with Mr Golding. There was comedy in discovering his Englished French authors on the shelves of the Sorbonne. A motherly woman kept me for much of my time in Paris, though not as a son. Which is how I survived. With so many starlings so much glossier then myself to warm her lap, why me? The *Golden Epistles* were silent on the subject of physical insignificance. Like most books, they assumed that to be young was to be lovely and, as one might have expected, they nagged-on about vanity. But when I read the following to my friend and benefactor, she pulled my hair and said, 'There, let that be a lesson to you!'

> I advise you not to lay up great confidence in your beauty, and much less presume upon the greatness of your race, for at court for one gentleman that makes love to your person, you shall find twenty that spend the whole day judging your life, since beauty without virtue, and high kindred without good conditions, are nothing but a green tree ...

It was the greenest of all green trees which found itself in the Regiment that moist summer of 1621. Father was all forgiveness. I was Joseph restored to Jacob. By all means a Lieutenant Felton must have means. In my new circumstances they were nothing less than my birthright. O happy warrior! And, God be praised, his Majesty was on the brink of making war to restore the Palsgrave, so military honours must fall to me almost at once. I would be – was already – the envy of the family. 'Dear boy of my flesh, brave scion of a noble house.' By now, as sons often do, I was beginning to love my father for his silliness.

I liked the Low Countries. They appealed to me in their level-headedness, in their gusty humour and their dissention. Their churches – there were every brand of them – struck cuttings from both Calvinist and Catholic roots when ever there was an argument. Did St Paul say this or that? And another congregation. Should one stand or sit or bring the dog? and a brand-new body, gowned pastor and all. There was a lot of Luther-music in the scrubbed choirs and the soughing and frouing of enormous garments. The fear was that the Pope or some elector or other would put a stop to it all. The Dutch prefer a kind of ponderous zest in their worship. Their God is not etherial but a solid presence not unlike themselves.

I was billeted near the lands which are called Holland, due to their woods, and through which the sea fingered its way. Tall ships apparently cruising through farms made an eccentric sight. It was a kingdom of walls and wallers, with the north ocean licking up to both and everywhere seeping into view. Very precarious, I thought. A Dutchman's fate is rather like that of poor Sisyphus, except that what he has to eternally shoulder is mud. Dutchmen are singularly urbane about drowning. Although the sea is always about to fall on their heads, they taunt it unmercifully and keep winning fields from it when they think it isn't looking. Half their kingdom has been filched from Neptune and half their lives are spent as beavers to ensure that they can hold on to the spoil. I was always being taken to see some fresh snatch of seabed where in no time at all the oats would flourish. Or a windy church. With so little regimental business to do beyond flaunting my hat and my new upright walk as a lieutenant must advertise himself, said Captain Lee – I spent most of my time trotting along the dyke-tops, exploring orange brick towns, harking to windmills creaking and clacking, and observing birds and skies which respectively had flown and stretched their way from Suffolk. That wet summer mired on and on to a soaking winter, and still there was not a bugle-cry to tell us where to go and what to do, although every ear was cocked. More officers drifted in to Arnhem during these negative months and so far as our mess was concerned we were soon at full strength. But where were our platoons, our men? Where were the rank and file which we were to add to Count Mansfeld's army?

'They will be with us soon enough', said the Colonel with a shudder, 'that malodorous rabble. Those unfortunates who at this very minute are being cudgelled and bawled into a scarecrow soldiery by the trained-bandsmen for the promise of a shirt and a stewpan of offal. And for the promise of a wage from his Majesty who, as everybody knew, did not have it to give. Why – I am addressing you, Lieutenant – why did endless thousands of such poor creatures fight, die, become mutilated and diseased, even cold and miserable, for causes which they can know nothing about? Why do they let us do it to them? Do you know, this question has only just crossed my mind!' He appeared gratified.

I at least knew why there was no money, not even for the Great Cause, as it was now being described, the restoration of the Palsgrave, Zeus's son-in-law, the re-enthronement of Zeus's daughter the Winter Queen, and the grand plan of a Protestant empire. What funds there were had trickled through those sievelike hands of James to cup-bearers, masquers, jewellers, palace-builders, gold-thread-men, horse-and-hound men and men who were just good fun. And to George, of course, the ultimate Ganymede. Although George's expensiveness must have an inventory of its own. His and the King's love too. We must not forget to include their love. It must never be left out in any totting up of the cost. Mr Golding's Ovid had instructed the whole of England in the varients of desire, although only kings, being gods, could find some of them legal. King James tried to make it easy for his subjects to understand by taking his passion out of mythology and putting it into scripture.

'The Lord Jesus had his John and I mu'n have my George'.

Well, if you put it like that ...

But we are discussing the economy. Being Scotch, there was every expectation that when his Majesty ruled England he would succeed the late Gloriana's stinginess as well as her crown. However, as we know, there were misconceptions on both sides, ours that James would be thrifty, his that in the circumstances of her famous miserliness he would find her savings. There were no savings; the cupboard was bare. The chief treasure was her immense wardrobe which James's play-acting wife ransacked greedily for her shows. I am told that there were occasional gasps of horror when some recognisable garment appeared; it was to some as if a sacred vestment last seen on the back of Bishop Andrewes was being worn by a morrisman. They say that Queen Anne sliced the jewels from Elizabeth's dresses to pay her stage-manager. King James of course lived miraculously as a spendthrift without funds. Never a skimp, never a horn drawn-in, never a pound withheld where a penny would have done. If a minister so much as hinted at bankruptcy, James would answer, 'But I am the King!'

The flight of the Palsgrave from Bohemia after the battle of Prague in that dark autumn of 1620 confronted King James with fiscal reality. As the Palsgrave was the husband of his daughter Elizabeth, both must be reinstated, and re-instatement costs a fortune. She was his artfully-wed daughter and the exactly positioned key to the re-making of Europe. Re ... Ré ... but I am muttering. This handsome Palsgrave in flight and his pretty wife captured the Protestant imagination, no inconsiderable achievement, and were re-titled the Winter King and Queen. Sadly for them, their romance came to a halt in the House of Commons.

'Parliament mu'n get me moneys', declared James.

Parliament said what it would always say, that Bohemia was a distant land about which it knew very little. Though it believed that the Winter King and Queen should have their thrones back, but how – without money? There *was* no money.

Meanwhile, on the drilling heaths of the English shires it was yells and promises, scarecrows and rumbling bellies as the trained bands did their duty. It was an uphill task, this knocking some bloodthirstiness into such dregs of humanity and convincing them that King James's shillings would arrive anon. Just think of it, clean slops and shirts and mint shillings, *and pride*, just for slaughtering Catholics! The captains of the trained bands (who never left home so as to protect the kingdom) only wished that they were free to fight for the Palsgrave and his Queen. And all this time, in waiting at court, there was George, whose only military experience had been to mount the great horse. George who, with hindsight, was waiting in the wings to finish off many a wretched life. Ganymede was waiting to become Hector, whilst they, the heathmen, were waiting to become maggots. Looking back on all this, as I must do now, I can see that all our tragedies, including his own, was when George metamorphosed from *mignon* to *privanza*. Or in good English language, when the lover turned ruler. To begin by holding the cup and end in holding the reins might sound like a successful career, but in George's case it was not the way to get on. I could have told him this but by the time my kind of advice was of use he was well out of earshot. It would have been like a rocket listening to what the earth was saying.

But I too race forward and must go back a mile. On the morning I left our mess at Arnhem to ride to The Hague to gawp with the rest of the world at their Winter Majesties, now in exile there, the Marquess Villiers was married to the Lady Katherine Manners, to the joy of King James, who liked his lovers to be family men. George woke up on his honeymoon morning to find a note on his pillow.

The Lord of Heaven send you ... all kinds of comfort in your sanctified bed, and bless the fruits thereof that I may have sweet bedchamber boys to play me with, and this is my daily prayer, sweet heart ... James R.

*　*　*

This must be the place for me to set straight the record of this notorious pair. If I do not, posterity will conclude that George was the unnatural successor of Esmé Stuart and Bob Carr, and God knows how many lesser lads who simulated feelings for his Majesty out of consideration for his towards them, which were always strong and genuine. They coped well enough with his lust; it was his love which was unreturnable. But George returned it – something which had never been done before. His Majesty, who had been a king since he was a baby, and whose life had been like one of those fields which are repeatedly cropped without any goodness being put back into it, was to experience as an ageing man in his late forties the devastation of reciprocated love. He was after all nearly half a century old when penniless George returned his love as gracefully as he returned service on the tennis-court. It demoralised James. After all, when love is so long withheld that one learns to live without it, or pay through the nose for something resembling it, to be suddenly and unbelievingly tossed the real thing by Antinous come back to earth is terrible as well as wonderful. Poor dirty, bandy King. Poor pedant. Poor flinching flesh before George's strangely loving eyes. So devastating was this return of love, it was said, that the King begged the Almighty on his knees to spare him from it. It was more than he could take at his time of life. He asked God to take this new cupbearer's cup from him as it held what he had never before tasted. The Court was agog.

It is said that personality can be trained to over-ride the shortcomings of our bodies. As a king James had never bothered about the one or the other. Each showed what had happened to him as a child in those dripping Scottish castles. A brilliant education and rough familiar depravities had been forced on him. There was little he couldn't learn and nothing he wouldn't do, and although it was always the polite thing to praise his brain, nobody ever drew the line when it came to reporting his habits. The curious nature of these went out to all the world and added, rather then detracted, to his reputation as a monarch, for men hope to see in kings those abnormalities which prove their divinity. From old Madrid to the young Plantations, faithful accounts of King James by those who had seen him were part and parcel of any letter. In Catholic realms the very fact of his being the heretic son of a martyr, as well as the successor to Elizabeth, made him an object of inordinate fascination and it gratified them when dispatches from their ambassadors contained ever more peculiar information about him. One such account by M. Fontenay to his master the King of France, like most documents marked strictly private, was being devoured right across Europe just at that moment when I set foot in The Hague. Of course I cannot recall everything it said but I will never forget how the monstrousness of our Majesty shone through. There was his untouchability – 'The absolute prerogative of the crown is no subject for a lawyer. It is presumption and high contempt in a subject to dispute what a king can do, or to say what a king cannot do' – and there was what should have disgusted but instead enthralled.

This King, it was broadcast, had no repose. He trotted and whirled his way through a Court which itself was never still, talking ten to the dozen. His vice was the hunt. So dedicated was he to the chase that he shat in the saddle rather than miss a minute of it. Although he paid full respect to the royal hunt of the deer, his passion was the hare, and he would match its screams with his own at the killing. He had been in so much fright himself all his life that this creature-fright seemed to be a kind of understanding in the poor animal, for which he was grateful. The bloody body would be handed up to him to mouth and caress. There would be rheumy tears and thick Scotch pityings. The hounds themselves, they said, would weep. Then off the whole hunt would rush, for one hare could not fill a day, and those with state work to do would be leaping alongside his Majesty craving instructions. He wore a hat which was lashed to his head with a silver chain, and one could sometimes hear his chest rattling in his corselet like a nut. Ours are the days of the swift, sharp ending – poniard days – and the King made sure that he was dagger-proof by wearing leather next to the skin. His constant cry was, 'Keep up! Keep up!' When he entered a room, if his legs were busy running here and there, so were his eyes. They rolled from face to face, and should in the course of this nerve-wracking operation to see who was present other eyes met his and then look down, he would shout, 'Aha! And what have you to hide? Out with it, out with it, my Lord!' His very red tongue tumbled from his lips and he liked to be reminded of this so that he could tuck it in again. His face and hands were like rose taffeta, and speckled like thrush's eggs. They said that he exuded his royalty in the form of a sweaty kind of honey, and that one always knew when he was around. The fountain of honour was sickly-sweet. It deluged George and his entire family. No one was left out. The King renamed him Stephen because he had the face of an angel (true) and made him Buckingham so that he could say, 'My buck ...' True enough.

All this and not more than half a dozen years since we shared the straw in Angers. I was told that the word Favourite no longer applied and that what Whitehall or Royston, and wherever the happy pair happened to be, was seeing was a love which defied description. The whole of Christendom hunted for a precedent but could only come up with the usual old couples, David and Jonathan, etc. Edward and Gaveston, some whispered, even if there wasn't the faintest resemblance. But it showed they knew about such things. Yet what kind of love was it which made his Majesty dedicate his Meditation on the Lord's Prayer to this Stephen neé George, it being short and simple thus 'fitter for you, since you were not bred a scholar'? He could learn from it how to 'pardon them that offend you'. The trouble was that almost nobody offended George; it was always the other way round. He offended practically everybody. It puzzled and worried him. How could he? But it was still some long years on in our mutually brief lives that he would offend me. All he was doing that springtime was hurting me. Hurting John Eliot too. For we are all in reverence for the comradeship which is our youth, and are injured when a friend is so thoroughly removed from us that we have to pretend that he never existed. Marquess George, James's George, Lady Katherine's George, do you remember me – Lieutenant Felton since February? No has to be the answer.

* * *

I returned from The Hague to a great turnaround in the Arnhem mess. The little April journey, touched with early sunshine and perfume, had itself spelled change, and it could partly have been simply the time of the year which had signalled a muster. Where I had left three officers, now there were twenty, each of them, bristling with mustachios and purpose. Their collective brio made the rafters tremble. They stamped their new boots and every now and then broke off from their confidences to kiss each other warmly. Mynheer van der Vollenhouens and his voluptuous wife had sprouted a large staff in my absence and the eating-room thundered beneath its ministrations. The food there had always been plentiful; now it was prodigious and required real attack to prove that we had done it justice. As well as swords, these new brother officers had armed themselves with lutes, flutes and mandolinos. Quite a few possessed sweet liquid voices, their songs pouring with astonishing feeling from red wet mouths. As we were still many months away from the outbreak of a war which continues to this day, and looks as if it is set in, like evil weather, for years to come, and as what was being said both in our own Low House of Parliament and throughout Europe was 'Peace, peace', this sudden flight to the colours by individual officers from every corner of England had to contain some intuitive element on a par with the gathering of birds. It was all very jolly. We were the Mansfeld boys on our way to regain the Palatinate for their Winter Majesties, a cause so romantic as to blind us to its impossibility.

'Lieutenant Felton has just left them'.

The table-roar subsided as if the Grace were announced.

Proud of this coup, Colonel Mathers swept a hand towards me and said, 'Ask him anything. He knows all the answers.'

'You have seen the Winter Ones?'

This from a wondering old chap too ancient, one would have thought, for carnage.

'Yes.'

'And they spoke to you?'

82

'Not to me, but I listened to their voices'.

Deadly quiet now. Just a sucking of crackling and involuntary wind. My tongue loose by so much friendliness, something of a novelty for me, I found myself reporting on the scene. I stood up, as King Frederick and Queen Elizabeth had stood up on the brown dais, showing themselves at a levee which was in fact a staring mob, myself part of it. How they just remained there both significant and pathetic. Three children joined them in their display. They were like actors after the epilogue has been declaimed, who were out of their roles and not yet into a personal identity.

'Every now and then her Winter Majesty, the small princes romping about her, made short sallies towards the front of the stage as though she was opening a masque. Then appearing to have second thoughts, she retreated to her husband's side. He looked well, humiliated. Now and then both of them seemed to grope for somewhere to sit, missing their thrones.' I grew metaphorical. 'The scene-changers had carried them off.'

'Should we discuss these Majesties in play-acting language?'

As the Winter Queen had done little else in her life other than theatricals, I thought that we should, but did not say so. She was, after all, our leading lady and the Protestant armies would follow her until death. Her death.

'Ask him anything!'

Colonel Mathers was eager to make a show of me. There was a Lieutenant Wemyss who had arrived only that morning who said, 'I would like to ask you about my Lord of Buckingham'.

'What about the Marquis?'

'About him and yourself'.

'I knew George Villiers, not the Marquis.'

'Will you tell us about him, then?'

'What is it that you want to know?'

'Anything – everything – something.'

'About us being at Angers together?'

'That will do – for a start anyway.'

The effect of this exchange on the company was sensational. I hedged; it was neither the time nor the place. In any case we were only students then. 'You know what students are – especially at horse-schools'. Although the questioning ceased, I felt unsettled. Ever since I heard about George's ascendancy I had taken great care to know no more of him than what was commonly understood. Wemyss had touched a nerve. The reason was not hard to find. King James would have to declare 'our' war but his George would be in charge of it. So, what was he like? Who doesn't know now!

That evening I walked with Angus Wemyss by the canal and offered my own explanation of George's rise to the heights. It was something I had worked out for my own sake. That the King had to find a way to convince Europe that a lover *loved* him, something he had never experienced before.

* * *

'Had you, Mr Wemyss, heard that Carr had been succeeded by an amiable youth called Sir George Something or other, you would not have given the matter so much as a second thought – now would you? Nor would have little King Louis and his Charlie de Luynes, nor Madrid, nor the Grand Turk, whoever he might be. Of course not. Are we not speaking of those ephemera of great courts, the man-toys who can now and then make a king put out of his mind the terrible knowledge of his divinity? Monarchs are allowed distractions forbidden to ordinary men.'

Wemyss thought that such toys would not distract him.

'Nor me,' I added hurriedly. 'But were either of us God-touched and set apart as his Majesty is, we would certainly be looking around for some light relief. Have you never wondered why courts are so frivolous? It is because of that awful personified seriousness at the heart of them which cries out for natural unregeneracy. George, to give him his due, could make anyone, male or female, forget one's sacredness for an hour or two. I remember him coming in when I was low at Blois, and that laugh of his which sent my black dog packing. You know, I think that if George had a face like Doctor Dee King James would still have adored it.'

'Tell me, where was it you first saw him, and if you yourself had any consciousness of his – his ...'

'His presence? Is that what you are trying to say?'

'His loveliness. Let's call a spade a spade. They are

mentioning Adonis in the same breath.'

I thought before answering.

'That isn't what struck me, I suppose because even then, when I was so young, I took it for granted that any man had to be fair in comparison with me. So everyone, Eliot even, looked good. What I could not but notice was the way in which Frenchwomen raked the shirt off George's back with their longing glances, and how he hated the way his body drew attention to his poverty. We were all in tatters at the time. And now he is the apple of his Majesty's eye – and more surprisingly, King James is the apple of his!'

'Rotten squashy old medlar, more like.'

'That is the point; George can only see an apple.'

'I should be sick.'

'And that is why George is now galactic, hanging there among the stars like one of those mortals who gave himself to a goddess, sparkling away with old Queen Elizabeth's sapphires, and made a marquis to boot. And why? So that he could ride so high that no one on earth could miss seeing him, the favourite who *returned* his King's love. There aren't many of them about.'

'It is an interesting theory, God give it substance.'

'Can he rise and rise, or is that it?'

Wemyss held up his hands. 'There could be a crown.'

'Jesu, no!' Now I was shocked. *Prince* George? It would break all the rules.

'Why are you so fascinated, Lieutenant?'

'Me? I'm not fascinated, as you put it. I am thinking of us, and what will happen to us when the Palsgrave has to be re-enthroned. If your old stable-mate goes any higher he will have to lead us, that is what I am thinking. How would you feel having *ci mignon* in charge?'

I already felt vertiginous. The Arnhem bridge swayed, the Dutch air clotted in my breast.

'Why...?'

'Why not? Or rather, how not? Hasn't he got his hands in both the honours and perks bins? It is what I am told. If we have a war, will he not have to support his rank by glory in the field? Might not he and his Majesty alone draw up the grand strategy, God help us! This is what I am thinking. You must think like this too, Mr Felton. He is your old friend after all – you must have a thought to him. Remind me of his elevation via the Milky Way.'

'Cup-bearer.'

'Yes, yes, Cup-bearer. We all have to start.'

'He must have been, let me see, twenty-one. It was August 1614. Eliot wrote to me, a have-you-heard kind of letter unusual for him. He said that cup-bearers are expected to be good conversationalists because his Majesty talked through his eating. About eight month's later – it was St George's day, so very suitable, George was made Gentlemen of the Bedchamber with Queen Anne's blessing. The very next day it was Sir George and one thousand pounds to keep his knighthood up. By January he was Master of the Horse, by April again it was the Garter and, four months after this, it was Viscount Villiers and Baron Waddon, plus £80,000 worth of land to nourish these peerages. There were no more funny letters from Eliot – I now know why. The next year, 1617, again during the twelve days of Christmas when the Court was rocking, George became Earl – became – Buckingham. In the New Year's honours twelve months on, it was Marquis George. And here we must stop to get our breath back. Three years from pot-boy to deputy ruler of England. Have you seen a play called 'Macbeth'? Will Shakespeare wrote it for his Majesty. In it somebody says something like, "If it were done," then it "were well it were done quickly". But now I come to think of it they were discussing assassination, not the honours list. But the thinking is the same. To take breath away you have to move fast. His Majesty took everybody's breath away when it came to young George, which is what he intended. You must have heard what he said to so many raised eyebrows? It wasn't blasphemous because of it coming from one whom God could call a god. James said, apropos George, that Christ had his John and that he must have his George. His Majesty would never blaspheme. In which case the Court was to understand that from now on this love affair was no longer Greek – Olympians and mortal lads – but Christian, and with safe credentials.'

'You have it pat.'

I tried to cover myself, unhappy to appear so well informed. I said it was common knowledge. 'Everybody is talking about it. You yourself had the main facts; what you wanted from me was a handful of recollections as a fill-in to the general gossip.'

'Don't be angry. I was intrigued by the way you describe things – people – that is all. That report of yours from The Hague, with the Palsgrave and his Winter wife exhibiting themselves like marionettes to the curious, it held the mess spellbound. Perhaps you didn't notice.'

'Perhaps they were all thinking, as you are now thinking, that I am a chatterbox.'

'I think you are an author, an originator of tales.'

'I am an officer, sir, like you.'

'Not at all like me – in fact, unlike any of us. But you will fight like us, and be brave like us.'

'Isn't that enough?'

'No.'

I stared into his broad red healthy face, wondering if it was his intent to upset me. Or to threaten me, even. But all I saw was a greater intelligence than I expected.

This I found horribly disturbing. Until this moment on the Arnhem bridge I had counted on our regimental codes to hide such oddities as I might possess as adequately as my lobster-tail helmet hid my vulnerable neck. It upset me to realise that Wemyss could 'read' me so easily. He struck me as the epitome of soldierly convention. If he could identify me, who could not? I felt suddenly unsafe and filled with regret. But then something clearly prearranged happened. A large woman elevated on patterns because of the mire clumped towards us. As she drew near I could see that the largeness was due to her voluminous clothes, then a mark of the Hollander bourgeoisie, both male and female, who moved around like stuff mountains. She approached Wemyss with an easy directness. A small white hand protruded from her tent-size cloak, and a small white face hung like a lantern in her vast hood. We each swung our hats as far as our arms would reach and bowed. As it was plainly an assignation, I stepped back to show that I understood and that there need not necessarily be an introduction. But Wemyss, with his Scottish manners – the best on earth when they have any – caught her arm and mine and said, 'Madam von Hol, Lieutenant Felton.'

'I am glad that you had your comrade to talk to – Mynheer –

87

so that you won't have noticed how late I am.'

She was not entirely looking at Wemyss. A fragment of her attention fled to me as she spoke. It conveyed the most fleeting interest but I felt it all the same. A thunderous response which was out of all proportion to it made me colour and I had to look away. My blood mounted and I became elated, not from lust but from simply being noticed. Really, truly noticed. I didn't mind making myself scarce and leaving them to pursue whatever it was they had between them. I didn't mind Wemyss's casual use of me as he waited for someone else, or that he had left me stranded so far as the evening was concerned. A ray of interest, like the most distant summer lightning, and as swift, had caught me and in the process had illuminated me, so that Madame von Hol had no option but to give some thought to me. Would she, later, casually but carefully, say to Wemyss, 'Who did you say your friend was?'

I had been chaste at Arnhem. Continence after whoring is a young man's treat. The gallant interests of the other officers seemed also in hibernation, flattened by food, maybe. How we gorged! Even my thin frame grew round as a bolster. The Dutch are the only race I have met who will say, 'Let's see your grossness. Unrestrict your poundage. Put it on show.' They are great displayers of the stuffed gut and the broad arse. Their coarseness blew into our mess with a kind of healthy effrontery, like a big fart, and soon we were as bad as they were. Drunk after dinner, the Colonel would collapse on all fours and yell, 'Jockey up!' and myself or one of the other lieutenants would have to mount him and whip him round the room, whilst the van der Vollenhouers watched watery-eyed from their hatch. There were other tomfooleries, but as they say, 'a gentleman remembers nothing after midnight'. Poor old Colonel Mathers, poor good-natured idiot. I would one day see him topple to his death from one of George's too-short ladders at the citadel of St Martin on the Ile de Rhé, his face all caved-in by a brick. His horseplay, or our grand horseplay at Blois, was it not all part of the same silly game? My *Golden Epistles* state that 'God suffereth absurdities to exercise their force against such as are most strong'.

* * *

88

'But who did you say your friend was?' It was I who was now asking this question, although not within Wemyss's hearing. He must tell me eventually. He must say 'Oh that lady, she must not be thought loose but she has an eye for a garrison!' Everything I had been told about Hollander women now returned to inflame me. How they invited their lovers into their great gowns and used all kinds of arts to preserve a full accessible nakedness undercover of their heavy apparel. How their appetite in this direction matched that at the table, and how strong they were with men. With Wemyss's friend's little glance teasing my imagination I let my thoughts run into blissfully uncontrolled lewdness. I put morality on the shelf along with my breastplate and kindled every kind of delight whilst those with whom I shared a bedchamber snorted and turned in the foetid air. I lifted the lady off her stilts and laid her beside me. I crept into the hot cave of her skirts. I found a small body at variance with its thick coverings. I found the little white bosom in its starched lair trembling at my touch. Best of all, I found the whole of that look of regard of which I had until this unspeakable moment only caught a fraction of what interested her in myself. Could it be possible that she might desire me as George so inexplicably could desire King James? Could she want me? Could she? Nobody had before, not even mother, not really. There was want in that look, if nothing else. It required something from me. It also weighed possibilities. What were they? But she had clumped and clopped her way to Arnhem bridge sans attendant, and I had watched from a distance she and Wemyss disappear into the heart of the town, admittedly walking stiffly apart.

I was direct with him the following morning. I could not be otherwise. Would he mind if I met her?

'Who?' He appeared fuddled. 'Oh, Beatrix my sister. Yes, of course. She wants to meet you.'

'Your – your sister?'

Wemyse caught on at once and gave his beet-face grin.

'Aha! So that's what all this is about! Well I am sorry to disappoint you. You will have all the answers on Sunday when you come to dine. Midday sharp. Don't wear a sword. I'll pick you up. Yes, she said, "Do bring him."'

And so I had my first glimpse of a *sancta casa*. It was not far from being the grandest house in Arnhem, with a vermilion and gold portico inscribed. 'This is none other but the house of God and the gate of heaven', which presumably meant that it contained its own chapel. A blue and white cupula on the roof reminded me of the Duke's chateau at Blois. It carried a brass Peter-cock which spun and flashed in the wind. From the corner of my eye I saw Wemyss looking at me to see how I was taking it, so I preserved a lack of the astonishment which I felt. And I hid my disappointment, which was great. At dawn that morning I had washed my body all over in the van der Vollenhouers' pond and scented it for quite a different house. This one was filled with the aroma of cedar wood and wax, and of wild flowers arranged in red pots. We waited in the hall for what I was later to learn was Sext, or the Little Hour, to end. Then out they poured, chattering in a devout way, high folk and lowly, from the equality of the altar. My lady – Wemyss's sister – led, more diminutive even than I had fantasized, with her tiny silk-shod feet on the floor and no bulk of damask to stand around her body like an upholstered wall. She was dressed in elegant black and white, and carried primroses. Her large breasts were hoisted onto her corsage and finely veiled. She had yellow hair like her brother but her skin was bone-pale. She kissed him and welcomed me, extending as I had hoped she would that first look of interest in me. She actually nodded to herself as if to say, 'Yes, I was right.' She apologised for keeping us waiting.

'You must blame the fifty-fifth psalm – I expect you know it – it is all about being let down by a friend. "Mine own familiar friend" whose words "were softer than butter" '.

There were so many servants of both sexes that some of them found little to do, although it was dinner-time, and sat in the windows reading books or sewing. One, a child, came over as we talked and asked her mistress the meaning of a hard word, pointing to it on the page, and it was explained as if it was her own daughter who was having the lesson. Wine was brought to us before the meal 'to fill a gap'. A group of musicians assembled in the gallery and tuned-up noisily. The atmosphere was peculiar, very free and easy and yet at the same time severe. Madame Beatrix, as they called her moved on to check her table, now and then re-arranging things with her own hands. After a

90

few of Wemyss's vague introductions, I was left to myself and studied the great saloon of the *sancta casa*, observing its deliberate beauty, the Scripture painted on the walls, the swags of lutes hanging from pegs, the family portraits gazing down, the enormous candleholders all burnished and swinging from chains, and books left all over the place. Then a commotion. Madame Beatrix's husband had arrived. Her face lit up with joy and expectancy. I have rarely been in the presence of such unconcealed happiness. It must have been the wall-texts which brought the ecstatic spouses of the Song of Songs into my head. I imagined her equal, white skin and questing eyes and all, and saw a snowy old man creeping towards us on a stick and pausing every yard or two to embrace both his guests and his servants. His wife ran to him and they met as though they had been separated for weeks.

'Now who haven't you met, dearest. This is Lieutenant Felton, one of Angus's friends from the Regiment. Mr Felton doesn't know it yet, but I am about to recruit him!' This was said with a smile which instantly filled me with the delicious sensations of the night. 'I knew it the second I set eyes on him, and so did he. Did you, sir? I think you did. Mr Felton is by way of being a bookworm, husband, so he will be someone for you to recruit too.'

Doctor von Hol held my shoulder in one papery hand and buried the other in the thick golden hair of the boy who had raced to meet him, his son, but he allowed his skimmed-milk eyes to accept us equally. At eighty there is no way forward except the patriarchal. And so he advanced, shakily but surely, like one of those time-obscured popes of the Catechumens in a ceaseless act of blessing. I had heard Mr Golding speak of him critically, and of his master the celebrated Jakob Arminious even more so. They would let any Tom, Dick or Harry into Heaven, whereas it was perfectly obvious that Paradise could only be a reserve for the elect of God. He, Arthur Golding was elect, and so he hazarded might I be. Being too young to demand, 'How do you know?' I had until this moment stayed doubtful. Doctor von Hol's trembling fingers against my neck destroyed such doubts for ever. I did not, never would, believe in a sheep and goats theology.

The Arminians were famous for domesticating their religion, for making it kitchen and parlour stuff. In their holy houses meals, sweepings, lessons, prayers and bakings all went round together in a kind of sacred clockwork, with the Servant Christ doing His share. They aimed at Bethany without the complaints, and their eating-rooms in particular were arranged as ante-chambers to the ultimate hospitality which God would provide in those 'mansions' above. The Calvinists found all this very frivolous and private-chapel-y. God knows what is going on, they said. They had found a technique for talking extremely loudly and their denouncements rumbled like thunder. They were dreadfully shocked when they discovered that although a place was laid for Jesus at every Bethany-house dinner, it was not always at the top table. And then they heard that a little Westminster clergyman – 'our Laud' behind his back – was busy restoring to the Church impurities which they thought had gone for ever. It was too much. But what could they do? It was the high-born who were choosing to travel 'the good old way'. The untouchable, George, born a gentleman like myself, now high and untouchable, it was a thought. It was different in the Low Countries, where few were above the burgher level. There were few at Arnhem who would have been received in Suffolk at our rankings. These were people who smoked tobacco-pipes, rollicked in song, stuck their legs out when they sat, painted canvasses and who insisted on enjoying God *and* life. People, Mr Golding would have said, who needed everything they wrote to be translated into a decent language.

Truth to admit, Beatrix von Hol's house bore out none of these generalisations. One could have been at old Lady Herbert's. These Dutch rooms were exquisite. Tinted window-glass admitted a pink and sapphire-blue light onto the black and white stone lozenges of the floor, creating a pattern on pattern. A youth played Sweelinck on a chamber-organ, or sang to a lute. There was a haunting scent of cowslip and wild violets, and it wasn't hard to imagine the Magdalen's broken box of spikenard releasing its pleasures. The Saviour's Prayer was engraved on brass and set up where it could flash unexpectedly before some drifting gaze. Some especially beautiful cats sidled around looking for laps. Poets spoke to dons and were appreciated.

Everything and everyone was innocent and sophisticated at the same time, particularly my hostess. I no longer dared look in her direction for even my most fugitive glance caught her eye. It was an eye which looked straight back, but why? Because I was her brother's friend and had to be repeatedly made welcome? Because I had to be hypnotised into her special Christianity? Because she felt as I did ... ? None of these reasons, I decided. Then why?

At table, with the Lord Jesus's chair between us, I knew why I could now no longer stop looking. I loved her. We do love like this, all of us, now and then, suddenly and helplessly. I loved her beyond the fair skin – beyond desire even, and without knowing her. It was this I thought which she saw in my face and had to keep seeing. But then in all the comings and goings of her house, and all her guests – including many young men – and with such a husband, must she not have regularly attracted love? And not just Bethany and Emmaus love either? Gospel imitation is one thing, human nature another. Just before leaving, she signalled the evening hymn, and there would be a crashing back of settles as we stood. It was the *Rerum Deus tenax vigor*.

> Grant us, when this short life is past,
> The glorious evening that shall last ...

And it was always, 'You will come again, Mr Felton?' Yes, Yes. And the rose-water skin of her hands faintly against my mouth. I could have eaten them. Wemyss watching and the company queuing. 'You will come again, Wybrand ... Willem ... Emilie ... Hendrik ... yes?' Baptismal names for some. 'She has shaken you to your shoes, little fighting comrade!' said her brother, and she had. I lived for her holy assemblies and her ivory shoulders. Often the party was spoilt by my longing to say goodbye so that I could taste her fingers and feel her breath. I imagined her giving me seconds – a minute – more time than all her other guests and would become as exultant as some fawner who had caught the royal eye. 'Poor friend!' smiled her brother, who had doubtless seen it all before.

Back at the van der Vollenhouers it was piggy-back with drums. Steeds and riders thumped up and down the mess to a crisp tat-a-tat from the regimental drummer, a skinny man from Wales, the Colonel, who liked to be ridden, first. There would be meat and gravy all over the place and much skidding and yelling. The contrast with what we had just left was appalling. Wemyss and I would both manage to put in an appearance and escape. Officers who cut the horse-play altogether were extremely unpopular and suspect. All the same, neither Wemyss nor I wanted to be paired as mount and cavalier among the spilt wine and tureens, and we brought the being seen and the vanishing to a fine art. Once I heard, 'Felton Felt ... on' following us into the blackness as we ran to the canal path. On this particular night we sheltered from the buffoonery, not to mention that cold humours which creep from the dark earth of places like Holland and Cambridgeshire, in the first windmill we found. She stood on a heap with stilled sails and we edged around her until we found a spot where the wind couldn't catch us.

'That was a near thing,' Wemyss laughed. He looked at me. 'They were married ten years in Edinburgh, Nothing would stop her. She is his fourth wife. Three died under him, but Beatrix won't. She has given him the son but she won't give him her life. Did you notice her joy? It is because she knows that she will live here for many years, then for ever. Her husband is not reconciled to these plans of hers. Old men aim to keep heaven waiting. He grudges my sister her earth time, having spent all of his. Otherwise what you witness is a happy marriage, for she adores him, God only knows how or why, body and soul.'

Sea-bound gulls fled in great numbers across the purple sky.

* * *

It was very soon after this that Wemyss delivered his thunderbolt. Hatless at midnight, the keen Netherlandish winds tore at our curls. Fetched out of the sea, what an uncomfortable country it is. We had begun by talking about Madame von Hol, with her brother amusing himself at my expense. First he would be percipient and sympathetic, then he would be mocking. Unlike Beatrix, there was no facial expression to go with what he said. Hers was all revelation, his a robust blank. How come the occasional mismatch of delicate understanding and fine intelligence which forced itself from his hard head? As one may have suspected, I was not going to allow his picture of a happy couple to destroy all hope of infidelity. Old men with young wives had to be cuckolded; it was what they were asking for. It was they who broke the rule, they whose coarseness must be answered with coarseness. Wemyss and I had by now attended a dozen or more of the von Hols' Lord's Day soirees, and my conviction that Beatrix would see the morality of slipping away from her silvery spouse to take her pleasures with me, grew. I was of that age when nothing could stop it. I warmed my body in that cage of clothes every night; we shared it. She was mine by right of fantasy and there had been times when I entered her presence when I think she knew it. Not that she crimsoned or shook, simply that she looked at me as women who have enjoyed a man look.

My desire for her made me set about apprenticing myself to her beautiful social religion. It wasn't difficult. Soon 1 was hobnobbing with the Saviour with the best of them, and sincerely, for I loved Him. Madame von Hols was so pleased. Her face met mine across the lectern when she took turn to read from the King's new Bible and even now, all these years on, I cannot turn to the Lord's Galilean walks without hearing her voice. Like me, like all of us in that Christian house, she practised the companionship of Jesus, even sometimes turning to smile at Him at her side. Every meal, every room, every conversation had to be fit for Him. She would say, 'We will be in the garden if you want us' and her servants would say how they found Him such a help in the kitchens. 'Her motto,' said Wemyss rather gloomily, 'is "Paradise now" '. I was bewitched by her voice, which was much clotted with Scotch like his Majesty's, so that we had to make a stab sometimes at what she meant. One of my awake dreams was to have her in my bed teaching me how to pray. I asked God to forgive me such distracting lessons. I became very dissolute – it was the only word for me in Arnhem. Dissolute. But only in my head, which could be worse.

One day when Wemyss and I were miles from the town and the sun was warm, and we seemed to have shed our soldierings with the hats and swords we had left at the camp - for the troops were arriving and the tomfoolery was over – he told me, 'I am not one of you'.

I assumed he meant an Arminian. I was myself having difficulty in acknowledging myself such, although what else could I be now? He realised my mistake and said that we had both better sit down. It was the time of succulence when nature is fleshy, particularly along water-banks. Later summer flowers were in waiting among the juicy stems, hardheads, bellbind, rampion, clary. Wemyss grabbed a tough rosette.

' "I will pick the smooth yarrow that my figure may be sweeter, that my lips may be warmer, that my voice may be gladder ..." Go on.'

' "May I be an island in the sea, may I be a hill in the land, may I be a star in the dark time, may I be a staff to the weak one ..." '

' "I shall wound every man," ' he prompted.

'Oh yes; ' "I shall wound every man, no man shall hurt me." '

The childish saw died away.

'Felton, what I meant when I said that I am not one of you is that I can no longer believe in the existence of God. There-is-no-God. There now, I have said it!'

There cannot be many who have listened to such a declaration and my fist shakes as I ink it down all these years hence. Horror and pity fought inside me, and must surely be struggling inside him, yet the red face registered little. It lay calmly on the crushed stalks. The eyes roved the curve of the universe, the mouth held a grass. Without turning his head Wemyss muttered, 'I have upset you.'

He had. I was too distraught to speak. I was also on the verge of a bilious attack and I remember the urgency of the bile in my throat. When and where it would throw itself out became more important than the words which had heaved it from its filthy habitation within me. Faintly, I heard him adding something to the baldness of his statement, something emollient, like the petty codicils which are added to an otherwise ruthless Will.

'Do not be sorry for me, sweet Lieutenant. Envy me instead. It is not given to many of us to see beyond or away from "God" – he is in inverted commas you will notice – but I do. Nor, now that he is no longer here or there for me, would I dishonour him in any way. To be honest, I never saw much of him and now he has gone, utterly, utterly gone, and leaving not so much as a gap as a window into space. Without wishing to hurt your feelings, Felton, that what you call God has necessarily to block the view.'

'Excuse me, Wemyss.'

He rolled to his feet and walked a few yards until I was all spilt out. When I caught up he said, 'Well, well, who'd have thought it would have got you like that! All the same, now that I have confessed my ante-conversion, I will need to tell the rest of the tale, for what it is, and so meet me tonight, when I shall have my blackboard. You look peaky. What are you doing, muddling along with these bloody soldiers? Your intelligence should revolt against their regulations. Mine has – and it is not a hundredth part of yours. I shall resign my commission, not because there is to be a long war, but because there is to be decades of your-God-or-mine war. There is only one thing I would fight for now – to keep open my window on the universe. Which I admit is another silly cause, for who can close it? No man – and no "God".'

Wemyss's blackboard was gloriously pierced. I have never known such a night. It was if the stars had put themselves at his service. He pointed at Polestar. 'Can you see him? He's my guiding principle, my "way" if you like.'

It was then that I made the error of knowing where I was, which was in that contrary country of the astronomers. It was very alluring. I used to read about in a mouldy old volume in Mr Golding's bookroom and which decidedly begged to be translated out of its barbaric poetry into some kind of science. 'The Sterre Transmontane that it clept the Sterre of the See, that is unmovable and that is towarde the Northe that we clepen the Lode Sterre ...' For clept read call. Doctor Gilbed called the 'Lode' – 'magnet'. He lived in Colchester and he and Mr Golding would meet to have starry talk which was tainted with anxiety. How far could one travel those luminous distances without leaving the Lord behind? Once men started to re-arrange the solar system, Mr Golding would say, they must go on to re-arrange everything else, and for him this would never do. This was not why we were put on the earth. I was not so sure. Signor Galileo Galilei, that teacher with a telescope who caused havoc among the papists, was for ever whispering, 'Don't be sure'. And it was Copernicus who had whispered non-certainties to him. All the sky-men, especially Tycho Brahe and his disciple Herr Kepler, were saying, 'worlds, worlds, worlds' when God so loved the *world*. Although this plurality was never such a worry to me as it was to some as every time I saw a new stretch of the universe I saw more of Christ. But trust the priests to fight shy of any extended vision. 'You must only see what *we* can see'. I loved Herr Kepler's music of the spheres which sang higher and higher the nearer they whirled to the sun. I am sure that John of Patmos heard fragments of their songs deep in his saltmine where, to console those who laboured in the white blackness, the stars would shine all day. Again, the priests are at this very moment furious with Herr Kepler because he maintains that the planets move eliptically, and not in perfect circles, to create their divine tunes.This is how they sing:

Again we sprawled on our backs, ignoring the night dew. We made sweeping arcs with our arms and aired our facts. There's Saturn! There's Jupiter! Gauzy clouds creamed the Milky Way. A million un-named constellations glittered across our puny understanding. My bones felt the pull of the ground.

'And there's Polestar,' said Wemyss softly, as to himself, with 'Cassiopeia and Celpeus just under him.' I had a double vision of God's hand everywhere, 'lighting the lamps' as we were told in the nursery, and of a natural phenomena so stupendous that there were no words as yet to give it meaning. Wemyss quoted Galileo:

' "Philosophy is written in this grand book universe – which stands continually open to the gaze, but it cannot be understood unless one first learns to comprehend the language and interpret the characters in which it is written. It is written in the language of mathematics, and its characters are triangles, circles and other geometrical figures, without which it is humanly impossible to understand a single word of it. Without these, one is wandering in a dark labyrinth".' He went on, 'I rather like this, "Improbable facts will on scant explanation drop their cloak and stand forth in simple naked beauty." '

I felt challenged to declare my position, my 'Polestar'.

'For me, Wemyss, God is the improbable fact who has dropped his cloak to show Himself the perfected man.'

'For you, as you say, Lieutenant, but not for me.'

'I wonder the earth doesn't swallow you up.'

'Where we happen to be lying, I doubt if physics would permit it. Under the Haarlem Zee wall maybe.'

Whitened by moonlight, the rubescence drained from his skin; he looked like his sister. He told me how that, for him, God had tumbled out of his heaven without a sound. There was nothing dramatic, as in the Revelation of St John, nothing like a Fall. The sky did not roll up like a scroll and there was nothing in the nature of wrath. God had gone quietly, as had the gods in the end. God's golden city and their high Olympus, they had joined the long list of the soul's poetic destinations.

'Then where will your spirit go when you die, Wemyss?'

'It doesn't have to "go" anywhere.'

'Your body then?'

'To the same places as yours. It will drip away, powder away, be soaked and blown away. It will granulate, it will briefly splash, it will seeth with life. Its skull will at last be cousin to the rock. You and I, sweet Felton, will be elevated to periwinkles and nightjars, and made to expand oceans. Such are all our resurrections. You see, my friend, were this all' – he made more arcs – 'God must reign, Christ must save – observe the love in my face for Him that still only Good One – but it is *not* all, is it? Improbable facts turned into great truths by mathematics point to more. If the ground-glass of a Prague telescope can find dozens of hitherto unsuspected worlds, how can a line be drawn – ever – under What Is? As for mankind, what has it ever been but specks of pollen, grits of sand, raindrops? Physically, I mean. Artistically it is all part of the Song. Nature wastes nothing, although it still hasn't made up its mind what to do with our skeletons, or they wouldn't hang around for so long. Petals, rivers, eliptical music and rattle-bags of ribs and knuckles, that is us. That is your horse too.'

A few weeks after this shooting-star display of his atheism, Wemyss took his leave of 'our' – meaning no longer his – war. The muster of the two sides of the Christian claim in the guise of the Catholic League and the Protestant League was going apace. Unholy battlecries filled the air. Shiploads of troops arrived, hoards of bewildered men from the hundreds and shires who had been knocked into something approaching soldiers by their local trained bands. They were sheltered and fed like cattle, and caned if they fell out of line. Then why had he taken his commission in the first place? If Wemyss knew, he refused to say. Perhaps it was to be near Beatrix. The Low countries were where armies traditionally marked time. Now he was off. I was bereft. It was like saying goodbye to John Eliot all over again. What would Wemyss do before he became a vegetable and a hymn? There would be a good many years until those immortalities.

'I could buy my own telescope – that should keep me occupied until mineralisation sets in. I shall certainly, for your sake, besides nodding to Polestar, say a few words to Jesus out of courtesy for His love. I daresay I will marry and breed. I will certainly write to you, Mr Felton. We are obscure men, Mr Felton, and few will ever know that we existed. I hug my obscurity to me and I advise you to do the same.'

I realised that Madame von Hol knew of her brother's atheism, although she said nothing. At least not in public. It may have contributed to the noticeable gravitas when she and her husband were together which was rather like that closed ranks bravery of having to accept a murderer within the family. During those final days at Arnhem before the commander-in-chief ordered us to march away to the everlasting war, I became intrigued by the positions taken up by the couple in the holy saloon, where they stood virtually poles apart, Beatrix at one end, Wemyss the other. They reminded me of the Winter King and Queen in the makeshift throne-room at The Hague who were close yet sadly disconnected. The company, of course, had no notion of Wemyss's godlessness and presumed that he occupied his end of the chamber in lieu of his aged brother-in-law so that he could take his share in receiving what was often an endless queue of guests. Their Christ-filled faces would meet his starry redness without recognising that it shed a different illumination. I wondered if he ever felt deceitful. They fell for his rough charm and his Scotch aristocratic-ness, qualities that were plainly deficient in King James, alas, although, with his parentage, who could wonder? I moved about in both circles, not so much out of politeness as out of consideration for Beatrix. Being a Christian doesn't stop one from seeing the beginning of an affair, which is what I believed was happening. The religious intensity in which it was being conducted gave it a further thrill. Did I feel deceitful? Not a bit. I felt what young lovers feel, a rising of the blood, a beauty in myself which must make me desirable in order for me to have what I desired. There must be something wrong in what we are taught, for I have never felt more sinless than when I have been in a woman's arms.

I watched Wemyss as he watched us. All through these last weeks he had become a breathing observatory, missing nothing. Having no great sense of humour – Edinburgh again – life didn't amuse him as it amused me, but he liked to take it in. He didn't care to miss a thing. Now and then it seemed to me that he had become 'god' himself, a teeny god admittedly, but a true deity all the same and one released from the pull of our laws. I saw him 'turning' in accord to his own balance or pivotal position, and thus inevitably becoming unaccountable to ours. How lonely he must be! But all of our way of looking at things hadn't left him. He still knew when to keep his mouth shut, which was a relief. So a sensible little god to cast his planetary gaze around theological London, which is where he meant to settle, and which was just as well, given the King's interest in witchcraft. Of course the propaganda pitch of the debate required to set all Europe off on yet another religious war made him air his blasphemous views and I would warn him,

'Be careful, Lieutenant!'

'You take care, Lieutenant!'

Why? I remember wondering. My future was safe enough. Unbearably so. It would jog to its close, where our armorials would mark the spot. Not a blameless life – who's is? – but not a watched life either. A book would crash from my hands and the cat would rush from the room. I would be old then – old Captain (General?) Felton up the road, brother to the Big House. Unwed but unneglected in other ways. This would do. I would be sorry not to meet Wemyss in heaven, but Sir John Eliot would be there, and I suppose George, being so close to a sacred majesty.

'What will happen to you, Mr Felton?' He paused. 'Let me tell you what is going to happen to me. You know how the watchers of the other worlds poke their lenses at the stars? Well it is my intention to pass my earthly scrap of time – the amusement part

101

of it – in observing the Court which, as you know, imagines itself the equal of the solar system, comets and all. I shall write these observations down and, as every author must have at least one reader, I shall send them to you. They will be sparklers among your guns. Warfare is mankind's most frivolous pursuit and you shall have some other nonsense to accompany it. I shall try not to be treasonable, if this is what is worrying you. Anyway, what is treason but another point of view? "All look my way" – that is what that old Jehovah of yours has been telling the human race since Genesis, a lovely, lovely myth, and quite my favourite when it comes to tales for beginners – but from now on I shall be looking in another direction, north, to that ultimate star. Ultimate where I am concerned, I mean, for if I look further, I shall be without references and sans a language. Which is perilous for all visionaries. You voyagers with Christ can plead, "Keep me as the apple of the eye" but we constellationers must find our own protection. I shall take some of your prayers with me – just for the sound of them among the planet music, just to provide the spheres with a lyric or two.

'If you whisper a word of this in Whitehall – if you so much as hum a line of a song which betrays your atheism, I tell you, Wemyss, you are done for. Your reputation will reach the King and it will excite him to examine you before torturing you to death. He is always on the look-out for some unusually troublesome fly to de-wing and is amazingly condescending as an inquisitor, they say. "Let me pour you some more wine, Mr Wemyss. Now take your time, don't let me hurry you." And his English bishops will struggle to understand your phlegm-choked Scotch accents and demand an interpretation. And, as you have good legs, he will admire them and be cross with you if, through obstinacy, you allow them to go to wrack and ruin. But he won't care much for your plum-face, so you will be safe there. He will put you in his witch-book. Now you wouldn't like that, would you – to descend in history as Wemyss the Witch? James is the maddest of the witch-hunters. He'll catch you and carbonise your minerals. He'll boil your liquids on a bonfire! So watch out!'

Wemyss said that I had mistaken him. That he was easily terrified and not brave at all, and that, don't forget, he had no

God to call on. So he certainly would not be foolhardy. A month later I received via the camp mailing arrangement his first letter. It was not a bit careful. Born journalists are dreadfully unselective and rash, piling it all in, a royal banquet one paragraph, crawling meat the next. We had moved on to the great muster. Before leaving Arnhem I prayed for Wemyss in the Grote Kirche because its arches always seemed to me to out-soar the Dutch skies. I prayed, 'Jesu, return thy servant Angus to his rightful sphere and me to Ovington-cum-Clare anon, if it be thy will'.

7

FUGITIVE PIECES

I should explain about these papers. I had been prisoner in the
Tower just under two weeks when the Governor brought my
mother to see me, and without notice. I had last seen her in our
Fleet Street lodgings by St Dunstan's. She walked through the
door and stood still. For a second I expected her to revile me, to
cast me off. For a second more I thought that she would break
down into tears. But she did neither; she just stood. The
Governor brought my chair to her but she ignored it. She looked
aged but sturdy. She wore gentlewoman's clothes, a thick good
gown with sharp lace and her chain. The Governor once more
went to her to relieve her of the parcels she hugged, one plainly
fresh linen for me, the other piercingly familiar, so much so that
I found myself staring more at it than at her. My papers. My
letters – soldiers treasure letters – my fruitless applications, my
Goldingesque notes, my Cadiz and Rhé Journals – all these
writings packed into a waxed linen pillow-case and lugged by
me in the wake of bloody Buckingham. Why be cautious now?
Speak your mind when the hangman is finishing his breakfast. I
had left them – my total documents – at Ovington after
staggering back home from Rhé last autumn, both my arm and
mind festering. My mother laid both parcels on the table,
continued to regard me, then made a tiny run towards me and
clasped me. The Governor dismissed the archivist who had just
entered, and himself turned away.

'I thought you could do with these, my son.'

'You went all the way to Ovington to fetch them?'

'Of course not, I sent the groom. But I shall be returning to
Suffolk in the morning to stay with our kinsman at Playford. It is

best to keep out of the way until you are released.'

'Released!'

'Of course. How can you not be? Have you any idea in this place what is being said about you outside? Here, I've brought a Felton-song – there are scores more.' She handed me some squib which began, 'To Felton in the Tower' and went on,

> Enjoy thy bondage, make thy prison know
> Thou hast a liberty, thou canst not owe
> To such base punishment ...
> Thine act may mercy find, lest thy great story
> Lose something of its miracle and glory.

Mother, I assumed, had read this far but not to the end where I was to be 'Of public sorrow the epitome'. I took her hands in mine and so we stood for a long time silent. How could I have done this to her, even for our country's sake? Martyrs, heroes (I consider myself, neither) have to be numbered among the cruellest of men for the tortures they inflict on their mothers. 'There now,' mine was saying, 'Here are your shirts and shifts, here are the bits and pieces you put at the back of the closet, and a book you began to read. What else do you need? Franklin can bring it. Your cousin Arundel is to see it fair when you come to trial. Now let me see that arm. We sat below the window and she unwound the bandages. They snaked grayly over the floor-straw. She called for a basin and washed the black flesh as though it was still the white and pink dimples of childhood. Faded hair escaped from her coif and the snowy starch contrasted with her grubby neck. 'Let me kiss it better,' she said. 'Does it hurt? No? Good.' She left after an hour. I would not see her again. I knew it.

I unpicked the thread and released the papers. Letters from Angus Wemyss the skyologer, from Sir John Eliot – four of these – one from 'Monsieur' Parmenter, many from father who never ceased to believe that I was hungry for bombast, a few from mother and enclosing lines from old Mrs Golding, a handful from women who never quite come into a man's story, and three Epistles from St Beatrix von Hol. And the military Journals, of course. Also an Ovington spider which scuttled up the wall, through the bars and out of the Tower. Miserably, there were too copies of my various pleas to be made a captain, all turned down. It was father's ambition more than mine, which was to find solitude in uproar. People telling their own tales need to pad them out a little, and nothing fluffs up the prose like a letter, so I shall at this point stuff in a few of mine. Once only I heard from George, and this in answer to a pestering request for promotion of which I am now ashamed. He by now a duke, I have applied in the flowery manner decreed by etiquette, and as this may well be held against me at my trial, I give the exchange in full for what it is worth. Me: 'Without a captaincy I cannot live.' George: 'Lieutenant Felton will have to hang if he cannot live'. My demands for back pay were those of every officer, every man fighting the King's wars. The Crown, by which we then meant George, declared, alas, that it was broke and that the army must march on its love for it. Somewhere in this letter-sack I have Wemyss's funny inventory of George's belongings. We'll see how it can be fitted in when we come to it.

The first and earliest letter was from Parmenter. In fact his only letter. It came to me in Paris and I remember being moved by it, but had replied in a way which implied that he need not reply, but gently.

From the farm at Frélaze in Loire.
(no date)

My erstwhile Lord,

I have taken this description of us from a book. Do you like it? It is now four years and four sons since our Thursday lessons by the brook. I do not forget you. I wish your Honour health. You will be a great man now. I hear of your Father's passing out of the world. I commend him to God. Did you know that he found out about the lessons and was wroth? I hear he took it out on my brothers, who took it out on him by vanishing to Dengie to lie low in that marsh. You will be in grief for him and I send you pity. I repeat what you taught me, including the Prayer. I attend the mass here with Madame my wife out of civility for her, not respect for it. I do not bend to the idols. Madame Parmenter's love for me is great. I command her vines but do not call them mine. We shall

106

take our grapes to the press today. Our black grapes are called Frontiniacs and are as blue-black as beetles. Our green grapes are Sercials and Verdelhos. We have sheep. Our grape-cart must pass the Horse School, when you will appear in my mind My sons' names are Achille, Henri, Gaston and (past permission, forgive me) John. My wife respects you and thanks you for me. I send the love of your erstwhile man, Parmenter.

I am lettered now, as you see. You gave me the hang of it. It is like sewing for females, a few stabs and then you have picked it up. Do you miss Long Melford fair, sir? I do.

More papers. My book-lists, my expense accounts and mess bills. Some Christ-haunted pages from Madame von Hol. Careful copies of all my applications for advancement. My stabs at journal-keeping. Sifting through them, the sight of so many Hollandish names made me realise how I had been virtually marooned in those low towns since receiving my commission and what news of England had filtered there had all been blown about, inflated, distorted en-route. None of us ever knew quite what was going on – and we the enforcers of our nation's politics! But thus it ever was. Statecraft must hold its nose and shut its eyes as the semi-controlled rabble called armies does the actual business. My main news came from Angus Wemyss, except that he was not a natural vender as news failed to interest him. His gaze was rarely on the ground and when something there did manage to catch his attention, he was inclined to laugh at it. For him the Court was a zoo for various species which would not be able to exist elsewhere, and the Church an upward-looking institution which took care to see but a single star, and the world generally a cheerful madhouse for ants. If Wemyss's letter-writing energy had equalled his amusement at life I would now possess more correspondence than a packhorse could manage from Ovington to the Tower. As it is, I flutter through a handful of well-intention leaves which peter-out wearily and thankfully into the wild flourish of his signature. His freed soul danced in my cell. Did the planets perfume the universe as well as provide its harmony? I sniffed the Rannoch paper but the smell was that of my Ovington closet, as I expected. Now that I have to tell my tale I would find it helpful to have been given some hard facts by those in the know – in London at any rate. What was going on when, in March, King James died? What exactly? Why wasn't he buried until May? Why at this moment (I have caught a glimpse of my *Cadiz Journal*) are we singeing the King of Spain's beard all over again? It must be close on forty years since we last did it.

Mr Archivist bends over me at this point, lusting for documents, his hungry gaze taking big bites out of the *Cadiz Journal* although it is still in its oiled wrapper. Both this and the *Rhé Journal* are sea-stained and blood-stained. Mr Archivist – 'please call me Wren' – makes a grab and has a book-list. As he will read this I must take care not to injure his feelings when I have, now and again, to describe him. He is after all the last person on this earth I shall be near to. Well, Wren, you are like a child, troublesome, unfeeling for others, yet openly affectionate, indelicate (the gaoler's prerogative), but not unkind. When I am gone and you have my papers all to yourself, you must study them for what they are, the sole property of an English officer who would have been promoted for killing a hundred enemies but who was hanged, drawn and quartered for killing one. My hope is that these few weeks spent in my company will put you on the first rung of the ladder of becoming a gentleman. A gentleman observes; he does not watch, he does not spy.

'Mr Archivist, go away!'

He leaves me, first giving back the book-list. He is clad in smart new cuffs and collar. Having a peculiarly retentive brain I hear him humming what was on the list as he locks the door. 'Pierre Gassendi ... *The Woman in the Moon* ... T. North's *Plutarch* ... Ben Somebody's *Poetaster* ... Astronomies ...' Unoffended, he trails away. He doesn't appear to have glimpsed the *Journals*, which is good as I mean to spin them out. If I simply attach them to what I have so far written and then add The Last Chapter I shall be taking the short cut to Tyburn.

8

STARRY WEMYSS

Ivy Lane by the Strand,
Near Westminster.
On a celestial day, August 1622

Dear Mr Feltoon,

My first letter to you, thus the correctness. I shall be warmer later. How are you, foolish soldier – old book-eater? I miss you. Has Madame my sister made you a true disciple? How is Antwerp after Arnhem? Have you rogered that Elizabetta? Do you drill and puff and swank? Has his honour your father cast you off? Do you miss me? May the stars enfold you.

I am in my London house, lent to me by a Northern kinsman. Ivy Lane, should you not know it, is not that thoroughfare by the Paternoster shambles but a good address between the Savoy and Somerset palaces on a road running down to the Thames. My house is a skinny wooden business with orange brick chimneys which scrape the clouds and triple over-sailings. Quite respectable for a young laird. I can see Lambeth Marshes from my bedchamber window. There is a slovenly garden, quite big, which will do for a man who enjoys dandelions. Martins live in the roof, as well as rats, I daresay. But we must all abide somewhere. The mud track by the river is hard this time of the year and I can walk to the Privy Stairs at Whitehall, and so up to Court. All in ten minutes. Oppositely, I can stroll through St Giles's fields and be out into the country in half an hour. But it is a long way to the Bridge (and to Martha Black's stew in Southwark which beats those Dutch dens we patronised hollow). Martha should not have made her entrance in this letter

– what a pushy bawd she is! Had I a gifted pen I would make your eyes water. I am locked in tiltyards and mighty dwellings, thick orchards and scurrying servants, and in ditches and horseponds which might be East Anglian were it not for what bobs in them. Sewage thy name is London. Yet the river knows how to clean itself and the only matter to bob there at this time of the year are the dark heads of swimmers. I adore the shipping, the most I have ever seen. The most which anyone in the world could ever see in one place. So many vessels that it looks impossible for them to get along, yet they speed on the glittering surface with élan and precision. Though when it comes to a gilded state barge – a dozen of these – watermen have to scull ahead like yelling heralds to clear a passage. Lots of fishes and water-birds, and Westminster schoolboys walking in crocodiles and learning as they journey.

I have something to ask you. I am turning this house into my first observatory, a temporary one until I get settled in Scotland, a plan which must not reach the kinsman who owns it, as he would have me out as a heretic the minute he heard of it, so not a word to Madame von Hol, the guileless one, who might innocently mention telescopes. You will see if you have not done so before that I intend to make myself an astronomer, a Highland Kepler, a scientist of sorts. Will you work with me? not out of your Faith, for I would never ask that, but as a writer? You know your way into the libraries, I must find my way into the solar system. Your Lord can follow you into both. Who made the poets? Who created the stars? I will answer Nature, you will answer God. We shall not quarrel. So, and I plead with you, turn in that commission, make a farewell bow to our rollicking Colonel, *have nothing to do with Count Mansfeld*, and come to me, for my good, for your good. We shall marry and keep our wives out of the telescope chamber, although let them see Venus once in a while. Do not dismiss my request out of hand. Brood on it by some canal. Roll off that Elizabetta, scratch your head and mutter, 'Why not?' Come to me, my Felton. You will like Scotland.

Yours in the Milky Way,
Angus Wemyss.

Dear Felton,

Your letter gives me hope. Yes, of course you must have time to decide. But see us as planets in conjunction. My sister writes, 'Oh poor Lieutenant F. We are more and more certain that he is not on the right track. More so since you have left'. So it is not only me who notices. I also have an intuition, and please never call me an astrologer, that something very terrible will happen to you if you do not cease trying to be a soldier. You are using the army as a hide. Come out of it. Now. Those old mess-mates of ours at Arnhem, they found you sullen, not understanding seriousness. When you are most thoughtful and subsequently most happy, the description 'malcontent' will lodge in their heads. In the field, you will have to out-hero them to stay within their admiration. Half my relations are regiment-men and I am an expert on their type, believe me. Creep from your tent to a higher roof.

Villiers. I have clapped eyes on him and I can only echo the Queen of Sheba, the half was not told. I went to Court via the slimy Privy Stairs, and there he was, the flesh in sublimity. I have never seen such legs off a statue, or such a beautiful face, or so many pearls on one man. He walks among sensation but having learnt how not to be impeded by walls of rank staring. So on he went, head turning this way and that out of courtesy to fawnings, though good-naturedly enough. I remember your telling me how kind he was at Angers. But he is well-loathed all the same. Hated. What a creature to be found in the dog-house! The King feeds him on honours and holds him by golden chains. The common error here is to believe that he has James in chains. James is more experienced than any other Christian prince when it comes to Favourites and never relinquishes his leading-rein. Yet it is my Lord Buckingham who appoints. His office has become these last three years the fount of all offices – and doesn't the Court know it! So it bows at his arrival only an inch less down than for his Majesty himself. Not so the Parliament-men, who are forging away at legal restrictions. Meanwhile Lord Buckingham's queue grows. It is please, sir, give me an earldom, a baronetcy, a see, a monopoly license, leave to lick your arse for the going rate. The latter is enormous – has to be because England is broke. Last January your George gave St Paul's Deanery to Dr Donne, who could never have afforded it. So his policy must be to fleece them if you can, if not take nothing. Yet when his appointees fall Villiers can do little to cushion such ruinings, Francis Bacon being a case in point. It was pitiful all round – except for his Majesty, who approves cool justice. Villiers sent condolences with one hand and took Bacon's palace with the other, a huge and decrepit old mansion by Charing Cross which is now being glorified. Repairs have been going on for a year or more, just as at the three other houses, New Hall, Burley-on-the-Hill and Wallingford along Whitehall. New Hall is near Chelmsford, not far from your country. I expect your family knows it. The cost of these four palaces is alarming everybody, and the price of this pretty man generally quite dreadful. Squibs are everywhere. Here is a sample shown me by one of Martha Black's pimps.

> When only one doth rule and guide the ship,
> Who neither card nor compass knew before,
> The master-pilot and the rest asleep,
> The stately ship is split upon the shore.
> But they awakening, start up, stare and cry,
> 'Who did this fault?' – 'Not I' – 'Nor I!'
> So fares it with a great and wealthy state
> Not governed by the master, but his mate.

Here is another.

> The King loves you, you him, both love the same,
> You love the King, he you, both *Buck-in-game*.
> Of sport the King loves game, of game the *Buck*,
> Of all men you. Why you? Why, see your luck!

But no more. Nostrils are slit for less. What I find curious about Courts is their insularity. What goes on outside them is unimportant. In James's and George's case, who in the measureless ignorance of common people would understand a love such as theirs? Who could know that monarchs and their great servants must live in glorious state as reflections of Heaven? Tell that to the Turks, they say.

112

I didn't mean to go on like this. I intended a short letter to persuade you from soldiering on. I add this delicately, but you shall have a salary. The bookman is worthy of his hire. I can afford you.

Your companion among the Spheres,
Wemyss.

Ivy Lane-by-Thames,
14th October 1622
My refusing Friend,

I am desolated. I counted on you which perhaps I should not have done. So you will not join me. I am angry with you – angry for you. Do you not understand that you have taken a big step in disappointing yourself? Let me spell it out; *you do not belong where you are heading.* Is that plain enough? Where is your perspective? These religious wars are a pygmy business when compared with the astronomical movements on high. I invited you to join me in our universe – yes, ours! Yours and mine. What drives you on to yet one more filthy little Christian massacre? It cannot be patriotism. Your father's memory? It grieved me to hear that he had died. Now both of us are fatherless. Is it your notion that you are carrying out his wish for you in preparing for battle? Something like that? From what you told me in Holland this honoured parent of yours regarded soldiering simply as a profession for a gentleman of small means and would not have minded you abandoning it after a respectable year or two so long as you did not descend on him for support. Mr Felton of Ovington did what he thought was his best for you at the time. This doesn't suit you now, admit it. So what drives you on? There is something inexplicable here, maybe. Your direction appears to be fixed like an out of kilter version of Dr Gilbed's magnet, pulling you towards some polarity which will destroy you. I fear for you. And all this when you are telling yourself that you are simply obeying a call and fighting for a cause. Phut! To perish – even to suffer a sore foot – for those Winter Ones at The Hague, how ludicrous. They are not worth restoration nor does Bohemia want them back.

113

But it is not them, is it, John? It is something else which makes you stick to your guns? Tell me when you discover what it is.

Although I hardly expect you to change you mind, I'll tell you why I offered employment. I am going to map the skies. Are you still upright on your camp-stool? I intend to call my planet-chart an Atlas after the brother of Prometheus who was an astronomer, and about whom there were fairy-tales about supporting the universe on his shoulders. (Atlas was actually sitting on a mountain watching the stars). Martha Black's well-trained girls and the Court are merely my entertaining side of London; I am seriously here to purchase astronomical instruments and books, which is where you were to come in. Oh, how I need you! Help! Won't you change your mind? You are one of those rare men who always have the right book to hand. Your eyes and brain leap through pages. What a blessing you would be to a sky-mapmaker. I would be the mathematician, draftsman, scientist; you would be the poet and philosopher and we would chart space. Only it is not 'space', is it? We would put in what is there. I won't go on. Neither will I in future letters scold or persuade you. I will remain.

Yours Wemyss.

Ivy Lane by the Strand, London.
Twenty-first Day in August, 1624.

Little Mariner

– for I hear that you may become a sea-soldier. Is this correct? If so, here is something to fill your sails. I have just this hour returned from the spectacle of a pack of Bankside players dismaying the Privy Council. You will know of Tom Middleton the mocking play-writer, well he has devised 'A Game of Chess' in which his Majesty and the Spaniards, Prince Charles, George of course, old Gondomer - everybody on the current political stage – take each other's pieces. Nothing is sacred, in particular majesty. It ran for more than a week, making Tom Middleton a small fortune, before the Court heard of it. In fact, it was Gondomar himself who complained. 'Summon the lot of them!' cries the

114

King. 'Chop their lugs off!' Half the town comes to see the show –
the Whitehall epilogue, as it turns out, of the Swan production.
Tom himself is missing. The Privy Council raves. How dare they
put on such stuff! Hopkins, who plays the Fat Bishop, holds his
fire until the Council is beside itself with indignation, then steps
forward with the Licence signed by Herbert, Master of the Revels,
who clearly hadn't read it. The actors, who are all standing in a
row, clap. The boygirls wink. The court collapses. We, the
audience, are weak with laughter. There are satirical requests for
Tom to put this scene in his play. Here is a sample of the latter – it
could take your mind off deck-drill.

I am your loving servant Wemyss.

> Fat Bishop: Here's *Taxa Poenitentaria*, Knight The Book of
> General Pardons, of all prices: I have been searching
> for his sin this half hour, and cannot light upon it.

> Black Knight:That's strange; let me see it. (Reads) 'For wilful
> murder thirteen pound four shillings and sixpence'
> – that's reasonably cheap for killing.
> Killing, killing, killing, killing, killing – Why, here's
> nothing but killing, Bishop, of this side.

> Fat Bishop: Turn the sheet over, and you shall find adultery a
> couple of shillings, and for fornication fivepence –
> Mass, those are two good pennyworths! I cannot
> see how a man can amend himself – 'For lying with
> mother, sister and daughter' – aye, marry, sir –
> thirty-three pound, three shillings, three pence.
> The sin's gradation right, paid in all threes too.
> 'Simony, nine pound.'
> 'Sodomy, sixpence' – you should put that sum on
> the backside of your book, Bishop!
> What's here, sir? (Reads)
> 'Two old precedents of encouragement. Given as a
> gratuity for the killing of an heretical prince with a
> poisoned knife, five thousand ducats ...'

P.S. George has been playing leading man in a masque, leaping
on the stage before his Majesty, and dressed all à la Thessaly,

and getting things going with a 'Make room for a sun-burnt, tansy-faced beloved, an olive-coloured Ganymede!' Encore, encore!

Ivy Lane by the Strand, London.
October, the first Day, 1624.

Little Mariner,

I suppose that it must be true what I heard, that you are going aboard or aloft or whatever it is? You have not told me your news. All I get is official troop movements. At the moment you seem to be trooping onto a boat. I am in fair condition for a man who has been through a London summer. Scarcely a rash. I have also been in your country – Ipswich-Harwich direction – and oh dear! It wasn't bringing the harvest in but scraping it in. Stooks were being carted as though they were the last treasures on earth and poor narrow creatures were in the fields gleaning with their finger-nails. Every ear counted. They told me that your peasants half-starve at the best of times, but this year – whew! You should return home and teach Sully-ism. Throw away your cutless, take up land management. What in your God's name are you doing? Your peasants are gaunt and destitute. Where is their Moses? The common graves are dug in lieu of a hard winter and, believe me, they will not lie empty. Most of what your ploughmen grew is already shipped to the cities, leaving them with more seed-corn than bread-corn. But I make no comparisons. I daresay that it is as bad in Scotland – though not among the Hollanders, if you remember. What eaters! And not among the likes of George, if such a glory can have a like. His new suit, they say, cost four thousand pounds. I think it included the hat.

Ipswich was busy with Puritans being harried by their bishop, who rides around fencing-in the altars, for fear of desecration by dogs, he tells them. For fear of their being able to see the antics of the celebrant, they tell *him*. Ipswich is very pretty, I thought, all flint steeples and river-sides, reflections and thoughtful children. I would have liked to convert them to Polestar but, with bossy Bishop Wren about, prudence caught my tongue. The cleared-out churches suit my taste and I especially adored the uninterrupted floods of colour pouring from the ancient glass in which your angels and saints continue to posture. Though for how much longer? Soon the daylight will get a look in. The lecterns are mobbed. His Majesty's version will wear-out at this rate. There are few prayers in these Ipswich shrines, just a continuous whip of the page and reading aloud of the Word. Decent women surround these scriptures by the hour to use them as a letter-book, learning to read with amazing ease and returning home to spout great passages at their families. I would not have guessed that your countrymen were such a cantankerous lot had I not made this journey – worse than the Edinburghians. Dinghies for the clothiers' ships bob and slurp by the harbour wall. There is talk that when they next set out it won't be with woollens for Flanders – or with wretches for mercenary Mansfeld's army – but with New Age families bound for the Plantations. I trust that your family is aware of this? I am scribbling on a ledge in St Mary-Elm-Street. Do you know it? Very dark and bogified. It is raining and I am sheltering and shivery. Silver runnels have crept in under the door and are making for my feet, already soaked. No elms but sycamore suckers penetrate the bone-hole. A white-head is reading out of the King's book to some little lads who sprawl on their bellies on the cold slabs. 'Go on – go on, sir. Don't stop, sir.' Now I shall listen until the rain stops.

I have something to tell you. I am to be married. Her name is Ruth Urquhart – Urquhart of Urquhart, although this will mean nothing to you – and we are cousins. We are not in love but are decently matched. We shall live in her castle with her loch all round us, and I shall turn its towers into star chambers and create consternation. 'Living well is the best revenge'. There is a book-room, so come and stay. Tonight I might, if I dare, get myself up the unsafe tower of this church, just to be seventy feet nearer the heavens. I hope the cloud lifts.

Are you kicking your heels? You know what they say, 'Soldiers in peace are like chimneys in summer'. I embrace you.

Farewell, your friend Wemyss.

Dear John,

What do you know of *Nanas* – dwarfs? Apparently they are very collectable and search-parties are out scouring Europe for them. The King has a couple, both males, and they toddle in his wake. They say that the Spanish and Mantuan courts have the best *nanas*, where they are much petted, and that manikin and ladikin dwarfs are mated at the Pope's court of Vatican. George is openly envious and has sent his chief shopper Mr Gerbier to find him a couple of *nanas* for York House, the interior of which is now one of the wonders of the world, they say. I haven't seen it. There are some in your Church who question their full humanity and who doubt if there is enough of them to be called Christians. His Majesty, ever curious, had his dwarfs stripped naked in private in the interest, he maintained, of science. They attend him in the new Banqueting house, at Royston, in Whitehall gardens – everywhere. The hounds are very fond of them and it amuses the King to whistle and have little creatures and a dozen dogs tumble at his feet. They have – the *Nanas* – large sad heads and tuberous fingers, and I suppose are about three feet tall. The Court women speculate on their powers without bothering to lower their voices, causing them to crimson. They say that the Duchess of * * * has them on her bed among the spaniels. They are said not to speak like us due to the constant note of regret in their throat-reeds. They detest being taken to laps and tickled, being at least thirty years of age. The King is exceeding proud of his *nanas*. He never touches them. 'They don't bite, sir,' says son Charlie. 'I know, I know, Baby. And I know that God made them and that the Saviour died for them, but do not require me to pat them.' He dresses them in ropes of pearls and cascading ear-rings, and has them washed once a week, and stuffs their breeks with Attar of Roses, the same as he wears himself. George's *nanas* should arrive by Christmas, a present from the Duke of Mantua, and he can't wait to put them into white velvet. I'm told that *nanas* can be mighty difficult, insisting that they are men, women, and so on, and so one of us. But consider: they face our groins in conversation and need steps for a chair. I would not write like this to Madame von Hol, would I? What am I thinking about.

It is the Capital, it minimalises me.

The leaves fall, the afternoons are golden. People are looking forward to frosts to kill summer distempers and cut off plagues. There is no point, I suppose, in me once more urging you to change your ways?

I am a friend Wemyss.

Ivy Lane by the Strand, London.
Your Feast of the Saints, 1624.

Little Mariner,

Well, you are in for it, and do not say that I did not warn you. All this year those Boys of his have plotted marriage and war, and the King has been unable to stop them. Charlie will marry Henrietta and Steenie (short for Angel-face) will restore the Palsgrave. 'A war at my time of life!' weeps his Majesty. The Boys are adamant. More to the point, they are as thick as thieves, and who is Prince and who is subject can be anyone's guess. They get his Majesty out of the way – 'Go and have a nice hunt, Dad'. First the marriage. Henrietta is thirteen, and so fit and ready – and extremely pretty. The Prince of Wales is coming up to twenty-four and positively pawing the ground, the Infanta having fallen through. No mistresses apparently, hence the strain. But, due to your religion, the situation hasn't altered a jot. Henrietta has to have the Pope's permission to marry a heretic and he won't give it if Steenie makes war on the Habsburgs. Steenie, – I must revert to George, the George you knew – who has switched the Infanta for Henrietta, has convinced everybody that she is the only girl for Charlie, and if he can't have her he won't have anybody. So there will be no heir and the Crown will pass to the Winter Queen's grandchild. This appalling certainty galvanises public opinion. 'Let's have the popish Frenchwoman then – if she's what his Highness has set his heart upon'.

Having got all this settled, George declares war. But this is a quite different kettle of fish. Princess Henrietta will arrive with a shipload of gold (and priests); Count Mansfeld will sail away from our shores with a hundred thousand of our countrymen and the

119

money to feed them. Well, we don't mind losing the countrymen, most of them being riffraff, but we do mind paying this battlemongering general one hundred thousand pounds. Come, says the Commons, take fifty. Now that it is declared, the Commons won't have the war. His Majesty is indignant; 'Who are they to make or un-make war? It is I the King who make war. God told me so in Isaiah – or is it Numbers?' I am addling, it is age. Steenie has come to put Frederic and Elizabeth back on the Palantine throne. What a long way my Buck has come! In the Commons it is 'Oh, my God ...' Anyway, dear Felton, there is nothing here for you and if you want my advice, stay out of it. There is nothing in it for you, believe me.

I am your real friend, Wemyss.

From my London house, off Strand.
A few days later, the year of Your Lord, 1624.
Little Mariner,

Count Mercenary is here and earning his keep. They have lodged him in the rooms at St James's which had been enriched for the Infanta, ghostly girl. The Count sets about him with a will. Having fought other men's quarrels all his life, he knows what to do. The efficiency of his preparations fills his Majesty with alarm. He knows all about the Count, and has not received him. Paying this person for help in the field is one thing, touching him quite another. But letters of condescension (no thanks yet) float from Theobald's to St James's and are well received. The Count knows kings and their dirty jobs, and is not offended. I went to look at him. Pretty old, fifty, I should say, though not scarred, which you thought he would have been. To any question of 'what do you need, sir?' his answer is always the same. Money. 'Give me money, lots and lots of it!' A great black smile like an open cellar door, and with a similar rush of released foul air. The infanta's chair creaks under his bum.

A tremendous army is to be gathered here under English colonels, plus Scotch and Welsh, I suppose. In fact, they are already scavenging it. Size, not quality, is the thing. Our dear old

Colonel Mathers is in London fitting himself out. The Count's beaters are in every Hundred and never was there such a ruthless flushing from ditches and shacks of human scarecrows, thieves, vagrants, loose-enders and no-hopers, some bollock-naked, all thin as a twist of hay, a few crazed. The Count's recruiters themselves, some of them, are no more than shittens in shoes, and I don't know who to feel the most sorry for, the drivers or the driven. Every road is a-trickle with volunteers as well, all the poor and the bored lured on by promises of meat, cockades, shillings if they are lucky, and trumpet music. The best sort are the poor weavers from the silenced looms, desperate, respectable men who have been reduced to starvation by the drying-up of trade. I doubt if the Count or his colonels will be able to tell these from the rabble, or would wish to. George's agents are out in every shire seeing that it produces its quota of fighters.

You have your holy-days, I have mine. And a double one which was first declared in the autumn of 1609 to celebrate Kepler's book on Mars and the turning of the telescope to infinity. What poor Bruno called *De Immenso*. Sad star-trekker, he was born during one of those moments of homecoming to the Earth, to the devil we know, and all that. To hell with *De Immenso*. And to ashes too with this high-flying Giordano! cries the Bishop of Rome who, should he look up, only sees nine orders of angels and a harvest moon. As I refuse your sacred honours system, I dub George Bruno star. You are potentially starry, Little Mariner. Even Madame von Hol noticed – which is why she looked up to you. I know, I know, you hoped otherwise!

I am proceeding to Augsburg in a few weeks' time to commission a telescope for Urquhart Castle, where it will be delivered as organ pipes rolled in hessian. Indeed, my fiancée Mistress Urquhart is paying for it as such, as otherwise she might refuse to have such a mighty aid to heresy in the house. It is still her house until I marry her. Anyhow, when I ride to Augsberg, I'll try to see you on the way. I don't expect old blood-and-snot Mansfeld will have marched you to Prague until next spring. Augsburg is pilgrimage-land for star-men. It is where Tycho and Ramus met. You would find Tycho *simpatico* – I say this without mockery – because he had real trouble in reconciling Copernicus with Scripture. I don't. For one thing I am not a Copernican;

Kepler is my man. I am scratching my head for some way to bring you together so that he can seduce you. Would it help if I could prove that you could take your Jesus far beyond that heavenly concert of Revelations to where He would lead the music of the spheres? The trouble is that, at this stage of my heresy, I am not very good at either theology or astronomy and I find it dreadfully difficult in letters like these to say what I am, what I know, where I am going, and where I came from. You have your prophets in revelationary order, Moses and so on, and I am about to line-up mine. Ptolemy (my Moses) first, then Pluto, Aristarchus, then Roger Bacon, who was not a 'wizard', then Copernicus, Tycho – then Kepler!! How I cannot wait to reach him! He must be getting on now, over sixty. I would like to come to him as Timothy came to Paul and hear him say, 'son'. I would ask him to hum me the *Harmonoes Mundi*. I'm told that it goes something like this:

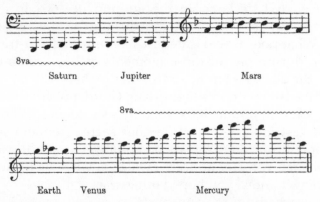

Such music eternally streams through the etherial air, like whale-song through the deep. These harmonies are the prayer of the universe, sweet friend Felton. Carry your Christ-hymns into them. Their purity will flow across Kepler's solar system which he has cleansed from all the errors of the past, and you yourself will find that you are released into that timeless space which is, contradictorarily, fully occupied by love. Be planetory! And not a word to Mistress Urquhart, whose God reigns from Schiehallion, her own Hebron. Our castle is near there, stuck in the middle of a loch island, and deathly damp, I daresay. Imagine the factor rowing my lenses and tubes across, and saying to himself, 'Wine for the marriage – is that it?'

I am in good health, thankyou, for a bespoke man, and am developing a respectable lust for the Urquhart. It is a struggle to stay away from the Southwark stews – particularly from the house of one great bawd, a Martha Black, whose new intake of Welsh girls has the town queuing up. But no risks at this stage, even if 'There are more men threatened than stricken'. I don't mind telling you, I rise just by strolling across London Bridge. We Scots are strong. Roll-on, Mount Schiehallion!

Thank you for your last letter – certainly, all your letters reach me. Will mine continue to reach you, now that Count Mankiller is on the shift? Take all care of yourself, for you have an appointment with an astronomer in Rannoch.

I embrace you,
your companion, Wemyss.

From London still.
The new year of 1625.
Little man-at-arms,

It snows. The Christmas revels have paralysed the town. Footsteps crump. The Thames is narrowed by thin ice. God help us, it is cold! Frawn, that's what we are – and you too, I expect. Heaven, I mean the solar system, help poor men. I cannot get myself broken-in to the sight of starving wretches. It is all the fault of your Saviour for giving me His conscience. Scavengers go about Westminster, where heartlessness is all the rage, pulling corpses from windbreaks and crannies, and piling them on handcarts. I saw three frozen children all stuck together, a wee maid and her brothers, all dead. They hung across the shafts like a frieze. They were found in a garden behind Wallingford House and the scavengers told my servant Job what a good thing to have discovered them before the thaw, when they would have stunk the place out. Every now and then the sun shines and the hungry and the glutted promenade, seemingly both alike affected by the brilliant wintryness, laughing and cavorting. No work is done; the twelve days have us in thrall. My people take out pies and puddings, and bread especially, but with such a sea of empty bellies they are no more than an apple-core in an ants' nest. Whitehall dances, and I expect that you and the other gentlemen are showing a leg or two. Christmas is Christmas. Whilst they were emptying the poor-boxes I said to myself, 'I must tell Mr Felton about the new craze of making a collection. From his wambling Majesty down it has become the vogue to possess more things than anyone else. Curious things. Well-I-never! Things. Such as a cock-a-trice's look, if you know what I mean. No sooner has one called on some lord or other than it is, 'Come and see my cabinet' – the object being to be outdone in rarities.

George Villiers – remember him as such? Is the maddest collector in the market. I say mad because, unlike Mr Tradescant, say, he is not remotely interested in natural history, or relics or bibelot, etc., and all he desires is to possess more objects of the cabinet kind than any other person in England. And of course he has five houses to fill. This Duke is an amasser, a man who must have all of everything, a converter of possessions who likes to call himself a Connoisseur, meaning knowledgeable. But he does not *know*. To have amassed so much, and not to *know*, will be his downfall. I try to see him as you saw him at Blois, but all that remains recognisable from your affectionate descriptions is the sweet temper. On a black day he doesn't rage, he falls sick. Becomes really very ill and those places of his change from treasure-houses into infirmaries. They carry him from one to the other as though the sight of all that he owns (has pilfered) will revive him. And I suppose it does, for who would go naked into the darkness at his age with such haystacks of fine objects to detain him?

I must draw a line. The snow has grown very deep and is banking. The Court is supposed to travel to Windsor tomorrow for some hare-chasing but clearly it will not get through. So there will be masques and more masques to fill the tedium. George will dance. They tell me he is so good that he might have made his living from it. His Majesty will lie a little to the left of his chair, as he does, head on hand, dreadfully tired, watching and wondering if he will see another winter. Should he nod off, slip, George will be instantly solicitous. This is his true giving. They say that the King, were he Solomon himself, could never adequately reward Duke Steenie for what Duke Steenie has given him. Unconditional love.

His Majesty hates London – never feels well there. When he does appear he takes to wearing a crown, walking about the passages and stable rooms with it on, to the amazement of those who crowd there. It is a gold circle with rubies and he wears it on a dusty cap which hides his ears and keeps him warm. He says, 'our arms and legs ache so, poor me, poor me!' When I bowed to him he said, 'Mr Wemyss, is it you?' limping on. He has written thus to George, astonishingly 'releasing' the letter as evidence of his continuing favour.

> Come and see me so that we may make at this Christmas a new marriage, ever to be kept hereafter. For God so love me as I desire only to live in this world for your sake, and that I had rather live banished in any part of the earth with you than live a sorrowful widow's life without you. And so God bless you, my sweet child and wife, and grant that ye may ever be a comfort to your dear dad and husband.

As his Majesty has been King since he was one year old, I can understand his exhaustion. He moves with sickly alertness and leaving a little stench as he passes. He prays when the pains are bad, holding on to whoever is next to him, a servant, a courtier, the Nanas. Pity follows him, pity and fear.

I salute you, my Felton, Wemyss.

There should have been more letters from him. Why so few? This is where I realised that Mother had forgotten to tell her man about a second cache which I had sent from Rhé, from which I never expected to return. These were Wemyss's journal-letters, his side of our pact to keep diaries. Had my own also been left behind? I felt a feverish desire for them and scrambled through the rest of the papers. There they were, the Cadiz and Rhé Journals, blotched but readable. They smelled not of carnage but of my little pippin-wood press. Some scents have no right to travel. They carry too much with them. This one brought with it a view of Cavendish from a window-frame, a bed in which I had devoured a thousand books and the farm-girl, and curled-up, icy nights. Not in the direst illness does one entirely give up a returning to where one could be happy again, but in prison one does. In the Tower one does. The Tower says, No more! It is why it exists – to drone No more! I felt the cord which holds me upright jerk. It was terrible and yet no more than a salutory twitch compared with what must follow. And that convulsion has to be expertly handled by the hangman if my sentence is to be carried out.

'What sentence?' asks Mr Archivist, that reader of terrified minds. 'Why, *the* sentence of sentences. That for treachery against the Kingdom which gives leave for the executioner to do to me what his late Majesty did to a brought-down roe deer when he was up to his elbows in its guts. And yet, like the poor animal, it is possible that I might feel more amazement than agony that death has to be so bloodied. I stabbed George and his blood flowed out of his mouth like a brook, yet only my knife touched him. The hangman will feel inside me with both hands, hauling me out before my own eyes.'

'You romance. You are also crying. Don't cry, sir. You weep out of homesickness, not from fear. My wife is constantly homesick for Tavistock, it is a great nuisance. She too is a crier. But you are not in the ordinary way, are you? You cry like a child who cannot open a door when you should be looking for someone big to open it for you.'

'Who?'

'We'll see. Meanwhile, to this confession, not a line of which will you let me glimpse.'

Wemyss's only other letter was the seriously comic one in which he had weighed the Duke of Buckingham's speculations in the balances and found them, frankly, ridiculous. Such favours as his should not have come cheap, there being none to equal them, but – well let the Teller of the Stars give a rough estimate of what it cost the country to have George.

Some pages missing.

... and two Caravaggios. An *Esther and Ahasuerus*, not quite finished though good enough by Jacobo Tintoretto, a stark-naked Lucretia grasping a dagger, a *Return of the Prodigal Son* by Dominico Fetti who himself returned to his almighty father only the other day, a full set of *Months* – sowing, reaping, etc. – from the Mortlake tapestry factory, and costing the earth, that horrible *Samson Slaying the Philistine with a Jaw-bone* by Bologna which, if you recall, King Phillip gave Prince Charles when he went a wooing the Infanta a couple of years ago, and which King Charles has handed over to George for his river garden; roomfuls of pictures from the sale of Mantua when that duke went broke, and Raphaels and de Vincis galore. All these and a million other things besides have been amassed for Buckingham by his pop-eyed cabinet-keeper, Sir Balthazar Gerbier, and by, of all people, his chief gardener, a Mr Tree Descant, a prettily named person from Suffolk. They were both at Rhé, only I don't expect you will have had noticed in all that mayhem. Mr Descant was observed collecting plants during a battle. Sir Balthazer explains his employment thus:

> My attendances was pleasing to my Prince-Duke because of my several languages, good hand in writing, skill in sciences as mathematics, architecture, drawing, painting, contriving of scenes, masques, shows and entertainments for great Princes, besides many secrets which I had gathered from divers rare persons, as likewise for making engines useful in war, as I had made those which might blow up the dyke that stopped the passage to the town of Rochelle, for it was the same model of that of the Prince of Parma, when the attempt was on Antwerp. He did put to me first the contrivance of some of his habitations, to choose for him rarities, books, medals, marble statues and pictures. I did keep his cyphers.

And as well as dragging half Europe's art-work into your George's habitations, Sir B. drove towards these mansions posses of carvers and painters themselves. Including poor old Orazio Gentilschi, that sweet Italian, but far too ancient to go up ladders to make Magdalens on ceilings. How Pop-eyes abused him! They say that the Cabinet-filler is currently offering Peter Rubens (another spy) one hundred thousand florins for his entire art collection. Where in the world can such a sum be found – for pictures! Money trickles, not flows. Parliament trickles some to his Majesty who trickles it to George, who trickles it to the auctioneers telling them that there will be a trickle or two more from where this comes. Tell me, was George Villiers picture-struck during your time by the Loire? You never mentioned it although those valley palaces must have been dripping with oils. Cannot somebody tell him that he will never be a Lord Arundel or a King Charles, or a true connoisseur as he knows nothing whatever about art collections? But then he knows nothing at all about government although this hasn't stopped him from governing, if one can call it that. Does he sleep with the new King as he did with the old? I believe not. His and Charles's love is of another nature, though love it is. Why cannot we *all* love him? No, do not give reasons; they will require pages.

These pages began as a catalogue and must end as one. I make such a list as one who dwells in a bare castle whose chambers hang with draft-blankets and whose only portrait is a severe Queen of Scots on the Eating-room chimneypiece, all long white fingers and rough diamonds. We in this Kingdom scratch our heads at your English cabinet-mania, your boxing-up of everything from a Florentine cartoon to a fern. And we in Scotland would never dare send our factors shopping in any case. Like us, they are used to a pared-down life and ask no more than a stool to sit on and a board to sit at. Holyrood itself is not cluttered. Neither your chief seat at Playford, I suspect. My cabinet, as you know, is the ebony night, my infinite box of stars. Kepler has lifted its lid.

This will amuse you. It is Mr Tree Descant's shopping list, sent on by him to Mr Secretary Nicholas of the Navy, who showed it to me. It reveals what your George is stuffing into his Cabinet of Rarities.

Noble Sir,

I have Bin Commanded by My Lord to let yr Worshipe understand that it is His Graces Pleasure that ye should In His Name Deall withe All Marchants from All Places But Espetially the Virgine & Bermewde & Newfound Land men that when they into those parts that they will take Care to furnishe His Grace

128

withe All Maner of Beasts & fowels & Birds Or If Not Withe Heads Horns Beaks Clawes Skins feathers Flyes or seeds plants trees or shrubs. Also from Gine or Binne or Senego turkye Espetially to Sir Thomas Rowe who is Leger At Constantinoble. Also to Captain Northe to ther New Plantation towards the Amasonians withe all thes fore Resyted Rarityes & Also from the East Indes withe Shells Stones Bones Egge Shells with What Cannot Com Alive. My Lord Having Heard of the Dewke of Sheveres (Chevreuse, he must mean) & partlie seene of His strang fowlls. Also from Hollond of Storks A payer or two young ons withe Divers kinds of Ruffes whiche they theare Call Campanies. This having mad Bould to present my Lords command I Disire ye furtherance yr asured servant to be Commanded till He is,

John Tree Descent.

Newhall this 31
day July 1625

Postcriptum.
To the merchants of the Ginne Company & and the Gouldcost, Mr humfrie Slainy, Captain Crisp & Mr Clobery & and Mr Johne Wood Capemarchant. The things desyred from those part Be theese

Imprimis on Elepants head withe the teethe in it very larg
On River horses head of the Bigest that canbe Gotten
On Seacowes head the Bigest that canbe gotten
On seabulles head witg homes
Of all ther strang sorts of fowells & Birds skines & Beakes, leggs & phetheres that the Rare or Not known to us
Of all sorts of strang fishes skines of those parts
The Greatest sorts of Shell fishes Shelles of Great flying fishes & Sucking fishes withe what els strang
Of the habits, weapons & Instruments of ther Ivory
Long fluts.
Of all sorts of Serpents & Snakes skines & Espetially of that sort that hathe a Combe on his head lyke A Cock.
Of All sorts of ther fruts Dried As ther tree Beanes, Littil Red and Black in ther Cods withe what flower & seed Canbe gotten the flowers layd Betwin paper leaves In a Book Dried.
Of all sorts of Shining Stones of Any Strang Shapes.
Any thing that is strang.

129

Now, my Shining Stone, littil sea-soldier Felton, what does this shopping-list tell you? What does it tell you about Sir Balthazer and *his* requirements? I will tell you. It is that cabinet-keepers collect what *they* like to possess, not what their master orders. Rich and important men have to be provided with objects which give a nod and a wink to the cultured mind. George has given his cabinet-keepers an open money-bag and they have laid out what was in it on what they themselves longed to have. That Mr Descant is a naturalist and would, with a small persuasion, see moondust. Should you on your wretched travels come across lens or sky-charts, buy them for me. I will repay the monies.

Signature obliterated.

9

WARNINGS

Dear John,

Yes, of course I remember you. How could I not? You should not
write, 'Do you remember me?'. It suggests that I have neglected
you or avoided you, or that you are unmemorable in some way.
If you and I have not written since France it is because of an
intelligence on both our parts which accepted that the kind of
student relationship we once had cannot be maintained unless it
grows into something more, which it hasn't. No fault on either
side, unless you call distances faults. And no, I haven't heard
what has happened to you, although I sincerely hope that it is
what you wanted. The King's army, wasn't it? Well rather you
than me from what I have seen of armies. Field-use and then
field-ordure. I saw what Cadiz did to English soldiers, not simply
wound them – that would have been a mild fate in contrast to
turning them into a muttering garbage to be trailed along the
Plymouth streets, like escapings from the night-cart. My dear, my
un-glorious countrymen! I trust, officer-Felton, that none of your
crew met this fate. I would have done more to help them but I am
stripped of all authority other than that which comes from my
knighthood and membership of the House of Commons. When I
witnessed the human muck which Villiers brought back to
England from Cadiz, and remembered the decent human beings
he had shipped to Spain, never did I so need to be a Justice of the
Peace and a Vice-Admiral of Devon! I would have washed down
those filthy decks and washed away those dirty men who treated
those who fought for them thus.
    They have locked me up in the Gatehouse because I refuse to

pay the forced loan which will allow Villiers (our nice George!) to make more war, more havoc of Englishmen's flesh. I grant him the cause but not the competence. Do you know the Gatehouse? It is where the old bishops of London used to incarcerate naughty priests. I can see the high tower of Parliament from the slit, and the members hurrying about. They will have to let me out the minute his Majesty opens his third Parliament. I am in the doghouse where Villiers is concerned, having in a spout of anger last May, when I had to summon up the debate for his impeachment, called him our Sejanus. It was the Tower for a few days after that – myself and poor old Dudley Digges who, like me, cannot be kept quiet – 'Unless we may speak of these things (Villiers' rule of England) in Parliament, let us rise and begone, or else sit still and do nothing'. So we spoke, and here I am, my language apparently still running like wildfire through the House and through the Court. I did not mean it to run so far or so fast; liberty-words run away with me. My wife is not best pleased. I might think of her sometimes, she writes, as well as the country.

How did you think that I could help you? I am not a soldier. I would help if I could, but how? Like you, I read all day, having little else to do. The bishops kept their bad shepherds warm, so I toast my legs with my gown up. Seriously, Felton, your concentration now should be on your social, not your military rank. We gentlemen must soon come together to save England. Our fight will be to keep George in his place, which is not the *council* chamber. Grit your teeth; I am no good at playfulness ... I shall write to you once more, but in deadly seriousness this time.

> I wish you well, page-devourer,
> your servant Eliot.

> The Gatehouse in London.
> Easter-tide, 1627.

Dear John,

The deadly serious letter. It will be short. It will be for you to finish it, but not to reply to it. For I will have stated my case and must do so in many quarters, and it will be for you and others to develop the theme. It will put the wind up George-Sejanus, Prince-elect of Tipperary. It will puzzle King Charles. I don't know if what I have to suggest is original; I certainly cannot recall reading it in a political book.

Charles is monarch, yes? All of us are monarchs by virtue of King Jesus – yes? Do not mutter. Not before you have given the theory all your thought. So we are a monarchy of redeemed men and there is not a royal crown between us. As monarchs we rule on earth but we cannot – or must not – over-rule each other. I don't mind telling you, Felton, I have never felt more kingly in all my life. Don't you see, our kingliness – the kingliness of English gentlemen – is what will save us? Those lacking this high quality, be they High Admirals, must not be allowed to reign. I write sedition. I will flatter you – few will have done, I suspect. I recognised the monarch in you when we shared the Loire country, though not in Villiers, which was extraordinary when one comes to think of it. For on the face of it he was all crown, all sceptre, his countenance virtually sacred with loveliness. Moreover he was my dear friend in wildness. Now he is my enemy and I his.

My dubbing George Sejanus was no slip of the tongue. I meant it. Although the ancients are bandied about in Parliament to convince each other that we went to school, there are names which are never mentioned. But we know them, we know what they stand for. Those benches shuddered when I cried, or rather murmured (oratory teaches us that the fall of the voice into softness as condemnation hoves into view can produce an unforgetable effect), *Sejanus*. You are a learned lieutenant, you will know those old Hebrews never dared to say God's name, – Yahwey, they mumbled. The Duke, we have muttered, the Duke, the Duke ... Then it came like a soft fart, stinking the House out. Sejanus. There was no retrieving it. It is why I am here, for letting that old tomcat out of the bag.

Elius Sejanus was the son of a Roman knight, a good man from Tuscany, all this about the time of our Salvation. Sejanus possessed the gift to please. Realising this, he set out to please the first Caius Caesar, then Emperor Tiberius. He went on to please the common soldiery, the senate, the Praetorian Guard

133

and everyone he met. He then pleased all their wives – so they say. The currency exchange for pleasing is esteem and Sejanus became estimable. The lazy Emperor gave him carte blanche to take over the chores of divinity, and so we next find Sejanus doling out honours and public money, and then, when Tiberius discovered that he could not spare a moment from what gave him pleasure, we discover Sejanus calling himself King of Rome and his master the Prince of Capri. This was too much and so the pleaser was strangled. All men agree that his Grace of Buckingham is pleasing. He pleased me so much when I was sent to confront him with his failings that I was struck dumb. We were in the bedchamber at York House, the room which is filled with Mantuan glories. He pleasingly brushed aside the real purpose of our meeting and chatted about old times – actually mentioning 'little Felton – what's happened to him?' I felt pleased until I ran down the Water Gate, when I felt rage. How – why – have we come to this pass? How is this person the ruler of the Kingdom? Tell me, King John. Ask the Almighty, you Parliament!

No more. I shall burst.
I am your servant, John Eliot.

Mother's letters, many of them, came next, but have no place here. She could not have known that the bulk of what she sent for from Ovington was making a repeat journey. She wrote impersonally, either because her hard Durham breeding came out in correspondence – which it did not in speech – or because she believed displays of tenderness between us would be bad for me. Mrs Golding's occasional letters, very newsy, were far more emotional. They swept me up to that large bosom. Somewhere among Mother's letters was the disastrous enclosure from Timothy the eldest, the brother who had succeeded to the property after Father's passing. Did he think that by tucking it into her's that what he had to say – icy tidings – would gain a little warmth? But it was, now that I look back on it, its frigidity which showed its honesty. It was to the point.

My beloved Brother,

Greetings from home. I must warn you, brother, that from now it
will be all that we can send. You would not know our country, for
such is the dearth of its prosperity. The crops do not pay for the
gathering and the markets are empty of buyers. None can recall
a time like it. Respectable men, even clothiers' men, trudge to
towns to join armies. Vagrants and honest folk alike besiege our
gates daily for food. Those yeomen which angered Father with
their new dwelling-houses are, they say, now planning a
migration to the Americas, taking half their villagers with them.
Our mother, as you know, has become a goodwoman and will do
anything with her own hands. We are plagued with goodwomen
from Sudbury to Bury. My wife would be one of them, given a
chance, but I do not give her this. I keep here where she promised
to be, ever at my side. Yet the great dearth of what has to nourish
us, and its consequences, strews sickliness in every lane. So we
remain within the park. No crops, no profits, and no Means for
you. You cannot be astonished at this drying-up of funds where
you are concerned. They have reached you regularly into your
middle years. You will have your Pay and, with promotion, more
Pay. And you have no wife and no house. Forgive this plain-
speaking, John, but we are living in plain times. And forgive
what must be plain to you, that the new King must bleed us
gentlemen for the cost of his new war. It is our money or the
Marshalsea for us. May I suggest a broad view? That instead of
subsidising one officer I am paying in full the war-tax. Many
gentlemen in Suffolk are not.

I wonder that you do not supplicate the Lord Duke, your old
friend (as I boast to the neighbours). His being at Chelmsford, we
feel touched by his glory. Sir Oliver D – is to visit His Grace's
title-shop to purchase an Irish barony, and thus swell the war-
chest. You have no cash for such honours but a colonelcy for an
old stable-mate should not cost more than a grin and a
handshake. You will find the Duke at New Hall. He must know
that he has come close to Felton country. Do this, brother. It

makes sense. Pray to God to fill our hearts and bellies with all that is good for them. I pray to thank Him that you at least cannot starve.

I am your ever Brother Timothy Felton.

10

FOLLOWING FRANCIS

The Cadiz Journal of a Sea-soldier, written down during the Autumn of 1625 by one John Felton.

September 22nd

Swaying, plunging, one minute in a vast runny hole, the next on the crest of a wave, why was not I sick like everybody else? I waited in, as it were, all morning for my biliousness but it failed to arrive and I stayed so well that I could lean from the rail to study our keel cutting through the sea. Its waters sped away in twinned arches. We came out of shelter near Helvoetsluys to join the Dutch contribution. It looked enormous. I tried to count but the flotillas had a way of gliding through and around each other, and getting their outlines merged. Fifty ships? I'll leave it at that. Ours was the *Dayspring*, an old vessel which we had sent to the Hollanders on loan and which moved as though it could not get back into English waters fast enough. Hundreds of men packed the decks in a peculiar mingle-mangle of relief and misery. Retchings could not overcome the contentment that the enemy was Spain – not Bohemia. Why change an enemy? This was the general opinion. Princes must make war according to the rules governing their hereditary foes, and the Bohemians were hardly this. But Spain! Every English generation must have a go at Spain. And now mine was. Now and then I lurched through the troops to give heart and reply to questions. The decks were all dark and bright with their hair, which they had cropped from each other's scalps and cheeks with shears. In their grey-white shirts they were sheepish and at our mercy. I knew what they were imagining – a pile of pay on the Hoe as high as Mount Edgecumbe. 'The King owes it to us, sir!' Well, yes, and to me. 'You will be paid' I tell them with God-knows what authority. I tried not to catch their vulnerable eyes. They are scarecrows. Their breastbones gleam through their skin, their bare shanks are like smooth wands. 'Will we have armour, sir?' Armour! 'You will be given what is needed.' 'It is warm for August, sir.' 'It is September.' The speaker, a man too old for all this, turns to his group and announces, 'It is September.' An unsteady youth gets himself starboard, clapping me on the back – 'We're all in the same boat, sir!' and a riot of laughter.

In the middle of the night, fitted into the sleeping-box beside the Lieutenant, both of us lying there like a pair of knives in a case, I dreamed that I walked off the *Dayspring* into a Devonshire lane, and continued walking. On and on into sanity. Panton – the Lieutenant – then squirmed about to seek comfort on our left sides whilst deep below our horses would have done the same, except that we had made certain it would be impossible. They fidgeted and whinnied sorrowfully.

September 24th

We are coming into Plymouth. It is a white town, as white as white roses, that kind of white. From where we are, far out still, it looks like an alabaster model half veiled in gulls. Somewhere in all that whiteness is the King. When we land it will be the farthest west I have been – nearly into Eliot country. The sailors are busy aloft, taking-in sail, freeing flags. Last night I dreamed of Opheltes luring the wine-fuddled boy Bacchus to his ship, not realising that he was pressing a god, and what resulted from this outrage. I dreamed it in Mr Golding's translation of the *Metamorphoses*, except that it was our ship the *Dayspring* which sprung ivy oars, and our crew which sprang overboard in terror when the god's lynxes and panthers appeared for his defence. As for us soldiers, in my dream we were as nothing, a mere ballast for those occurrences we call history. I would like to unpack a book or two but I hesitate to disturb the baggage. Never have I been so ravenous, so famished for a read. When I saw a soldier, a neat man, making out what I took to be a squib, I borrowed it from him, just to see words in print. It was part of the Acts book from King James's Bible, much fingered and fumbled. I had a read and handed it back to him, rather like having a puff of a pipe. The religious light in his eyes looked for an equivalent in mine. But I turned away. The pages I read told of St Paul's voyage to Rome in a ship containing two hundred and seventy-six souls, and its running aground on Malta and the barbarians taking him for a god. These sea yarns curled in and out of each other in my head all day. In the late afternoon I went fore to watch Plymouth coming towards us. Our arrival, and that of all the Dutch ships, was slowed to the utmost by the presence in the huge harbour, the loveliest I had ever seen, of George's armada. Our sea-soldiers and landsmen alike crowded in silence as we anchored in its midst. Why sail to Cadiz? Invite Admiral Spinola to Plymouth simply to look at what Spain is up against. What Catholic could take this on?

September 25th

All ashore. White Plymouth is actually white with rage, but keeping it in because of his Majesty's visit. The fact is that the billeted troops have behaved like a plague of locusts, eating the port bare and infesting it like vermin. The mayor has complained to the Privy Council that these soldiers exist on promises and threats, and that no one in the town has been given a penny for their keep. Worse, not only is Plymouth stuffed to the attics with these devouring creatures, but half Devonshire, all waiting for the Lord Duke's enterprise. It is even said that Mr Evelyn, who has the monopoly, won't send any more gunpowder until the government pays for the last lot. As our contribution to the armada disembarks, the townspeople mass on the Hoe, horror-filled. More of them!. Thousands more of them! And all hungry and scant in rags. More of that stink of an army passing. Only not passing in Plymouth's case. Captain Hawkins from this town, slaving on the Guinea coast, encouraged his men to 'Serve God daily, love one another, preserve your victuals, beware of fire, and keep good company.' Mercifully it is summertime and we can sleep in meadows and on sands. Although our stores have for the most part become 'creeping food' a good boil or bake should

139

be able to get it into our bellies. I found a field and ordered my platoon to live in it until morning, none to leave on pain of a thrashing. Some lay down in the clover, some danced. There were hard curses. Where was the pay-pile? I left them to it. Strolling towards Mount Endgecumbe, I saw, let us call it, a house of industry and put a woman to work. She bathed me, relieved me and bathed me again in a clear runnel which splashed along a rift in the kitchen floor. I gave her the minimum for her services, not apologising. She brought out a pie and we both ate. Summing me up she said, 'Have they pressed you, sir? You are not a soldier.'

September 26th

I saw the King. Like most monarchs, he is a short man on a tall horse, and wears a tall hat. A priestly face and a remote gaze. A man who can only breathe the upper air. Charles, the King of half a year. Younger than me, younger than George. The crowds quieten as he rides by, never doffing, and accepting homage in the form of little outbreaks of clapping with just the apparition of a smile. No movement of the dark head. It is still very warm. The Sound glitters whether the sun is in or out. For these inhabitants their Hoe is a perpetual grandstand which demands their presence. Were they French or Italian, they would parade it, animate it. As watchful English, they stand in a great still block, just looking. Not a day passes now when I do not say to myself, 'walk away from all this – what is to stop you?' A viable alternative is such a luxury. 'Think straight', as Wemyss would insist. I do not think that this Spanish expedition is at all necessary – other than to display George as Lord High Admiral. So walk away. I feel so well. The industrious woman along the Mount Edgecumbe road – three visits now – tells me I look well. 'It is these arms, brave officer, I admire, so rounded, such nice skin!' And she kisses them in the bend. Saying my prayers in the parish church, I ran into the parson. Like myself, he is a bookman and has opened his shelves to me. 'You knew Arthur Golding ... ?' The parson's eyes filled with questions. How to get myself from the house of industry to the Rectory, to accommodating woods and meads, and other private destinations during what is now turning out to be a hiatus in George's naval plans, and to run into the troops, this requires artfulness. I – we the officers have been paid – but they have not. It is a secret. To be exact, I have been half-paid, so it is easier to pretend penury. I miss my Ovington means. Knowing how corn goes up and down, I have written to Timothy today, reminding him of this. No means at the moment – but it must not be for ever. When it comes to maintaining the seat, old families are ruthless. Although their heads would not dream of cutting away the relationship in a loving sense, they are quite pragmatic in encouraging younger brothers to sink or swim. Timothy's cutting off my means has left me bobbing about. Colonel Mathers has arrived – on a boat called the *Seamew* – and we have set up mess in a part-roofed chantry, every other building being crammed with men and equipment. He is thrilled by what is happening. Says we must trust the Duke, fight for the King, count ourselves lucky to be here. Thumps us on the shoulder. Bawls snatches of army-songs. Jigs.

27th September

Wemyss's birth-day. Autumn mist swathes Plymouth. Only the tip tops of things show. Masts, steeples, weather-vanes. I don't know why it reminds me of the Loire, but it does. Probably because of the way those palaces drew the gaze up. They say that his Majesty is fretting. Why haven't we set sail? Why are we eating up all the supplies before we so much as weigh anchor? Shoo, shoo, gallant birds of passage. Float off to Cadiz. There, have your King's blessing. Now go!

28th September

My first sighting of George. He looks older – must, of course. Ganymede has become Hercules. There was no seeing me in the crush. He jolted along the cobbles, a horse's nose-length behind his Majesty, the small King in black and white mourning for his father, the Duke in gold silk, and decorated rather than protected by garments of silver-inlay armour. The King so stiff and still, Duke George remaining grand to look at in spite of all his twists and turns. They rode to the Hoe to bless – and urge out – the Fleet. The crowd saw that something was wrong, that there was no flagship decked out for the Lord High Admiral, and that he had not been aboard any vessel since he arrived in Devon. Being closer to him on the Hoe, I could tell he was ill, just as he used to be at Anger, the picture of health one day, wan and pulled down the next. 'Leave me alone,' he would insist. 'It is how I get better.' The King was ministering to his right-hand man miraculously without moving, allowing his divine dealing to cross the narrow space between their nearly-touching bridles. If this tender show was apparent to the onlookers, it in no way softened their opinion of the Duke of Buckingham. So there continued what I had at first believed to be some mechanical use of an enormous kettle under steam, a sissing which fluctuated from being the kind of sound one thinks impossible to the all too inescapable sound which follows some men about and has to be lived with. There was a great commotion of church bells as they descended from the Hoe. Civically, all that could be done was done. But who can halt the travelling hiss? As it continued, I saw George half-raise a hand, as if to strike out at a pestering fly, then re-grasp his rein. He and the King were clattering up the High Street by now and at one point so close to me that I could have said, 'Your Grace' and would have been heard.

I said my Evensong in the church all by myself. It was St Michael's eve. I read, 'There was a great battle in heaven: Michael and his Angels fought him with the Dragon, and the Dragon fought and his Angels, and prevailed not, neither was their place found any more in heaven. And the great Dragon, that old serpent called the Devil and Sathnas was cast out, which deceived all the world ...' Went blackberrying.

Michaelmas

All is explained – by Colonel Mathers officially. The Lord High Admiral is not to be our captain. He is to hold the fort, so to speak, whilst we, the country's hope, repeat Drake's triumph at Cadiz. And what is even more amazing, a hero of Drake's time will lead us. Sir Edward Cecil. *Who?* Don't all ask at once. To be honest, I actually thought he was dead. I got the living facts from the parson, who is one of those clerics with an infallible memory for kinsmanship and precedence.

'Yes, dear Lieutenant, now let me see. Sir Edward Cecil. He is a naval person, the second Lord Burghley's third son. He is over sixty and ripely experienced in all military matters. As a youngish man he fought at Nieuport under Sir Francis Vere, a gentleman from your country, if I recall rightly. He – Sir Edward again – he raised the siege of Ostend and Queen Elizabeth dubbed him knight. What else? He was a politician for Aldeburgh, wherever that is, and he tried for the Duchy of Lancaster, I believe. The Duke tried to get him the command of our troops in Germany, but it was given to Sir Horace Vere. More you. You seem to come into this story from all directions. Anyway, the Duke has his way this time, and Sir Edward is to be your "Lord Marshall and General of the Sea and Land Forces", as well as Viscount Wimbledon, wherever that may be.'

I strolled round Plymouth gauging how this extraordinary news was being received. With bewilderment mostly. Had the Duke been hissed off the battlefield? – Do ships have battlefields? Battlebays. Old Cecil, not young George.

'Did I hear you say that you once knew his Grace?' asked the parson of Plymouth. 'Not well, sir, and not recently. His body? What can I tell you about that?' We returned to literature, in which the parson had secular preferences. Half way through the evening he rose suddenly, left the room and returned with a little slip of a book and told me to let him know what I thought of it. Almost asleep on my camp bed I remembered it. The title swam before my eyes in the feeble light – *Prodomus Vindictae* by a Doctor Eglisham. Or in plain English, *The Forerunner of Revenge*. I read it with a crib, avidly, though shocked by its gist. It asked among other things that the Duke of Buckingham should be tried for poisoning King James. What was there about me to cause the Parson of Plymouth to bring such a work to my attention? I returned it with affected casualness.

'No, keep it.'

Not a glimmer of why I should do so crossed his skinny face. Its author, he explained, was the old King's doctor – in fact had been brought up with him in Scotland. They had been boys together. Eglisham knew it all.

'I won't take it.'

'But you read it?'

'Just – with the help of a primer.'

'I know you read Latin better than that.'

I did, of course. The Parson was unsettling me and he knew it. He was making me furious. Who was he to find and touch a nerve? To push so far?

'I must go. Busy times ahead.'

'Then you know when the Fleet sails?'

'Not the day, but it has to be soon. Nights pull in and battles have to be fought before Advent – isn't that what they say?'

I hurried from his Rectory, leaving *The Forerunner of Revenge* but not its message. This had accommodated itself, rationally, reasonably, in my head. Not that George was guilty of the regicide it described; he destroyed kings another way.

October 2nd

One of those wordless instructions which sets the military into epidemic action blew across the camp just as we were finishing breakfast – oatmeal and water – and we all began scratching our belongings together, pulling down tents and getting excited. All aboard! In half an hour it was an embarrassed 'as you were', again with nothing said. Just an osmotic recognition of error. The soldiers fell back on to the grass they had soured, and the distinctive smell of the camp, which, like that of the humanity which had created it, had been thinned by our sudden movement, promptly re-thickened itself inside the hedges. The problem with soldiers is that they have to be kept in clover – well beanstalks – for years as the price of a battle which might only last one day. None of us knew how to keep them occupied. I marched my battalion up and down the lanes with the same result as exercising dogs. Enhanced appetites. Some of the officers put their men to road-work, ditching and similar labour, but I saw the wear and tear of their clothes and knowing the great hold-up of supplies, allowed my troops to loaf about for this reason. It had taken the Colonel months to get them a shirt, some breaches and a blanket a-piece. Every roll-call found some missing. They ran – walked – away to God knows where. Most stayed to follow me blindly. They were landsmen, and yet here I was, leading them to a ship. This multitude of ships to float an army of landsmen to Spain.

All this for a raid! For what can only be a raid. Certainly, replies our Duke. And he reminds us of Sir Francis's immortal raid of forty years ago and how in future it will be seen but as the rehearsal for *his* raid. *His* Cadiz – George's – would have as its prologue Drake's Cadiz. That famous singeing was about to burst into a conflagration which would show Europe who was boss.

I like chatting to my men, finding out where they come from. Today I asked at various groups where they thought they might be going. My fellow officers were amused by these solicitudes and would brush imaginary lice from my hair when I returned to the mess.

'And where are we off to?'

'The Catholics, sir.'

'And why?'

'To kill them for his Majesty, sir.'

'And why?'

A blank. Then I heard the word 'cause'. It was thankfully taken up. 'for our cause, sir.'

'And what cause is this?'

They looked to each other for an answer.

Eavesdropping one night, I discovered them to be disturbingly well-informed on some matters. Lewdness and hatred fought for the uppermost as each man put the Duke through his paces – as a buck. The loathing was lashed with a knowledge of matters which it amazed me to discover they possessed. Repeatedly through the licentiousness, the sensual charades of George in action, came the angry question, 'How was it that fucking Buckingham had been allowed to pollute two Kings? Why had not the great men of our land chopped him, like poison ivy, from their Sacredness?' They vied with each other what they would like to do to him. Once I hollered 'Treason' in the blackness and there was that immediate sucked-in silence as when king-rat touches a bare foot in the night.

October 3rd

A bright day but tinged with warnings. A day which says, 'watch out!' a day which says it is no longer summer and do not be

145

deceived. Enterprise must either be under way or put in mothballs. However, its just the day for a grand naval review and to watch a thousand ships going nowhere. For surely they would have sailed by now had they a destination? I and the entire population of West Devonshire take up our theatre-box positions on the Hoe for the umpteenth time. We are getting to know even the flimsiest of these craft by heart. There is absurd interest in the least movement, in the hitching of a rope, and in any fleshy figure on a poop deck. The autumn gulls scream around the rigging in white clouds and the sea's surface looks suddenly and dismayingly prinked with ice.

We show off our familiarity with the fleet by explaining to newcomers its order and procedure. There is no order or procedure; what we see below us is clearly unmanageable and outside any kind of naval strategy. The King has cried, 'Go!', the Duke has, as Lord High Admiral, ordered his unparelled armada to be on its way, and now poor old Sir Edward has to obey. But he puts off taking the plunge, like a swimmer in May. A poet could forgive the inactivity because of the beauty created by hundreds of ships at anchor. Surely that is the *Anne Royal*, Sir Edward's flagship, and that is Colonel the Earl of Essex's *Swiftsure*? Of course, of course. Their pennantry is gaily held out by a stiff wind. Banners flap and crack like muskets, silks billow luxuriously. Know-alls point to the *Peter Pomegranate III*, the *Christ*, the *Ferret*, the *Mighty George*, the *Hero of Shoreditch*, the *Pippin*, the *Jesus for All*, the *Runnagate Dick*, the *Landrail*, the *Corante*, the *Autolycus*, the *Newcastle Fiddler*, the *Good as Gold*, the *Southwold Corsair*, the *Virtuous Boy*, the *Queen of Hearts*, the *Just Woman*, the *Salvation*, the *Sue Dehnbigh* ... 'She's his sister.' Name-spotting is our order of the day. I feel aloof, passionless. They say that aged men become indifferent to events, and this is how I feel. Very soon, tomorrow maybe, what is enchanting in perspective will be a vile hold under sail in which man and vermin will share quarters and rations, and then what will I feel? That I must soldier on? What else? At the moment even the northern colliers look fit for Helen, and those spanking new ships which George rushed through the builders' yards, and which still aren't paid for, are those of dreams. Flotillas from every high port and muddy creek of the kingdom are here at Plymouth, all glorious without, all rotting within. How many know what I know – that we are not waiting for winds but for supplies? That what has gone aboard has the weavily strength to crawl ashore? The very ordnance, the *apparatus belli*, they say, is far from being up to scratch, and contains much old stuff from castle walls, church armories, etc. They say that when Sir Edward protested about this in London, some creature in the Lord High Admiral's office reminded him that he was going to Cadiz 'where all that was needed was to give a fright and light a match'. Sir Edward, they say, then carried his protest to the provisioning. It would be uneconomical to carry an army all that way and then find it too starved to take the city.

Sea-captains continue to ride around town begging for bread, meat, anything. They kneel to farmers and merchants, promising all kinds of things if they invest in the expeditionary force. Colossal sums from the captured Silver Fleet and booty without comprehension. All, all in vain. It was please take yourselves off. Please, in the Lord's Name, leave our wards and our shores. Leave us the leavings of your dreadful visit, for if you do not we shall have nothing. There would in future be, said the Plymouth citizens, a rider to their petitionary church prayers – 'And finally, O Lord God, in Thy mercy spare our city from being ruined by the Lord High Admiral Buckingham's adventures ...' 'Take care,' warned the sea-captains.

He was there on the Hoe this morning, pale as blossom. We each of us came inescapably into view and his mouth shaped my name – with a grin. I bowed deeply and when I rose up his head was turned away and fixed with enormous interest upon something or other, I couldn't make out what. Was I to approach? Metamorphosed George had decided no. It was reasonable. The soundless recognition had been friendly enough. His glorious clothes hugged his beautiful person. Like Saul, he was head and shoulders above the rest of us, and, like Jonathan, there was evidence in the glances of many males promenading the Hoe that love of him might well exceed their love of women. Kings apart, George's love-lust – 'luvst', he once wickedly described it when we were in France – was exclusively and obsessively for ladies. Some of these, catching on to the realization that the great Duke and Lord High Admiral, and the modest army officer were old friends, swivelled round to drop curtsies to me. All this in a few seconds. Some inferior must have dismissed my plea for promotion out of hand. Now that George had acknowledged our old friendship, I would write again.

I fell in with his entourage and only gradually saw that he was agitated. I was too far back to hear what he was saying but the gist was clear enough. We must *sail*. Once he looked down on his gorgeous naval achievement, the thousand ships on the October waters, with open disgust, as if he wished them on the ocean floor, somewhere where they did not advertise his dilemma. Scared, his captains excused themselves with talk of waiting for prevailing winds, when what they must wait for was food. But I could see the urgency. There are red and yellow trees among the hanging gardens of the Dart and Tamar, and Mount Edgecumbe is creamy with fog. The harbour too has that tell-tale slopping sound where the breakers push forward, and the Cornish distances are lurid. It is the time for laying-up, not for setting out. Yet set out we must.

He himself set out – for London – that afternoon in a golden coach with pretty painted shutters and feathers on the roof. The troops stuck fingers in their mouths and whistled as he passed. Worry spoke from every rattle and horse-beat. Last orders in his own hand were spread across the headquarters table for everyone to see. 'Go the hour supplies are stowed. A fast stowing – and then Away! For God's sake go to Cadiz!'

October 4th

We wait. I was presented, with a great many other officers, to the Lord Marshall and General of the Sea and Land Forces, Sir Edward Cecil. He is a little old man, well over sixty and looks seventy. He nods at each name but doesn't speak. Thick mists.

October 5th

More presentations, this time to Colonel Lord Essex and a Sir Henry Hungate, a Duke's man. Afterwards I sit on the wet grass and write to Wemyss. I must choose reading for the voyage. Some lines from the poet Aeschylus buzz around my head - where did I learn them? Something apposite to our situation, something about dark ships with black prows which struck, split, filled, and sailors and soldiers alike 'haled to that far shore!' and he did not mean Spain, but Salamis. Everything has been done before and will be done again. History is mainly repetition. Wemyss has extracted himself from the repetition, I have not. I am going round in the worn groove. George is following Xerxes' watery rout. Not that he would know that. I slipped off to the industrious woman and tired her out. Or so she said. One doesn't have to believe flattery, only hear it. Her great smooth crupper. Yes, the poet Aeschylus for the trip. If I am to go round with some old sea-battle, I may as well go round with Salamis. Two and a half thousand ships fought at Salamis and managed to strike, split and fill without an ounce of gunpowder. Those were the days. And all the Greeks and Persians waving with the seaweed, dead men and plants alike the playthings of the currents. Salamis was all prow-ramming and oar-splintering, a beaky business, a tipping over if you could. And then the splashing and churning and drowning.

> Full fathom five thy father lies;
> Of his bones are coral made:
> Those are pearls that were his eyes:
> Nothing of him that doth fade,
> But doth suffer a sea-change
> Into something rich and strange.

This is from a play by Mr Shakespeare out of a book by Mr Golding, his Ovid, of course. The play is called 'The Storm', if I recollect. 'Knowing I loved my books, he furnished me from mine own library with volumes that I prize above my dukedom.' This is in the play too. I have to collect my sword from the sharpener's, and my linen from the starchers. Idiot George to know nothing of Salamis. And little enough about Sir Francis Drake.

At nightfall I stood by the groyne to pray to the Lord Jesus Christ, my blessed Saviour. I knelt to Him on a dry rock.

149

October 6th

Is it nearly a month since George brought his Majesty to the Hoe to tell him 'Sir, you may see all that you gave me floating in your service?' Shall we never be gone? Some ships went out yesterday but met hazards and are turning back. Sir Edward says that in his opinion English soldiers are prone to epidemics because 'they are raw men and by nature more sickly, even in summer, than any nation in the world'. 'Pooh!' retorted George. His Majesty passed a white hand before his face.

October 10th

Immense confusion. I haven't been able to write and do so now only with difficulty. We got away at last the day before yesterday – I think. Time itself is awash. I have lost my battle reading – and my hat. And Colonel Mathers. Instead, a Colonel Sir Henry, the Duke's-man, and a bewildered Captain Lee. Plus a hold full of malcontents and a deck controlled by Barbary hands – or this is what they look like. Lee says you have to laugh! The Duke's-man high and mighty. O, Salamis, Salamis! The October waters are liquid sunsets turning our spew to jewelled skeins. The Duke's-man is rude to me and Lee says, 'Tell him who you are – Mr Felton of Ovington-Pentlow.' It reminds me of our antics in baby Orleans' palace. Who is Captain Lee? 'Nobody, sir, nobody ...' I have my doubts about this. How long can we keep the soldiers subdued before we unleash them on Cadiz? Who are they? 'I often ask myself that, sir,' one of them answers surprisingly. Gulls are taking rides on the rigging. This pen swells like the sea, gulping up the ink and throwing it out. What a page. Spillings. Splatter.

October 19th

It was impossible to write. We plunge on. Not nearly as many ships as I said – maybe two hundred. But a tremendous show all the same. I have enjoyed the multitudinous crackings and snappings of the rigging, and the pistol shot of the sails, and the singing, all blown about from deck to deck. Sir Edward and the other leaders are in spasmodic conference but putting a brave face on their ignorance of what to do and where, exactly, to go. The sea-captains try to hearten them by running up all the flags and putting on what they call a show. Show it is. All show. I am not alone in fearing this. Will I perish in the Bay of Cadiz? It is a strange thing about the military life that one never numbers oneself among the casualties. Cadiz is the head of a peninsular hanging a couple of miles out to sea. Shall we chop it off? Burn it off? But then what? All go home? Will that do for Duke George?

The weather is delectable and the air is nicely tainted with oranges and stirred by beach birds. An old hand sniffs and tells me, 'Oh no, sir; it is not Spain, it is Africa.' Some vessels sunk to the gunwales with whatever it is they are carrying slink between us, sailing the other way, looking like kicked cats. I am informed that these are our own traders to Spain who are getting their stocks out of the country before the carnage. The merchants themselves lie low and their cargoes are not explained. Are they pressed fruit? Tongues run lightly along lips. A skulking figure is sighted. A Jew?

'Christ-killer!' yells Captain Lee.

Something more important is happening. What military commanders most dread is happening. I have no logical words for it but the conviction that we are not being – cannot be – led is informing the entire expedition.

'Here,' says Captain Lee, 'have you heard this one?'

He draws me aside in his leary way and recites, again,

> When only one doth rule and guide the ship,
> Who neither card nor compass knew before,
> The master pilot and the rest asleep,
> The stately ship is split upon the shore.
> But they awakening, stand up, stare and cry,
> 'Who did this fault?' – 'Not I!' – 'Nor I!'
> So fares it with a great and wealthy state,
> Not governed by the master, but his mate.

October 20th

There is Spain, here are we. The new government-shirts and boots have been issued below deck, the weapons have been un-roped. It is hot for Luke's-tide. Many retch and the surgeons go up and down. My soul for a book. O, helmsman, helmsman! Rumours fly about like gnats. The fleet tilts this way and that, though pulling generally in a common direction. Yesterday the *Anne Royal*, Sir Edward's flagship, came in so close to us that we could watch him pacing about – could see his agedness and, what was worse, his unwillingness. Surely he should have drowned this by now?

I have taken to mumbling *Salamis*, raking-up all I can recall, pages of it. Cold comfort is comfort of a sort, and it solaces me to realise that the human race will never be any different. One sea-battle has to be much like another, and Salamis is as good a description of what has to come as any plan of Cecil's. The poet declares that never before between sunrise and sunset perished so vast a multitude of men. But poets always say this; their epics demand slaughter on an ungrudging scale.

A poor lad climbs from the hold, shivering in the Spaniards' heat. He topples towards me. 'I believe I am sick, sir. Am I sick, sir? How sick am I?' He shakes his way to the rail. There is shit on the government-shoes. We can see Cadiz plain. 'Look – Cadiz!' The sea-soldier does not look, cannot. Kitten-film will be sealing his eyes. I have seen it before. 'Look – Cadiz!' Helmsman, helmsman, back in your Chelmsford palace, where are you landing us? In what?

October 23rd

Still we wait. I do chaplain-duty below, but not well. I short-cut the prayers and am ashamed. It is because these sea-cooped creatures need other nourishment. Nine of them tipped overboard this morning, youngsters well-hung with cannon-balls to send them to the bottom. Captain Lee does orison-duty, omitting nothing. Two friends who, I have observed, are Greeker than the law allows, turn away from these splashes, terrified that death may separate them. We stagnate. Lee thinks we should turn back. Sir Henry Hungate, the Duke's-man, is short with me. I have only to be in his line of sight and it rankles with him. I am careful to ask him nothing. Last night I dreamed of Belchamp and the high road which runs to Cavendish. I could hear its songbirds, its incessant larks, its thrushes ... its nightingale. I must not be *drowned*, I must not slide from Lee's corpse-plank, I must survive the shattered helms of Salamis. I wrote to Mother and fastened the letter into my hat.

Some days later

Journal, I do not know how to tell you this but we have accomplished what was required of us, to make fools of ourselves and our country. For what else did we set forth? Nothing which made sense. We are tacking home, every ship for itself. A god's-eye view of us on the broad Atlantic would register a fair enterprise. All the white sails, the gilded figure-heads caught in the sun, the churning paths of our progress, even bursts of music. But we are floating infirmaries and those bales which we so lavishly cast from deck to wave, twisting as they fall, are young men with weights. See how they dive! What clean entrances to the grave! How these diseased bodies rush to their purification! How glad they are to abandon ship! Some won't go down; they bob on the water and are drawn into a tow. O Christ, dear rotting lads. But they saw Cadiz! That they did! as we say in Suffolk.

I have stayed healthy, although I do not know how or why. I have only been sick at the sight of others. I have been chaplain-surgeon-comforter, up to the elbows in pestilence, a closer of eyes, a presser of hands. So, to give him his due, has been Captain Lee. But Hungate does nothing but roar-on about us letting down his Grace, and what will he, Hungate, say when he comes face to face with that excellency, that Jove returned to earth? That for all the vigour of his Grace's enterprise, for all its being divinely wafted on by his Majesty himself, the greatest fleet ever sent to Cadiz had left that waiting prize *virgo intacta*. Untouched. Hungate storms along the decks weeping, too disappointed for words. We have to ask him about the burials – it is an army rule – and he snivels, 'Yes, yes, get on with it!' There is no longer sufficient sailcloth, so the corpses and shot have to be rolled up in anything which can be spared, and as economically as possible. There is human seepage as I read the service. 'Cut it short, Felton! What a pile of prayers. Is there a rubric which says that you can't do three at once? Push them off starboard – can't you see that you bury into the wind? Failure, failure, and with the Silver Fleet just *waiting* to be taken like the whorish thing it is.'

Eight funerals this day, if you can call them that. The last of an old man from Shropshire, too aged for anyone's army. He requested the Lord's Supper and I told him that I could not give it, nor now could anyone on this ship. The chaplain was himself reaching out for it in the desperation of his own condition. The old man begged a word from it – 'Just a word, sir.' It would do no harm to share this word, I thought, and began, 'Almightie God, father of our Lord Jesus Christ, maker of all thyngs, Judge of all men, we knowledge and bewayle our manyfolde synnes and wykedness, which we from tyme to tyme moste greuously have committed, by thoughts, woord and dede agaynst they deuine Majestie ... hauve mercye upon us ... forgeuve us all that is past, and graunt that we maye euer hereafter seuve thee, in newnesse of lyfe ...' The soldier's voice ceased here. His bowels broke and he died. We tied him, palliasse and all, in the cloak he so valued, thrust in a weight and slipped him still warm into the Spanish sea. 'Heare what comfortable woords our sauioure Christe sayeth, ...' I washed my hands in rainwater.

The first day of our flight was singularly lovely. The scent of grape-mast hung in our shrouds. I was reminded of Angers. I also reminded myself with equanimity that I was a thief, a pillager, and no better than any other man-at-arms. Needing a safe place for my pillage – safe from the elements, that is, for it was the kind of loot which no one on board was likely to cover I discovered a kind of carved nook below the main-stay collar and the headrails which was sheltered from spray, and into which I could crawl. Books are heavy things and I was relieved to put them down. They looked as though they were waiting for me on the table of Senor Pablo Salvador y González Pallarès, whoever he may be. My prayer as I crept under the main-stay was that one volume at least would not be in his language. There were six of them and all marked with his name. Hungate, Lee and the other officers, and the crew and the men, were all stowing away their prizes. On the whole, these were modest takings as no permission had been given to spoil the straggling peninsular with its surprised forts and handsome villas. Precious little permission had come down from on high to do anything, and once disembarked the troops and their captains milled around more in wonder than at a loss. So this is Cadiz! Huzzah! for Sir Francis and for that other, better Lord Essex, and for the Lady Queen! Spicy days! First-footing on Cadiz quay and in the town's plaza, we were back in better times and it was quite some while before we realised that the Spaniards too were spinning with *deja vu*. Where were they, anyway? A handful gasped from doorways, and petrified children could not throw the stones they had grabbed, or their mothers the curses from their hearts. It was not so much our presence in their city which froze these inhabitants as the quantity of our sail, which whited-out their ocean views. If this garrison had been capable of second thoughts, it would have returned immediately to cut all our throats, not as military invaders but as threats to the public health. Every other man among us shook with fever. Instead of which there was a general vanishing of Cadiz's defenders to debate, one presumes, what to do when history repeats itself. The Fort Puntal garrison which was situated further down the famous harbour met our snowy canvas with a frenzied waving of handkerchiefs through the crenelations, whilst furious gulls yelled their derision. Now, if warfare is to remain among men's high arts it must retain a deadly seriousness. There must be no jokes. It would be preferable for a mighty commander to lead his battalions to annihilation than into the ridiculous. Those who have to fight them will never forgive a captain whose battles raise a smile. The Duke's man soon saw what was happening and were silently begging the Almighty to take the humour out of it. Fifteen thousand men, ships, ordinance, what have you, all loose cannon in Spain's Plymouth, rolling around whether on water or on land, and far more dangerous to us than to the enemy. Anyway, what 'enemy'? Was it not only yesterday that George and Charles were courting the Infanta herself?

I must spare myself the politics.

We shall be voyaging home now, every ship for itself. The troops have been saved from slaughter in order to die from food poisoning. The ships' captains, being also shipowners, have only one thought in their heads – how to get their property to England in one piece. The fifty, or is it the hundred colonels cover their faces with their hands on the sterncastles. What will they tell their wives? Devout singing rises from the orlop decks where the worst of the sick lie, and I am reminded of our plague-house at Pentlow where, as boys, we crouched in an orchard to listen to dying peasants psalming their way to God. The chaplain has pulled himself together and he and I have been stumbling about in the skull-cracking interior of the *Peter Pomegranate II* whispering disconnected texts, dodging physical contact, holding our noses, making wild promises to burning eyes and seeing that bodies are baled and removed. We emerge to unnatural October heat and to lads calling to each other as they pursue their monkey duties on a sprit-top and mizen. I tell the chaplain that one can almost imagine the souls of the departed soaring past them in the rigging. He studies me queerly. But then he has never dined with Wemyss's holy sister.

'I do not understand you, Lieutenant. Not in any way. Excuse me.'

There being nothing else I can do, I retreat to the solace of my stolen books. Gratios, Don Pablo Salvador y González Pallarès. The space under the headrails is sweet with salt and tar. I can sniff new oak. Also print. A fine *Orlando Furioso*, but still in Italian, the poems of the Queen of Navarre, all in French, God be praised, the *Works* of a Luis de Góngora y Argote, an English grammar and – who could believe it – Mr Golding's *Metamorphoses*. How bliss travels! I read of Arethusa stripping herself naked and swimming violently in the clear river which had to be the Stour at Sudbury, crashing her arms on its surface so that the water flew against the overhanging poplars and willows. Arethusa, goddess of the fertile fields, trying to escape Acheous, but hopelessly. Soon they were a common stream, the kind which, as children, our pestilential cargo of ill soldiers would have cupped and swigged. It may not be an acceptable fact, but pestilence can be life-stimulating to the healthy and this reading from Ovid is marked in my mind as one of the last delights in and of myself. I unlaced and my hand turned into a woman's hand which explored and loved me. I felt my strong arms and narrow belly, and soon it was making me catch my breath in the pleasure it took in me. I know that one is supposed

156

to fall to guilty prayer after self-love but I lay back among Senor Pablo etc.'s books with trembling joy. 'Whatever is made by the hand of man, by the hand of man is overturned,' so used to say Mrs Golding when we dropped a dish.

The *Peter Pomegranate II* rolls among the corpses like a cur in dirt. Many have shed their anchorages and have bobbed back into the sun. I watch them through the rails. I bless them and commend them to the Saviour. I lash safe my stolen library. The weather is on the turn and becoming what it should be at the close of the year. The demon heat of Africa backs off before a sharp little wind. It is suddenly cold. We are going home and just as suddenly I am overcome by the reality of my position, now that the expedition has failed. This abortion of a military enterprise will have cost me my promotion. I have to remind myself that I am no lance-knight whore, selling his services for any old cause, but an English gentleman-at-arms fighting for his King. It is my profession to be so. I am also thirty-three years of age and *must* proceed to a captaincy – to the captaincy which would have by right awaited me had the Cadiz raid succeeded. Colonel Sir Henry Hungate shrugged and muttered something like, 'What could stop it?' when I had the nerve to mention my promotion. He himself was taking further honour for granted as the price for his hand in making a bonfire of Spain's navy and looting the Silver Fleet. Or so he claimed. It was about the only civil thing which that carcass said to me the entire voyage.

What will happen to me, to him, to all of us, now? Or indeed to George? This tremendous question dances on my lips. Mismanagement and ordure, the two things slime together to cover us all. Parliament and the people will reel away from what has happened. His Majesty himself will be reviled for his part in this messing about with history. The stars are appearing in the Spanish sky and a winking constellation west of the coast becomes Wemyss's face. There is the Scottish option. I ponder it. How luxurious to possess an option! Wemyss should cease grinning at the universe and preach his doctrine of futility. Most of the actions being taken by Europe's leaders, by its legitimate kings and its mignons-in-armour alike, are futile. Wemyss could direct his telescope until it focussed upon the laughter of God. Once our lords saw this they would think twice before taking to the field. But there was the difficulty, of course, of Wemyss knowing that there was no God in his heavens. Was God sending me to Rannoch to point Wemyss's lens in His direction? As I ask myself this, scribbling it down as the *Peter Pomegranate II* heaves, I feel very missionary. If our arrival was, to put it politely, individual, our departure is a blatant every ship for itself. By the look of his flagship, our Vice-admiral is issuing orders, but who cares! Hundreds of vessels are turning tail and fleeing in all directions. A Newcastle collier bumps alongside to announce that she has lost her charts and please which way to Scillies? The Vice-admiral, seeing that he has lost control, adapts his commands to fit what is actually going on, so as not to appear impotent. 'Set sail for home!' Home, home. We have done what we set out to do. Something of this nature ripples suggestively from quarter-deck to quarter-deck. A realisation that when we docked at Plymouth we must all tell the same tale. We would have put a match to this or that - but here at least, on this blank page, I shall have to say what I saw, if not what I did.

The long arm of Cadiz vanishes in the dark but the scenes of our damnation surface like oil-paintings on the waters. We plough through them all over again. I can hardly bear to look down. The keel cuts through them but they form up in our wake. They are not to be missed. Does Hungate see them, does Lee? Do the boys clinging to the giddy yards look down in discomfort on these sea-pictures of what happened to us on the peninsular? There is defeat and there is degradation but they are not synonymous. I have observed the special nobility of conquered men, what the Salamis poet described as having 'steered in the path of doom their unwise King's argosies'. We are not such men. Our foolish argosy ended in what none of us will in future want to talk about, in what is called a shameful act. The shame of English ruffians in Spain. Even as I write this by the timber-head's lantern, the Cadizers will feel that they cannot sleep until they have shifted the last of our shit from their doorways, picked up the pieces which we made of their altars, dried-out what we pissed on, and buried deeper the diseased creatures we left behind. They will kneel before their bloody Christs and beg an explanation. Burn their navy – that would have made military sense – but to arrive like carrion-flies gorged with sickness to get drunk, to shout in unison, to strut arse-bare before our women! Pigs, pigs! They will pray to their decked-out Virgins to spare them from anything catching which we may have left behind. 'Cadiz, sixteen-twenty-five,' they will be telling themselves, 'what a filthy day for the calendar!' It will be entered in the imperial registers of the Escorial, 'This day the land and sea forces of his sacred Majesty of England, commanded from afar by the Duke of Buckingham, invaded Cadiz in their search for an emetic.' O Salamis, Salamis!

Let me remember the Bay of Cadiz as God formed it, let me allow for its loveliness from when the watch yelled, 'Land ahead!' to when I was left to wander (what else could I do?) along a wild strip of country between the capital and Fort Puntal with no orders, no command, no notion of what to do other than to occasionally prod myself with the amazing truth that I was *walking in Spain*! Enemy-land. The county of Cadiz spreads past Cape Trafalgar until it squeezes the great seas to a mere crossing between Spain and Tangier so that the pungency of Islam blows straight into our Christian senses. Mediterranean herbs too had crept along the Atlantic seaboard and I strolled amidst biblical plants. I wondered that the peasants did not rush at me, and at other of our confused men, with pitchforks, or their wives with vituperation, seeing that we were heretics of long standing in their view of the world, and hereditary foes of their King. But there is a moment when the real is never more unreal, and it was so with both of us. The Cadizers stood stock-still; I passed by. Behind me I could hear Colonel Burroughs' men behaving as though they had won Agincourt, singing and dancing and crying, 'all for good King Charles!' and other mottos. All that had happened was that the garrison of Fort Puntal had walked out to welcome them. This fort is prettily placed on a knoll, which like the landmass by Gibraltar, narrows the water, so that the Bay of Cadiz is in fact a pair of bays, the inner of which now held the Spaniard's grand fleet. Their ships are taller than ours and have high gilded castles with Jesuses and saints and Manes all standing in fretted golden balconies, and enough flagging each for a Whitehall procession. All their gunports were open. They looked beautiful, cornered, indignant, like swans. With Puntal surrendered, I thought it could only be a day at the most before

159

we torched them and I felt a twinge of pity for what we soldiers have to do.

An unseemly sun, forgetting that it was not in Africa, parched the ring of land round the Bay. I could just make out with creased eyes the rivers which fed it – for many harbours are the labour of rivers, not of oceans – the Guadalete, the Saint Peter, the Trocadero, the Zurraque. They shimmered like pearl-thread.

It was then that it happened. Remember that our's were sick men and that the ill crave drink. Remember it was Luke the doctor who knew all about burning thirst – 'Send Lazarus that he may dip the tip of his finger in water and cool my tongue' – before you utterly condemn. I am telling myself this. Remember too that men do not go into battle with a whoop but with consideration. These men packed below should have been the job lot with which any commander has to contend, but they were not. Just how they were not I still cannot explain. I did my best as a gentleman to restrict them to being no more than the necessary assistance to our victory, as I had been taught, but none of us could keep them in their place. It must have been the sickliness. We imagined that the ocean air would blow it away but instead it blew it around. God cared for me and kept me immune. A few hours before disembarkation I called the low-deck together and lectured it on providence. I wore my helm and breastplate and carried my sword, and fired a few eyes. I called the men my friends. I was truthful, reminding them that although they had not been paid, they had been fed, and though not fully provisioned by way of uniforms, they were far from naked. And I told myself that although they were clearly not of Hector's choice comrades in arms, the trained-bandsmen had set their shoulders back and made them handy with grenades. A few youths struck heroic poses but, I was sorry to note, with undisguised irony. The greyheads – quite a few of these – looked already defeated. A weaver my own age begged to ask a question, '*some* questions, sir.' This did not surprise me, knowing what weavers are, with their loom-learning and argumentativeness, but I was astonished when the usually lip-sealed ploughmen also *demanded* to know what was happening. I told myself that Parmenter was taking his revenge – or putting into effect what I myself had taught him, a tongue beyond

160

servitude – so I gave them a short account of what had to be done for the King.

'The *King*, sir?'

Uproar.

There was the customary health-dancing on the main-deck on the morning of October twenty-three, the day on which we boarded the skiffs and rowed to the beaches so that George could suffer a sea-change and be the new Francis. Lee and I were cast ashore from a lively little craft, neither of us wet above the knee. Thousands of sea and land soldiers poured onto the sands, laughing and chattering, waving honourable weapons like pig-sticks at a fairground. Troops from a raft further down the beach had utterly unclothed for a swim. A trumpeter and drummer, between them, were trying-out a song. A colonel was wailing, 'It is not a picnic. Let me assure you, it is not a picnic!'

But it was.

Salt water and sun like a stove laid on an almighty thirst, and our commanders were forced to listen to the pleadings of what had become one great parched tongue. 'Give us drink your honours!' It was worse than Lazarus in hades. 'Just a sip, your excellencies. We swear by Jesus not to touch a drop more!'

It was against this whining prattle that I heard Drake speaking to Walsingham across half a hundred years, and knew that we must not only fail, but fail ignominiously. For although we had three times his ships, we had nothing else of his, not his God, not his nerve. Men were breaking ranks to run towards the wine vats as I listened to that confident letter:

> The wind commands me away. Our ship is under sail. God grant that we may so live in His fear as the enemy may have cause to say that God doth fight for Her Majesty as well abroad as at home ...

Our regiments were storming the diegos' cellars as the *Elizabeth Bonaventure*, Sir Francis's pretty flagship was, in my head, storming the inner harbour, igniting terrors which ran like racing lightning all the way to gouty King Philip, and dispiriting all Spain. Since Sir Francis was in all our heads – those belonging to the better sorts – I did notice some captains trying to stem the rush to the trough. But they were hugely outnumbered and unheard in the cheering. The vats were wine-ponds. Never had we seen so much wine, some old, some mostly new from the harvest of a few weeks previously and filling the atmosphere with its skull-hammering presence. The vats stood four to a room on stained wooden platforms. The rooms were cool and whitewashed, with paved floors which had purple cracks. An amiable air blew through, which was odd as there was none outside. At first the soldiers gathered in rings round each tun, lapping the dark surface like cats, drawing up the liquid in noisy gulps. But as the wine sank below the reach of their mouths, they reached in with helmets and hats – any receptical – and carried it out into an unseasonable sun. Soon there was one of those gross scenes which the Hollanders allow in their parlour-pictures in which everybody is either silly-drunk or passed-out in the highway. Meanwhile, the Cadizers watched in wonder, drawing close and genuinely amazed that men should either wish or be permitted to drink so. Our officers behaved as one does when cattle have broken into the rose-garden and can do no further damage. Scores of our men had sucked up so much wine that when it levelled them it spilled from their throats as if they were tipped-over jugs. Hundreds were dreadfully sick, as if their bowels would fly through their lips, others were too happy for words. A few had heightened wits and spoke shockingly equally to us, cursing the Duke for a man-whore and talking unmentionably to the Cadizer women before their husbands hurried them out of hearing. All this under a blue sky and by a blue sea. Some stayed upright and managed to roll from vat-house to vat-house like sack-connoisseurs, advising each other to 'try this'. By evening many, being diseased in the first place, either drank themselves to death or into health in a kill or cure fashion. In one vat-house the stopcocks were kicked out and red wine rushed through the doors until a little plaza was flooded.

None of the officers drank. We might have been less impotent if we had. I found myself idiotically preserving cast-off tunics and cast-away weapons putting them into neat heaps, as though I had to salvage something from the mess. A bombadier lurched up to me with his coat, spreading it on my arm as though I were his servant, before returning to his guzzle. When Sir Edward arrived to see the abuse of his humane decision that thirty warriors could have a cup of wine, he looked like a man who was almost relieved to find himself at the nadir of his misfortune, for surely nothing more ghastly could be in store for him? Wine-fumes and vomit turned his stomach and he broke through the watching enemy ranks, shooing them from his path, and incoherently raging against God, King, Duke, scum and all. Having no other choice, he returned to order us to let them sleep it off. An entire army to sleep it off. A day later we were chasing our men into the shallows, into boats, into holds. And there they rocked and spewed their way to Ireland, to St Mary's, to Devonshire, some landing with no idea at all that they had set foot in Spain.

Yet this much has to be acknowledged. That England sent its greatest ever naval might against its foe and it held a bacchanalia! No need to add more. Best not to. We gathered in our messes to word an agreed report for the Lord High Admiral, quite forgetting the Spanish ambassador. What a tale was to reach him! Don Pablo Salvador y Gonzàlez Pallarès must have been out watching our conquest of wine vats, leaving his door ajar, when I stole his books. Senor, your pardon. Oh, Don Pablo, you too will have to think of Salamis. Think of the world's high adventurers, your own armada, if you must, when it was *blood* which ran out of men's mouths, streaking across the golden decks, and when it was your saints which looked down on the ruby spillage, not in revulsion but in pity, and when it was your prince, intoxicated by Masses, collapsed before the Escorial altar at news of your defeat, less by Pirate Drake than by our English August weather. Put out of your noble mind the St Luke's little summer of 1625 when our Duke decided to mimic his betters. Tell me, did you read that Ovid? It looks suspiciously clean to me. Would it interest you to know that his translator's star pupil thieved it from your villa? Possibly you did not need to plunge into its pages as your unregenerate religion is filled with transformations. Ours allows but one, a single metamorphosis into innocent childhood. We have to be re-born. We are urged to prefer our child-shape to our man-shape, the former being more grown-up, spiritually speaking. Mr Golding has written extensively on this simple subject, should you wish to study it. I

163

trust that you can follow me, Don Pablo, a mere bookish lieutenant that I am, and no true scholar. Count your books on loan, to be returned when another Admiral Fool decides to chalk-up Cadiz. Or, who knows, I may come back to Spain alone and walk to your libraries, and call on you with a bow. And these volumes.

11

TO THE OBSERVATORY

A near-month has passed but now we scrape homeward with dragging feet. What awaits us? We have no pride. Our ceremonial is cut to the bone, our banners are pulled in, our canvas has a way of looking flaccid even when filled. We throw the dead over the rail without rites, holding our nose, some lacking sinkers, so that men become surface flotsam and gull-food. The surgeons warn of a catching distemper below. The stores are putrid and, irony of irony, there is little to drink.

A dispute rages between the sea-captain and our commander the Duke's-man. It boils down to this: the sea-captain must run to Kinsale in order to save his vessel and Sir Henry must make all haste to Plymouth if he is to save his reputation. The sea-captain must patch the *Peter Pomegranate II* with all speed, and Sir Henry must put what gloss he can on our disreputable venture. So there is roaring argument all day long.

I am gravely detached and relish it. I no longer mind where we land. I am recovering from the worst fate which can beset a soldier, which is to be marched to a battlefield and then, without striking a blow, to be marched from it. I and all those on this vain enterprise. Were we not shipped to famous Cadiz in full expectation of warfare? To perish in Spain for England? If we must. Or to return to our shires knowing that we *fought* the deigos, win or lose? Either way it spelled honour. Either way it would have been something. It would have been something even if the plague carried one overboard. Also, it is not healthy for a man to be brought within a yard of what the military profession allows, and then for him to put his sword or pike away. I listen to boastings from the black hold where the sick lie.

'I would have given those bastards steel – I would!'

Phlegm-thickened frustrations. The chattering teeth of young would-be warriors.

'Water, sir.'

Biscay Bay lunges at us, bringing down shrouds. Scores of birds ride our cross-masts. The look-out boy hangs fast. The sea-captain steers for Ireland.

'Is your course for Devon, sir?'

'It is, sir.'

'Liar!'

We travel on to home waters. All our brave flags have been long taken-in. There are days when, in spite of the naval immensity of our enterprise, we never sight another ship. It is uncanny. But now and then we bump into their dead, this afternoon a golden naked figure with outstretched arms which were not imploring but resting on the green surface. He looked well. Sickness ceases when we die. Our crew is sullen but I am not. Because of this farce of a venture, I regard myself as being honourably discharged from my military vows. Last night, peeping through the chinks of a cloak – the temperature fails – I saw a falling star, then, as it were *all* the stars. I was given a privileged look at what existed above me. Planets. One (it was half a dream) was called Rannoch and it sang. My conscience has begun to haggle, arguing Wemyss against the regiment. I must be mine own advocate. Item, I entered the King's service in good faith but I come back from Cadiz with no faith at all. Ditto most of us on the *Peter Pomegranate II*. I would have died for England at Fort Puntal, but the Spanish men waved white cloths and cried, 'Oh, for Jesu's sake, don't do anything so reckless! This old fort? It isn't worth it!' I offered my life to the conquest of Puerto de Santa Maria and to Cadiz itself, but the offer was brushed aside. Now I offer my resignation. I cannot go on offering my life. The fish-food corpses are persuading me to value it.

We are hauling ourselves towards Kinsale and I am packing for Scotland. My battle clothes and habiliments, this journal and the Don's books. As we enter, I see that Kinsale is Cadiz writ small, a port whose little arm thrusts from the mainland and whose long neck of harbour swallows all kinds of craft. We anchor close to a slovenly quay beside other disgraced ships from George's armada, and are met with dismay from the Irish.

'Are ye plaguy?'

'No-oooo ...'

'Are ye catching?'

'No,' we lie

Those who can have climbed on the deck, and there is a descant, 'Water ... water ...'

'Water, is that all ye want?'

I hand my letter to Sir Henry Hungate and descend. Which way to Rannoch from Cork? I am a rat leaving a stinking ship and it feels good. I must write at once to Wemyss.

* * *

His answer is waiting for me at Ovington – the only answer in my brother's house. Otherwise it is all questions. Why this, why that? And where to now? He did not hide his anxiety when I spoke of extended leave. So where to now? *Scotland?* This answer runs through our villagers like sparks among the stubble, as the saying goes. My brother considers it. To the best of his knowledge 'no Felton had ever gone to Scotland.' 'Then I will set a precedent,' I tell him. He is pacified – mollified – when I speak of my friend Sir Angus Wemyss, and none of your mint-new Villiers' creations either. My brother knows this – it is the kind of thing he would know. He softens towards me, is less embarrassed. Now it is, 'My brother *Captain* Felton (he raises me up) is between wars and will soon be on his way to join his comrade Sir Angus in Rannoch.' But he speeds me on my way with questions about roads and weather. The reality hits him. It is February and I can hardly be seen off until April at the earliest.

'You are welcome, dear brother, of course, but how deadly dull it will be for you after all your adventures!'

At this point Mother intervenes to welcome me to her dower at Cavendish. Mrs Golding had given it to her with a 'take it' and that wise grin of hers which so unsettled father. Mrs Golding, they say, is now a notorious goodwoman with a hand in everything. My brother is unnerved by her and shows it. She is on his mind and I hear him repeat things like, 'The trouble there, of course, lies in her keeping her own money. It is a disgrace to this kingdom, the way in which fortunes do not always pass from wife to husband at the porch door when the marriage is pronounced!' When Timothy talks like this, our mother, with not a penny left of her own, stares down, whether to conceal her amusement or her rage it is impossible to tell. However, in all fairness it has to be said that my brother sees to it that she receives funds enough to keep up her state in Cavendish.

'Come to Cavendish, my darling, and live with me until the roads dry-out.'

Much relieved at this solution, my brother orders a velvet suit for me so that he can show me off to our great relatives at Playford. And so I spin-out the waiting-time until the highways can take a horse by walking to Paul's Belchamp to read in Mr Golding's now cobwebby library, to stand by where I think his grave is – no tomb – and by writing more letters to Wemyss. No answers. This does not grieve me, knowing that our starry partnership is secure. I visit father's tomb at Pentlow, which is all that the St Edmundsbury tomb-maker said it could be. It is not marble like the envied tomb at Long Melford, but colourful alabaster. Father lies in full armour – which he never possessed – under a magnificent tester, and there is a good likeness. Plus room for mother. Timothy and I, rigged in old-fashioned ruffs, kneel either side a plaster pre-dieu and lack all likeness. Our ancestry pours down on us from a dozen shields, all very pretty. I bow to father as he looks up to God. Near him remains the plinth on which the Virgin stood. She came down leaving a little stone foot behind. It is unshod, pure, perfect. The rest of her made rubble for a path. I bow ever so slightly to her foot but when I attempt to call-back her face it becomes that of Madame Von Hol.

Less than a week before I am able to ride north comes a letter for Wemyss. '... thank the devil for Cadiz, I say, old friend. Thank him for being so disillusioning! Thank him for making such a mess of it. For had you been Drake's men and not Duke's men you would have gone burling on to more victories of the kind. Instead, you have come to your senses like the Prodigal and are on your way to becoming my bookman. O praise your God in his firmament! Felton is to be a Scotchman. Arrive as soon as you like, bookman.

I shall set a chair for you by the telescope in Kepler's church. You and I will follow the planets.

Advice from my wife the Urquhart, who welcomes you as a friend "you can talk your nonsense to" and who is queen of the local goodwomen (tell Sir Timothy). You are to bathe away every mite of Cadiz unwholesomeness from your person and bring none of it here. You won't be admitted if you are unhealthy. So make your sweet person – sweet.

My advice. Do not ride north without your man. It is not safe. Otherwise, bring neither "silver nor scrip" or thin woollens. Have you heard the latest about Duke George? - I'll tell you when you come. Hey, lolly! etc. what times we shall have together! Your Wemyss, polestarian and master of Urquhart.'

* * *

North and north and north until at last the black dank castle soars from its water-spot on wintry Rannoch Moor. My servant Forrester eyes it uncertainly. He is no Parmenter, no Lavenham-man either, but one of those straight-natured Suffolkers who are at ease with themselves. He is large without heaviness and has a gaze so strong that he can peer into neighbouring shires. So this is to be his home, he is telling himself. He surveys the castle thoughtfully, summing-up both its and his own position. Will he like it? Will it like him? To me it registers its original meaning, which is one of violence. What a violent land this is, even if, as it happens, I have seen no violence being done. This castle says, 'Watch out!' Whatever immediate impression it makes on Forrester, he keeps to himself. It has no grandeur but serves its purpose, which is to harry the resolve of anyone foolish enough to think of settling within half a hundred miles of it. Forrester hopes that it will be warmer inside than out, which is not always the case – *vide* Belchamp Walter church. He feels the chill badly, says that it eats into him – 'Always has, always will.' He notes that the castle flag sags low on the mast. So do I, but out of a strong desire to find that all is well I squint it to the top of its pole and hold it there. We trot towards the castle. Its standard is now plainly half-mast. So Lady Wemyss has lost her child. It is sad but usual for the first-born. I explain to Forrester who is truly sorrowful, having lost so many sons at birth.

'In and out of our world so fast, sir, that there is scarcely time for a shout.'

We ride to the lake's edge where there is a stone caunsey and a half-naked man wearing a checkered blanket. He leads me across the caunsey by the bridle but without having first made obeisance, which rankles a bit. But why isn't Wemyss on the doorstep? His servant takes our mounts and waves us towards the door like somebody who does not have our language, which he may not, and we enter the first room. It is like a cathedral galilee, a chamber in which the progress of the foot and the eye must be delayed so that they can adjust themselves to the marvels which lie ahead. An unseen piper wails. It is freezing and I can tell that my old enemy the outside cold which comes inside is creeping about to find an exit. I pity Forrester; I can at least demand good fires. He must take what warmth is offered – not much, unless he dosses in the kitchens. Enormous but still heatless fires spit on the hearths, having just been lit, and are dragging in the draughts. Black draperies balloon in the rafters, furled banners waver. Hangings bulge with wind. But being familiar with such initial stages of comfort at my uncle's house at Pentlow – though never at Ovington, a snug place – I feel certain of durable temperatures anon in Urquhart Castle, if not in its extremities, such as the tower which Wemyss commandeered for our telescope-room. But I will put a stop to hardship there. Forrester stares at the festooning mourning, listens to the tragic piper and takes note of the strickenness which engulfs the great hall. He sees excess.

'All this for a stillborn?'

It is what I am thinking.

'He (such grief would hardly have been accorded a girl) may have lived for a week.'

The far chimney now honks like a water-spout as the flames lick up it. Where is Wemyss? I am now groping around for words which will go with these elaborate signs of lamentation for the death of an infant. Tomorrow, in the star chamber, I will have to cheer him up. He must begin all over again. Begetting must be his immediate business. But where is he? I catch Forrester's eye and nod towards the funeral curtains, meaning, 'Try to look a

170

little more upset'. He takes the hint and hangs his head like a hound. I think I hear Wemyss but the steps die away in one of the many labyrinthine passages which link each main chamber. The piper comes closer and a door under the gallery opens ceremonially for what amounts to a procession. First him, the skirler, then a pair of waiting-women, black as stoves and heads more hang-dog than Forrester's, then, after a dramatic pause, Lady Wemyss herself, a rangy dark tree of a woman whose weeds slip and slide as she makes her awkward way to me. She is breeding and is at the stage when she must lean back to balance her belly. She stretches her arms emptily towards me and is saying my name, but I cannot hear her. But I see that she is done with crying. I kneel and kiss her hands. Now I am holding the backs of them to my eyes to block my weeping. Now she draws them in to hold me nervously by the shoulders. Her women and Forrester turn obliquely from us at this, like attendants by a catafalque, and her piper and his coronach encircles us. Her explanations come tumbling down to me like rocks, knocking me silly.

'Last Saturday (is that what she is saying?) Last Saturday.' And then something like, 'chilled to the bone, and not for the first time either! Did I know that it was true what they are saying about him? That he was tampering with God's heaven? Well, you can guess what they are saying now! Puer mon, and his child fatherless! My puer laird!' She would have sent a servant to break the news to me along the road, but which road? Those to Rannoch were multiple and devious and who knew which way we would come?

When after what seemed like hours I drag myself to my feet I am so robbed of Wemyss that I can neither think of her or their child, only the disaster which confronts me. Me – myself – John Felton alone once more. I am insulted to find Lady Wemyss speaking to me in the tones used to some kind of professional, a disappointed office-man or other. Then I realised that Wemyss would, of course, have explained me away to her, and to the neighbourhood, as a secretary or the like to still the suspicions. But it rankled. As though sensing she may have gone too far in this, she added to the nightmare by explaining that she had managed to reach Madame von Hol with the terrible news of her

171

brother's passing, and that she would soon be in Scotland.

'Pray God I will have given birth before she arrives!'

She grins gauntly. Her women turn her towards the door and propel her gently out of sight. Their inky scarves float in the trapped gale. Forrester leads me to a window-seat.

'Your Sir Angus – dead?'

Wemyss having been all the life of our long journey from Suffolk to Rannoch, I can only share in his incredulity. Then the piper returns to wail out, 'Dinner, your honour!' But I am unable to stand, and nobody comes to ask why I do not go in.

*　*　*

Moorland turf smolders hotly in my bedchamber. Seeing my servant's envy, I tell him that he can sleep on the sheepskins piled by the grate. Everything indicates that this is the room chosen for me by Wemyss himself. There is a press for my books, a table to write on, a fat feather-bed, a painting of a naked woman in a park pretending to be Diana, a butt crammed with sweet-smelling heathers and much else for my pleasure. By the hearth a torpid mastiff with running-gold eyes, a dark mask and a beating tail welcomes our invasion. I wait until both man and dog are sound asleep and then do my weeping. So it was my friend, and not his wife or her steward, who set his hand to this hospitality. Full of tears, I ransack my memory for something from *The Golden Epistles* to comfort me. Something like this:

> I do not say that it is evil to have friends, but that it is dangerous and painful. To require of me to be your friend is to bind you to love me all my life, dividing my heart with yours, and making you another moiety with myself, the friendship being none other than an unfeigned will and affection. One friend ought not to say of another, I will not or I cannot, because it is the principle of all friendship to find nothing impossible.

I think I hear wolves. I must enter the bed and draw-up the coverlet. The fire is blazing merrily when I wake and I sit by it to add a dream to what was written last night. Forrester and the hound have gone. Pale spring-light has entered via the little

172

window-glass to announce 'day' – no more. This dream. The woman in the painting comes to me step after step from her park. She is neither Diana nor Eve but Beatrix von Hol uncaged from her clothes. She tells me that I was mistaken when I took her look to be entirely evangelical during my visits to her holy house at Arnhem. She says that her husband must soon be in one of her Lord's many mansions and that we – she and I – being of an age, must, because of the principle of friendship, find nothing impossible. But when we embrace, it is within the frame, so to speak, and her body, though bare, remains art, and no longer feels like the flesh with which I was so familiar in my imagination.

Forrester has returned with the bounding dog, on his arm my brushed cloak, in his hands a tray of breakfast, in his mouth the news that Lady Wemyss has given birth to her son. We remain in the castle a week, this being the shortest time one can be a guest, then we ride away. Lady Wemyss lies in the family great-bed looking torn between the requirements of widowhood and the triumph of maternity. She holds out strong hands to be kissed. The teat-nurse holds out Wemyss's boy and I touch his fingers. The bagpipes have been silenced. Without having asked permission – I was frightened that it might be refused – I find my way to the star-chamber where we would have worked together at extending the bounds of creation. I swivel his telescope about in probing arcs, and the stars cascade into my eyes. At last - it is night - I fix the lens on those three moons of Jupiter which Signor Galileo Galilei dubbed the Medicean Stars and I know that Wemyss is well. But this room *is* cold. I recall how he would laugh-off damps and chills and empty grates and draughts, and how I accepted this unconcern as being something which every Scotch gentleman had to have, their being in their country nothing to be done about it. His tower window rattles on a wire, inviting the Rannoch agues in, or was fixed in such a way to let his Polestarian self soar forth – who could tell? I write my name in the dust, 'Felton was here'. I find all my letters to him and retrieve them; I believe such things remain the property of the sender so it is no theft. I close the door on a partnership. Forrestor, who has stood outside, hugs his arms and remarks that you would catch your death in such a place, and hopes that this late lord knew Christ's salvation. I must close here and be on the road.

* * *

It is not easy for me, bent over these piecemeal confessions in the Tower of London, and this two or more years later, to describe what happened next. Anyone seeing me ride out of Scotland and take the highway south would not have witnessed a horseman all in chains, and with every impediment in his way. Forrester and I covered the ground in a fair lick. But even so, my servant was constantly ahead and keen to get back to what only a few weeks ago he hoped he had turned his back on for ever. He sang and whistled the praises of Suffolk without stop, but took care not to vilify Scotland because its inhabitants now terrified him. Savages with proud wooden necks – never a bow – strode from their hovels to watch us pass. When we travelled through the granite canyons they call their cities and around their mucky farmtouns, nobody spoke. When we crossed the Border it was a crossing of the Rubicon. I remember how we contrived to take in the bare white legs of the women, like mayflower in the dusk, without turning our heads. The Scotch race live in tribes under chiefs. Kings to them are an after-thought and bishops no thought at all. Yet I could see the makings of both Wemyss and his sister in this northern society. Somewhere on his side of the Cheviots I took formal leave of him. I galloped off to a small circle of rowans picked out by the May moon, and there I laid sky-facing on the grass so that the stars could read me. I turned my head to many unidentifiable planets and asked to hear their eliptical songs. I said prayers to God the Star-maker and composer of universal music, and I thanked Him from my heart for Wemyss, commending my friend's soul to him.

Now I come to the hard part. If my words become too baffling, then you should recollect those of the prophet Amos who was told to keep his mouth shut and reminded 'for it is the king's chapel and it is the king's court'. But was it then as I rode from Scotland? And was it until I struck with my healthy hand? And how am I to describe what every man knew but dare not or could not put into

174

sentences? Amos said he had no particular right to speak, to act; that he was just a young herdsman and fruit-farmer, but somebody had to say, to do something! I did what I did on the spur of the moment. Such a moment never occurred to me once during my long trot through his Majesty's realm, but I worried that business about it being 'the King's chapel and the King's court' round and round in my head. Was it certain? It was not. The loveliest cuckoo ever hatched sat plump in the sacred nest. The hungriest too, swallowing hours and houses and offices and jewels and pictures and gardens and the best of everything within the gift of a consecrated monarch. This cuckoo reigned, but without divinity. He did what only a king could do, and not without some competence. Fair is fair. He lived as only a king should live and thought as only a king should think. And he the bed-boy. There were plenty of precedents for a union running the show, but none for them sharing the sacredness of him who is God's anointed. This was the reason why, as I journeyed through the lakes and mountains down into Yorkshire, and after three weeks on the road to London, that I choked on a stench new to Englishmen, that smell released by the usurpation of the Divine Right by a commoner. Everywhere I went I heard the same question. Having already taken so much from these great Kings, what was to prevent the Duke taking a little of this, should it be offered him? There was no record of either King denying him anything. George Villiers was the Lord's high recipient, the man who was to be given all things. The sacred receiver. I am the man who has been given one thing – a taste for reading. 'Isn't that enough?' asks the Lord.

Such acute anxiety as I rode through the kingdom. The question was everywhere. I fancied I saw it in the wondering glances of dumb creatures and it was certainly on the tip of everyone's tongue. Might not his Majesty, one happy day among his paintings, say to his friend,

'Look at all this kingship which Almighty God shares with me. See the endless flow of it. Allow me, sweet taker, to divert a little of it in your direction!'

To make matters worse, this horrible and blasphemous question happened to coincide with overflowings of another sort, those sewers of poverty and pestilence, of starvation and of national wretchedness. How we picked our way through these

175

miseries as we came south. And how the question of the Duke's royalty leered unanswered in the trees, from the belfries, in the markets, on every rough face. It gave weavers and ploughmen knowing looks and it was no secret to the gentry. As I travelled, I knew that where the Duke's business was concerned, it was all out – starkly out in the open. The lowest sort, thinking of King James, thought it was all Sodom stuff. Alas, had it only been that! Yet the bonding of King Charles and his father's lover defied easy exploration and was too enchanted to be interpreted. It was said that George had bewitched Charles during their gallop to Madrid to bring home the Infanta. It was also said, Mr Golding's *Metamorphosis* still as familiar to many folks as the tales in the *New Testament*, that the King, being the fount of change, could change the Duke into anything he fancied – the Duke's fancy, that is. He must fancy a crown if it is all that is left. It stood to reason.

At York Forrester amazed me by demanding to know where we were heading, was it to London, the ports or to Pentlow?

'To London', I replied shortly.

'Then', said he, 'it will be "fare thee well" when we come near our homes.'

'You were willing to stay at Rannoch'.

'Not for good, sir.'

'You were unwilling to work on our estates.'

'I will not be working on my lord's land.'

'Where then?'

'On my own. I have been gathering parcels of it here and there since I was thirteen and, with the willow wood I closed in at Borley just before we set out, I reckon I might make the "fifty acres of freedom". Mind you, sir, my brothers helped me. We have to put the house up. Its framing is all but done and we have made our own bricks for the sills and chimney. It will be *warm* – I promise you that! We shall live by Holy Writ, and the devil's arse to kings and parliaments.'

I then told him about Parmenter.

'We aren't Parmenters, sir.'

He seemed offended.

Not being Parmenter, he was indifferent to what was to become of me. Yet why should he care? Who was left to care? Army-men cared for one another because they knew what it was

176

like to be out of care.

'I wish you luck, Forrester.'

'I wish you the Saviour, honoured sir.'

This level exchange occurred on the Great North Road. Forrester's addition to life was to make those he was with feel lonely. It was a power of sorts.

So that is how it went, the retreat from the galaxies, clump, clump.

* * *

Colonel Mathers had set up his standard at Elstow, a village touching on Bedford. The situation was not unlike that at Arnhem, the dull city, the broad river, the muddy plain. Except that the pearly ranges of the distance were not clouds but the Chilterns. He welcomed me with pleasure but not surprise. And without reproaches. Old mess-mates had been drifting back all the month. His headquarters were his own mansion, a shambling affair with gates and doors everywhere. I was presented to his wife, I remember, before she made herself scarce. Later, as summer came, I bathed in the Ouse. I read the time away, propped against the pollards on its bank. Constant posses of mounted gentlemen clopped across Bedford bridge, and the town itself had no other business but the Bible. It was drunk with scripture. Peasants and burghers alike cast it at each other in the orchards and yards, and God was mayor. I would remind you that this shire is best part loving-land for most of the year and that the walker steps the miles with a pound or two of it on each shoe, and there is no shaking if off. But in summer even the pug-pits and sloughs dry out under robes of flowers, vetches and tiny potentillas, enchanters' nightshade, buttercups, tansy and clary. Foxgloves, the fairies' plant, were everywhere. I saw women digging up elecampane root for hair-dye whilst capping each other's quotations from Revelations. And I saw a little shepherd hiding in fireweed to rehearse his portion for the Sabbath meeting – although he may have been making himself scarce because our pressmen were rounding-up people like himself for the regiment. I kept my lieutenancy low when I had to enter the town as it was wounding to have folk pull away from me and eye

177

me without turning their heads. At Elstow, almost within hearing of these cautious citizens, lengthy straggles of pressed labourers and jobless weavers were being drummed along by hour. Colonel Mathers, myself and the other officers took turns to record their names and skills, and then to give them over to the sergeants for drilling. It left me with plenty of time to myself. As Bedford was stuffed with dissenting books, I read those. They were often outrageous. It soon struck me that unless all literature was properly licenced there would be nothing which would not be printed and bound, and thus endure. It was all right for me to read anything because I had 'read everything', as they say, and could make a judgement. But what of a lettered goodwoman inflamed by these tracts? Would she not be wrongly swayed? Seduced via type?

By a common process of reasoning, such thoughts led me to a never-ending harping on Beatrix von Hol as to whether she had forgotten me, or was in the process of forgetting me, or was having to make herself forget me. I actually found a small aperture below Bedford bridge where I could crouch unseen to contemplate her – us. She came to me there in the vast Dutch apparel and with the old invitation of 'there is room for us both'. I would love her under her brocades whilst homing dissenters clopped and argued their way back to the villages amidst scraps of Colossians or Ephesians, and gradually it came to me, as their saving texts came to them, that I must write to her. I must stop the forgetting. And so I wrote her two letters, one from a gentleman who used to come to dinner and one which – well, I will come to that. She would be at Urquhart Castle still. The flowering boy would by now be beginning to obscure the dead brother. She and Lady Wemyss might hazard a little cheerfulness on their heathery walks. She would show my letter to her sister-in-law and hear about my visit. There were no reasons why Lady Wemyss should not be complimentary. She would certainly in her outright Scottish way tell Beatrix – I have to call her this to get her away from that Methuselah of a husband of hers – of Wemyss's opinion of me, which was both high and original. Beatrix would listen and, with what she was now hearing and with what she already knew, I would come to new life in her memory. I wrote to Scotland:

At the Headquarters of Colonel Mather's Horse,
near the City of Bedford, in the month
of August, the 17th Day, to the honourable
Lady Madame von Hol at Castle Urquhart. In
the Year of our Redemption 1626.

Madame,

I am bold to write to you because of your Brother's love to me. I
last saw him – and you – in the Holland house, that exquisite
abode where the Lord Christ found another Bethany. Except, as
you know your dear Brother and I met continually by our long
correspondence, and in those mutual plans which would, had not
the Grave intervened, have brought us together in a learned
fellowship for the rest of our days. Since the world is a chattering
place, and you may have heard to your anxiety that my Friend
your Brother was no true companion of Our Lord Christ, allow
me to assure you that such speculation is vile and that no man
lived who had a greater regard to the goodness of Jesus. As for
myself, dearest Madame, my existence would be immeasurably
the poorer, and my Faith itself fractured, if I had to believe that
we, you and I, Madame, could not see each other again, and until
that time, write as young people may about a Brother and a
Friend who was to vanish into Paradise leaving only them. Pray
tell the Lady Wemyss that her hospitality still leaves its sweetness
at my heart, and that I wish her well. I have the honour to remain
your friend in the Lord Jesus and your brother's sad relic,

John Felton.

I wrote for myself:

From the House of the honourable
Mistress Felton at Clare in Suffolk
(this being where we shall dwell).
On a Summer's Day in 1626.

My perfect Beatrix,

Beata immaculati! Peerless girl, my Queen-apple, I lift you out of
those watchets and lawns, I free your flesh and its musks. As the
linens fall, I have your mouth, your closed eyes, your hardening

179

breasts. Knowing only slow-coach desire, you stiffen at the swift pleasure of my fingers at your delta. Knew you this before? And *this*? We are young and so we go straight to the point. I retract and you breathe again as the roving embassy of my hands takes to the soft hills. How pretty you are – such a pretty woman with that golden brush on your belly and those peeled-willow knees, and that sparkle in your armpits. I must eat you. Your warmth is the warmth of the disturbed nest. I heat you up more by the furnace which you have lit in me. What a pity it is that I am not a poet. With your themes a few alexandrines would have sifted out my dirt. Holy, cunty girl, my own Beatrixissima, mine and none other's. Do I love you because of my lusts? I do, yet for other reasons. You know these – I do not have to spell them on this paper. I know you know them because of how you looked at me, not once but every time. 'Ah, Mr Felton', you would say in that bell-voice as I crept into your saloon at Arnhem. Do not think I did not notice. 'Ah, Mr Felton', and the look to match.

My Queen-apple, consider your young Lieutenant. Consider him as we are bidden to consider field-lilies, and for a similar reason, that, being crafted by God, he cannot be without glory. Compare him with that Anabaptist who shares your bed when he should be sharing a churchyard. Lie me beside that old man with his satin shanks, his collapsed rump, his time-warts and dribbles, and make an honest pick. I am quick to concur; of course, like us, Doctor von Hol was made in the image of God, but too long ago to stand much reflection. I tried not to notice his gait, the general flutter of his person, and I admit an evensong beauty. But I saw too - we all did in that holy room – his mortality at the fore. And so what I am advising you now is to do what he dare not do, look ahead. I am in an absolute fright and terror of losing you, which is why I am so indecent. Don't forget that your brother's wife was widowed in less time than it took to get their child. You must be hurried to me in the short time; you must know where you are going before you present duty allows you to set off.

Come to me, my Beatrix. You do not deceive me. I have sense enough to have seen that you are not all texts. Let me be lewd. Come and see what must be a novelty for you, a young man out of his shirt. Come to cuddle against a firm skin, a springing wand. That ancient your near-late husband would have to be told in as many words that you were touching him. And, *foutre*, his breath! Fenny air. You know, young men's breath, provided they are not drunken or been at tobacco pipe, smells of buckthorn. I am telling myself that you will inhale me, and I your musks. I am telling myself that the moment will come when I shall lay you down, open you, close you with myself. *Beata immaculati* – my pure happiness, my white girl from Scotland, this is the way men dream – all of them. They lay women in their heads. My dream has to come to pass. Make it come to pass, Beaty. Let me stir a dream in you. Imagine that we have tumbled like naughty angels out of Heaven – but into heaven! Imagine your shouts (do you shout?) when I become rutting Jove. Imagine, afterwards in that matchless quiet after spending, your pink fingers trotting like mice along the furrow in my back. Think of our content.

But to be to the point. Madame, you cannot be wife only to that old good man. It cannot be. Admit that you still *want*. There is an old author of whom you would not have heard because his English is now unreadable who had a tale about a Sir January marrying a Miss May and how, after his senile attentions one dawn, she sat up to see that his slack neck was still ashake. I tell you this in order to rouse enough disgust in you to bring you to your senses and to make you want. It worries me that you may not want what all young wives *want*. Want me.

To be practical and remindful. I am of good birth and intelligence. Also kind and your own age. I will love you for ever. O my Christ-girl, forsake all other and come to me when you can. Make no bones about it. I am waiting for you and will make a life to suit you, holy house and all. My courtship passionings apart, I am convinced of the necessity of you. When Doctor von Hol – ignore my cruelties, they were born of fear – when he goes to God, then, White One, come to me your lover John Felton.

I should have sent it. There is balance. *Il faut savoir garder le juste milieu.* I suppose she is teaching some other man how to do this. Pray for your Lieutenant, St Beatrix of Armina. How could you know without a letter? How could you want what you were not shown? But a curious and, as it turned out, a correct intuition told me that this was not the moment. For within a month, or return of post, came a reply from Urquhart Castle. It was brief, Lady Wemyss being the sort who do not mince words. No pre-ambles and post-ambles. But a nice start:

From my Castle of Urquhart at Rannoch
To Mr Lieutenant Felton. Michaelmas
Sixteen-hundred-and-twenty-six. Greetings.

Sir, I am bidden by my sister Mistress Hol to answer for her thus. That she was delivered yestereen of a female bairn of good parts but lies in childbed still, though well enough, God be praised. My sister says to tell Mr Felton that her cup runneth over (Psalm 23) as does that of Mr Hol. Pray be glad for them both. My sister arrived here like the Lord's own mother carrying her salvation, which I hope is not a wicked comparison. But this second child, she says, will re-awaken all Mr Hol's first delight in her. He is to follow her to Scotland. What a blessed family we shall be.

Item. It was disagreeable for us not to engage when you had travelled so far. But you saw how it was.

Item. My bairn thrives.

Item. The turret-room has been emptied and cleansed at my instruction, and the books and papers bonfired. I could have delivered them to you, but what would I have said on Judgement Day? False prophets, Mr Felton, false prophets.

Item. The tellyscopp is taen down and put away. 'For now we see through a glass, darkly, but then!' (Paul to the Corinthians). We shall look into Heaven soon enough, Mr Felton, without poking about with tellyscopps.

Item. I shall widdow away and wear my doole-weeds for a twelve-month, no more. This is to give notice of my intentions.

Item. Your friend my husband did not die of our damps but of a distemper given him in a Southwark blackhouse. This confessed in merriment to his physician whilst staring at stars. I tell you for a Lesson.

Item. Who is Dr Kepler?

No signature.

12

THE FAVOURITE'S TAKING WAYS

And now, my page, my bellman, what follows is what we scribblers call a linking passage or essential reading. But you will know all about chains of thought and breaks in narrative. How late it is – half-past October. Leaves begin to drift on my unreachable sill and the afternoons are turning yellow. I fancy I hear boats plying on the Thames. I steel myself for the plash of silver oars and thoughts of dripping blades. I do not have to tell you that spinning-out my tale I add to my days. You are a good handler of writers – do you realise this? So encouraging! You burst in every morning with a 'Take your time, sir'. My time? I have no time. What time is mine, young Wren, tell me that? If you are straight with me you will reply, 'None to speak of.' And this time twelve-month will you not be urging my successor in this room, 'Look, sir, lots of lovely paper and ink, and lots of time. Put it all down, what you did, who you are, your motives, your innermost feelings, that sort of thing. Pour your heart out – and don't give me any of that remorse stuff. Begin – now!' And see that he puts in a nice linking passage where necessary. This advice should not be hard to remember for someone whose parish is St Peter-in-Chains. Do you know what I would like at this moment? A walk to Teddington, keeping to the bank. I would like to stare at the red sycamore hands with their five lobes as they sail down to waiting skiffs. I would like to watch the autumn gale-wood riding the currents and sit in the church porch and listen to barley-birds, or to a good old man at his evensong. That is what I would like. You are new to your gaol business, my insistent Wren, and it will take you some time to realise that with we felons there comes a moment when much of what has been and what is to come is irrelevant to what is actually happening at a particular moment in between. Like walking to Teddington to hear the barley-bird plus a nunc dimittis.

Where are we? Oh, yes, George Villiers stops being fun and starts being monstrous. But first this caveat. It was not entirely his fault. I put it on record. Are we not to allow for a degree of helplessness in all our lives – yours, the Duke's, mine? If, like me, you can count on a few fingers those who have shown affection, there will always be a handful of men who, whatever their faults, will continue to hold one's gratitude. How your interest rises when I come to passages like those. How you just ask to be teased. How you long to know anything whatever about George Villiers of the Horse School which pointed to his fabulous career. Nothing – not a thing. Even his beauty was in such tight bud that I at any rate hadn't an inkling that when it unfolded it would shake the crown. What did come out was that there was insanity in that family. Brother John showed the early promise of a full-time lunatic. Was George dismayed? Yes – and no. It was odd and we all felt it to be so at the time. Yes because John's mad fits would always prevent society from having in the Villiers the perfect English family, and not because George had learnt one lesson at least from that impoverished education of his, which was to ride-out shame of all kinds. As you know, Turnkey Wren, the Duke's shamelessness was so great that people were beginning to believe that he had some royalty in him. At Angers he taught us his own art of guiltlessness. I remember we thought it was well-bred to do without a conscience. With us it was a temporary loss but George could hardly be expected to put his back in place, not possessing it in the first instance. But he had heart. It was when he lost 'heart' that things began to go wrong. You and I, Wren, are lucky fellows. We plough a decent enough furrow with no great credit to ourselves, God putting us straight when we lurch out of line. But his late Grace was forever being tugged askew by forces unknown to men like us. How bewildered he was when he was criticised. 'I am the Favourite'. What do you expect? Do not favourites take all? I don't suppose he read enough to have read Kit Marlowe, but had he done so he would have agreed with much of that poet's apology for Gaveston, even if he would have shuddered to find that a favourite could come from nowhere. But he would have found that 'I here create thee Lord High Chamberlain, Chief Secretary of

State, Earl of Cornwall and Lord of Man' etc. quite normal. You – the way you are going – will be made Chief Secretary of Confessions at H.M. Prison, the Tower, but all I will be made is old bones at the crossroads. I will swing and creak and fall knuckle by knuckle to the mud – that is if I am not H.D. and Q'd. Dear merciful Saviour, see that it is just the rope. Put it to my credit that George felt so little. Assassins aren't cruel. They are simple removers.

The Duke's cardinal error was to inherit a king. He should have known better. He had been at Court long enough to learn that in the nature of things favourites must have a short working life. They must take all they can get and then step aside. Who ever heard of a monarch inheriting a favourite as well as a throne? Father's boy. Was not that monstrous in both the new king and the old lad? Ask anyone and there will be but a single answer. It was monstrous.

You probably will not know, nosey-parker Wren, that in my tutor's gloriously Englished Ovid Hebe had to fall from grace before Ganymede could succeed her as cup-bearer to her father King Jupiter. To be frank, she actually took a tumble while waiting at table, showing more than a father would wish to see, so she had to go, and making way for a young man of whom his divine majesty could never see enough. Who came after Ganymede? No one. He is the eternal wine-waiter. He started at the bottom and he remains at the bottom, and is topping-up nectar at this very moment, could we but glimpse that Olympian feast. And what has he got out of it? – why immortality! Puritans may scream, but it is my opinion as soldier-of-the-world that had George Villiers known his place, as we say of our best servants, which should have begun and ended in King James's arms, our sweet country would not have had to endure its recent disasters. Why do you think the crops failed, the plagues blew in, the armies mutinied, the money ran out, honours to have become a stew to be ladled forth for a consideration, and the kingdom itself a laughing-stock? Was it because, when the curtain went up on King Charles's reign, the Duke was revealed standing behind the throne? Not at all. Perhaps you did not hear the gasps. It was because King and Duke together were seen amicably squeezed side-by-side on the ruling-seat. 'But we thought we had got rid of him!' Did you hear the disbelief? And again it was – and from the father's *son*, mind you –' What can we give darling Steenie this bright morning? A parcel-diamond to go with the sun? The Chancellorship of Cambridge University? A Titian or two? My word, little Steenie, where do you put it all! You'll burst.' King James was religious but this King is *spiritual*, they tell me, and I could see him comforting this Favourite II with biblical reassessments such as 'Forget all that consequential business in the Garden of Eden, Steenie. It was not intended for an anointed king. Go on taking all you can get. Grab what fruit you can, particularly that which ripens according to the hereditary principle. Forget your modest ancestors, think of your mighty descendants. And certainly put it out of that lovely head of yours that *malum* happens to be the Latin for evil as well as for apple. Let not your acquisitive heart be troubled. Take, take, take. Take the poor man's ewelamb if necessary. Your sailors, Lord High Admiral, sicken and riot. Take their lives. The Parliament, for the King's sake, doles out shipmoney for your adventures – take it for a ride. Glut yourself, doubly favoured George, and the murrain on your critics.' And what can I give to the boy who has everything, I John Felton from the student days – do you remember? Do not answer. I wish that you had found God interesting, your Grace, but you never did, did you?

You know, Gaoler Wren, that what kings find interesting is a favourite's taking ways. They vie with each other in the lavishment of their giving. Titles, baubles, palaces, fortunes slide into the man-mistress's lap, although up to now it never occurred to kings that they might be persuaded to throw in a scrap of their divinity. The glorious Duke of Buckingham managed to wheedle it out of King Charles, although he got nowhere with King James. All the same, the truth is that Favourite George nudged and fidgeted to be royal – to be James's son and Charles's brother, which was monstrous. No wonder the night skies have been so upset by shooters and the country laid low with famine. Why did the Lower House begin to impeach this Duke? It was because, having taken all that a favourite could legitimately take (the biggest all in history, it was believed), the Duke had ceased to walk with princes but as a prince. He was often run across talking the kind of rot which only princes should talk and, what is more, keeping his hat on in the Presence. Parliament was beside itself at his hubris. In vain did his Majesty reassure it, 'No, no, my beloved Commons, my Lords, no, no, well-meaning and faithful, you mistake, his Grace is our servant, our right hand.' Aha! It replied. Now we see!

A pernicious fear now spread over the kingdom like slime over the jakes-ditch. It was said that nothing like it had been felt since the Bishop of Rome had interdicted the kingdom and dangled it over Hell. During those few months separating my journey from Rannoch and my setting out for the Ile de Rhé I watched this dear country of ours slithering like some turd towards a midden, with nothing to grasp on the way, neither policy nor plan. England just slipped, finding no footing. I saw men openly crying in the streets and at plough. I saw reading-women with Lamentations and Job open at every have lectern, and protesters in the churchyards, listless boys and girls who no longer sang, played or laughed, and naked multitudes warring over a crust. The land stank. So many mourning-cloths flapping on maypoles, so many gallows on the go, so many clergymen standing between the porch and the altar beseechings, like Joel, 'Spare they people, O Lord, and give not thine heritage to reproach, that the heathen should reign over us!' it was because of the metamorphosis of favourite into monster the change from plaything into 'prince'.

Many declared that all was up and began fitting-out vessels for Massachusetts and a Christ-governed life on the plantations. That brave new world, as Duke Prosperous described it in the play. But most sank into apathy and depression and dolours of the soul. Lewd scrawls passed openly:

> Man-queen of England, ruler of our earth,
> It was the Cockatrice who gave thee birth.
> Snapper-up of Places, Lord of Me-me-me,
> Prettiest gentleman of the Admiralty,
> Obliging Buck, planter-out of peers,
> What must I be or do to attract they cheers?
> Who emptied two kings' exchequers,
> And steered the ship of state to the wreckers?
> Dear George, when you are gone they'll say,
> 'This little grave embraces
> One duke and twenty places.'

Bankruptcy, epidemics and the most frightening thing of all, a frightened people, colluded. The kingdom was poisoned. There had to be lancing. It was Eliot who took it upon himself to bring the Duke down. He appeared to have consulted some book – 'How to rid the state of monsters' – something like that. It wasn't pleasant for him. It was like having to destroy a dangerous dog which one had loved as a puppy. Eliot's finger ran down the monsters-list until it stopped at a 'beast called by the ancients Stellionatus, a beast so blurred, so spotted, so full of foul lines, that they knew not what to make of it'. I remember at the time that it sounded like one of those dreadful creatures which are thrown-up from the boiling waters of a Cornish cove. But it was Sir John Eliot's clear use of the word 'beast', rather than the name Stellionatus, which caught the public's ear. This beast, said Eliot (he had become a mighty fine speaker since he stammered out his lessons at the Horse School), this beast was the very worst kind of vampire because 'by emptying the veins the blood *should* run in, he hath cast the body of the kingdom into an high consumption'. And then, in full pursuit of monsters by now, he caught at Aelius Sejanus, the favourite of the Emperor Tiberius, and of course more of a household name than old Stelly. Sejanus, like George Villiers, was a knight's son who bewitched the army, thus extending the rules of favouritism throughout the ranks. Imagine such a begetting of favourites from the throne to the barracks that no one of any consequence was out of favour. But then – unlike George – over-sugared his luck by favouring the wives of the senators. All of them. He should never have let the women in. They don't understand about favourites – about the male bodypolitic, as it might be put. These Roman ladies brought Sejanus's wondrous pyramid of favouritism crashing down. Matters were made worse by his putting Tiberius on the stage. Now if there is one thing which may not be done to a king-regnant it is to make him a common entertainment. Flatter him, worship him, cheat him, roger him, if that is his command, but never, never make him a spectacle for the groundlings. When Tiberius, who lived at the seaside, found out that he was in a play, it was the end for Sejanus, who was strangled for the Epilogue. Sir John Eliot was on popular ground when he raked-up Sejanus and put the Duke of Buckingham beside him. There was quite a likeness. *Comme deux gouttes d'eau.* No wonder at court the day went dark.

As you know, Mr Wren, since you lived through it, George's answer to being loathed was to go to war. It never fails. A prince – he was beginning to accept himself as such – a prince on the beam-ends knows that he has only to raise his flag for his people to cheer him and his spirits to rise. It never fails. But neither does it succeed for long. As usual there were no funds and war-cries turned to groans and discontents, mutterings and mutinies. Where I was concerned, the new war, the Duke's war of rehabilitation, meant riding to and from Bedford with dispatches for Count Dirtybum's headquarters in London. Lists of pressed men, supplies, etc. This is how I came to see the King.

* * *

I am writing this in a window-frame of the Painted Chamber, having just left Count Mansfeld's office. I am to see my King. Say what you will, it is something for an officer to see his Prince. There is a fluttering and a catching of my heart. They have put up a dais for him and the enormous room smells nicely of shavings and glue. There are *two* grand chairs, so the French lady will be by his side. There are hundreds of people, the Parliament, both Low and Lords, the Court and gentlemen like myself. I have to lean back into the case so as not to be jogged. It is a sunny noon and the King's pictures look well. Enter his Majesty. No trumpet. He is small – short – and walks on tall heels and in a tall hat, and on a swaying stick. An uncontrollable love burst from me to him. It is the same for others standing near, who blink and touch the corners of their eyes. King Charles Stuart, aged twenty-six. He is apparelled all in black but with a profusion of snowy point-lace and here and there are diamonds. The Garter makes a sparkle at his knee. It is only a few weeks since he was crowned, but it is the chrism which still hangs about him. We have crowned a clergyman. The Painted Chamber is silent as he clicks his way to the centre of the dais. My God, we have crowned a priest! His long face makes other long faces. Prince of Seriousness. Dear Lord, what solemnity he asks of us. Already, at twenty-six, he has exhausted eyes.

No wife. It is the duke who comes in *with* King Charles – not

189

after him, not a step behind him, but by his side. A rippling fury runs through the room. Side by side like a consort. In contrast to his Majesty George is so magnificent that those nearest the stage step back a pace as they would to an on-coming sun. Whilst everything else might be new about him, he wears the old smile, making me return it, although he could not know that I am there. Here, only yards from him – and Eliot. It is an old boys reunion. George's face is inexpressibly beautiful, those of the King and Eliot – I can just make him out at the head of the contingent from the Lower House – are saturnine. Eliot's black Cornish eyes are all a-glitter. He is the Baptist come to berate Herod Agrippa and is angular and stormy. He and George, they say, have been good friends but have fallen out. Eliot looks as if he has slept in his clothes, and he probably has. George shines in rose silk, very quilted and spoiling to the figure, but it must be so to support the jewels. These are a kind of sapphire and emerald armour. Only his armpits and privates remain unencrusted. He is well over six feet tall and he *wears* a plumy hat. Thunder. He removes it to make a bow and makes it appear that it is for his own convenience that he doesn't return it to his head. Hatted, he was Buckingham, uncovered, he is Apollo.

The old man who has clambered up beside me to get a better view says that he means no disrespect but that the last time he saw such a magnificent person it was Gloriana. 'Can there be man-Glorianas?' if I know what he means. 'Yes, sir.' I will not allow George to distract me. I concentrate on my King. Beloved little King with a face like Matins! You are God-touched – I can see it. If monarchs and minions have to be, who could hope to see a more complete King or mightier servant? The King shows his sacredness, the servant shows off. Listening to Sir John Eliot as he determines to chop master from man, I tremble for both. The Painted Chamber seeths with danger. How are we three here? Why does it come to me that a fourth gentleman – God's elect – has joined our fateful trio? The room is shouting – neither they stand before them. It is too much. There is as much weeping as temper in the Parliament that this holy King, still damp from the holy oils, should be in the hands of the man who pleasured his father and ruined the state by his greed. King Charles touches the petition for the Duke's removal with his finger-tips as though it was his duty to touch shit. They leave. I kneel on the window-seat and pray to Christ for King Charles. God save the King. The Parliament bangs its way out.

The morrow. The talk of Count Mercenary's house is of the King's fugitive nature and of his discrete habits. He has to be watched, for like a shy bird although, once seen, he doesn't fly away. Usually it is his finder who beats a retreat, overcome by this Prince's privacy. The talk is of his Majesty's liking to be in some chamber hung with paintings fresh from Italy, and of standing before them, one by one, in mystical admiration. It is said that the King's fascination with pictures must be papistical, a contemplation of the Holy Ones – that kind of thing. But such comment is brushed aside with assurance that 'he just likes art'. I could fill this sheet with what is being said about King Charles at this moment. Fact or guesswork, all I hear makes me love him. Do I not hold his commission? Have we not a bond? Would I fight and die for him? Fight, certainly. Where is the King to be found? He is not to be found, they say. He is to be come across in Whitehall gardens as he passes alone through the box-walks. Or seated on a bench with his dogs. Or strolling through a pleached alley. What does one do – what does a lieutenant do? 'Make yourself scarce!'

Same day – noon. I am hunting my King. He is the angel I must encounter unawares. I shall kneel on the sward when he passes and not look up. My posture will be 'count on me'. It is chilly in these enclosed walk-ways. The earth deadens all steps and all I can hear are squarks from the royal duck-pond and a guard being changed. And then suddenly there he is, all by himself and leaning against an ash, Charles Stuart, my King. He is wearing the same black suit but no Garter this time and less lace. And flat off-stage shoes. His dogs scamper at me and of course he does not call them off. I fence them in my arms trusting they won't bite. His beasts! They pull in my embrace, they pulsate, whimper with joy, leap, lap my face. Unable to proceed because of them, I kneel where I am. At which the Scotch animals, four of them, mount me in a frenzy of what I hope is liking. The King does nothing – just continues to lean against the tree, and nobody comes in spite of this barking hullabaloo. I rise, bow, rise once more and edge away. The pack follows me. He does not call. We take another path in a blissful flurry and unable to not look back, I meet his hooded gaze. I salute him – my King! – and find my way to Mr Jones's great Eating House, to sit on the steps.

'Are they not his Majesty's dogs?' asks a servant. He chases them back to the park.

By knowing that the King saw me, I am changed by this distant tête-a-tête, irrevocably altered. King Clergyman, I kiss your ermined Cloth, although what would my friend Wemyss have said? I suppose that I must have ridden from Elstow to the Mercenary's recruiting office six or more times that year, 1626, but I only saw his Majesty once. It was when he was at tennis with a lord – not George – and his hair was tousled and flying about and his thin shanks all a-jump. He was able to stay sombre whilst volleying and his movements were part-running and part-dancing. A curious game-playing to be honest. Many gentlemen were watching but what this view of the King did to them I could not discover. I had made it my regular practice to pray for him on the journeys home. Dismounting in a Chilterns beechwood and holding myself like a Felton knight in our Suffolk window-glass, I prayed 'That it may please thee to keep Charles the First, thy servant and our King and Governor in safety, that Christ may rule his heart in all faith and fear and love, and that he will give him a victory at the last.' And then, as did all the gentlemen of England at this time, I prayed what could not be omitted - that Christ would keep the King from the Duke. 'Spare them – thy people – O Lord, spare them, spare them. Let not thine heritage be brought to confusion. After the multitude of thy mercies, look upon us.'

* * *

My book-making, my pasting-in a scrap of journal here and some old impression there, has been disturbed at this point by a letter from holy Madame von Hol. Her 'get free soon' notes from Arnhem or Scotland had been far from comforting, the release which she had in mind being that of the soul from the body, but until today she had not entirely upset me. Now, in the middle of her recommended serenity of the spirit, her commands to prayer, and her general solace, she quite casually informs me, 'that as it

192

is Sir John Borough who is in charge of the Records of the Tower, he will be sure to lodge whatever plea you make in the best hands, being meticulous in such matters. He will carry whatever you write to the King's merciful eyes.'

So it is out, Wren – that you are no more your own master than I am mine. You have deceived me. You somehow seduced me into thinking that I might do some final good in this world by helping your bookish career with a thick volume one for the Wren Library. Now I discover that you have been handing in my manuscript, my day's work, to that born archivist Borough himself. Do you imagine that I do not know of such things? That I am a firebrand who is ignorant of such learned appointments? I know Sir John exceedingly well. His father is a Dutch gardener of distinction. Now he will have planted almost the whole of this history of mine, slip by slip, in his Majesty's way. How am I to go on – tell me that, fool? I am coming to the terrible words – how shall I put them down when I know how terrible they will be to read? They must hurt the King whom I would never hurt. Yet as I am so near to going west, I must state my case. Your trickery was found out just as I was about to paste-in the journal I kept at Rhé. I assure you it will not make good reading for the King. Do you not still understand, artful gaoler? I am coming to the chapters in which I have to justify the murder of Absalom – now do you see what you have done? Sweet King, that severe mind of his has to have the plain facts but not the horrors which must now go in. The trouble with your sort, Wren, is that you do not understand autobiography. How, once the pen takes that direction, it is unstoppable. We can do what we like with our own life-stories and I cannot at this late page check the direction and pace of mine. I don't know that I would have told it all had I known that it would have been run, piecemeal, from the Tower to St James's. It appals me to realise that his Majesty must now be on tenterhooks for what he knows has to come.

Sire, this tale was told to a young Tower creature, not for you. That distinguished author your father would have taught you that literature has to be addressed to some person or other – we cannot spin words towards space. And so I cast mine to your Royal Records Dungeon via this man Wren, and in good faith. But it is your sacred glance which has caught them. What a lot you know of me. Now I must choose another reader and forget that the King will be peeping over his shoulder. How else can I go on? I write now for a dead gentleman who has gone to the stars – his notion of heaven. As it may interest you, a *Scottish* gentleman. As he would have dreaded little which kept him out of the planetary system, I have to confess to your Majesty, before we part on the page, I shake and shiver as the time of my dispatch draws nearer and nearer. I am sick in the corners of my cell. Tears rush from my mouth. I sweat – I stink with fright. Rope, Axe, Knife – will this be the sequence? *My dear flesh* – it is only the arm which is past loving, the rest is smooth and white. A king has God's particular attention. Will you please mention Felton to Him? Will you say to God, 'Let Mr Felton not be frightened.' It might do us both some good – although you will never be where and as I am, imprisoned, waiting for an executioner. Please forgive me for taking the Duke from you without a warrant.

Wren, I am back to you. Wren, when your teeth have blackened like those of the rest of us, when your back has humped and your nerves have been blunted by the ghastly trade which goes on here, I see you hobbling through the bookshelves to take down 'Felton, J. Assassin, Malcontent, Reader, Gent.,' saying under your breath, 'Bloody fool – but he gave me my start'.

Your Majesty, a word more. I am not one of those writers who have a clear aim. When I write it is like a child stamping in a puddle, sending its contents all over the place. This book will soil you but, believe me, when I began it I had no idea that you would be in its path. I beg your forgiveness. I kneel on this filthy floor – in my own vomit - and I say to my King, 'Forgive me'. And whilst I am so down, let me thank you for not racking me, as you would liked to have done, not only because of my crime but because it would have been a legitimate way of satisfying the cruelty in you. May Jesus enfold you.

13

ISLE OF RUE

The Journey to the Isle of Rue by Acting-Captain Mr Felton.

Midsummer-day in the year of our Deliverance, 1627

This is different. Myself – everyone – thinks so. It is
preposterous, but different. We are to invade France. We rake
each other's faces for a shred of belief in this enterprise. There is
none. But at least we are not miserable, not condemned as we
were when they God-speeded us off to Cadiz to repeat an old
adventure, the sorriest sight on a high sea. No, we are quite
different now. I am different because I appear to have
transmuted into that dangerous person, the detached
participant. It is hard to tell what is the sharpest, my interest or
my weapon. And I feel so well, part of this comes from
discovering that what I thought was a touch of the Southwark
distemper was no more than an extra touch of louse-rash. Now I
am as clean as Naaman in that quarter. I breath again. Like our
pretty Duke, who by rights should be standing in the dock, I am
undeservedly reprieved. Another healthy sign is that I have
stopped carping. I *watch*. What a world it is to watch! The new
world of Duke George and itchy Richelieu. I'll give our Duke
this; he is a procession which can come round a hundred times
and still draw a gasp. He passed this noon in a beautiful red hat
of a mocking kind. Next came – a coach. A red coach to run
aboard a ship. 'Upsidaisy!' laughed the sailors as they swung it
aloft. Boxes followed, scores of them. Wardrobe fillers. We must
look our best when we invade France. Sapphired breeches for
Paris and lots of body cambrics, and a gold ewer, if you please,

for the shaving-water. And instructions saying that if the worst came to the worst and Hector fell, his corpse should be returned to Westminster Abbey. All this is public news. I dedicate this journey to my difference, old star-man take note. I continue to miss you, Sir Angus, but less wearingly, which I hope will please you. Can you see France? Bordeaux in particular? We are to swarm in there. Is it possible to see the Duke of Buckingham from the nearest singing planet? I expect he thinks so.

This is a true Summers-day. This is the weather for enterprise! Our Lord High Admiral Duke is rowed to the *Triumph* amidst a boat-load of musicians and had removed his hat to let the Portsmouth breezes tangle his black curls. We trust that this time he knows what he is doing. When he steps ashore, all the Protestants in Europe will rise against the Cardinal and will make a corridor for their Winter Majesties to ride through all the way from the Hague to the Palatinate. Well that is the plan. We look into each other's eyes with a silent, 'what do you think?' Talking of watching, I must watch out for my ship, the *Poor Jane*. I must not be left behind with so much to see. Where do we board for the *Poor Jane*?

'What you, Felton?'

It is old Burroughs himself. Our General.

'So it is France, Sir?'

'Who told you that, Felton?'

Nobody with a name, I had to admit.

'Then do not speculate, Felton. You speculate, sir, that is your habit. Break your habit, Mr Felton. It is not a healthy one. Get aboard and count the pikes.'

He is thumbing down his list. I might well be another bale. I observe him. He looks alarmed. His arm shoots out.

'There, there in front of your nose, Mr Felton, the *Poor Jane*!'

As I bow I notice his sick feet in their bindings. It is a misfortune which causes my own health to blaze up like a puffed flame. General Burroughs's misfortune is to be the only man in England with real military knowledge. He stinks a little. It is his age and feet. I give him a cake which a girl gave me and he devours it without thanks.

'Now get *aboard*, Felton.'

He hasn't changed.

But the Duke has. That brush with the impeachers has altered him. This business with France is to rehabilitate him. Or finish him. This is why everything is different.

22nd June

His Majesty hovers about, ringed by the Court. It moves when he moves like a sea-urchin on a wave. He mounts, dismounts, takes a few steps, stands stockstill. The finery of the small group is thrown about by the shore wind. Gulls form its wailing canopy.

More and more troops march into Portsmouth by the hour. Contrary to the policy for the Cadiz expedition, they are already wearing their army-shirts and shouldering their pikes. Far from full bellies underneath, of course. But soldiers soon learn that they cannot have everything. The long slog and sunburn have tightened and polished their frames. Again unlike Cadiz, it is impossible to tell the vagrants from the unemployed weavers. Old Burroughs's recruiters have done a good job. Through the lanes from Southampton, Cosham and Guildford it streams, the army which will open-up a Protestant highway from the Hague to Bohemia. Or so the Duke has told the King. A peculiar development. These thousands of marching men occasionally release an inchoate roar. It is animal and uncivilized. It could bring a church-tower down, one thinks. Why this great shout? Who can stop it? I noticed such a thousand-throated bawl check the King in his tracks. He was by the Round Tower and shading his eyes against the glitter, strolling and, I suppose, wondering when he should go home. Then the army-shout and city and gulls in brief turmoil. Then the extra silence. When I inspect my platoon I will forbid the shout.

Every dwelling-house for miles around has been bolted against the troops and at Portsmouth itself all the valuables and temptations – girls, boys and horses – hidden out of town. The city hates the Duke, nearly hates the King, hates every sea-soldier and land-soldier alike, hates the Parliament, hates, as one might imagine every fresh trick to raise money for the King's war and hates itself for being where it is, behind the kingdom's best harbour. It hates the befouling we must necessarily leave behind when we sail and it dreads our return

197

with cargoes of horror. The Duke is put up at the Greyhound, his Majesty at Southwick. Once an hour at least the whole region is rocked by the Shout. A chaplain said, 'Do you not think it is like the pagan roar of the Colosseum, sir, when the killings took place?'

We wait amidst one vast inhospitability.

The regiments still expect to find a mountain of shillings on Portsea common. They dream of shillings – shillings, not shirts. Their tongues are thickened by the roarings. They are to sleep out. Each day saved from their ordure aboard ship is day added to their health. The barges which will carry us all to the war vessels roll and slop at the quays. George has thought of everything.

24th June – the Sabbath

I have taken the Sacrament and repeated a psalm. Lovely weather. Flags, banners and martial tunes for the Duke as he climbs aboard the *Triumph*, every inch a prince. An hour later he is barged back to the town, having been told that there are those, officers among them, who don't fancy a trip to Bordeaux. It is said that he went in person to their kennels and bedchambers and rustled them out half-naked, and drove them like pigs to the quay, himself all in pink silks and laughing.

27th June

We sail. There is glory in this hour, let me not decry it. It is anchors away for *Poor Jane*. The sea is like lapis, endless coloured segments of water keeping their hues and flowing together. We are in the *Triumph's* wake. I know no one, I should not be on this ship. I have been told wrong. 'We shall each find where we should be anon,' says the captain, a Mr Sawstonhall from the north. Does he mean religiously?

July 4th

Eight days out and the war council changes the invasion point. Not Bordeaux but La Rochelle – Huguenot-land. Confidence begins to be not quite what it was yesterday. 'We have to give it a boost, hey, sir!' says Captain Sawstonhall. 'How shall we do that – hey?' He makes the *Poor Jane* swing over the new course.

'Will it still be France?' asks the lad.

10th July

We have arrived, all one hundred shiploads of us, and the glorious Duke in person. There is – France. Le Rochelle looks nothing much from this distance but we can see that it is unwelcoming.

'It is the Protestants,' explains the Captain. 'They repress joy. They won't put up a flower-arch, not even for Buckingham.' Having little else to do, I while away time reading Boethius on the poop. 'In every adversity of fortune, to have been happy is the most unhappy kind of misfortune'. I puzzle this.

12th July

Mr Golding's birthday. *Sit tibi terra levis*. Dear Belchamp earth. How shall I write what must be written? In what way? It is dark and I crouch by the poop-lantern. The *Poor Jane* rocks its sleepers. I can hear the sea sucking her planks. She is at anchor but not at peace. How can I write this? Take heart, Felton, and take your time! There will be enough sleep for you after midnight. Your ink has kept well. No grouts. So write. Start with what happened this morning and then draw your conclusion.

It takes a Huguenot not to be thrilled by a floating army. I had met these rational believers at the holy house of the von Hols and I must have been the only man in the Duke's army who had been to La Rochelle. For him it was the gate of hope, for me it is a memory of dull streets and sullen principles, reminding me of Lavenham. I swam in the Sèvre, its compensating river. Until noon, when the blow fell, I found it powerfully interesting to realise that in an hour or two I would be there again. Also there were the bookshops – you have to go to a Protestant town if you want a good bookshop.

About midday an intelligence spread from ship to ship that the invasion of France was off. (Sailors have an affinity with windmillers when it comes to spreading news). The twitch of a sail, a word spelt out in spins and halts, and in less time than it takes to walk a mile everybody knows what is going on. Captain Sawstonhall could not believe his eyes and had to check with his officers. All the landsmen were lined-up on deck, piked and ready to take to the barges. Moreover singing. For there was to be no beach-battle, just a grand Protestant march into town, into a reformed world stretching from La Rochelle to the Palsgrave's throne. Our great navy was so near the Charente Maritime cornfields that harvest scents filled our canvas. And there was this warm, shimmering summer light which one gets along the Stour.

A poleaxed Sawstonhall came to me and said,

'It is all off.'

I saw that he meant Buckingham's rehabilitation. If the Huguenots of the French coast told us to go home, that is all we could do. Where else could we land ten thousand men? For what purpose? Arsehole Mansfeld might have suggested an alternative, but he was dead.

It was late this afternoon that we observed a boat being sculled from ship to ship. The tall soldier in the rough white government-shirt had evidently been ordered by the Duke to tell the fleet to turn-tail. The rowers whirled him from vessel to vessel and he stood up most of the way, and was still yet even at this distance inwardly restless. Indeed, his visible anxiety was such that it appeared to blur the summer's perfection. As we had watched him shouting something to nearby ships, a handful of us went to the rail to receive his message. The boat flashed towards us and the standing man held his hands to his face against the sun. Featureless, burning like a nimbus, he disappeared beneath our gunports. We heard the splashings and clumpings of oars being raised, and then – 'Your ladders, for Christ's sake! Get me up!'

We did not need to see the speaker to know his identity and our entire company was on one knee when Buckingham swung himself aboard. For a second or two it looked as though he would observe the traditions of a Lord High Admiral – or even offer some kind of explanation for his uncouth dress and breathless arrival – but then he brushed all this, and us, aside, and without a word to anyone he turned his back on La Rochelle and gazed on the fish-shaped islands which guarded the town. To the right, Rhé, to the left, Oléron. Still we knelt. But when the Duke ran to the mainmast and began to swarm up its rigging, we ourselves were stretching upward as far as we could, our necks taut, our mouths gasping. I knew then that what the Duke might see as his salvation from the upper fighting top of our mast would be our graveyard. He was graceful in his descent. His heart had lifted. He had discovered a direction which was not straight home to Portsmouth. He was now like one of those lonely finger-posts which point the way off a terrible moor. He was also an object of grudging admiration for his courage and skill in climbing from the lower to the upper fighting top. Also for proving that although emeralds and sarsenet were required to show his great rank, the lowliest slops merely emphasised the excellence of his person.

I saw all this from where I could not be seen. I saw Buckingham stroll slowly to a huddle of youngsters.

'Who can swim?'

Petrified silence.

'Come on – who can swim? Answer!'

A lad raised his hand. The Duke spoke into his ear, then propelled him to the ropes. In minutes the tiny craft in which Buckingham had been rowed to the *Poor Jane* was heading towards the tip of Rhé, a wretched promontory called the Point of Sablanceaux which stuck its finger towards France. In an hour the naked boy was back before the Duke. The seawater still ran from him. He did abasement. He muttered what he had glimpsed on Rhé. To Buckingham it was like receiving confirmation of a promised land. He patted the soggy head as one would a wet dog.

'Get up, little Lysander!'

I report all this. I report my misgivings. The Protestant sweep of our armies through Europe's Reformed kingdoms was what was intended – was what was understood. But shipping ten thousand Englishmen to a marshy isle, stranding them, playing soldiers with them, going the Lord High Admiral over them, not knowing where else to march them ... O Salamis!

I spoke to Captain Sawstonhall but he could not speak.

201

15th July

We have invaded Canvey – this is what it looks like. But there are greater defenses here than Lysander knew and some of us have been killed, including poor Heydon. Wemyss used to make fun of Heydon's father, Sir Christopher, on account of a book he was supposed to be writing called *A Recital of the Celestial Apparitions of this Present Trygon*. I'm told that it never saw the light of day.

16th July

It is raining heavily. We buried Bill Heydon – in mud. We march on. For a Canvey, there is a long way to go.

17th July

We are now about half-way along the coast road of Rhé and the sun has returned. St Martin the capital has surrendered but not its garrison. This fort is made like a stone star by the sea's edge and would have been no consequence were it not that Richelieu sees it as a means of holing us up. Quite suddenly, the might and majesty of England and of his Highness (sic) has to be put to the test by the capture of this stoney star. There before us in the water rides our navy. Here on land are massed our regiments. Their trumpets and whistles cry all day. Between them, horrid as a Portuguese-man-of-war, sprawls this besieged star. Who dares grasp it? The Duke must. How fastidious he is, we think. How reluctant he is to have such a minimal victory. St Martin – where did you say? That *sand-dune* known only to kites and Dunkirkers! O Buckingham!

Journal, who do you think I saw today? Mr Herrick the chaplain running after girls.

'Mr Herrick!' I said.

'Oh, you know how it is Mr Felton.'

'I do, I do – know how it is.'

He and I are of age, I should say. He would not do for dinner at the von Hols. He showed me a pretty verse which he fished from his shirt. Others fell out, and he fished these from the mud.

'I say my prayers too, Mr Felton.'

A rounded life. Mr Herrick is one of those hapless slummochy men whose sash won't stay up and who is forever rescuing parts of himself. Cassock awry, I once saw him giving the Sacrament to the Duke as one might give a child a tart, patting it into his mouth. His eyes cannot miss a girl. The St Martin's girls remind me of Parmenter in their vagueness concerning sides. Women are so bad when it comes to taking sides. So unprincipled. They bob to Mr Herrick's cloth, otherwise they don't notice him. He calls after them as one would to lambs running wild and they la-la back. He also goes on flower-hunts with Mr Tradescant, whose name I have now got right. They talk gardening, if you please. Surely gardening is something for hands to do, not for us to talk about. The gardens on Rhé are dreadful, as they generally are on islands. Middens with leaves. I am severe.

25th July

We are dug in. Why the Lord Christ alone knows. Mr T. has planted us like a manned park, so many hundreds here, fifty there. The summer blows hot and cold, but mostly wet. To drill, or to do anything, we have to march two miles from the entrenchments. They are water-logged ditches between mud-slides. Mr T. has plucked some early flowering Death-come-quickly and also some Rampion and Elecampane, and has sent his assistants into the miserable St Martin gardens to see if they grow medicines. Wound-herbs such as Yarrow and Aaron's Rod.

1st August

What do we here? The Duke has had his pictures and fal-lals shipped from the *Triumph* to a farmhouse and has turned it into a little Whitehall – it is said. We are kept away by his guard. Our Angers horse-school masters taught him well, for (they say) he is all chivalry. Chivalry in the circumstances has to be his only activity. He and the Maréchal Toires, cooped-up in the star-fort, pass the time by pretending to be King Richard and Prince Saladin. Courtesies make a bee-line between their respective traps. The Duke has to wait until a second army arrives from England so that he can break out of Rhé. The Maréchal has been ordered by Richelieu not to surrender by any means because it will look so bad to the Catholic allies.

I hear from gossips that the chivalry goes something like this: 'Noble and worthy opponent (*antagoniste*), we beseech your Excellency to accept this fragrant handkerchief whilst we starve you out.' – 'Matchless *Adversaire*, increase my joy in having you as the enemy by wearing this collar-point stuff worked by my Mother. Is not the weather better? Shall there be more rain? Forgive if any stench adheres to this communication, but I have been assisting in heaving the corpse of a horse, too rotten for further eating, over the wall. Twenty-three of our men have perished honourably from hunger. Such is war!'

23rd August

Rain, rain. This morning we heard from our Duke's farm palace that we are to poison the wells and shoot-down the windmills of Rhé. Buckets of killed rats and other bumby-heap muck are to be tipped where the streams wander towards the star-fort. The Martinese are now at Mass all day long and now and then Buckingham joins them. l am more moral than I was in Cadiz and haven't looted a thing. Strangely, little has gone astray since we landed here – including female virtue. It could be the mud and the idiocy, but we are not soldierly. Other matters cling to us. Yesterday I approached M. le Curé for a read as he stumbled from his church and he opened his hands in emptiness. No library. No print but this; he tapped his *brévaire*. 'Who then?' He said, 'Find out.' The French used to be known for their politeness. In the evening an old lady tapped on my shed with a little volume entitled *Androgyne* by the poet Héroet and said. 'Bring it back!' She returned later with a whore and said, 'Bring her back.' Myself and Captain Benskin, my shed-sharer, had her all night. She was practised and agreeable and had no principles. But when I read to her from *Androgyne* she coloured. It is what I have always maintained, the printed word has powers above all our actions.

19th September

Despair, despair. The Duke's fright is now ours. The smell of it has reached Whitehall, for his Majesty urges him to come home. Forget the expense, Steenie. Just come home. But how can he – the Duke? He knows that this Expeditionary Force has cost England all she had – ever penny, every serviceable man. I will not say every hope, for not much was hoped for it. Our costly Admiral-General-Chancellor-neo-Prince walks by the sea. He scans where Portsmouth might be. There is a hissing other than that made by spindrift but this he does not hear. The Duke's ear selects pleasing sounds. Remotely, like the waves in the conch, he hears that he is not loved. A detestation of him is now the staple attitude. It is 'the Duke – ha!' is he wounded – cut? He seems not to be. What is becoming deafeningly clear is that no one except his circle at Court and his enchanted wife now gives a damn for him at home. Through its many-thousand ears we his army know that the King stands by both the Duke and the Cause. I can hear the loyal reminder. 'What cause? Why, that of our dear Sister and Brother of the Palatinate. And – oh yes – of our Protestant neighbours in the Huguenot lands.' And him very nearly a papist. But we know that this vast wreckage on the minimal rocks of Rhé is due to George's steerage. That he had been given his last change and has muffed it. Which is why spindrift seems to hiss inland. Yet more regiments are to be sent, further monies, more love from his sovereign. All that I can see from my admittedly low view are the vermin eating their heads off in the deserted fleet – George has brought all the sailors ashore and, to their horror, turned them into landsmen – and some hundred of French Catholics hungering in the star-fort. Also a Cardinal biding his moment like a cat.

22nd September

I have been put in charge of the east diggings. Mr T. marks them out and my men dig. Slime and water wells up. 'We'll have another trench here, and one over there,' says the grand gardener. I put it to him, 'Does his Grace believe that Richelieu will leap up the beach and fall into them like a badger in a badger-trap?' These crazy ditches collect mucky liquids from which my men catch their deaths.

'What, are you digging a trench here?'

'No, sir, we dig graves.'

So many war graves when there have been so few shots. And how my ruffians grieve for each other! Who would want more of the life they have? Yet how they weep when it is death. Mr Herrick buries in sixes to save his tongue. He too weeps easily, but then he is a gentleman. His tears add further messes to his front. 'There, there,' he adds comfortingly after he has muttered, ' "I heard a voice from heaven saying unto me, Write" ' ... etc. He gets on well with rascals.

The Duke writes to the Maréchal, 'We very much hope that when you come to sign the surrender that you will stay to dinner. Ordinary dress.'

The Maréchal writes to the Cardinal, rolling the letter into a tube of horse-gut and ordering a lad to swim to the mainland with it, 'For pity's sake, your Eminence, *send food.*'

I write to George:

> Your Grace, because this place is small our eyes have not met more than once, and with recognition. Must we not release ourselves from feelings of obligation because of who and what we were at Angers? It would be better so. I ask no favours because we were boys together. Not so much as a 'Why, Felton, how are you?' I am a professional soldier at the pinnacle of my career. You, your Grace, were a friend – this much cannot be unsaid. But let nothing more be added. There are matters which cannot be brought up to date. We had some mutuality long ago but if we meet further, my bow will not be for that but for my General. Permit me to clear the air for both of us, sir.
>
> I have the honour to be, sir, John Felton, Gent.

He replied within the day. 'My youth remains as precious to me as what has succeeded it, John. Let me wish you well. Buckingham.' I put this note in my hat, where it crackles beside one from Eliot and a proper letter from Wemyss. It was like laying a ghost – or exterminating a grudge. I shall fight the better for it. M. de Montaigne said, 'If you press me to say why I loved him, I can say no more than it was because he was he and I was I.' Let us be faithful in the past tense.

26th September

Our old Colonel Mathers has arrived. Quite how I do not know. He rollicked in, cheeks aglow. 'What a show, my boys! God, I'm glad I am here!' he has brought letters from Beatrix von Hol. They describe the good company of the Lord. She is to bear a third child. I bury my face in sour blankets as I try not to think of that white ancient on her. She has a request which neither of them would like refused. Will I be Godfather? A proxy can be arranged. She and her husband earnestly desire me to reconsider my return to the regiment. It is not what the Lord Christ would have of me. Arnhem is hot. They would ride to Scotland except for the breeding. 'I love my great belly.' I can hear her laughter – like icicles warmed off eaves and falling on bricks. She honestly believes that I – anyone – can have her kind of happiness. Pregnant immaculata! Lady-traveller on the Emmaus road. Bedfellow to Tithonius! Rich woman. Girl who should be mine. Smooth white kernel of those huge Dutch dresses, I nibble where your white arm bends, where your white legs part. Do you imagine that I have not made you mine? But what do you know of that lust which carries a man to a once and only love? I can smell your fingers on the paper. Could he – your husband? Can he smell? Can he quite see? Hear? He is eighty-two, you tell. Just a bit junior to Simeon. And still lecturing, you say. *Étonnant!* I read of your bliss on a chilling afternoon, lying on a spat of goosegrass known as sweethearts in Suffolk. We are all going to die here, my girl, because the Duke daren't go home. Yes, I will sponsor your child at the font. I will give him his spoon. It shall be made of guelder-rosewood and he can stir his porridge with it. But should he be a girl like you I will not forgive him.

27th September

Paralysis. Spellbound on Rhé. Suspended from all action. The year cools and this twenty miles of rock near Biscay Bay is in change. The common conviction now is that no help will reach us, nor should. His Grace was given a grand navy and a grand

207

army for his grand strategy and that seems to be that. He is unable to believe it and bombards the King, the Duchess, his mother the Countess and all his old friends with desperate pleas for more of everything, particularly men and money. He calls officers' parleys, which is how I know such matters. His physicians are fearful for him. That heroic frame belies its look and contains much that is gossamer. There was a dancing-day at the Great Horse School when we saw all the strength leave it.

Strength – such as there was of it when our scarecrow men were press-ganged into this debacle – has certainly fled the trenches where they crouch out of the wind. One can almost see it rising from their bodies like marsh-gas. They die in the night and are pulled out from their comrades in the way weaners which have been overlaid are pulled from the sow. The physicians peer at each corpse without touching it, holding their noses as well as their opinion. Have we plague? There are no plague-marks. Have we a distemper? No sign of it. Why did they die? Hunger and cold. But they were always hungry and cold. All their lives, hungry and cold. Some have stripes from being whipped to the pick-axing of the trenches in which they were to perish. In a north entrenchment the corpses this morning are of the naughty bathing party which the Duke himself had to break up. The sea was warm and these men swam and forgot when they could, and the Duke discovered them and bludgeoned them back to work. It was a mark of his efficiency not of his cruelty, which feeling was, for so great a person, low in him.

Near enough to the trenches for their occupants to hear the milk squirt into its pail and the hens cackle as they lay is Buckingham's farm. He floated it from Hampshire in a collier. Four fat oxen, two milch cows, two goats and coops of poultry, plus stockmen and dairymen and a nice little flock of Suffolks. To perish from hungering to the clank of churns and the drumming of butter-making, and to hear wine-casks run up the ramps! And to watch the Duke go in and out of his glorified quarters, bopping his head under the lintel and gathering a thick cloak around him, and at night to listen to his music-band, well it was extraordinary!

Rumour. The star-fort will surrender today. His Grace is incommunicado as he studies the protocol of capturing a castle. I

208

can see it all. The business of magnanimity. The return of Saladin Toiras's sword, the receiving of his suite, the drawing-up of the terms. They say that a thousand of the most decent soldiers are to be scrubbed and armed to attend his Grace when he makes the victor's entry and that he will be wearing his parade plumes and the Spanish cloak, and that pipes and drums will lead the procession. I have laid out my own parade dress, there being none to do it for me. The Duke is anxious about his servants; that if one go down, all go down. He has indicated that seconds may have to be trained to keep up his state. Tonight I will light my own fire.

28th September

Anything but rumour. The star-fort has been relieved, not surrendered. We woke to cheering and laughter. Trust the French to work wonders with food. Whilst our sickly host slept, a supply flotilla made up of small silent boats managed to outdo us. At dawn the besieged were feasting. Feasting on our chagrin, on our utter disbelief. The Cardinal's provisioners had delivered. We are nonplussed. The supply skiffs ran under our galleons – which are mostly unmanned anyway – on watery tip-toe and not only enough food, but delicious food had been carried up to the citadel before it was light. And not only this, but these siege-breakers were back to the mainland in an hour. St Martin rings with 'Richelieu' and 'Vive le Roy!' Toiras himself as well as his garrison have been larking on the ramparts with turkeys and sirloins on pikes, and beside themselves with happiness. Worse, our men rejoiced with them. It was such a good joke against the Duke that mirth made them weak and they had to hold each other up. They sang seditious songs but were not rebellious. When loaves and cakes appeared on pikes, they stopped rejoicing for – others and became silent for themselves. We have to pack up and leave. What else?

29th September

The ashen Duke takes stock. All St Martin's go to church for a victory Mass. It is the feast of St Michael who, reminds the Curé, won the war in Heaven. Their introit *Benedicite Dorninum, omnes Angeli ejus* seems to be spired to the clouds in hearing of our whole camp. Michaelmas at Ovington and father sending his tithe to the rector, plus a mite more for the look of it. Mr T. came to my tent with a list of Rhé trees – much stunted by ocean winds, he said – and what he excitedly calls 'finds'.

'Did you see the Cardinal's larder?' Mr Tradescant.

'I was flower-hunting around La Couarde, Mr Felton.'

'So you missed what happened?'

'I heard what had happened.' replied Mr Tradescant. 'Now look here, sir, howsomedever (he comes from Walberswick), put your gaze here, sir, and tell me what you see.'

Wilted stems.

'This, sir, is the Broad Leafed Sea Wormwood, and this, sir, is the Greatest Sea Stock Gillowflower. So it was worth the coming after all.'

He helped me to supervise the burial of forty-seven corpses, eyes for ever on the look-out. A grass here, a fossil there. Why, a buckle from Julius Caesar! The bodies slide into their companionable grave like herring, silvery cheeks and fingers touching. Mr Tradescant's grief is tempered by his passion for curios. 'A minute, sir', he interrupts the filler-in. He reaches down. It is a tile. 'From Constantinople.' Virgin earth thunders across sky-facing heads. 'Farewell all,' says Mr T. I came back to the billet. Mr T. followed and asked, 'Have you anything which should be collected?'

2nd October

In retrospection and disgust. I left the following out because it was shameful. Mitigation: being greatly thwarted and the suffering there of. The madness. My Lord Buckingham knows nothing of being held back and his frustration is not to be measured by our disappointments. His mighty enterprise is braked by a half-built, half-manned garrison which might take to Christmas to starve-out. By which time we shall be dead. So he turns to what must disgust and in the same way, I expect, in which we would, in extremis, roast and devour a corpse.

About a fortnight ago, when there was not the least sign of the star-fort surrendering and he and Saladin were at the zenith of their billet-doux, my valiant enemy this, my worthy adversary that, the Duke's thwarted ambitions burst from all decency, as military requirements often do, and he was seen running this way and that to various officers, pointing furiously, first to the garrison and then to the town, and barking orders, all of this entirely unnatural to his character. There was some huddling among them when he calmed down, some debate, some swift planning, and it was then that I heard my name. Felton ... Felton. We are dogs when it comes to our names. We turn back. We come to the caller. I spoke French, was not that so? The Duke, shaking like a man who has shown to the world what he did not know he had, walked slowly home. Old Mathers then arrived to tell me what I must do.

'You have only to explain – nothing more. Be methodical, sir, and go from dwelling to dwelling and explain.'

'Explain that all the Catholic ladies are to be pulled out of their houses and driven to the star-fort so that their men will have to feed them, and so, by next week if we are lucky, run out of food – explain *this*?'

'Mr Felton, you have not languages only, but grasp.'

It is how war disgraces us. It is war, it is war, we say. It is disgrace. It began to drizzle. I put on sword and hat, took two men from a game and began in the chief street. It was called the Rue Ste Geneviève after the patroness of Paris. It was trim – and quiet when I started knocking on doors, a hubbub when I cease. When the troops marched down, all I could think of was one of Master Rubens's 'Nymphs Surprised' or of a popular rape – the Sabines. Except that the men were forbidden such soldierly treats on pain of death. The women begged for time to put out their fires or fetch warm clothes, to collect children. A great lady from the house by the church thrashed a loon with her cane when he dared to hustle her. M. le Curé stood on the church step and cursed the English with terrible comminations. Women were thrust from the surrounding streets and from the *place* to the Rue Ste Geneviève until, what with soldiers and females and crying children, we were all locked together between the house-walls. Impacted. It now rained steadily. The Duke appeared on his horse and looked shocked. He went away. An infectious fright now took hold. The vile *Anglais*. The *Duc – monstre! Jesu, défendre!*

211

They were to be ravished then murdered.

The great lady seized me. *'Expliquer!'*

To the fort? – but it was roofless! I amazed her. *'Heretique!'* She slapped my face. A big dirty pikesman then slapped a rump as he might have done to get cows on the move, and it began, a helter-skelter down the steep Rue Ste Geneviève to the aghast star-fort, each of its points lined with husbands, brothers, fathers. There was no stopping the terrified flight from home to castle. No stopping, either, of a mounting excitement in our troops and of racing lust. But there was nothing more than opportune handlings. In less than an hour from when I visited the first house, the doors of the star-fort received the Catholic ladies of St Martin.

'Another little mouth to feed,' said my servant as the last one was tugged in. It was good strategy, he thought. With all those women inside, the larder would run out in a week, the fort would surrender, our Duke would have a victory and the bloody Rochellois would have to welcome us, and Pope's man Richelieu would have lost, and what more had we to do?

I described this revolting day to Mr Herrick at dinner. He was silent. He told me that he had been burying up by the marsh close to where we must go out. It had never occurred to me that we would not leave Rhé by the same way we had come in.

'Mr Felton, there is a French army on this island.'

He ate enthusiastically as usual.

As we left the mess there was a kind of guard of Protestant women to curse us and throw their chamber savings at us.

'Criminel!'

'Oh, I don't think so, my dear.'

Herrick mopped his cheeks.

I cannot go on with this. I haven't touched on what really happened today. There are no words for what I feel. Dragging girls and grandmothers from their houses and chasing them to a camp. It *is* 1627 and we should know better. I hope George is sick. It pours and the roofless star-fort will be a star-pond. It was Buckingham who threw the innocents into this tank. He must fish them out. Woman-luster, I hope that this won't get back to Whitehall. Your cunties won't like it.

* * *

212

Two more days and nights, and they are out. The landgate swings open and they emerge in a deliberate procession of two-by-two, the great lady leading and holding forth her neck-cross. The rain has ceased and the sands steam in the sun. the procession plods on to where the approach road begins and there is an ordered stamping of feet. Loiterers from our camp straggle towards the Rue Ste Geneviève to take note and reel back from the stink. It is not rainwater that clogs these passing skirts, it is not mud which squelches from these small shoes. So the star-fort is a pismire. So they stand in shit. So the weather pours through its rooflessness and stirs what it finds there. We are told that not a mouthful of the precious rations have passed the women's lips, and would cold deny it? Hungry children, covered in filth, suck their thumbs. The Duke is appraised of this exodus and says it is just as he intended. The women have told him just what he needed to know about the state of the besieged enemy. They were his Caleb and Joshua returned from spying-out the Promised Land. I see quite a different thing from the balcony of the *école* where I am allowed to read. I see the kind of blunder which puts resolution into men who are at the end of their tether. And I do not mean our coughing crew.

The smelly crocodile dispersed before the steps of the great lady's mansion. Her husband, so ancient that he made Doctor von Hol look a sprite, trembled his way down twenty leafy steps to receive her and to kiss her hand. The women went to their houses and for a while silence absorbed the town. Then M. le Curé sprang from his church like a jack-in-the-box and poured forth comminations so foul that they complemented the smell left in the air. He shook his fist and crossed himself. It was at this most moment that I knew all was lost.

Another matter. We had assumed, and then taken it for granted, that whilst Rhé's chief defence was incarcerated in the star-fort we had little to fear. To be sure there were snipers and raiding-bands, and certainly further troops had been run-in from harbours along the Charente-Maritime in the same way as the food, but these too could hardly threaten his Grace's army, that vast and heroic concourse whose transport alone, as it dipped and fluttered in the roads before La Rochelle, spoke of power in the utmost sense. But it was beginning to dawn on us that as many of the Cardinal's men were at war outside the star-fort as those confined in it. Considering that we had been on Rhé since mid-June, and that no more than this fish-patterned sliver of France which an expeditionary force the size of ours should have captured in a day, it was uncomfortable that we had not taken it. It was – tell it not in Gath, publish it not in the streets of Askelon – the Duke who was holed-up. And he knew it would not be long now before those old-fashioned lessons we had both been taught at the Horse School would be brushed aside, and he, and all of us, would be scurrying from point to point of this rock like minivers, searching for where we could jump off.

So many of us killed when there had been no battle! His Grace's best advisors shot or sworded, not on the field but in some field. So many funerals without a deserving rhetoric. Although we spoke of heroes all the same. Hero – that would be me if, poking about in search of old throw-outs for Mr Tradescant's cabinet of rarities, I should be struck in the back. A last wish in my hat-lining. Boil the flesh of my bones and return them in a fair sack to Ovington, England, for my sepulture. More Horse-School rubbish. Where is all this boiling of gentlemen's corpses being done? I have never found where. George would not like it. He owes everything to his body, to the clothing of his bones. He will insist on reaching the Abbey in one piece. Wemyss once told me that we might all be burnt. Of all his turn-things-on-their-heady sayings, this most appalled me. I am morbid because of this death without battle. I shall pray to the Lord Jesus after dinner. I shall ask him to save me. God of battles ... King of Peace. It is troubling. Sense will be made of it in paradise.

25th October

Autumn hurries on. Biscay gales batter the camp. The Rochellois light their lamps early across the straight. The sailors called to be landsmen have been sent back to the fleet to protect it against rough weather. We must soon do something or do nothing and go home. Diseases without titles roam the entrenchments where thousands of our soldiers still lie. Rats and raindrops dance on their faces. We can hear them bellowing old country songs.

I have done it, I have written to mother to tell her that I will marry Jane Crane. I have said that I like her enough to come to love her, and that she is appropriate and cannot demean us, or we her. I did not add that she has always reminded me somewhat of John Eliot's Rhadagund of Treburaye, for that would be too long a story. But she did – does. Passion and sense. I have asked mother to ride over to Chilton to make the first moves. She is not at this stage to tell my brother Blabbermouth. I feel, well, exalted. As I have never felt before. I have shifted a block and made all the rest fall into position. It is so unlike me to do such a thing. The Biscay tempest is blowing me into a house - a Crane house. God knows, there are plenty of them. I may write in the house. I'll see. There will be a home for me with a wife and a dog. We shall live on wild birds from the shoots, hares and the like. My letter is in the courier's bag with a score of others all begging for more money, more men, more thought for what is happening here.

Last night was the first time since we landed that my rest was not prefaced with a dream of Dutch skirts. Last night I set aside *Androgyne* and took up my neglected *Golden Epistles* and read myself to sleep. I woke very early when it was still dark and evaluated myself as one might a healthy enough creature from a good line. I added up to more than my own estimate, and this without vanity. I felt my worth, such as it was. Ridiculous assets such as my Paris mistress's opinion of my arms piled themselves on the scales. She would kiss me elbow to shoulder and whisper *beau!* after I had covered her. She adored the languor after the engagement, as Frenchwomen do. She was old for me and good to me, and my best lover. I shall never forget her roar of merriment when I came to her door to enquire if she took students. She said we could come to an arrangement (holding her sides by then). How good she was to me. *Madame, salut!*

Jane Crane – Jane Felton. It will be all over Clare. Mother won't hold her tongue. I wish I could say that it was the Holy Ghost or an old desire which brought her into view, but it was one of those fragments of an otherwise lost conversation which mentioned her. Some thing about her having green eyes. I cannot quite see them but I can her crooked smile. When shall we sail from here?

215

26th October

Mr Herrick on his round. Specimen: 'Take my word for it, heaven is paradise and paradise is a garden. The Gardener is Christ – the Lord Jesus, you know. Oh, the periwinkles, violets, daisies, the marigolds, columbines, paigles, lad's love, the roses, the lilies, the perfumes and tendrils, the tall trees and primulas of paradise!'

He is chaffing a blue hand and squatting on the soldier's shield. 'But what of Hell, sir?' enquires the dying tongue. 'A misunderstanding, sir. A misprint most probably. Hell is here – not there. No, we all go into the Garden of God. His Son tends it and will tolerate weedy creatures like us to fill its walks and lawns ... do not reply. Breathe as easily as you can. What, no more?' (like a parent when the child pushes away the spoon). Mr Herrick allows the last breath its time, folds his dirty fingers in prayer, closes the staring eyes and retrieves his grubby cloak from its service as a blanket. He writes the corpse's name on his list and moves on. His shirt gapes and his belly shows. He murmurs a tune. He looks wonderfully old for thirty-six.

'Mr Herrick!' I call.

'Oh, Mr Felton, you startled me. I am at my Matins.'

2nd November

How ill I am – too ill to write, and that on damp paper which makes the ink run. I am very, very ill from a wound. 'Four hundred and thirty dead. Many wounded.' When you read this think, 'Lucky wounded', which is quite a mistake. It is terrible to be wounded. Dreadful. My wound beats like a second heart – a heart in my bicep which leaps with its own agonising life. I thought it was crying, 'Let me out!' and I did my best to release it, this pulsing pain. I touched the purple shining plum of a bicep with the tip of my dagger and I imagined the pain would fly out with pustulance, but it did not. Or rather the deflation gave the cramped conditions required by a different pain, a grimmer pulse. One near to the bone. The sea-surgeon has examined me, for what it is worth. I ordered him to lay down his instrument first. I cried when he unrolled the rag.

216

'Yes, sir, you will cry,' he said.

'What do you see – Mr Cartright, is it?'

'Not a musket-ball ... not a slash, not a jab.'

He straightens himself.

'Sir, your's is a mangling. You are mangled – Mr Felton, is it?'

He lifts my arm and I faint.

When he comes again – he is assiduous – he announces what he calls good news. The arm will hang on without feeling, so no pain. I move its hand. Screaming pain.

'You will encourage it just to hang on, sir.'

How fortunate I am to keep an arm. Many have lost their heads, sliced off when they appeared over the parapets. The scaling ladders didn't reach to the top but the heads and hands did. So off they went, craniums, fingers flying.

'Over the top!' yelled the Duke when he stormed the star-fort. But his ladders made that impossible. Saladin Torais scarcely needed to give an order as we presented ourselves to be decapitated, chopped, stoned, strangled or just pushed to fall fifty or more feet. After an hour of this, we hardly needed our scalers. With enough victims and a little more time, we could have captured the garrison by running up the ramp made by our own dead. It was such a disappointment to the Duke. He could return as the victor of St Martin. It was not much but it was something. He could have worn his parade helm. He could have been seen in a different light.

I should not be writing. Just the actions of a pen is enough to set my pain on its travels. I should be lying tense on the hard deckboards and willing their elmy health into my body. But I find the mere sound of paper a distraction. It cannot drown that in-breathing roar of torment but it offers a friendly scratch and rustle in which, if I do not try, I can occasionally lose myself. The noise of physical suffering is as individual as speech – or laughter. Each of us makes his own recognisable groan. Mine are never held in. For what purpose? I am quite dreadfully ill. A mole is at work in my gut. My skin is taut and by eyeballs burn. I would not have to try very hard in order to die. Although my head is bent to the page, I notice that our peculiar attendant is at his business once more, trotting to and fro with considerate steps and taking care not to skid on anything we may have

217

drained onto the freeway. We call him Mariner.

'Mariner, on which deck do we lie?'

'Why, the orlop-deck, sir.'

'Mariner, do we lie aboard the *Poor Jane* – she that brought us all to the Isle of Rue,'

'It is Rhé, sir. Are-Haitch-He. And no, sir, you do not lie in the *Poor Jane* no more, but in a ship of special hospitality brought here for the comfort of injured men, something rarely done before. Six months ago, it was no more than a Deptford hulk but the Lord High Admiral in person, anticipating your hurts, had it all fitted out for your recoveries. I will have them mended, he said, "spirit and flesh". Free gentlemen such as yourself, sir, or pressed-men, it means nothing to his Grace when your mending is the consideration. The name of this ship is either the *Oberos* or the *Umbrios* – after the Faery of Shadows, you know. Something of the kind. I haven't as yet counted how many hundreds of you lie aboard, but hundreds there are of you without a doubt. And few so hurt as to perish, thank the Lord Jesus. And, talking of Him, there are sacraments for the asking. Send for a Reverend Mr Tomkins, once minor clerk to his Grace himself and fully licensed to cure you souls. Another thing; may I politely suggest that those among you who have the strength to do so, might care to go to the heads. The less the shitten the fairer a deck you know. Farewell now. Call me if you need anything.'

Three days later – I think.

Although stoutly anchored, the *Umbrios* has a kite-ish way of climbing high and then falling back. It mounts a water-wall and then plunges into a well. We rise and crash and are never still, never firm. But with so little in our bellies, we are more dislocated than bilious, which is a type of mercy. We are beginning to sling rope-beds from the ceiling for those who are most threatened by instability. And I have managed to crawl to the forepeak, where they usually keep the spares, to find all kinds of stuff, deadeyes, spars, parrels, axel-spokes, lots of nettle-rope, etc. and have organised a party to carry them down to the orlop for splints.

We do for each other. An officer with a crushed thigh splinted

218

my arm and I laid his leg safely in a cage of spars. Each of us howled like dogs. After which I decided to leave this putrid hole for a cupboard I had emptied by the forepeak. Mariner, who had returned, saw me dragging my baggage to the ladder and demurred. I would be cold. He was in charge. I must stay where I had been put. What if we all picked and choosed? I took no notice. Having only just enough strength and one hand to climb the ladder, I ordered him to bring my goods after me. and so I have escaped certain disease. I lined the cupboard with my cloak and I lie like a curiosity in a cabinet with pure air cutting into me. Let me perish from exposure, not suffocation. My two hearts race, with my arm getting in the most beats. But my hand is numbing nicely. I relish the smack and flap of an unsecured sail and the shriek of the gulls as they glut our slops. When Mariner does his meal-round, he stops when he reaches my windy box and tells the dolers-out of skilly, 'One here.'

Another day of Rhé

George has sent his band to cheer us up. Lutes, rebecks, a drum and a singer. They are required to play in concert on each deck in turn, which they do all the morning. They wear his livery, and have flowing curls. We interrupt their tunes to hear their news, as they have come from the flagship. It is incredible news. In spite of our being massacred, first at the star-fort and then as we felt the island, in spite of us now being unprovisioned, unpaid, unfit and expecting to go home, we are told by these musicians, and with some astonishment at our defeatism, that the Lord Duke has contrary plans for us. That he sits at this moment surrounded by spread maps and charts planning to invade - France. Another army is on the way, so is money. So is his Majesty's trust in the Duke of Buckingham. As I listen to this, the absurd features of poor old Colonel Mathers roll into my recollection, just as I witnessed them roll at my feet when, grinning like a boy who has climbed to the top of the apple-tree, he simply offered himself to one of Saladin's pruners. Down came Mathers's silly head, bump, bump, bump, bravely smiling from rung to rung, gallantly smiling in the ditch. But the rest of him gripped his parapet, and had to be pushed off.

Whether we rush the beaches of the Vendee, whether we make the gleaned fields of Charente Maritime or the Biscay coast of the Gironde, we must all be cut down – a late harvest for the sickleman Richelieu. George's musicians protest. We have not understood. Reinforcements are on the way. So is cash. So are weapons, food-ships, clothes-ships, horse-ships. And – what did we think – a special ship carrying all the glory by way of suits, jewels, furniture, etc. our Duke would require for receiving the beaten princes of Catholic Europe.

A youth with a half shot-away arse leans up to enquire of the musicians whether they know this one? He sings with a piercingly beautiful voice a Strand-song which has been going about the fleet in the strange journeying manner of such ditties which, once sung, are on everyone's lips, the wide seas no silencers. The song is called 'Welcome home, George'.

> And are you returned again, with all your faults,
> Great Commander of the All-go-naughts?
> And left the Isle behind you – what's the matter?
> Did winter make your chaps begin to chatter?
> Could not the surging and distempered seas
> Your queasy stomach, George, with sweetness please?
> Or did you hasten headlong to prevent
> A fruitless hope of needful parliament?
> The Frenchmen beat you, and you ran away.
> Can this be true? Could not your glorious boasts
> Before your going, fright them from their coasts?
> But is the Duke come safely home again,
> Triumphing o'er his conquered countrymen?
> Leave, upstart greatness, ere it be too late;
> Submit yourself, be governed by the State ...

Dozens more verses. Scribblers of such stuff never know when to stop. But a threatening air. Get it out of your head if you can.

What date?

We retreat. The high enterprise is on the turn. This is no Cadiz rout but a rich funeral with sails. How many dead – four – five – six thousand? Among them great men gone, Burroughs, Brett, and poor Billy Heydon who got drowned stepping onto Rhé. All are left behind. A few score bodies which have been washed out of their clothes and weightings are in naked pursuit, face-first in the water. Their pure white limbs plunge in the wake of our squadron in particular, the *Umbrios* being the wooden cliff from which we threw them. I doubt if we would recognise any of them even if they could look up. Sodden, shining creatures with all the sickness laved from them with seaweed hair and starfish hands, and with here and there a big clean cut.

The *Triumph* appears no less triumphant as she heads for Portsmouth. We are bound to admit that she remains a lovely sight. As a fleet we are intact. The Duke has brought his expensive navy home with not so much as a scratch. Nor has his expedition broken the exchequer because what it cost has simply not arrived. As for the five-six thousand casualties, well who is counting? Not admirals and generals. Did Alexander count? Did King Harry? Of course not. When this kind of counting starts – goodbye the gospel according to Mars. We shall return to re-plan, re-stock, to show to King and Parliament that there is always another day. Rumours from the flagship are of the Duke in good spirits. The only deep water which he has to steer through at this moment is that of the Atlantic Ocean. They say he has the charts out and is busy drawing lines for next year's argosy.

A day later.

I am woken by (a) the peace of my wound, which is saying nothing, and (b) a hullooing to starboard as a drowned man turns lazily onto his back, and it is Finch the weaver, eyes, teeth and legs wide open, and a bird of some unknown breed riding on his genitals. 'Come away,' recommends Mariner. The formless sea reminds me of Ovid homesick on the Euxine shore and the first line of *Metamorphosis* – 'I intend to tell of bodies which have been changed into bodies of another kind.' I've forgotten quite how Mr Golding put it, but it was fairly scientifically. Better than Genesis. In one of the tales a ship's crew jumps overboard and turns into seahorses with spouting nostrils, and horny spines. Finch the weaver bobs about. 'Finch, my agony has gone. It was just my arm, you know.' Many pages gone into the sea.

221

Fragment:

We are reaching the end. I have been strolling the pestiferous decks to tell the sick about disembarkment. Some trembled with weakness and delight. Others were morose. At noon I found myself by the mainmast pondering the incompetence and the illegality of the Duke. How he does what only the Anointed may do. This is where our disaster has crept in, like bilgewater through a crevasse. The most ignorant aboard knows this much. They ask, 'How can the Duke be the King?' Did God give him leave to do what he has done – is doing? Could his Majesty? The answers are No. A king cannot give away any part of his anointed self. King James knew this but does King Charles? Such talk is all the rage with us at this moment. It breaks off when I or any other gentleman appears and resumes when we are out of hearing. And we suspend it when our servants enter. It is rumoured that there has not been such universal disquiet since the Bishop of Rome laid his ban on us eighty years ago. This isn't treason-talk, it is really a popular debate about blasphemy. The Duke is not treasonable – so is he blasphemous? What is happening puts me in mind of the woman who dared to touch the hem of the Saviour's coat, causing the strength to drain from Him. Buckingham has *borrowed* the coat. He is turning this way and that crying, 'See how it fits me!' there's the blasphemy. And the little King so drained of energy that he has closed himself up with his pictures. When he reaches Whitehall, succubus George will stride past the Rubenses to plant a kiss on the King's neck, drawing yet further powers from him.

Portsmouth glimmers through the fogs. Contrary to what is said of them, great harbours are not in themselves welcoming. This one is so crowded with shipping already that from this distance it looks impossible for it to accommodate us. We smell sullenness. The very size of our fleet is the dimension of its failure. The *Triumph* flagship is bedecked with silks and is braving it out. The Duke's musicians even play and charming songs hang in the air. The pest-ship *Umbrios*, however, is even more shadowy at this moment than its name. She sways and slops.

Those with permission to walk away – and who have the

222

strength to – are noisily stating their destinations. From top to bottom one hears nothing but towns and counties, and in these spoken maps a touching love for these places. This is sure to die when the speaker limps into his parish. I have seen it all too often. Many will not get that far and will die in a ditch, to be grudged grave-space in the nearest churchyard. But how we all long for the land! I shall do what I did after Cadiz, buy a horse, find a man and mount for him, and make my way home. I am lucky, having a wound to show. I may hack by the by-roads. They won't be impassable as yet and I won't have to respond to all the questioning which one gets on a highway. Should I be asked, I shall say that I wasn't there.

'Where, sir, Rhé? No, sir, I am a gentleman setting east to Suffolk.'

Mariner and his gang are checking to see that nobody is getting away with ship's gear. I have just managed to stop him unstrapping splints and seizing cripples' sticks in his zeal for honesty.

'They are the Lord High Admiral's property, Mr Felton. You cannot deny it. I am only doing my duty.'

'His Grace would not wish it, Mariner.'

Give George his due. For a martial-man he has some odd tenderness. I observed how less moved he was by casual death than by casual woundings. How his mind writes-off the lifeless in a way which does not allow them to trouble him. But his own inexplicable bouts of illness seem to make him one with any sufferer. His eyes would fill with fear and warmth by any sickbed. He would have no wounded aboard the *Triumph*; his constitution could not have stood it. They say he asked continually after the *Umbrios*, his special Ship of Wounds, and that he had chosen Mariner especially as chief carer because he had heard that he had been a man-midwife, and would thus be experienced in pain and blood. There was not one instance of gratitude on our ship for anything the Duke had done, only sheer hatred.

14

THE REMONSTRANCE

It is always a temptation where contemporaries are concerned to see two lives running side by side from beginning to end and touching at every salient point. To be accurate, the lives of George Villiers and John Felton were close together at Blois and Angers, but never again. When we heard each other's names spoken at Cadiz and Rhé, we heard what cannot continue – student talk. The Duke was not above flinging me a grin during the landings at Rhé. It was a brief smile which said, 'That is all. Expect no more.' At the moment his name is filth. I never thought I would live to hear it so soiled. It is on everyone's lips, but disgustingly glued to them like an unsuccessfully spat-out fly. We are August children, born in heat and stagnation, the very last Elizabethans, Virgo boys, country gentlemen on the make, military incompetents the pair of us. His fate and mine only came into conjunction, as Wemyss would have said, when I was kept waiting in a Holborn printers. Desperate for a read (it was over two hours since I had turned a page), I picked out one of those debates which the parliament-men are increasingly fond of having set up in type. Who would read such stuff if there was an essay lying about?

'May I?'

Bookseller Willoughby gestured with inky hands.

I read *A Remonstrance*, skipping the preamble, then, realising the importance of every word, going back to it. I leaned against the wall, I sank to a stool, I stopped hearing the printing-press. I read the accusation, this 'grievance of grievances', this passionate appeal for the King to sack the Duke. I could hear John Eliot's voice, clear as a fast stream, rising up from the smudgy letters, and via him I could hear remonstrating England. Ganymede was calling himself Jupiter and the unnaturalness of it, not to mention the expense of it, was ruining the country. As the squibs said,

> The King loves you, you him,
> Both love the same:
> You love the King, he you,
> Both Buckingham.
> Of sport, the King loves games,
> Of games, the Duke.
> Of all men – you – and you
> Solely for your looks.

If George was not born to reign, I was not born to kill. Yet each of us had grown up to be the changelings which we are, he the Duke, myself the Lieutenant with the knife. On an August morning in Holborn, a remonstrance became an injunction.

'I never noticed you reading it, sir,' remarked old Willoughby, taking it from me and returning it to the pile. 'They will get that pretty Sodom man – you'll see!'

He glanced round his shop. His was still a chancy business even if he had got to sixty without paying ear-rent. His apprentices sang catches and jigged type. Deserting soldiers and mutinous sailors collected beneath the eaves to join in. They sang of love. The fishwomen screamed, 'Fish!' and the salt-lad hollered 'Salt!' The normality was appalling. I could hear John Eliot saying, 'So we have come to this. You, myself, Mr Villiers and the dancer.' Sorrow gripped me. This is what contemporaneity means, some ultimate involvement.

'When?' I asked.

'When what?' said Willoughby.

'Mr Willoughby, you know the world, has it escaped you that there are men who would sooner have a read than a woman? It is something I had to disguise in the officers' mess. Messes, Mr Willoughby, are dinner-rooms where a man's singularities are better paraded than hid. It is an impoliteness among soldiers to be lost in a book. When they try me and have to dredge up the worst to be said about me, and come to my reading, it will be, "Ah, chronic reading, did I hear you say? H.D.Q. for that". But by then, Mr Willoughby, I shall be longing to get on with the metamorphorical business, agonising though it will be. Do you think it was painless for the naiad to become the damsel, and the damsel to become the dragonfly, and the dragonfly to become cuckoo food?'

'Bloody poets,' said the printer.

Apparently – various hints and rumours I had heard were beginning to add up to make sense – the parliament-men had gone in a body to the Court to tell his Majesty what they intended to do. He was genuinely amazed. More amazed than furious. He clopped up and down before them on his tall heels and beating the floorboards with his walking-stick like a stage-master.

'*Remonstrate*? Against what? Against whom?'

The Duke then came in and produced more theatre by falling at the King's feet and looking up at him, Steenie-fashion. His Majesty pulled him up, using all his strength, with the Duke still kissing his fingers. The pair then faced the parliament-men, their complexions discoloured by their exertions, and panting. The King then burst out.

'He is raised too high – is that what you tell me? Then watch, I raise him all over again, my chief servant, my dear friend. Return, sirs, to your rancorous Chambers to thank the Lord Jesus for such a patriot.'

That night a mob went to Whitehall to chant,

> *Who rules the Kingdom? The King!*
> *Who rules the King? The Duke! !*
> *Who rules the Duke? The Devil! ! !*

Untrue this last. Which in a way was a pity. I could have put down evil without a qualm.

Whenever I read history I am struck by the lineage of persuasion. To give an up-to-date example. Sir John Eliot was persuaded by Sir Walter Raleigh's *History of the World* to persuade England by his Remonstrance. They say that Sir Walter was persuaded by all the authors who ever lived, for, like myself, he glutted on pages. It has always been my belief that when an idea arrives in style on the page, the die is cast for taking steps for bringing it about. Readers are not supposed to be men of action; it is against the rules of the un-read's game. Who persuades *them*? Men with banners, men with shouts. Men without a decent paragraph to their name, you may be sure. George read little beyond his own honours' list, which was a long enough tale. He liked lists and headings. They said that when Gerbier the house-furnisher fitted-up his palaces, George would be found browsing through the lists of what had been hung on his walls and rarely at the paintings. So unlike his Majesty, who must not be disturbed at prayer or before a Carracci. For us book-eaters, George was a marvel of self-persuasion. How has it happened that we, people, government, King and all, were led into treaties, wars and penuries by this lovely ignoramus in a silver suit?

I had walked into Willoughby's as some might walk into a tavern or a stew because of my tongue, or something, was hanging out for, in my case, a good read. Willoughby was used to us word-fanciers and would print away with us cluttering-up his space. Now and then he would snatch a galley from our hands with a 'Secret List, if you don't mind, sir!' It was a constant amusement among us that the Government had to pass most of its banned material through Willoughby's shop before putting it under lock and key on the Rolls shelves. All Willoughby's dirty boys were wicked readers, ripping through the prints of the day with their keen interest in pretty-well everything. He directed them with little sharp smacks and 'Get ons'. Willoughby himself read only to print. He had made a fine job of the *Remonstrance* and had himself chosen its top and tail woodcuts. These depicted the prophet Jeremiah's remonstance to King Jehoiakim being burnt before that majesty page by page by his favourite Jehudi.

> Now the king sat in the winter-house in the ninth month and there was a fire on the heath ... and it came to pass, that when Jehudi had read three or four leaves, he cut it with a penknife, and cast it into the fire ... until all the roll was consumed ...

When I read between these pictures that the cause of all the troubles that now beset our beloved country was 'the excessive power of the Duke of Buckingham, and the abuse of that power', I thought, 'Poor George, your dancing days are darkening.'

I shall not convince the ancient on the bench, nor anyone alive now or later, that there was anything personal in what I did. In fact I was persuaded by Sir John Eliot not to step back from the public fray into private happiness. I was in the Low House when he asked,

'Shall we forsake that sweetness? Shall we neglect that fatness of our peace, as the fig and olive did of old, for the public use and service? Yes! No difficulties may retard us, no troubles may direct us, no exception is admitted to this rule: but where the greater good is extant, the duty and the office there is absolute, without caution or respect. No danger or hazard may deter us. The duty and the office stand entire.'

It was this last sentence, and then discovering what had been spoken brought into the glorious authority of print, which sentenced George. As I read it, I reeled against the press, to be slapped off it by Willoughby and the galley torn from me. I saw George in the *place* at Angers, kicking a ball by the fountain, and the sun burning down. We two summer men – and now our last August! We two with a month to go, for he was already at Portsmouth, Rochelle-bound for the second time. We must need leave on the same tide for what I must do. We had come into summer together and would go out into the dark together. As Raleigh said, death would cover us 'all over with these two narrow words, *Hic Jacet.*' For I was convinced that Felton blood with its tricklings from Plantagenet and Capet springs would in the brief carnage bleed into Buckingham's bran-new quarterings. In less time than it took to hang a wet broadsheet on the line, I was telling myself, 'A month, a month!'

Outside all was as usual. Mares swigged from Holborn brook. Bells crashed. Women traded. The sun was delightful. Children paddled in the Fleet, their legs orange from tanneries' effluent. Thatchers were busy above, preparing lasts for the new harvest straw. The Lord Mayor passed by in pompous procession and was jeered. People smiled, frowned. Dust rose in clouds. I could smell the bakers' ovens. The scent of late haymaking drifted into town from the Surrey meadows. The jakes stank. London in August. Who would take deep breaths then? Only those who knew their breathing time was brief. I opened my mouth and drank August in. It tasted Arabic. The streets were filled with the lesser kind. It was August and the Court was in Hampshire to say Godspeed to the army. The clergy were hiding in orchards. Which only left the Londoners, and they were like boys out of school, or mice when the cat is away, sunburnt and hardly able to believe their luck. Make the most of it, poor peoples. Deserters from George's cause, sea-soldiers, landsmen, will soon arrive to burn his house down, and eat up everything you've got. Lock your doors, conceal your wives. Enjoy the Bethnal meadows before they become squatting grounds for malcontents with tarry arses.

* * *

It was when I was walking up Cornhill that a remarkable things occurred to me. I had to take leave of my life. I was the wrong end of town for this. But a voice inside me said, 'Say your goodbyes now, John, then you will be finished with it. You will find it such a help later on.' They were sweeping the granaries and flour barns, making them ready for the first corn-carts from Middlesex, and painting the steelyards blue. I can remember the exact moment, the hot afternoon being deliciously stroked by zephires and a labourer on a ladder singing 'The willing one' ('She was the willing one who ... etc.') I noted, as if by a necessity, that drapers were lugging bolts of cloth towards Candlewick Street and that young men were setting up a quintain on the rough ground where the wagons turn, and that martins' heads were hanging out of their nests in a cornice. I strolled to the maypole by St Andrew's and placed my good hand on its warm shaft. I could see the Tower and the river. The last time I had stood on this spot was with mother. It was St John's eve and I had brought her to see the lamps and cascades of St John's Wort, fennel and birch branches which hung from every lintel.

'Resign your ccommission,' she had advised for the hundredth time. 'Come back to Clare with me. You have some books. We have some fields. Your arm is your honourable discharge.' Her Durham directness. She was drably dressed as a goodwoman but her rank showed. Midsummer London with the Court in residence. I had taken her to St Mary Axe because it was also dedicated to an Ursula (and eleven thousand other virgins), only to find that it had become a warehouse with a pump where the altar was. Mother

229

had approved. The church was being useful for a change.

I swung round the maypole with my good hand. Farewell, virgins' shed! Farewell, roaring boys and bonfires! Farewell, hunting-grounds and pismires! Farewell, little hungry London birds! Farewell, Tower, should it come to that, and myself all out of joint. Except it won't. It will be, 'After the outrage, the loyal crowd seized the culprit and tore him to pieces'. There is no more justified a laying-on of hands than those on an assassin. This a Persian word for a murderer who drugs himself with hemp before pursuing his victim.

I wished that mother was still in London. That she was waiting for me off Fleet Street in the lodgings. She would have been writing her endless directions to the land agent, to her steward, to the tenants, who couldn't read them. Cut this, pickle that. Collect all. Take heed. See, I come quickly! Lots of threats and orders. She would unwrap my arm and entice some feeling into it by drawing her fingers down heavily from shoulder to wrist, causing a dull ache to be a lively throb, and me to cry out.

'Am I hurting,'

She hopes so, for pain is a sign of life. She would bathe me with a cloth as she did in the courtyard when I was a child, holding my hair up to get at my neck, then dry me with pats. Rough, kind, northcountry lady.

'Am I hurting?'

It satisfied her that I had no bullet or cutlass hole, only a bicep like a bursting plum and an elbow like an ivory knob. So many of us are armour-marked. It is not a valorous wound. It is difficult to dress it myself, so I leave it be. Out of sight, and often out of mind. Neglect is my pain-killer.

So goodbye, my Ursula, goodbye, St Dunstan's and Dr Donne's bell. Goodbye, that girl from Foxearth, even if it never came to much. Goodbye, the Spanish lad who had the grace to weep. Madame von Hol and astral Wemyss, your partings shall not be on this list.

'Saint Ursula and eleven thousand virgins,' remarked mother. 'What ever had got into those silly women?'

From the St Andrew's maypole I wandered aimlessly. Knowing how little time I had left gave me all the time in the world. Reaching Tower Hill, I found a cutlas and purchased a tenpenny knife.

15

NEMESIS ON THE
OLD PORTSMOUTH ROAD

The Journal of my walk to Portsmouth

I am writing it on the paper which Willoughby allowed me. It was generous of him. Last night I managed to make a sheath for the knife and hang it above my right hip. One-handed Jack. Went to the Fleet creek before it was quite dark and washed all over. Others doing the same, pallid sticks in the gloaming. A little over three shillings left of mother's gift. The army must owe me hundreds. Forget this. Eke out what you have. Bread and spring-water should carry you to him. Use the knife to slice off three strips of paper, two to fit into my hat like concealed crowns and one to leave in St Dunstan's for Doctor Donne. Viz:

Hat one. 'That man is cowardly and base, and deserveth not the name of a gentleman or soldier, that is not willing to sacrifice his life for the honour of his God, his King and his Country.' From the immortal *Golden Epistles*.

Hat two. 'Let no man commend me for doing it, but rather discommend themselves as the cause of it. For if God had not taken away our hearts for our sins, he would not have gone so long unpunished. John Felton.' John with the long J which Mr Golding insisted. 'A flourish to a name, boy!'

For Doctor Donne: 'Sir, next Sunday pray you for one who was disordered and discontented of mind. Do you pray for departed men, sir? Pray for me, now dead, and who died in confusion.'

231

I have put my necessities in the bag which mother left behind. It has our arms and E for Eleanor, her font name. It was Mrs Golding who called her Ursula 'like me'. She said it would make a change – and it did! Packed *Golden Epistles* at the bottom, but very heavy. I must carry their weight. Who will find you, fat book? I shall wear soldier's dress and be inconspicuous among the laggards shuffling to Hampshire for Rhé the second. I shall be saluted. It will be the usual favour-seeking. 'Can I thieve you a horse, sir?' I shall answer, 'Please do not trouble yourself. It is such nice weather. I prefer to walk.' The dagger pricks. I must tie it a little higher.

Tuesday 19th August

So yesterday was the feast of Colchester Helen and it is just over a week to George's birthday. The great formularies of the skies are in motion. What is La Rochelle to Mars? Two eggs for breakfast. Set off at dayspring. Walked forth. The sun shot up above the houses when I crossed the river to Southwark. Farewell prison-land! Clink, Marshalsea, King's Bench, Compter, it is not you who will confine me. The smell of gaol-country. Goodbye, Olave Street whores. I salute your tolerant stews, your stag-bags and enticers, but don't move. It isn't nearly time for you to get up, birds of the night-shift. This was the kind of stuff I was humming when I was on the bridge. I saw the Thames sulking along between the cracks. I thought that the knife would only have to tumble through one of them to entirely disappear, and for me to stroll towards Surrey for a holiday. But my sheath held. The blade will be warmed by my breast when it enters his. What an errand! I kept to the river till Kingston, where I am writing this. I am not tired but the journey will do for the first day.

Expenses nil. Green apples and ripe blackberries, and a cake from a goodwoman. It is an oppressive late afternoon. Hammersmith and Richmond were full of plague-doors and keep-away signs but I have seen these warnings before where armies are mustering. These are the dreaded pestilence, not bodily afflictions. I saw two young brothers standing like Eden seraphims before their uncut corn, guarding it with pitchforks against locust troops. All the orchard fruit has gone, ripe or not.

Fowls and other stock are locked in barns and cottages until the Duke sails. Hammersmith village is a woebegone place, very rotten and wasted. Thames-bank land all dry as a desert. Saw corpses in a ditch. The gallows busy at Richmond. Saw a state-barge with silk flags and a lutenist, and a lady under a canopy. She was beating the midges away. Feel well. Not a bit weary. Could go on. May God have mercy on me. Everywhere is so silent. England has lost its voice. Its tongue has been torn from it. Speak to me, blessed land, speak to me.

Wednesday 20th August

Slept in a hayshed two miles out of Kingston. Persisting scent of scythed flowers in the hay. Soft grey cobwebs. Mice chasing through them. The soft peace of field-dust. The mice touch me delicately, face and hands. The smell of meals from the evening hearths made me hungry. A barn-owl soared in and out, terrifying the mice. I took off my uniform to keep it uncreased and lay in my shirt. Before this I prayed to Christ for forgiveness – meaning understanding. Surely He must understand? He who cleansed the Temple? I could not walk on wearing the knife, it scratched against my heart in spite of it being on the right side. I wrapped it in butter-bur leaves and tucked it under my book.

A bad night. Should I tell it? I was in the holy house at Arnhem. So was Wemyss, so were we all. A thousand mice animated the tapestries and a piper skirled. The Lord was in his chair by a fine roast. Wemyss debated the Milky Way with him. The servants jigged to a psalm, smacking their palms together and twizzling giddily. The room reeked of hay and Doctor von Hol rose out of the floor smothered in grave-clothes which became cobwebs. His hand-bones still hung together but were fleshless. They clinked when he took the servant-girls' chins in his fingers, chucking them, poking into their corsets. 'Won't you give me some of your flesh?' he was asking each of them in turn. They shrieked when he touched them, calling on their Saviour to protect them. I waited for Beatrix to come in and restore the goodness.

But when she entered it was as the great Trull of the north whose appetites were on display. She advanced nakedly and was not at all the white wand girl of the Dutch skirts. She was a female from one of Mr Rubens's canvasses, all a-sag and mighty in her flesh. Below her belly flared the burning bush, the sight of which was blinding. So we all hid our eyes. I saw it through my fingers as she strode towards me, arms outstretched, my name on her mouth, and I recognised her brother's mop of ginger Scotch hair. I ran and would have drowned in the Arnhem canal if I had not woke up. Even so I was soaked. The hayshed mice which had gained shelter in my armpit woke too and fled perpendicularly up the wall. I beseeched them to return. Tremulous animals whose mouse-breath joins human-breath in every bedchamber of the kingdom, I would do you no harm. My heats subsided but minus the usual shame. Some lines from a play which Wemyss remembered hardened my purpose. I should know who wrote them:

> How easily might some slave be suborned
> To greet his lordship with a poniard,
> And none so much as blame the murderer,
> But rather praise him for that brave attempt,
> And in the Chronicle enrole his name
> For purging of the realm of such a plague

I fetched out the cheap knife and examined it. It has a long handle. Rose and took to the Godalming road.

Thursday 21st August

Walked on from Godalming because it was full of angry sailors marching on London where (they were yelling) they would burn down the bloody Duke's houses – all of them! I heard that they had received no pay for a year and had mutinied. They jeered me as I passed in my lieutenant's hat and swept me fancy bows. 'Hurry, hurry, fool! Don't keep the Lord High Admiral waiting.'

The sandy soils of Surrey. Not a berry on a hedge and the orchards stripped. Rabbit skins and charred sticks where meals have been eaten. A dead child. I carried her into the bracken and washed my hands in a brook. Light as a plover. Thought her braids might fall off. Walked on. Spent a shilling on fresh bread and some carved meat. Thought 'enough for tomorrow, my last

234

full day on earth.' My arm-ache has run into my legs, so I ache evenly. It could be the army potholes and cart-ruts. Made me think of Parmenter's description of the ploughman's lolloping progress, one foot on the level, one foot in the 'furrer'.

Hung about in the back lanes of a village until it was dark then made a bed in the church porch. Sheep munching the grave-hummocks all night and something clattering now and then in the nave. Door barred. Because of the troops, I suppose. No nightmare. No pain either. Having run into my leg from my arm, it seems to have run out through my. toes and away. Pain is a strange thing. Very capricious. Also, once gone it cannot be remembered. A sexton arrived at dawn and started to dig. He nodded at the porch and said, 'It makes a decent sleeping-room; I have used it myself.'

I say – to test him – 'Have you heard of the Duke of Buckingham?'

He spat.

I continued, playing the gentleman's part, that I supposed spittle was not treason?

He dug. Grave-dirt flew around. Was it for the girl? Watching me eating the bread, he brought across a morsel of cheese. Poor men share. I had a sudden crazy impulse to confess to him, as one would to a papist priest. I beat it down. Instead, I drew him out on parish matters.

'You don't know where you are, do you stranger? Witley, stranger, is where you might settle, had you a mind to. Did the church rattle disturb you? Some say it is a fiend, others a loose catch. I cannot myself say what it is. Finished, have you? Then you had best be on your way for what you must do.'

I was paralysed.

'For what I must do?'

'Your soldier's task, sir.'

'You puzzle me, sexton.'

'In that case I will have done my task for today.'

'You are a philosopher, sir.'

Although not much further down than grass-roots, his spade was smashing skulls. He looked up, 'You will have witnessed our birds, sir. We have beautiful birds in Surrey.'

Walked on.

Friday 22nd August

As Portsmouth via Petersfield can be only twenty miles, I was correct to reckon this my final full day on God's earth. George's too. We shall depart in violence and together. Let us claim soldiers' deaths. Let us each die for our country's sake. Let my blow be one struck in battle. Let his fall be sacrificial. Knelt by the wayside and begged God to attend to the decencies of tomorrow – begged Him above all things not to allow England to see George as a pricked tumour when the tenpenny knife lets out the breath. 'Let him give his life for his King', as the saying goes. Me too. Let the pair of us do proxy for whole armies. Felt better after this intercession. Felt that I had exorcised 'assassination'. Felt much relieved.

Heavy traffic from Petersfield on. Hundreds of carts and milling people. Whore-camps all along the highway. Trumpets calling. I swung through it all at a good pace, returning salutes and knowing that I was inconspicious. Was handed plumes for my hat and would have visited a shag-tent were it not for meeting Jesus on the morrow. Instead, read from my *Golden Epistles* for the last time, kissing the page. Seeing Mr Golding's hand made me cry. Seeing that it was a book which was so evidently not in the best style made me love it the more. It had never left me since I left Ovington. After tomorrow they would read into it what it did not contain. I had read from it to George when we were in Blois – I've forgotten which bit. 'It's no good, old friend, I can't take it in. Tell me a story instead.' Eliot and I took turns to tell him stories, the taller the better. 'When are you going to grow up, Villiers?' The lunatic brother sprawling in a stupor by his side and George pacifying his interruptions. 'Book', I said, 'shall I bury you by this sycamore near the turning to Southwick? Shall we all three, the Duke, you, myself, all go under the earth together this August weekend?' The *Golden Epistles* made no reply. I replaced them in the bag. A closed book.

Magnetised by the pull of the road towards Southwick, where the Court lay. Every inch of the ground covered with tents, carts, beasts, equipment. Saw the eighteen wagons which had brought the Duke's tapestries, plate and clothes from Whitehall. Silver hubs to the wheels. This second expedition is designed to irradicate the disaster of the first. The belief is that it cannot fail. The money and supplies are at Portsmouth, which they certainly were not last year. The Duke has been making a show of being positive and himself saw to the hanging of some malcontents. They say – the town is all talk – that he is cock-a-hoop and that all his beauty is back after the defeats which ravaged it. Needing to know where he is, I made open enquiry. 'At the Greyhound.'

At the Greyhound.

'And his Majesty?'

At Southwick big-house.

Late August shadows. Seabirds. Saw some officers dining in a meadow and sat with them. Food passed to me without questions. Familiar mess talk. Except, 'where is your baggage, sir?' and a slurred reply which raised no further enquiry. I am alone now with several hundred men lying in a summer field, newly cut. We each stamped down the stubble where we were to lie, then spread a cloak. It is warm without humidity, and light enough to write. Some gentlemen are writing last letters to their wives and sweethearts. A youth comes to beg a letter to his mother who lives in Winchester. A carrier is to go there after we have sailed. We! 'What shall I put, sir?' 'Put that I am her dear son, sir, and that she must pray Jesu that I will come home again. And that – if it is not too much for the paper and your hand – that she will do well to care for Graceful the dog.'

'Shall you make a mark or shall I put your name?'

'Philemon – a name taken out of Scripture, your honour.'

'God keep you, pikeman.'

My final exchange. Cannot sleep. The dreadfulness ahead. I fight to block out wicked analogies such as Gethsemane but now I know a fragment of His passion. Idiot thoughts chase each other. They will hurt my arm – such thoughts. They will hurt me wholly, that is what they will do. It should be fast. Quick. There will be a stillness when the Duke falls, then a turning upon me, then the stamping of me out. Then a stillness again. 'It was all over in seconds, sire' – to the King I had widowed. A madman, of course. When necessary, the patriot may kill thousands to save his country, the assassin one. Still wide awake at midnight, I got up to look for a church, only to discover that at Southwick busy with some Arminian vigil which required blazing altars. It was packed with the Court and local gentlemen. Clergy in golden vestments were requiring from God victory, no less. So I hid in elders by the tower, smelling their virulent greenness and feeling their cool plates of fruit, taking them in my hands as I once did at Belchamp. I muddled my way through a Peter's Day psalm, the one which goes,

> Blessed be the Lord my strength, which teacheth my hands to war and my fingers to fight, my hope, my fortress, my castle and my deliverer ... Man is like a thing of naught, his time passeth away like a shadow ... Send down thine hand from above, deliver me ... take me out of great waters and from the hand of strange children ... and I will sing praises to thee upon a ten-stringed lute.

Going up to the big-house earlier must have put this in mind. There was the King in the open air, sitting on a terrace listening to music. Great people stood around him but not the Duke. The gardens echoed with the calling of night-birds and were hung with lanterns. His Majesty was dressed in pink, silver and black. He sat forward in a state chair several times too large for him, now and then shifting for comfort. His eyes shone in the lamps. Tomorrow – O poor King! Tomorrow – rejoicing England! The King insists on absolute silence before musicians, so the company stood like statues. The musicians were five viols, a small organ on a dais and a theorbo in consort. The theorbo sported ribbons. Harmony and gravitas. Waited until the King went in and the music stopped. I bowed to him in the darkness. O poor King! Watched his light moving from room to room as he passed to bed. Watched the musicians pack up and the frozen audience stroll away. Heard nightingales taking over and water splashing. Distant brawling.

I would not be scribbling all this if I could sleep. My soul fleeth unto the Lord, before the morning watch, I say, before the morning watch ... Catch at it, Wemyss, should it lose direction you won't mind being second best.

* * *

Tower-bird Wren, am I back so soon to you? Is there a space for Disappointments among your records. If not, make one. Every confessor of the deed itself will let you down. Better go for the eye-witness. The murderer with the knife has only a partial view of what he is doing and this is instantly filmed over in the subsequent chaos. To be honest, I should know far more about what happened after breakfast at the Greyhound if you would give me your version of the business. For by now you will have shelved scores of 'I was there' statements. I was there, though in no position to watch what was happening. So you must not take my version as the authentic one – not of the stroke itself. But what came before and after it is fairly trustworthy. I was pretty lucid then. To be candid, my own expectation of death so over-powered me that I had constantly to force myself to remember *his*. Some fear had gone. The cutting me down, the head blows, the kicking me to shreds, the wild butchery had become as nothing to the actual *piteousness* of dying, of being no more. There was a second after the killing when nothing sustained me and yet, looking back, I don't doubt that the Lord Jesus and His star-minder Wemyss were in catchment together. Boys ask men what it is like to slay the enemy in battle, and are put off - so the children think – with a 'I don't know, son.' But they *don't* know. When the executioner comes for John Felton, no one will come for him. He will kill me with no danger to himself, and so he will be able to see what he is doing from first to last, not being clouded in his own dying. Mr Golding, my eminent schoolmaster, you know, said that since few of us can do other wise, we should be egotistical about our own death and let it eclipse all others, even those of the saints and great men (he would have meant poets) when we bring ourselves to think about it. But walking up Portsmouth High Street on St Bartholomew's eve, as it happened, diminished my death. The manner of it rather than the matter of it was what preoccupied me. When I pressed my way into the Greyhound Inn, into the reek of soldiers and breakfast beer, I had all but forgotten the Duke of Buckingham's imminent departure, so dreadful was the thought of the way in which I would go minutes after him.

It had been my habit to concentrate on Wemyss when things were bad, to speak to him in my heart. 'Wemyss,' I said silently in the uproar, 'Wemyss, I am at this moment reminded of what you once told me about Tycho's star, the one by which he proved that the firmament was in perpetual change, and not fixed for ever as Aristotle declared. How Tycho had made a lense through which could be seen a star beyond the Casiopeian moon which until then was accepted as the Ultima Thule of the heavens. "Go beyond the known order, Felton," you used to insist. "There is always something further on."' The trouble with George was that he had always thought of himself as the ultimate limit, that there could be no going beyond him.

Tower-bird Wren, allow me to call you a Tycho of sorts, always wanting to go beyond what is called 'confession'. You actually want to *know* how I could have done it, not just did it. This is your interest in me. The people cry, 'Hero! Saviour!' but you ask with true curiosity, 'How could you find the efficiency to slaughter with a single blow, not the Duke, but an old college friend as he danced? Was it because he had climbed so high out of reach of your love? Was that it?' I know you, Wren, you are an explorer, not a bureaucrat, a nosy-parker of the soul. Have you left a space for Disappointment? Killers themselves will often let you down – better go for the eye-witness. They have nothing else to do but look. Remember that the assassin himself can only have a partial view of the action. I thought at first that listening to your account of what happened at the Greyhound on St Bartholomew's eve, and adding to my own, that I would have a full story of a now famous crime, but apparently not. Something is still missing. Let me go back on the event step by step.

I woke about six by the town gate to recollect that it was Bartholomew-tide, which was not helpful. Assassination is not massacre. Beyond the wall the wasteland seethed as an army rose from sleep, swearing, stinking, clattering its pewter feeding-ware and weapons, defecating in the gorse. Trumpeters were tuning-up. My last morning on earth, I thought, and a regimental one like thousands of others in the Low Countries. Only this was Portsmouth, that sink. Gulls soared high above the human pollution in the purest blue. I found some inlet sea about a mile away and washed. I went back to my niche by the gate and read a portion from the *Golden Epistles* then concealed the book in some dry bracken. Now and then a man would wander past and give me an ironic salute, one of those 'We're all in it together, mate' greetings which preceed battle. I now had no need to hide the knife so I stuck it in my belt. I remember thinking – prospective murder can have all emotion wrung out of it – that I could use it for breakfast first and that it was in fact a cheap table-knife. I settled my hat after making sure that the confession was still safely sewed into my lining. I knelt and prayed as much of the eighteenth psalm as I had been able to hold in my head, petering-out when I got to 'For in thee I shall discomfort an host of men', which was good going. I strolled to the High Street feeling serene. The Greyhound Inn was to the left. It was heavily guarded. Only yesterday (I had heard) some enraged unpaid men had tried to drag the Duke from his coach. But today was different because news was rushed through to say that the seige of La Rochelle was lifted. O joy! A lie as it happened. Or possibly just a cheerful mistake. But – the *joy*! Was it fair of me to prick it, there being so little of it about? Or, alternatively, could there be a friendlier act than to end Buckingham's life when his policy proved right and his critics proved to be jealous dogs?

I glimpsed George the minute the guards let me through. He was dancing. No impeachment. Instead, possibly Prince of Tipperary, who knows! Place-seekers hustled him, the giver of all things. He must tell his Majesty. He must ride to Southwick. 'Your Highness's toilet.' I watched him disappear to a scullery, dance steps all the way, and then return, still being combed and his white shirt gaping, as if being prepared for sacrifice. Yesterday he had hanged two young men who had rocked his coach to demand pay, ridden behind them to the gibbet to see it done personally, and to canter back to the Greyhound and breakfast 'aweful in his might'. It was noted for the thousandth time how easily he took life. I would have to take his easily; it would be what he had earned. I did not believe that Rochelle was open to the Protestant armies or even if this was true that George would cease marching, sailing, 'conquering'. But I was glad that he believed it. For it allowed me to send him to hell on the crest of a wave, he who had dispatched so many. And it would allow the Parliamnt to teach the King his role. He could find it very interesting and better than anything he had imagined. English gentlemen would legislate the country. One English gentleman from Suffolk of some learning and little worth in his own eyes, would speed this fresh course. Would die for it, in fact. But I must not go on. You, Wren, want to know what occurs exactly when a man knifes an old friend.

So back to the Greyhound. Hubbub, back-slapping, breakfast smells and compliments all round. The Duke has done it! Or let us say that he has. He certainly looks the part. I sat at a side table with other officers and we were brought some bread and beer. I found myself wondering, could I see the sea from the roof? In spite of the good news, the roaring all around me was how to round-up deserters and scare mutineers. There was chat of George's lovely ship and its out of this world furnishings. It was named the *Swiftsure* and was lined with damask. The officer stared at the state of my uniform. 'Do you come from Wales, sir?' I went into the backyard or garden of sorts. It was then that the blackness which attends terrible deeds engulfed the inn. Lacuna. A missing page. Fill it with your own reportage, archivist. Make something up. When I return to the main downstairs room George, always a showy bower, is returning congratulation after congratulation, bending always a fraction lower than the person who is praising him. Men will forgive a lot of things for such sincere condescension. Colonel Fryer – I knew him slightly – does the best bow he can in a crowd and whilst he is low down and George bare-breasted still and upright, I reach across and thrust. He takes all the ten inches then pulls the knife out shouting 'Villain!' like a Southwark player. During the pandemonium I find myself in the kitchen with more knives and slaughtered animals. And here is the unlikeliest bit of the tale, when I hear my name being called, 'Felt-ooon! Felt-oooon!'. I discover later that they were actually shouting, 'Frenchman, Frenchman'. I return to the dreadful room, some obedience to God willing it. Also I had to find my hat. 'Hat, hat, where are you. Inside you is my reason, my purpose and my apology.' It lies just below George who now lies on the table. Blood continues to gush through his teeth. The knife lies near the hat and is skewing about in what it released from George's heart, when I bend to retrieve my hat something warm and rich like mulled wine pours across my hand. Picking up the knife, I find that I am not tempted to use it on myself, as is done in the best Greek tragedy. I look on George, so close and still. His eyes are wide and made of sapphire. A nipple stands up like a raspberry on the daubed

242

porcelain of his naked chest. His beauty is draining from him, leaving a kind of sack. A shoe dangles from a big toe. He looks cumbersome and ruinous, and in urgent need to be put away. Such is death in August I remember thinking.

The commotion then grows enormous, but is suddenly over-ridden with cries I never hoped to hear. A woman in her bedrobe, hair down, stands before a bannister-rail above my head. Her condition is plain to see. Her shrieks lacerate the morning. She is drowning it in her grief, in her disbelief of what she is seeing. It is George's wife. That she should be in the Greyhound astounds me. I had thought her with the King at Southwick Great House, her time being near. She raises the roof, I my well arm in some automatic gesture of regret. We are thus momentarily arrested in those attitudes which suit Greek carnage when in hurries Colonel Fryer to take hold of me, saying thoughtfully, 'I will come to your right side, sir. It will be easier for your old wound.' The screaming Duchess then half-tumbles down the stairs to her murdered husband, sees what she can no longer kiss, and faints in his blood. She lies like a range of soft hills where he had collapsed, her belly mountainous. O madam! I too should have fainted, but so many battlefields, etc. I wait to be pulled limb from limb and have spurred heels ground in my face. Many hands are indeed on me but they are pulling me from the Greyhound to Portsmouth clink. I am no sooner there than another officer turns up with my hat. The lining hangs torn and loose, the message has gone. This man studies me gravely. I rush to him in tears. 'His lady, his lady ...' He holds me. What else? They take George back to London in the King's coach for Mr V. Dyke to make a picture of him as soon as he can. The *Swiftsure* all lined with damask waits in the bay. I, as you know, Mr Archivist, am waiting for the best torturer, the best trial and the best scaffold the law can provide, and as best I can.

16

RELICS OF THE DISEASED

Tower-bird Wren who lives for information, you too will perish before you can collect all you need to know. Fill that wife of yours with chicks. Leave us with more than a file. Discover a single book which will stand the re-reading. Docketing men is sinister work, leave it to the parson.

It was suffocating in Portsmouth clink. They embalmed George in the August heat – did their best for him, I suppose. Since one hears everything in prison, I heard that Mr V. Dyke is commanded to paint him though his face falls. I heard the Fleet sail and the subsequent hollowness of the harbour. I heard that we in gaol were in clover compared with what lay outside, the foul residue of a thousand emptied billets, the plague in patches, the bawds packing-up. The Duke's last rioters still dangled from the gibbets and the stench was so bad that none could walk along the Point. My own suppuration made fitting company for all this. Let me tell you this, the assassin should not live a moment after his work is done. He should be dispatched before the world can be thankful for what he has achieved, himself put down in a mindless revulsion. Let him not have a second in which to meet with his self-loathing. Be merciful and stamp him out. Leave him bloodied and unrecognisable. Out of charity, tear him to pieces. Then wash your hands. Do not, as is being done to me, give him time to think. Dear God, who only lifted a finger against moneylenders, do not lift me from the nauseous mess of my crime. It was your prerogative to destroy the Duke of Buckingham, and I usurped it. Dear God, who knows it all, remind yourself of the assassin's nature, which is a peculiar one. Dirty necessary work which can't be celebrated. August 23rd –

kill George. This time last year he was killing half the English army on Rhé. What was his great sin? His not being qualified for anything he did. He knew how to love kings, I'll give him that. I, John, pushed him from the stage. Who qualified me to do that? At Tyburn, my Saviour, let me be turned off into oblivion. Desert me, yet do not add to my lot the inferior horrors of hell. You are the Creator, make me nothing.

I wish Wren could find me a copy of Mr Golding's *Metamorphoses* – says he can't. I said there *must* be a copy in the Tower! He looks surly, not knowing how to take me. I woke this foggy day – it is November by the Thames – wanting to follow Orpheus through the Taenarus gate to the Styx, to pass with him the ghosts and wraiths until we reach a lower world. Orpheus's wish was to be strong enough to endure his grief. It wasn't much to ask. The lower world has no sound and no order. It is a chaotic silence. It is measureless depths in which isolated souls cannot drown. Orpheus played his way out this black and terrible emptiness to become the singer under shady trees. If Christ's mansions are barred to me and Wemyss's galaxies refuse me, filthy man that I am, let my dust blow around trees. There is a wooded knoll near Long Melford where hulvers, oaks, elms and sycamores reduce the light. May the soul of an assassin, such as it is, find its way there. Whilst I remember it, I give leave to the Feltons to clip me from the family-tree and to fill my space on the monument with a text from Corinthians. Where will you eternally blow, George? You never thought of that, did you! You would have answered, 'Westminster Abbey', that mighty dust-bowl. The Royal Box of the departed. Was it an assassination when you hanged the young mariner? 'Which one?' you ask. Which ever one. Yet you did not die because of him – of those. You died because you were the *unqualified* king, because you never knew your place. Dunce George.

It has become so cold. You grumble, Wren, when I ask you to board-up the window because it means a ladder, and neither can I stand all-day darkness. I must keep the fire in. Here is a Portsmouth poem to divert you. (There are lots more).

Some say the Duke was virtuous, gracious, good,
And Felton basely did to spill his blood,

If it be so, what did he then amiss
In sending him the sooner to his bliss?
All deaths seem pleasant to a goodman's eye
And badmen only are afraid to die;
Changed he his kingdom to possess a better,
Then is the Duke become John Felton's debtor.

* * *

I, Master Wren, chief assistant to the learned Sir John Borough, Garter King of Arms and Record Keeper of the Tower of London, thought fit to stitch into Lieutenant Felton's *Book of Himself* the following tributes, although he would not have agreed. Some were carried by skiffs to the Traitor's Gate and pasted to it. When documenting felons, nothing must be lost. Some are browned by fire when the Lieutenant attempted to burn them. I rescued them.

Item

Can thou be gone so quickly, can a knife
Let out so many title and a life?
Now I'll bemoan thee. O that so huge a pile
Of state should perish in so short a while!
Here is Buckingham,
Fallen like a meteor, and it is hard to say
Which went the straighter way,
Thou or the hand that slew thee!

Item

(Charon) Great Duke, which are commander of the seas,
Make haste to Portsmouth, if thy Highness please,
For there my boat is ready to convey
They soul to the Elysium – come away!

Item

This little grave embraces
One duke and twenty places.
Live ever, Felton, thou has turned to dust,
Treason, ambition, murder, pride and lust.

Item

Immortal man of glory, whose brave hand
Hath once begun to disenchant our land
From magic thralldom! One proud man did mate
The nobles, gentles, commons of our state;
Struck peace and war at pleasure, hurled down all
That to his idol greatness would not fall.

Item

Thy fetters, ransomed England, and they fears
Triumphant like trophies stout Felton wears
On him like seemly ornaments. They deck his arms
And wrists, and hang about his neck
Like gingling bracelets ...

Item

(In the prisoner's own hand) Behold, I show you a mystery: we shall not all sleep, but we shall all be changed – in a moment! In this twinkling of an eye! Starry Wemyss (?) you went fast enough? I look up to you at midnight and see Ursa Minor framed exactly in the window – the same through which Sir John Eliot would have stared. A fool of a boy attends me. I cannot be long now. They are to trie me at the King's Bench. It won't take a moment. Shorter than what will follow. Implore for me, Wemyss. Let me go twinkle-fast.

Item

'To John Felton in the Tower'

Enjoy they bondage, make they prison know
Thou hast a liberty thou canst now owe
To such base punishment. One kept entire, since
Nothing like guilt shackles thy conscience.
I dare not attempt thy valiant blood to weigh,
Or enfeeble it with pity, nor dare pray
Thine act may mercy find, unless thy great story
Lose something of its miracle and glory.

I wish thy merit studied cruelty –
Short vengeance befriends thy memory –
For I would have posterity to hear that
He who can bravely die can bravely bear.
Torture seems great unto a coward's eye,
But 'tis no great thing to suffer, less to die.
Should all the clouds fall out, and in that strife
Lightning and thunder send to take thy life,
I should applaud the wisdom of my fate – one
That knew to value me at such a rate,
As at my fall to trouble all the sky – the
Emptying upon my Jove's full armory.
Yet sure if every artery were broke
Thou would'st find strength enough for yet another stroke.
And now I leave thee unto death and fame –
One which will shake ambition at thy name.
And, if it were no sin, the Court by it
Should hourly swear before a favourite ...

(More – but sufficient, surely?)

Item

(Marked 'Ah yes' in the prisoner's hand)

Though he did good, he did it the wrong way.
They fall into the worst of ills,
That act the People's wish without their wills.

Item

Indecency.

Item

Indecency.

Item

In Latin.

Item

(Pinned to the chimney-breast)

The Poets when they went about to advance chastity, feigned a transformation of chaste persons into trees which are always green, such as the olive and laurel. Into such trees were transhaped Lotus and Daphne, signifying by their continual greenness virginity undefiled. They compared men to may trees. In like way they compared all young men dying in the flower of their age, and having a sparkle of virtue, to flowers, and transfigured them into blooms green, tender and delicate. Ovid turns to flowers Hyacinthus, Adonis, Narcissus, Hermaphroditus and other sweet princes. But he transforms dissolute and licentious men into brute beasts. The Poets changed tyrants into hawks of prey. They converted Daedalion into a bittern. Effeminate men they transfigured into seamews and cranes. Is thirty-six the flower of my age? Has there been a flowering? Who witnessed it? Not I. I shall repeat what the *Golden Epistles* say: 'You break your body with the toils of this life, and adventure your honour to fill one jar with water. Yet soon after your death it is broken against the wall by a prodigal heir who will laugh to see it run as a river.'

Item

Man-queen of England, ruiner of the earth,
Was it the cockatrice who gave thee birth?

Item

(In the prisoner's own hand) The dead cannot bite.

Item

An old book by one Dr Fenton entitled *Golden Epistles*, much thumbed, broken-backed, soiled and of no further use. Tossed onto the Wakefield Tower bumby, along with the Lieutenant's straw, which was fear-soaked.

Item

The Journey of a Wicked Man, written by Himself.

Portsmouth Gaol is a funnel. It is not to be praised. It is an up-ended brewhouse and those condemned to it slither like dregs down its slimy entrance. It was already full enough when they pushed me into it – 'But for your own safety, sir' and I discovered myself to be hugger-mugger among deserters and just another drip to be added to humanity's guilty lees. It was preposterously foul, even for a prison. The deserters were all crying because of their going to be hanged. The captain of the guard hung his moon face in the hole: 'Bear with us, sir. We shall clear a space for you on the morrow.' I dried the wet faces and said the Litany, as much as I could remember. The night passed with the deserters huddling together like puppies. When the fleet had sailed, the carts came for them. The guard was right, I did have space. Outside, more crying and git-ups to the gallows-horses, cracking of rims on cobbles and, 'Oh, my God, my God!'. As we parted I had said that they must not shake my foul hand, that they must not carry the stench of it into heaven. I had to tell them that, alas, so unforgiveable was my crime, that we could not meet again. Ever. I convinced them that they would be with Christ, who knew all about desertion, but that I would be in Hades – where else?

'No, no! sir,!'

Yes, yes. I waited until I assumed they had been hanged, then I tidied-up the cell, piling what they had left behind into a corner. None of it warranted a will. I then occupied the entire rooms I tasted my new loneliness, I let its darkness lay on my tongue. I listened to the sea-winds honking in the tunnel. The only light I possessed poured through it. It was about the size of a plate. I sat in it until I realised that it made a nimbus, then I moved away. I missed its musty warmth, but was resolute and kept out of it. Then I waited for the King's prosecutor to arrive. The town magistrates too. I knew what they wanted to know but in all truthfulness I would only answer, 'No, no.'

Lawyer's malarky. Most tedious. A punishment in itself. First question. 'Surely Sir John Eliot was in on it? Were you not old comrades?' No, no. 'Who, then?' Would it not take more than a lone lieutenant to finish a duke? I thought I could be frivolous at this and cite the case of Monsieur Ravaillac and the King of France (one of their best). Except that Monsieur Ravaillac, being insane, had the advantage of someone like myself, a rational being from a notoriously rational countryside. Oh, to have been mad, your honours! How convenient for England. It could embalm Buckingham with a 'thank God for lunatics' under its breath. Alas, poor nation, you have the sane assassin on your hands, the worst of all political problems. You have the leader on the gallows, the best leader of all. But – you do not believe me? I can see it in your faces. Heroic wastrels are not to be hurried off the stage by a slatternly soldier with a tenpenny knife. George, being a Caesar of sorts, required the protocol of a murderous delegation, a multi-bladed dismissal from office - not my single cut.

My interrogation, when it arrived, included all of the above and more. They drew me up from their Baptist's cistern and marched me to a comfortable house next to the Greyhound. I faintly recall Ovidian panels and a table which looked as though it might have been looted from a church. We all sat around. Wine was brought, food was passed, the sudden change in the weather noted. Then they all leaned forward to demand, '*Who else? Give us their names.* All the conspirators. The King himself would have them, and nothing less.'

'No, no. No one. Forgive me if I repeat what you read in my hat. Let no man commend me for doing it, but discommend themselves as the cause of it, etc.'

I watched them redden and slam shut their papers. A few days after this – terrible actions muddle time – they came in a body to tell me that I was for higher examination. The little King was mentioning the rack. I was advised to take advantage of my long cart journey to the Tower by drawing up a list of my confederates. Names, names, names. I might just as well, said the Portsmouth magistrates, 'as you will be like any man in agony, loquacious.' His Grace had felt no pain, just astonishment. Say what they will of him, his death had been poignant. He had said nothing.

'He cried, "Wound!" '

'Wound? Was it an invitation?'

'It was "wound" after my wounding. Oh, Christ forgive me for hurting him so.'

I know it was noon but not if it was August or September when

251

we left Portsmouth, the filthiest, most horrible town in the kingdom. I went on my knees to the wardens before I mounted the Tower-cart. 'Cover me in sackcloth and ashes. Put a halter round my neck. Let my feet go naked. Let the cart be that of the night-shit men. Placard me with, "Felton, who did what only God may do". Let us take the potholed way. Leave splintery boards where I must stand. Chalk "anathema" round the wheels.' They stripped and washed me, and smoothed my hair, then brought my uniform. A goodwoman who tended to prisoners shaved my face and renewed my arm-rag.

'My halter! My ashes!'

I was erect in the scrubbed cart when they arrived with the rope – of roses. Late roses. They hung it on me. I had become a late-summer May-king. 'How about this as your neck-verse, Lieutenant?' I imagined I heard my name being called, 'Feltoooon ...' My brains became fluid and slopped around in my skull. My cheeks ran with tears. I ran from person to person in the prison courtyard imploring each by turn to debase me. 'Burn my uniform on the Point and let its charred ribbons blow into the sea. Let the world gawp at my body. Let it remind it of that divine likeness which it destroyed. Let it have no protection when the refuse is hurled at it. Let women caterwaul and screech in mockery of my manhood.'

'Yes, yes, sir.'

More garlands.

We swung round towards the turning to the Portsea gibbet and I tried not to look. Those the Duke had strung up still twizzled there, but not my brief companions of the tunnel. Three corpses entirely covered in horseflies, so that they were clothed in a living velvet, tremulous and black, shifted. What had happened to the Litany men? I prayed; 'Dear Lord, let such be my portion, though let my evil flesh not brush against them, let it not contaminate.'

'Where were those others hanged?'

'Those others? Oh, *those*! I believe they got away.'

A gaoler by the cart sucked in his cheeks.

'Will I – get away?'

'You will not, sir.'

All the rest of our setting forth to London was a madness for me but plain sense to them. I remember demanding, 'My halter? My nakedness! My ashes!' and their, 'All in good time, sir. First things first.' One of the first things had been to deck the cart with fireweed. Another first thing had been to run it over strewn blackberries – they have them early in Hampshire – so that fruit-blood ran through the road stones towards the Greyhound. People had put the crush into their mouths and then spat it out with an, 'Ugh, Buckingham!' Their spittle had crawled down the Greyhound door. But would they have done what I had done? No, they only hated. Had I only hated him, George would be aboard his *Swiftsure*. Great men are not removed by hatred. It is a more logical hand that sends them packing, a hand which cuts through the argument. My hand.

* * *

On we went in a creaking, crazy celebration through the Forest of Bere into Havant, 'A town after your own heart, Lieutenant, being big in the parchment trade.' The sheep on whose flayed skins would be written our words were tearing at grass below the beech hangers. The Havanters came out to meet me and I cowered from them. Their women sang wildly from Samuel's book, 'The Duke hath slain us in our thousands and our little David hath slain *him!*' What would I have for such a killing? Gold pieces? Do no stint yourself, sir. Ask and it shall be given. A fat woman: 'Why, look at him, our Jack the giant killer, there's not tuppence of him. And he's hurt himself, poor lad. Have they hurt you, sir? Tell me, and I'll nip him in his buds.' Puddings, squibs, fresh linen, a downy cushion were tossed to me. 'Stop, halt, fools! Don't you see our David must have rest? Tell us, hero, where did you stick him?' Lewdness. 'How many holes did you leave him with?' Dancing by the Havant harpies. Their parson arrived to bless me. A turbulence of mockery, heart-felt prayer, silky knees and dirty thighs – and a sudden break in the weather. We were all drenched. I hid my face in a new taffeta scarf which somebody had thrown in. I bound my eyes with it and held its tassels over my ears. I had imagined nothing like this, and there were sixty-six miles to go. A girl climbed into the cart and pulled the scarf away. 'Let us look at your face.'

253

They let me walk between the high cliffs of Butser, half a dozen soldiers hedging me in for safety. There had been terrible threats from London about what would happen to them if I failed to turn up. H D and Q for everybody. The soldiers took the full force of the driving rain. As we splashed along through the gully, I could see swallows and martins gathering for their autumn hides. So soon. I was by now very ill and tired but was glad to be out of the cart and its motion. The Havanters fell away once they got out of their own country and we were able to rattle through Butser ravine unharrassed. Although I stumbled, I found myself relishing my weariness. Fancifully, I hoped that all my remaining strength would imitate the downpour and drain away with it, and that all of me to reach Traitors' Gate would be a bundle of diminished white and stiffening sticks. 'Here he is, Constable, your enemy of the state.' I also discovered myself biliously adrift between my dear Saviour and starry Wemyss, both of them kind and encouraging, and urging me to make a gentlemanly choice. I plodded into heresies. It was 'My Father's house' versus the firmament. I remember giving Hell a miss. My faintness could not have been all that evident or they would have made me ride. I must have kept my pace. I was chilled through and through with a raw cold, and my wet clothes chaffed. Those of the men squelched and they looked all in. I had seen this marching misery in Holland. My own had become so bad that my other predicament no longer held its importance and I was able to free my thoughts from it and turn them to other matters – travel, for example. All discomforts and fears take a back seat when one is *travelling*. I had been told that Wight can be seen from Butser. Salisbury spire too.

'Halt. I wish to turn round and view Wight.'

My guards, who had been striding and splashing, piled into each other when I stopped.

'For God's sake, sir!'

There it was, Wight, eggshell-brown behind the driving rain.

'See – Wight!'

'Come along, sir. We've all seen Wight.'

I had to push through them to vomit. The Havant puddings, the rocking cart, the perishing cold. Behind my back I could sense their worry. Better, I searched once more for Wight but huge pencil-strokes of moisture had scribbled it out. It did not matter. I had seen it beckon me as Skyros had beckoned Achilles – I was sure of this. O islands!

'Come along, sir. That isle was not in our direction.'

For the first time since I was arrested I knew myself to be secured, as they call it. A dreadful fate. My legs shook.

'I must ride.'

They heaved me gently into the cart. I was frightened and nauseous all the way to Liphook, where we took the bedchamber space in an inn called the Merry Harry, a sober establishment with a frugal board. But warm. I was given the bedstead and my guards the floor. I lay looking out at the twists of the Old Portsmouth Road. Who among the Belchamps could have imagined that it would play such a part in the small drama of my existence! But I must not go on taking it step by step in this narrative for the tedium of it. Our tale, like our lives, must have pace. And the ignominy of mine has to be stressed. I cannot be 'Felton at Liphook' in the style of 'Claudius at Colchester'. I was the great culprit of the kingdom. In a week – maybe less – I would dangle at Tyburn. This certainty made me busy. Men of our rank always settle their earthly affairs. I demanded paper and ink and some tallows. I had the fire banked up ('But it is still summer, sir') and by dayspring there were four letters under my seal. I wrote to Miss Crane of Chilton, releasing her from our alliance, such as it was, a tepid business, and giving her leave to speak ill of me should this be necessary in defence of her family's honour and her own sanity in having anything to do with me in the first place. (She would not, of course. The Cranes were a mild lot and great head-shakers at the follies of the world. I could see them as I wrote their address, talking on the moat bridge, and saying things like, 'Who could blame him?' But would this be the Duke or myself? You never knew quite where you were with them.)

I wrote to Mother at Clare, just a few lines. And to my presumably aghast brother at Ovington. just a few lines. And to Madame vol Hol. Pages. The light entered the Merry Harry windows as my pen sped. Then I wrote an extra letter to our kinsman my Lord Arundel, but a careful one, knowing him to be a patriot who had managed to hide his politics under the frivolity of connoisseurship, and knowing too that he would be under some obligation to me for freeing George's stupendous cabinets of rarities for the market. The Arundels, like most of our sort, saw no disgrace in the scaffold, just a temporary hiatus. None of us apologised for the executed relations or took down their portraits from the gallery. Mine would never have been there in the first place. In this respect I would have been marginalised, not hung. My existence would have been contained between natus and obit. Having not slept a wink, I arose refreshed. I jumped up from the wobbly table with a good night's work in my hand. Authors, I daresay, know the feeling. I was myself. I touched each guard with my foot and they groaned.

'Get up.'

They leaped to their feet. We were all back to normal. But then the abnormality returned and it was I who would have to get going. Civil orders but orders all the same.

'Into the cart, Lieutenant.'

We dragged on to London. Everybody now knows what happened at Kingston, how the legions of the destitute and the hopeful set up their standards by the Thames, how the new Pure Men in their plainclothes filled the square, how the detestable Kingston poets who mouthed their stanzas from stages, and not wrote them down, 'sang' my praises. I was lifted from the cart and enthroned in a meadow. Old women kissed my hands and feet, young women wept their thanks. It was 'Little David, little David and Jack the monster killer!' I was festooned with Traveller's Joy and fed with curds. Madrigals and psalms filled the air. Stock-doves were released, trumpets blown. It was Feltooon ... Feltoon ... from there to Southwark. In all this madness could be detected incoherent longings for a new dispensation, something 'other', though impossible, for the King remained the Lord's anointed and must always do so. But the Villiers poison had been sucked from him – from England. And the mortification of the state had been checked. They stripped me of my journey-suit and dressed me in blue watchet and lace falls. They trimmed my hair and beard and hoarded the cuttings. Boys with rebecks and drums rat-a-tatted my way. They made me central to their corporate prayer and fastened an amber carcanet round my neck. I was cheered enough at one point to borrow

George's lines – 'Make way for a sunburnt, tansy-faced beloved!'
But make way they did. Their parson said it was Isaiah's broad
and holy highway which I walked. All I know is that from
Kingston to Southwark I trod on flowers. And there, holding the
Bridge against the People, stood the massed garrison. Its Duke's-
man general saluted me, a simple chap.

'Are you Mr Felton the felon?'

That's a nice way to meet a saviour.

He had me firmly roped and led to the Gate-cart, then driven
off to a landing-stage below St Olave's where the Gate-boat
waited. But why tell you all this, nosey-parker interlocutor? Now
I come to think of it, I watched you watching me arrive at the
awful Gate. I watched you watching your poor murderer get wet
feet in the sullen slap of the river. I saw you seeing me scramble
into the Tower and my face as that cockney Charon yelled, 'All
change! Next stop Tyburn!' But God keep you all the same. He
will need to in your profession. And you may keep my Kingston
lace. Get your wife to launder it. And study gentlemen, even if
you can never be one.

17

THE ARRAIGNMENT AND PASSING OF THE LIEUTENANT

A Report by Mr Wren,
Keeper of Confessions for the learned Sir John Borough,
Recording Angel of the Tower and Garter King of Arms.

Late November, 1628.

Sir my benefactor,

I have done all you bid me. I have watched and encouraged, and have been unhindered by pity. It is all over. Finis to the enclosed and finis to him. He was not easy with me – and not on account of his predicament, which I allowed for. As your honour will see, the Lieutenant's confession is a book and before we enter into such a business with another condemned man, we should first find out if he is an author. Mr Felton was known in the streets as the Officer in the Tower and we have been unable to established his feloniousness. He was so uneasy with me although I was good to him. He was not courageous, nor did he trouble to hide his deficiency in a soldier. He hid nothing except his body, of which he was quaintly modest.

Less than an hour after carrying his confession to your honour's office, the Constable set about the arraignment, to the prisoner's very great distress. Those who have their just condemnation long postponed begin to believe that it will never come. Which is why, sir – and I hope that you will praise me for this – I believe that a hanging should tread on the heels of a crime. When told, the Lieutenant said, *'Tomorrow?'*

Oh, sir, his credulity!

'Would the examination be here?'

The Constable's errander could not say.

'Should the Ordinary be told?'

'Told what, Mr Felton?'

'That I stand condemned.'

'How "stand condemned" Why rush for salvation when like the rest of us you may be given all the time in the world to collect it.'

The Lieutenant got onto his high horse at this (I am scribbling it all down behind the door) and dismissed the messenger.

'You can come out, Wren,' he tells me. 'Did you hear all? I am to be sentenced tomorrow morning.' He then looked around for his book like a hen-partridge will look around for her next-chicks after the cat has been. I had removed it for safe-keeping. 'That is authorship for you, Wren; birth then robbery.' The arraignment then began to tell on his spirits and he shook.

'Come to the fire, sir,' I said, carefully misrepresenting his fright. I then led him by his good hand to the chimney. I waited for him to thank me for what I had done for him, this being the time for it, but being a man who was always out of gratitude, he said nothing. He just trembled. He cried as I stoked up the flames. He used to tell me that he was an easy crier, which was a sign of gentle blood. 'You must have noticed the peasants, Wren, they *never* weep.' He told me that the late Duke, and his Majesty, and especially his late Majesty, were copious weepers and always carried a tear-bottle with them. 'Don't cry, sir,' I said.

He said, 'Tomorrow!'

I said the rain had set in and that we would get wet. This seemed to cheer him – the going out of the Tower and into the rain. He held his best hand before him as one does to tell if it is spitting. We then both stared up at the window and saw it fall in sheets, and he looked satisfied. (I remember you honour instructing me that nothing is inconsequential in a description of a man's last moments).

The Constable errander, who had returned, informed the Lieutenant that breakfast would be at five and that he must be ready to leave at six. He also said that I had to remain with 'the prisoner' until the morning. Whereat the Lieutenant grew overbearing and said that he would not have it.

'You *will* have it', retorted the errander, 'so let us have no more of it.' He meant the temper. I knew why I had to remain – to prevent him from self-murder should such desperation seize him. It is God's prerogative to say when he should enter his presence, even when it is via the scaffold. Where do we go by our own hand? Out of this world – but where? 'I am here to stop you from doing anything silly, sir' I said lightly. He said, 'You are an idiot, Wren.' But he slept and I did not. I couldn't sleep for the cold. The fire died and the cell-stones ran moisture. I was in an ague of cold. I have heard that Sir John Eliot is still broken-backed from his residence in that room – that he is spiney from its damps. There is a joke, 'Have you been racked?' – 'No, I have been a month in Wakefield.'

There was a furious to-do at dawn. The Lieutenant had dressed himself as an officer, hat and all, but the Captain of the Guard (it was Grigg) had fetched with him a common shirt and slops for Mr Felton to wear, to make him unrecognised as we walked through the town. He threw them on the floor and said, 'Get into them – sir.' I explained about the crowds, but it was no use.

'Mr Wren,' said Mr Felton, 'I am about to walk from this prison to a place of justice, and then to suffer, and then to stand before God. Am I to be hustled along in those things?' And he skewed the slops on his boot and kicked them into the ashes.

I then had a brainwave. 'Captain Grigg, sir. Do you not have a posse-escort of a dozen soldiers outside? Let all be in uniform so that no prisoner is discernible among you. March to the King's Bench in order. I will follow in a casual manner.' And so we went out into the rain. I saw the Lieutenant holding up his face to drink it in. It was so early that there were few about as we splashed along, first to a wait at the Gatehouse and then on to Chancery. I noticed that the prisoner, as we should call him, was invigorated. There are those who complain of the harshness of our prisons but the harm they do is superficial, as can be seen when a man is released and flies into his freedom like a bird. I myself do not blame the Tower for crippling Sir John. We have to remember that he comes from Cornwall, where everybody is bent by fogs. It is my intention to make our Tower a byword for prison perfection. You will be glad to know this. Did I say that we marched to Chancery? I was mistaken, we marched to the incomparable justice of Westminster Hall, where it would normally be handed down before a mighty concourse. But there was nobody there and the rain dripped through. No fires, no lights, nothing. After a while Mr Justice Jones shuffled in, still putting on his robes, and after him Mr Attorney for the King, and after him, in the wrong order, the Sheriff and various court-men, and after them enough guards to protect a prince.

Mr Felton was put at the bar and indicted in a wearily, let's-get-it-over manner. Did he not in the city of Portsmouth on 23rd of August last kill the Duke of Buckingham?

Mr Felton: (Crying) 'I did, I killed him. Oh my dear Jesu, I killed him! It was I who slew the friend who had become the enemy of this land. It was I who followed through the Remonstrance of the parliament and the wishes of the people, a Brutus on his own.' Then something in Latin which I could not catch. It is my opinion that the Lieutenant would have been a happier man if he had learned a soldier's language. Then, 'Do not doubt, there will be plenty of talk of my ill-will, when I have gone. Whole theses on my malice, grudges, and the like but none of it will be true. I never possessed the energy to pursue that kind of thing. Ask anyone.' Then a digression about the plague at Aegina, when the very bulls waiting to be sacrificed at the altar collapsed from sickness, to fall bloodily on the knives laid out for their ritual slaughter before the priests could wield them.

Old Mr Justice Jones perked up at this and cried, 'Book Seven, Book Seven!' and his and the Lieutenant's eye met. The latter then seemed to lose his place and there was a lengthy pause and a great accompanying silence throughout the Hall. Oh, sir, the grandeur of our law, the lack of rush to the scaffold, the civilized taking of time! Had I my way, I would invite the legislators of Europe to stand in our galleries to obbserve it. The Lieutenant then raised his hands like cups and confessed, 'I am guilty of the death of George Villiers.'

Mr Ancient Jones: 'That is that then.'

He began to pass sentence. But he had not allowed for Mr Attorney for his Majesty who, like any lawyer, meant to have his say. Marvellously attired in Court clothes as well as a gown, and speaking without notes, he filled the murky Hall with the poor

Duke's glory. Oh, you should have heard him! It was herald's stuff, I know, and you will need to be told the gist and drift of it, but, sir, to actually *hear* it trumpeting around those bat-draped rafters was thrilling and unforgettable. I never understood princely might and precedent until that moment. Such prosecution told on the Lieutenant too. He was forced to hear the magnificence of what by a single gesture he had utterly ruined. The tears poured down his cheeks and he clung white-fingered to the rail. He struggled to appear the vile creature who had dared to gunpowder so divine a handiwork - I write metaphorically. The Attorney went on, 'had not his Grace since his youth lain in the bosom of our sacred Kings of England? Must not their divinity have touched him? Had he lived, "Oh, stygian day for the realm!" would he not at this very moment be routing the Catholic armies and carrying their Winter Majesties to the Palatinate? These are not rhetorical sweeps, my Lord, they are only a small part of that inventory of what might have been had our dear Duke lived.' And so on and on. And more spectators in the Hall as the news of the trial spread, and all soaking wet and running puddles on the dusty floor. And rowdy singing, soon quenched, at the back. And a monotonous hum of 'Feltoooon, Feltoon' from just within the Great Doors. It infuriated the Attorney, and he sought to drown it in oration, his voice now in full swing and much interest in how long he could keep it up. I have edited his beautiful rant so as not to weary you. He sprang questions. 'Who, *who* in all literature was a match to this Villiers, this prodigious Englishman?' Dead silence.

'Who will answer me? Speak up! Give me a name, a name with the Buckingham ring.' This brought, as you would expect, some filthy parallels from voices hidden behind posts. 'I will give you names,' cried the Attorney. 'I give you that the late lost Duke was our Alexander, our Jove, a knight from Arthur's table, our hope, our hero! If in countenance he was a second Stephen, in the righteousness of his wars he was another Michael. Remember, remember, that our shores could not contain him; he was Admiral of the Great Seas and the honour of all men.'

The Lieutenant listened intently, but like one who had overshot the mark. He looked desperately sad. His prison-blanched features appeared to shrivel at every title until they became a kind of hearing nut. The Attorney (I recall your saying, 'They are Bankside men, the lot of them') came to his peroration and giving the judge a look which said, 'See what you would have missed if I had not insisted.' He also came to his *coup d'theatre* by whipping forth the now celebrated knife. He held it up and there was a universal gasp. As I was sitting between him and the Lieutenant, I was able to feast my eyes on it. I saw the hardened blood at the hilt which had halted at the tender pap. I saw the long white handle and I found that I was asking myself, 'What had such a knife been made for, if not a murder?' The Lieutenant covered his eyes at the awful sight. I heard him say his Grace's font-name 'George, George ...' Over and over. The Attorney, quite carried away by drama like an actor in Webster, was howling, 'Ravaillac! Ravaillac! Ravaillac!'

Confusion.

Mr Justice Jones to the Lieutenant, I mean the prisoner, 'Is that your name? You have to answer, you know. Answer.'

'John Felton.' Said in a whisper.

The Attorney: 'He killed the King of France.'

Mr Justice Jones (surprised), 'As well?' And then not waiting for a reply, and turning to the Lieutenant, 'Do you desire Counsel? A jury? Pray instruct me as to what you desire.'

The Lieutenant. 'I desire to go from here to a merciful and forgiving God – but that would be desiring the impossible. So send me on my way, terrible way that it is.'

The Attorney then jumped up to demand H. D. and Q. And that he had to remind my Lord that those who raised a sword in the King's presence must have their hand chopped off.

The Judge: 'His Majesty was not present and anyway it was a knife, not a sword, which had been raised. Pray do not further interrupt my sentencing, Mr Felton, you must suffer death by hanging for murdering his Grace of Buckingham last August. Tomorrow?'

'Tomorrow,' agreed the Lieutenant.

It was over except the rope.

* * *

18

THE HOURS OF THE LIEUTENANT,
AS REQUIRED BY YOUR HONOUR

Thursday, 27th November, anno domini 1628. Trial-day.

11am.
Back in the Tower. Prisoner wet and silent. Sat at table. Fire out. Both shivering. Attempted to place bed-blanket about his shoulders but he said, 'Leave it, leave it.' Sent for sticks.

12 noon.
Governor himself arrived and I said, 'Stand up, Mr Felton.' Took no notice. Governor: 'Why are you so cold in here, Wren? Lieutenant, you shall not be cold!' To the turnkey, 'Get that fire going immediately.' Expects the prisoner's thanks, but instead more silence. His Excellency then enquires why the window-shutter is down and I answer that it is how Mr Felton would have it – 'to hear the rain.' The Governor: 'Fill the hole – you will catch your deaths.' Mr Felton: 'Leave it, leave it.' He then said, 'Tomorrow?' The Governor looks astonished and corrects the prisoner. 'Tomorrow is a Friday. We do not hang on a Friday, sir.' The prisoner argued, '*He* said, "Tomorrow".' His Excellency (to me) 'Was it old Mr Justice Jones?' He smiled. 'Saturday, sir, Saturday.' This added time cast the prisoner down.

3 pm.
The Lieutenant reads by the hearth.

4 pm.
Ditto.

5 pm.
Ditto.

6 pm.
'Pull up, Wren,' says the prisoner. 'Warm your feet – its got going at last.' He tells me about the hearth-keepers at his family-hall. 'They must feed a great blaze and stamp out young sparks!' Being an army-man, he is accustomed to being private when others are in the room. He gets lost in books. He holds on to his bad arm.

8 pm.
You should just hear the rain! It is sizzling down the chimney and crashing on the ramparts. 'Nice weather for ducks, Wren!' Soldiers can be very childish, I find. I hoped that the Lieutenant would soon be finding his bed. When I enquired if he was tired, he turned to regard me in his soft way and muttered, 'Very'. Yet he read until past midnight. I slept when he slept, taking the palliasse and in terror that a rat might walk over me. Woke to hear, 'Weems! Weems! (?) look at what is happening to me! Oh, friend Weems, your star-pupil is so frightened. He is so all out of character.' Sat and waited for more. Then, 'Mother, I am your John – do you remember me, your son John? Mother, *see* me.' Noisy sleep and then, 'George, I am sorry. Do you know what they will do to me tomorrow?' Screaming. Rose and turned the Lieutenant on his undreaming side. Then, 'Saviour, Saviour ...' and further rigmarole.

Friday 28th November.

5 am.
Myself: 'Good morning, sir.'
   The Lieutenant: 'I have had a rest of sorts between falling-dreams and terrible realities. That was my night. What of yours?'
   Myself: 'I was worried about rats.'
   The Lieutenant: 'Only rats!'
   I said that I had prayed for him and he said that it was good of me, and was sincere. He asked me, 'Do you know what today is? It is tomorrow.'

I was silent. I practised objectivity, according to your Honour's teaching. I recalled what you told me – 'On the way to a gallows always repeat to yourself the prisoner's crime.' Yet pardon me when I show heart; coldness will come with experience. I forced the prisoner to speak of the Duke of Buckingham. He looked surprised.

'What of the Duke, Wren?'

'That he is no more, sir.'

'The Duke was a taking man. He took what could only belong to kings. He took all. He took my blade. He was a rarity in nature, fair as a flower and not unkind. But he was taking. He took all.'

Had he heard the rumour that his Majesty was planning to fill half the Abbey with his monument?

'It is the nature of his dust to take space and precedence. He was a great man and great men have great tombs.'

I should mention at this point – it was before his Excellency arrived – the Lieutenant's unnatural tranquility. I confess that I was all of a-shake. Was I not seeing for the first time the last full day of this man's lifetime? I could not get this thought out of my head. Yet he appeared, well, satisfied. He repeated, 'Today is "tomorrow", my Recording Angel (he was fond of such silly pat-on-the-head names). How did Mr Justice Jones put it? "Will that be all right – tomorrow?" and do you remember how I agreed? Listen, it has stopped raining.' He held a finger to his lips. There was this different sound when downpoor ceases but the water is still running through the pipes. He asked me if I thought that rain passed the stars on its way down to us? Your Honour forewarned me of the strange humours of men under capital punishment and in this, as in all things, you are undoubtedly correct. Mr Felton is different since we returned from the King's Bench.

6 am.

Breakfast. Meat as usual. The Lieutenant slipping into misery. Said that he was not a fool and that tomorrow was 'tomorrow'. Myself: 'Yes, sir, Saturday.'

He said something about it 'being no mercy, only dragged-out horror.' And I reminded him that it was not the custom of a Christian land to execute on the day of Crucifixion. He replied, 'Tell that to the Mansfelds' (?) He was bitter.

7 am.

A kind of dull roaring outside and thumps from muffled bells.

The Lieutenant: 'They are taking George to his sepulcher.'

I told him that the Duke had been buried these weeks ago and that the passing-bells were for him. 'All of them?' (Every London steeple was being rung). The roaring increased and the turnkey rushed in excitedly to announce that not only mobs and rabble were gathering on Tower Hill, but many gentlemen also, and that from Aldgate to our postern it was a sea of heads.

The Lieutenant, at every fresh ring and shout, 'What is that? What is that?'

I was hard, 'Sir, they have come to see you die.'

The Lieutenant: 'Tell them it is Good Friday.'

I drove the turnkey from the cell and put out what was needed for farewell letters ('What is all this, Wren? Are you demanding another chapter?') The prisoner then sat down and wrote rapidly a series of brief epistles, none more than a line or two, and it seemed to be carelessly, banging them shut with his seal. 'What now, my paper-bird, how shall you and I spend Friday?' I urged seriousness. Was he not a step from Judgement? He thanked me for reminding him and told me that I would make a good secretary. I said, 'Be serious, sir.' I implored him to consider his salvation. I said much that would deserve your Honour's praise and commendation. I also felt scaffold-sick and hoped that I would be better tomorrow.

9 am.

Gave the prisoner a prayer-book but he ordered a basin of water and oil to wash his head. Enquired would he have the barber? No, he would not. Vehement. Thick, dark, gentleman's hair not washed since he came to us. Combed it wet for him and thought of our Lord's humility with the apron round him. The Lieutenant asked after my wife's colouring – he had often wondered, etc. He repeated, 'Yellow going to red'. What a curious person he is, usually distant then coming too close. After the washing he told me to go away – 'Make yourself scarce, Wren, go away. Come back tomorrow!' I told him that I could not. I told him that I must be with him now until the end. He said, 'Must you, by God!' He appeared suddenly tragic. I said

267

that I would try not to get in his way. He thanked me. I began to pray for him inwardly.

10 am.

Commotion. First Doctor Sutton came in to administer Holy Communion. He bowed low to the Lieutenant, who was furious. Why had he not been told? He would not have eaten meat at breakfast. The Tower was a heathen place, scandalously administered, and with nobody knowing what was what. Such slights. They hurt me, for I love our great prison and know its worth. The Lieutenant, who seems to know every book in the world, enquired, 'Sir, if you are the author of *Learn to Die*, then let me congratulate you, for I read it at Mr Golding's when I was a boy, and found it fascinating. I have been learning how to die ever since. I trust I will pass the test.' Doctor Sutton, a rickety past-sixty, took a seat and the Lieutenant fell on his knees before him. Doctor Sutton held his damp head and blessed him. The Lieutenant wept into his lap, gasping over and over again his regrets for his crime. I heard him say something like, 'Should any man benefit his country at the most evil cost to himself?' there were other demanding questions which the Doctor sought to answer through his own tears. He told the Lieutenant that he would never forget this moment and that he was teaching him, Christopher Sutton, how to live as well as to die. I too was much affected and knelt. A page set out a Holy Table under the window, placing lights, a cruet, the cup and the dish. When it came to 'Draw near with faith', the Doctor opened his arms to include me and I took the Sacraments alongside the prisoner. Your Honour, is there anything comparable in all the world to our Religion? I felt at that moment if my visit to Tyburn had to be more central than what it was, I should not have cared. I had my Saviour, I had my Heaven. I was *exalté*. But the Lieutenant was ill. He shuddered with chill and took to the wall for support. It was as though the holy bread and wine had been some useless potion. He prayed aloud for strength. The Doctor: 'You shall have it when you most need it. God may not be hurried.' The Lieutenant, 'O, Christ!' The Doctor: 'Shall I accompany you in the cart?' The Lieutenant: 'You shall not, sir. But I thank you for the kind offer.' The Doctor: 'May the Comforter be with you all the way.' The Lieutenant: 'Maybe he will.' They parted. The Lieutenant (to me), 'How certain he is. A certain man, which I am not. Are you certain little gaol scribbler?' I did not answer.

11am.
The prisoner crouches by the fire.

Midday.
Much hollering and stunted bells from outside. London is seething. They say that the disaffected land and sea soldiers are marching on the city. The Lieutenant: 'What is it all about?' Myself: 'It is about you, sir.' The Lieutenant to the sparks, 'Weems, how shall I know your star?' He seems disordered. The hours dawdle. This is when condemned men scratch on the walls to leave their mark. The Tower is still and sullen.

Long hours.
Each sixty minutes a month. Between one and four nothing at all said or done. I cannot get warm.

4 pm.
Door flung open for his Excellency and the prisoner's kin. These are the Earl and Countess of Arundel and their son my Lord Maltravers. Why was I not told this? The Lieutenant is not much less amazed, and bows and stares. But I can see the connection and I notice that he has their manner. They embrace him and lay their presents where the Communion cup stood, a white linen winding-sheet and a purse for the hangman. The lady tells him not to be offended – 'It is merely the etiquette of Tyburn.' She is robust but her noble companions look white and upset. There cannot be many such aristocrats who are unacquainted with the Tower, but these search around with dread. All the Earl can say is, 'Bear up, bear up, cousin!' His wife is practical. She shakes the purse and asks him if he is certain 'that this is the going rate'. Then they all get talking about gardens and late apples, and someone called 'poor Miss Crane'. And Ship Money, and rarities, my Lord the Earl calling himself a chronic collector. They are about to leave when the Lieutenant says, 'Collect these, sir, if you will', and thrusts the sack of papers which his mother brought

him into Lord Arundel's arms. These are, as you know, your Honour's State Papers, and I would have grabbed them back, but dare not. Everybody too great. Brushed past me. Something to the prisoner in French from Lord Maltravers and a kiss. Then they were gone. Dinner was brought in and the Lieutenant ate much meat. I could not touch anything.

2 pm.
The wind is rising. Brings soot down.

3 pm.
The Lieutenant has his book. Reads it then rushes his fingers through it in desperation. Myself: 'Could it be that what you are looking for is in another book?' Looks at me blankly.

4 pm.
There he sits, peaceably now, turning pages, drawing back a bit from the fire when it scorches. I cannot prevent my thoughts racing ahead, I fail to hold them back. They roar along. This time tomorrow he will be cold. He says, 'I will read to you, little Wren, what I once read to another. Pay heed.' Reads:

> Consider that the theatres or scaffolds of this world wherein we children of vanity do walk, do have their foundations upon sand, and therefore their strength is but frail, though the pillars be of gold and are held up with the images of kings. They are subject to shake. What do we leave behind us if we die not with renown? We live in vain if our life be infamous, since a man of naughty reputation, being dangerous to himself, cannot but be also dangerous to others.

I said, 'I have seen how you love your book but, forgive me, it is unoriginal. It paraphrases the Holy Scriptures – can you not see it?'

He did not reply.

7 pm.
Prisoner has been silent these three hours past. He has now said, 'I hope they will not hurt my arm.'

Myself: 'What is that?'

The Lieutenant, 'My arm, my arm ...'

Myself, 'The bandages, sir, have they grown tight? Your flesh has swollen with the heat. Let me loosen your rags.'

The Lieutenant: 'Go to the shitten-house!'

8 pm.

Doctor Sutton returns to enquire whether Mr Felton would have him with him in the cart. 'It would be no trouble.' The Lieutenant asks is this usual? 'Not for me, sir. It is the Ordinary whose usual task it is.' The Lieutenant then says, 'Does there have to be a clergyman?' and the Doctor says he is not quite sure but will find out.

The Lieutenant: 'I know someone who will be standing close beside me on that dreadful journey.'

The Doctor believes that he refers to the Crucified One and his eyes flood with tears, but I am less sure. I follow Doctor Sutton to the door and whisper my sudden realisation. It is that the prisoner's soul is in peril. The Doctor whispers back, 'Never his soul, young man.' What do such divines know of heresy? They will themselves into charitable attitudes. Where is their ferocity? I would not have the Lieutenant lose his soul. In a few hours he could be in Hell. If it be not Christ who accompanies him in the morning, then he goes into darkness. Someone – something – is with him. Who? What? I would ask him but, for a serious person, he treats me frivolously. The Doctor turns at the door at a thought. 'Mr Felton, tomorrow is the Eve of St Andrew's Day.' The Lieutenant, 'So it is. How does it go, the Andrew-psalm, "So that they which go by say not much as the Lord prosper you, we wish you good luck ..."' The Doctor answers, 'Sir, they will say more than that. The Andrew-collect insists that when we take and esteem all the troubles and adversities which shall come to us for Christ's sake, they will add to our chance of obtaining immortality.' The Lieutenant, 'I did what I did for my country's sake – not His. There's the rub.' The Doctor, taking caution because of my being in the room, 'The Andrew-psalm has these words, too: "The righteous Lord has hewn the snares of the ungodly in pieces. Let them be confounded and turned backward as many as have evil will at Sion. Let them be even as the grass

271

growing upon the housetops, which withers before it is pulled up, whereof the mower fills not his hand."' By this, your Honour, this learned divine would seem to be saying that the Lieutenant could not have taken the life of one who was already dead. I watched him – the Lieutenant – grasp the implication, and saw that it was new to him. But I saw no sign of relief. Ever since he reached the Tower of London he has remained inconsolable to the plain fact that he murdered a man in cold blood. He cannot bear being a murderer although he must know from the clamour which leaks in here from the streets that he is popularly regarded as the saviour of the state. This strange man's unquenchable grief, sir, is for his having become a common murderer. He cannot bear it. He wants neither heaven nor hell, but oblivion. He wishes he had not been born. Doctor Sutton seems to have discovered this in his penetrative way. He was telling the Lieutenant that if the ungodly (I mention no name) is already 'dead grass', then he cannot be mown down by the reaper's scythe. Should Doctor Sutton be examined?

It is black and I cannot tell what hour it is. I wish the Lieutenant would sleep, then I could sleep. But he stands with his eye to that arrow-hole in the corner grumbling because the clouds hide the stars. He is an adorer of the skies. He likes to tell me tales out of Ovid and has done since September. At God knows what hour he says, 'Here is a tale for you, Master Wren.'

Myself: 'Sleep, sir, sleep if you can. We are keeping the rats up.' As your Honour knows, it is a tradition of the Tower that it's rats visit those who are to be hanged in the morning. It is a kind of sympathy of the despised. There do seem to be more of them than usual tonight: they watch from dark ledges. Tiny glances like struck flints. These pinpoints vanish when the Lieutenant begins his Ovid-tale. It went something like this.

'There was a fine city set by a river where the ground was beaten flat by constant horse-riding. Those who rode were the glorious sons of gentlemen who, after these disciplines, were to rule the universe. They sat on strong horses and their princely riding-clothes and studded reins glittered in the sunshine. One of the gentlemen, Ismenus, the Lady Niobe's son, was skilfully wheeling his mount in circles over the trodden turf, guiding it with his sure touch and pulling hard at the foaming bit (an early indication of how he would govern his people), when he suddenly slipped from the saddle with a wild shout. An arrow had pierced his heart. Why? Because both the horseman and his mother were over-reaching mortals, and the god Apollo had seen them off, Ismenus to the squalor of the riding-ground, Niobe to the high ground where she squats and mourns everlastingly.'

'Sir,' I said, 'you are a poet.'

Even later. I sense your Honour's just impatience. I hear you prodding me, 'What of Tactic? When will you obey me?' Well, sir, Tactic depends on sleep, deep sleep, and for nearly all that last black night there was none in that room. Yet eventually it arrived. The Lieutenant, who was reading his *Golden Epistles*, fell askew on his straw and was out like a light. When he was still and regular I opened the door a crack so that his Excellency's witnesses could see and listen. Then I did the filthy necessary business for my King's sake. I roused the Lieutenant with rough shakes. I bawled an inch from his at first frightened face, 'Who was in it with you? *Who told you to kill the Duke of Buckingham*? It was Sir John Eliot, was it not? Sir John was in it with you, wasn't he?' A dozen times, with shakings and abuse. Very disgusting. But only the following:

'Get off me, Wren. I would not have thought you such a fool. You have made my arm seep. Bloody Wren!'

The witnesses will bear this out.

The Lieutenant added, 'Ask them to find you a copy of Dick Topcliffe's *A Beginner's Book for Torturers*.' I roused him tenderly at six by the Peter-clock for his ride to Tyburn. He asked, 'What shall I wear?' and was docile. Meat was sent in but he did not eat. He, asked, 'Does it still rain? Shall I need my cloak?' When he was ready the guards lead him to the postern, myself following with the white cloth and the purse. It was foggy and cold, the river all wraiths. 'Why, it is my cart,' he said, climbing in. 'Take a seat, Wren.' Nobody about. 'Look, is not that the Morning Star, Wren?' It cheered him curiously. A full posse of twenty kingsmen around us, and more in train. We went the usual way, Eastcheap, Poultry, Cheapside, Holborn and out into the fields. Some early farmers scouring ditches. The Lieutenant asked, 'Am I not allowed to visit a church?' We pulled in to St Giles's and he knelt just by the threshold. Then along the Oxford

273

road where we had the first inkling of our reception. Many hundreds of silent walkers going our way. The Tyburn Ordinary met us about half a mile from the scaffold and trotted ahead bleating 'Man that is born of woman,' etc. and the Lieutenant said, 'I don't believe that, do you Wren – that we have a short time to live?' I could not reply. He said, 'What do I do – do I remove my hat and cloak? What else? What do I do?' I could not answer. The horse steamed in the mist. A vast concourse round the stage. All quiet as in prayer. At the scaffold, which is a diamond of beams, all the ropes except his were draped. No other hangings, which was unusual for a Saturday. He said, 'Goodbye, dear caged Wren. Take my advice, fly away from that Tower.' I gave him the purse. 'What is this?' I told him that it was Tyburn-custom. 'A *tip* – is that what you are telling me? Dear Christ, a tip for my executioner!' And he emptied the coins into his palm and let them drop through his fingers, one by one. 'Twenty-five are missing.' He embraced me and a little while later I watched him climbing the ladder, he and the hangman together, his shirt fluttering. The crowd began to chant, 'Feltoooon ... Feltoooon' and women sobbed. He looked wasted and slight, which was not good for what was to happen. Big men die fast. The mob saw his dilemma and started to yell orders at the hangman – it was Barker, that villain – but he was careful not to hear. He noosed the Lieutenant and swung him off in a single quick movement. I can't remember how long it took - an age to the watchers. It was the twizzling struggle of a fly in a web. This way and that he kicked, his darkening face coming round and round again, his bowels emptying in the air. After it was all over, Barker had the impudence to come to the cart for the purse – he had watched the money fall. I had the kingsmen throw him into a ditch. We collected the body and rolled it in the Countess's linen and were about to return to the Tower when a message arrived from his Excellency for the cart to be directed to Portsmouth for public warning. It was attended on its dreadful way by many of the better sort as well as by the mob.

Having completed your Honour's orders concerning the murderer of the Duke of Buckingham, I await your further instructions. Merely as an odd appendage to this shocking business, I am sending you the enclosed 'poem', one of hundreds, it is rumoured, which float like goose-feathers about the Portsmouth gibbet. My wife, who is breeding, asks to be remembered to your Honour and to thank you even again for our Tower Green dwelling. The carcanet you sent her fits her pretty neck. Neither she nor I can find words to express our good fortune. A Madame von Hol has applied for the Lieutenant's remains to be released for burial but has been denied. His Majesty's own intrudence, apparently. But there can be little left. Seagulls.

* * *

Upon John Felton's hanging in chains at Portsmouth For Killing the Duke of Buckingham.

> Here unintered suspends, though not to save
> Surviving friends the expenses of a grave,
> Felton's dead earth, which to the world must be
> His own sad monument, his elegy
> As large as fame, but whither bad or good,
> I say not. By himself it was written in blood.
> For with his body thus entombed in air,
> Arched over by heaven, set with a thousand fair
> And glorious diamond stars; a sepulcher
> Which time can never threaten, and where
> The impartial worm – which cannot be bribed to spare
> Princes when wrapt in marble – is unable to
> Reach his flesh, which often the charitable skies
> Embalm with tears, doing those obsequies
> Which belong to men, he'll last until the pitying fowl
> Contend to fly his body to his soul.

a few engraving mistakes
(Great man)